ORDRAM'S LEAF

M.L. DUNWORTH

COUNTRY BOOKS

Published by Country Books/Ashridge Press
Courtyard Cottage, Little Longstone, Bakewell, Derbyshire DE45 1NN
Tel: 01629 640670
e-mail: dickrichardson@country-books.co.uk
www.countrybooks.biz

ISBN 978-1-910489-21-5

Also available as an Ebook
ISBN 978-1-910489-22-2

British Library Cataloguing in Publication Data.
A catalogue record for this book is available from the British Library.

COVER IMAGE:
Every attempt has been made to identify the copyright holder
without succes. If you are the owner, plase contact the publisher.

Printed and bound in England by 4edge Ltd. Hockley, Essex
Tel: 01702 200243

DEDICATION

For my parents Patricia & John,
and my sister Christina,
thank you for everything, all my love M xx.

CHAPTER ONE

At the edge of the valley, beyond the villages and meadows was a rocky ledge. From this ledge, Rose was at the highest point she could be without crossing into the mountains which encircled the island. Far below her, Rose could see children playing in the tall grass near the woodlands which spread over the lower lands of Cragfeld like a blanket. She could see farmers working the land, animals grazing, and people going about their daily business. Rose would come to this rocky ledge every day to escape the feelings of never fitting in, or understanding the people around her. She had her grey cloak wrapped over her shoulders and she was quite camouflaged amongst the boulders and rocks. She was sitting with her legs crossed under her, playing with the golden locket around her neck. Her soft brown hair curled and danced in the breeze which felt cool and crisp on her soft white skin. It was quiet and peaceful, just how Rose liked it.

Cragfeld was a small island in a magical world. It could be walked across in a day or two but the only ways to get around the island was on foot or on horseback. It had been many years since Dragons or Fairies had ventured to Cragfeld. Clouds clung to the mountain tops and cast long shadows into an already dark valley. There were few places where Rose could find solitude, so she had to go where nobody else dared go, near the mountains which the old witch had cursed hundreds of years ago. Rose didn't see the mountains as a threat, she did not know what she would find in them but she had always been curious about what was over the other side. Since she was a small girl she'd been told by the elders of Cragfeld that over the ridge of the mountains was a sheer drop into an endless ocean. Other people would believe this and not question the elders, they all lived and died on Cragfeld without questioning a thing. Rose was now a young woman and she had many questions but nobody with answers.

Rose's gaze was drawn over to the Dark Castle which was in the centre of Cragfeld on a hill looking down on the surrounding villages. Wherever you were on Cragfeld, the Dark Castle was always in sight. The Castle walls were made of stone, which, since the Ice Queen took her throne one hundred and fifty years ago had thick black ice shimmering over them. Some days the Castle seemed quiet as if plans were being concocted, other days a thick red and black smoke plumed out of the North tower. Only a few people had been into the Dark Castle, not many had seen the old witch and the Ice Queen, who between them could summon powerful dark magic. They had cursed the mountains to keep people from wandering into them, making it seem safer to stay in the Lowlands of Cragfeld. Rose was now grown up and it seemed to her that everyone on the island was under a spell; not to question life on the island but to accept that was the only existence there could be. Rose had a vague memory of when she was a young girl and she had been summoned to the Dark Castle. She and her friend Amber were bored one day and had been thinking about venturing into the mountains. The old witch had sensed their idea and needed to put a stop to it. The one hundred stone steps up to the Dark Castle were frozen and slippery, making it difficult for the girls to climb them and by the time they reached the top their legs were aching. A chill went down their spines as they walked under the frozen archway into the main hallway. Rose and Amber stood in front of the Ice Queen who glared at them with cold blue eyes before giving them a false smile. The Ice Queen stood tall in a shimmering robe of silver ice, which draped elegantly around her as she strode across the room. Ice crystals sparked all over her dress, creating a dazzling effect as it caught the light. With a tall frosted crown of diamonds and shards of ice, she was a powerful figure standing before them. She was, to anyone who did not know her quite beautiful, with ice white skin and blood red hair pouring over her shoulders. She clicked her fingers and the old witch came scuttling out of the shadows. The old witch, known as Orme, appeared small and hunched over and was walking with a limp as if it were her aged joints making her hobble. She hid her haggard face beneath the hood of an old faded crimson cloak. In her bony hands she carried a slice of cake for both Amber and Rose. The Ice Queen stepped forward and held her hand a few inches above the plate and sprinkled a red dust which frosted the cake. Amber thought nothing of this and saw it simply as a kind gesture so, without thinking, ate her cake with gusto as if it tasted sublime. Within seconds, Rose could see Amber's eyes had glazed over. Rose knew the cake had been tainted with toxic magic. Rose had no choice but to take a bite of the Ice Queen's offering, it tasted bitter and scratched her throat as she swallowed. The Ice Queen seemed satisfied that they had taken enough and let out a sigh as she walked away, leaving Rose and Amber to be escorted out of the Dark Castle by her sour faced servants. Rose could see in her friends dull misty eyes that the poison had taken her, taken her free will and zest for life, she was just like everybody else now. Rose didn't feel any different after the bite of cake she managed to swallow. Neither the Ice Queen nor the old witch had noticed that the poison had not effected Rose. Her mind was still curious but she was simply learning to be curious on her own. Rose felt a tear run down her cheek as she missed her friends sense of adventure.

On the rare occasion when the sun shone on Cragfeld, Rose tried to see things differently. It could look beautiful with the grass and trees in the Lowlands looking bright and lush. However, on most days like today, there were dark clouds circling above and the lands looked dull and grey. The Dark Castle had a silver glow as drops of rain hit it and immediately turned to ice.

Rose lived alone and was in no rush to go home. She pulled her grey cloak tighter around her and pulled the hood over her head, if you didn't know she was there then you would have failed to see her, she blended into the rocky background perfectly. Her bright blue eyes watched as each of the five villages lit its lanterns as night washed over like a black veil. The seven watch towers at the top of the mountains also lit their fires, these were the lookout posts of the Ice Queen so she could watch over her Kingdom and ensure nobody would leave. Any "incomers" would be escorted straight to the Dark Castle where few were ever seen again. If any incomers were released from the Dark Castle then they would have a familiar glazed misty look in their eyes, just like everybody else. Incomers would be put under the Ice Queen's magic to believe they were born and raised in Cragfeld, they forgot all about where they really came from.

Rose was an orphan and had no memory of her early years. She was raised in the same house as Amber, whose parents took her in and raised her as one of their own. As much as Rose loved and appreciated being part of a family, it was not her own family and she never felt as if she belonged to any-one or anything. She certainly did not feel part of Cragfeld. She was told that the gold locket she wears round her neck had belonged to her mother and she cherished it dearly.

The grey clouds circled over the mountains and there was a pitapat of raindrops hitting her cloak. Rose felt something strange about this night, the sky looked blacker, the air smelled cleaner, everything seemed quieter. Feeling tired but comfortable she lay back against the rock and covered herself completely with her cloak and hood. Her mind wandered back to when she was a child, she tried to remember what it was like to laugh and have friends but it seemed a long time ago to her now. She closed her eyes and let sleep wash over her for a short while. Rose had often stayed here all night, sitting quiet and camouflaged, listening to the mountains shift and come to life. She had never known what resided in the mountains but she knew things were moving around her. Rose thought if she left them alone then they would leave her alone and so far this had worked. She had only had one close call where she felt she had been found, she hid beneath her cloak and could hear the slow and heavy breathing of an animal much greater in size than a horse. It slowly approached her, sniffed at her cloak as she sat not daring to move or breathe, it let out a huge snort over her before walking away. To this day she had no idea what it could have been.

As Rose lay on her rocky ledge drifting in and out of sleep, she felt a relaxing soft breeze waft over her. She knew she ought to go home but there was something calming about the evening. The night darkened and she could feel the mountains shifting deep in the ground below her. Apart from the seven highest peaks where the watch tower fires burned, the mountains would shift in the night and never look the same as the day before. Whether they did this on their own or whether it was part of Orme's curse nobody really knew. Villagers got used to waking up each day with a slightly changed view. Rose thought it was one of the tricks of the Ice Queen of keeping her people out of the mountains, by scaring them with magic and making them think they would get lost in the ever changing rocks. Deep rumbling sounds from the mountain belly groaned their way through to the surface. It wasn't a sound Rose was scared of, in fact she found it soothing as she drifted off into a deeper sleep. Whilst she lay perfectly still and quiet, she had learned to ignore the noises of the night.

Out of the darkness, shadows started to move. Two Grocklings had been watching Rose as she lay unaware of their company. Hundreds of Grocklings had lived in the mountains long before the Ice Queen and Orme had taken hold of Cragfeld. They lived below the surface of the mountains and came out at night, often in pairs. None of the people of Cragfeld had ever seen a Grockling before, though the village elders portrayed them as nasty little creatures who would rob you as soon as look at you. They were in fact quite the opposite to this and very wary of strangers. Grocklings were similar in size to a large domestic cat but walked on their hind legs. Their upper body was similar to that of a small human but their lower body was like that of a cat, covered in thick black fur and with a bushy black tail. They needed to move around the mountains quickly and quietly and their large soft paws made this easy and effortless. Even though Grocklings had a fine fur over their upper bodies, they chose to wear long black coats for modesty purposes. It was very difficult for a human to spot them in the dark. Their size should not fool you mind you, they are quick, strong and incredibly clever. They had similar facial features to humans; their ears were slightly pointed and lower down the sides of their heads compared to a cat and incredibly sensitive to sound. Their large green almond shaped eyes give them clear vision in both daylight and darkness. The Ice Queen of course hated Grocklings because they are immune to her magic, which cannot penetrate through the mountain. It was only the spell from Orme that would kept the Grocklings in the mountains and out of the Ice Queens way. The Grocklings weren't bothered by this as the mountains were their home, where they prospered and were at their best. Grocklings did however miss the company of human beings as they used to interact very well before the Ice Queen banished them to the mountains and brainwashed the human population of Cragfeld.

When these two young male Grocklings saw Rose, they were both fascinated and excited to get a closer look. They had actually been watching Rose come to the same rocky ledge for the last few days and wondered what she was doing. They crept down to sit beside her on the ledge.

"I wonder who she is?" asked the younger of the two, "do you think we should poke her?" He gestured his arm towards her.

"Fiddy, don't!" said the second, grabbing his friends hand to stop him "We don't know who she is, best not startle her eh?"

"That's true," said Fiddy "but what's she doing sitting here by herself?"

"I don't know," said Furdon "it's been a long time since we've interacted with the people of Cragfeld."

"Do you think she's one of the Ice Queen's spies?" said Fiddy, getting slightly closer and sniffing Rose's cloak. "She doesn't smell like a spy, she smells quite lovely actually."

"That answers your question, if she was one of the Ice Queen's little puppets there would be a vile stench coming off her."

"Do you think the Dark Castle knows she's here?"

"How should I know! I doubt the Ice Queen is worried about one stray sheep from her flock. She knows none of the villagers dare go into the mountains, even though this one here is very close to the border."

At that moment Rose woke from her sleep but was still drowsy. She didn't move as she quickly became aware that she was not alone on her rocky ledge, she could hear Fiddy and Furdon whispering to each other. She slowly lifted her head a fraction so she could see through the gap under her hood. Rose could see the two Grocklings standing at the other side of her ledge. As Rose's eyes adjusted to the light, she was amazed at what she saw as she had never seen a Grockling before. Fiddy and Furdon stopped whispering, stood still for a moment and then slowly turned to look over at Rose, they had heard her breathing change as if she was no longer sleeping. With their nocturnal vision, they could see her looking straight back at them and they jumped back, partly with surprise and partly with excitement. Rose pulled the hood of her cloak back off her face.

"Oh she's awake, she's awake!" said Fiddy, jumping up and down.

"Calm down, you'll scare her," said Furdon, who was just as keen to meet her but could contain his eagerness a lot better than his young friend.

"I'm not scared," said Rose in a soft calm voice "Who are you?" She sat up and leant forward feeling wide awake and keen to meet these strange looking characters. She could see their half-human half-feline features and was becoming more interested in what they could be.

"We were going to ask you the same question," said Furdon, approaching her shyly. "My name is Furdon and this is my friend Fiddy."

"I'm Rose," she put her hand out and the Grocklings politely shook it. Their small hands were soft against her skin. She smiled gently as she could feel her new companions were not a threat to her. She continued "May I ask what you are? I've never met anyone like you before."

"That is a shame to hear but not a surprise," sighed Furdon "The Ice Queen stopped us talking to your kind when she took her throne."

"We're Grocklings," interrupted Fiddy excitedly "We live

in the mountains."

Rose looked closely at the Grocklings and admired the glossy black fur on their hind legs which puffed out into a wonderful tail. From some angles their facial features were more human but definitely had feline qualities. Rose could tell they were quite warm and friendly, not at all how they had been described to her by the village elders when she was a child.

"Miss Rose," said Fiddy "Why do you come here by your-self?"

"Don't be so blunt," said Furdon firmly "she's only just met us and might not wish to share that." They both turned to look at her with inquisitive eyes, glowing emerald green in the moonlight.

"Do you work for the Ice Queen?" asked Rose. She was not sure she could trust these strange new friends yet and did not want to let them know too much about her.

"Oh good grief, no," said Furdon "We keep out of her way. We're happy to stay in the mountains as long as it means avoiding her."

"Plus she can't stand the sight of us," said Fiddy "we've been here for hundreds of years, long before she came along and cast her dark shadow over Cragfeld. She may have some powerful magic but it is useless on us. The mountains are ours and they shield us… there's nothing she can do about that."

"Which is why we stay in the mountains," said Furdon.

"The people of Cragfeld have been warned about coming up to the mountains," said Rose "The Ice Queen tells people the Lowlands are safe and that is where we should stay."

"Yet you choose to come to this spot every day, as close to the border of the mountains as you can get?"

"Yes, I choose to do this," she whispered "The Ice Queen has everyone under a spell, a curse to stop them thinking for themselves and believe everything she says."

"But not you?" asked Fiddy, slightly confused.

"Not me," said Rose "Which is why I come here to this ledge, I don't fit in down there. If I'm going to feel alone then I might as well be alone." Her eyes looked over the villages which were now lit up below her.

"Interesting. Odd but interesting," said Furdon, looking Rose up and down.

"What about your family?" asked Fiddy.

"I don't have my own, I lost my family when I was too young to remember."

This made Fiddy quite sad. Furdon handed him a hand-kerchief and nudged him with his elbow as if to tell him to pull himself together. Rose smiled at them both, it was nice for her to meet someone who was curious and had their own thoughts, she had not experienced it for a long time. She definitely wanted to find out more about these little Grocklings and where they came from.

"Why are you out on the mountain watching me?" asked Rose "I didn't think anyone would find or even see me here."

"That's because you didn't expect us coming along, did you?" said Fiddy with a cheeky smile. "As the sun sets, hundreds of us come out of the mountain and watch over them. We happened to come across you a few days ago and, well… we had no idea what to make of you."

"Yes… and though you think you're hiding under your cloak," said Furdon "We could see you from a mile away." Rose blushed, she thought she was hidden away from on-lookers but apparently she was wrong. Only human eyes would fail to see her on the rocky ledge.

Fiddy gave a gentle nudge on Furdon's arm to pull him close to whisper into his ear. Rose could tell they were talking about her as they both looked at her from time to time between their exchange of words. After a couple of minutes the Grocklings turned to face Rose, Furdon cleared his throat nervously.

"Miss Rose," he said edging closer to her "we were wondering if you'd do us the honour of allowing us to escort you up the mountain to meet the rest of our troop?"

Rose initially felt uneasy at the idea, she had never been over or dared to go over the craggy border into the mountains. She looked up into the darkness and could feel the mountains rumbling as they shifted, as if they were groaning with age. She could feel her heart pounding faster at the thought of going beyond the comfort of her rocky ledge. Fiddy sensed her worry and jumped over to her and held her hand.

"You'll be perfectly safe with us," he smiled. "It's been so long since our troop's even dreamt of meeting someone like you."

Rose took a deep breath and looked into her new friends large shiny green eyes, she found herself smiling and nodding in agreement. Fiddy and Furdon jumped for joy.

"Oh, thank you," said Furdon "This is very exciting indeed."

Rose looked down over Cragfeld and could not help but wonder why it looked different to her somehow tonight, just as there was an odd feeling to the whole night. The villages were quiet and the night was the darkest she has ever known. The Dark Castle shimmered red and silver in the moonlight. She wondered if the Ice Queen was watching her as she got to her feet, ready to cross over the border into forbidden territory.

"Don't worry about them," reassured Furdon, as he held out his hand to guide the way "You're with us now."

Rose carefully wrapped her cloak around her and followed Fiddy and Furdon up into the craggy border. In the dark she could barely see where she was going and the ground beneath her feet was unpredictable. The surefooted Grocklings confidently guided her along and up the narrow pathway which gradually got steeper and rockier. As they walked along and chatted, Rose could tell Furdon was the more serious of the two. Fiddy on the other hand was young, fun and quite excitable. A few metres above her, Rose could see a layer of what appeared to be silver fog which every now and then pulsed with a red glow.

"What's that?" she asked, pointing towards the layer of fog.

"Oh yes," said Furdon "I forgot you're so much taller than us. For the next few minutes you'll need to lay as flat as you can and crawl. If human skin touches that when it pulses red then the watch towers will know to send out the wardens to find you. Then the Ice Queen will definitely know you're here."

Rose did as Furdon said and lowered herself to the floor. The three companions moved slowly up towards the silver fog which was glistening with ice crystals. When they were half way it felt cold and Rose shivered as the ice lingered over her. The red glow came round and surrounded them, none of them daring to move or breathe. It was as if it was scanning the ground and looking for trespassers. Would it pass over them and they could carry on unnoticed, or would it sense the human trying to pass beneath? They looked at each other while the red glow lingered for what seemed longer than normal and time seemed to stand still. It was as if each lingering ice crystal was an eye, watching every movement and wouldn't move on until satisfied there was nothing to see. The red light gradually faded and with a huge sigh of relief they continued as quickly as they could through the fog to the other side. Rose rested on a boulder and looked down on the island. She could tell she was high up and could see the speckled lights of Cragfeld glimmering far below like glitter.

"Do you think we got away with that?" asked Fiddy.

"I think so," said Furdon "But I was too nervous to be sure

of it. I say we hurry along, better safe than sorry."

"Is it much further?" asked Rose. She knew she was at the point of no return now, she needed the Grocklings to help guide her through the shifting mountains. If she turned back alone now, she could barely see the path in front of her let alone find the right one home.

"Not too far now," said Fiddy, helping her up.

"That's easy for you to say," smiled Rose, "You're used to scampering about these mountains every night."

The air so far up the mountain felt clean. The poisons emitted from the Dark Castle at the hands of the Ice Queen and Orme did not seem to reach this far. The clouds had cleared slightly and the light from the moon shone like a torch over the mountains. There were some strange noises coming from both the air and land around her, noises which Rose had never heard before. She knew there would be all kinds of animals living up here which she'd only ever read about in story books. It was clear to her that she had stepped into their territory so she had to be respectful. She was also confident that her friends would tell her if there was anything to worry about.

The Ice Queen had been standing on the balcony looking out from the main hall of the Dark Castle. She gazed over her realm, watching her people moving around the lantern lit streets and villages. She wanted her people to believe they were safe here, as long as they stayed within the Lowlands and close to the Dark Castle. Since taking her throne one hundred and fifty years ago, she protected her island by never letting anyone in or out, every single person was cursed by her magic and power. The Ice Queen had fought too hard against her sister for Cragfeld and would do all she could in her power to keep it. Her sister was called Rika and wanted to share Cragfeld but the Ice Queen was selfish and wanted her own Kingdom. For one hundred and fifty years she had held Rika captive, frozen in ice and time in the tallest tower of the Dark Castle. She had always been jealous of her sister who was beautiful, strong and kind. The Ice Queen always felt second best and over the years became bitter and vengeful. It had been said the Ice Queen's heart had frozen solid at the same time she captured her sister in ice. Just thinking back about Rika enraged the Ice Queen and sent anger through her poison filled veins. Cragfeld was hers and there was nothing that could change it; her sister and her people were to respect that, her magic would make sure of it!

As she stood on the balcony, she too sensed something strange about the evening. The sky looked darker and the air felt crisper than ever before. The whispers on the breeze sent down from the mountain watch towers were that there was some unusual movement on an otherwise still night. They could not tell her what the unusual movement was, so she summoned the old witch and her Crystal bowl for deeper insight.

Orme came scuttling into the main hall and placed the large heavy Crystal bowl on to the stone plinth in the middle of the room. Her footsteps echoed around the great hall which was cold and bare. There was a time the Dark Castle was full of life, light and warmth but all that was a distant memory now. There were only a few servants who dared to stay in the Dark Castle when the Ice Queen took power, all now as dull and as grey as the frozen stone hallways they walked in. The Ice Queen strode majestically over to the old witch and looked down into the black oil-like liquid glistening in the Crystal bowl.

"Orme, my friend," she said in a soft low voice "I can feel something strange is happening, this night is making me feel restless."

"My Queen, my friend, don't worry," said Orme quite calmly "I'll soon put your mind at ease, the Crystal bowl will show you anything you ask of it." The Ice Queen dropped one of the ice stones from her necklace into the bowl. The liquid started to churn, swirling around the sides of the bowl as if it were coming to life. "It is ready," said Orme, looking up at the Ice Queen from under the hood of her cloak, "Ask what you wish to see." The Ice Queen stood tall, lowering her eyes she peered into the bowl.

"Show me my people."

The liquid cleared and showed images of people in their homes, in the pubs, or walking between the two. They were generally looking oblivious to the strange night air. There was nothing untoward about anything they were doing.

"Show me the mountains."

The black liquid frothed in the bowl and after a few minutes cleared again. The mountains were shifting and the creatures that lived there were high up and away from the craggy border. The Ice Queen glared into the bowl, she wanted to see what was causing the whispers in the wind, telling her there was movement.

"Show me what is unusual about this night!" she demanded. The liquid shimmered red and silver as the blackness stirred round and around the Crystal bowl. After a few moments the liquid settled but nothing could be seen. "What does this mean?" asked the Ice Queen impatiently with a furrowed brow. "There's something I must know and I want to see."

"My Queen, there mustn't be anything to see, the Crystal bowl has settled."

"It's hiding something from me!" Her voice boomed around the main hall. "I can feel it, the sky, the air, the whispers on the breeze." She strode back over to stand on the balcony and glared into the mountains. She knew there was something being hidden from her. She had strong powers but could not use them on the mountains, which displeased her greatly.

Orme stood still next to the stone plinth, looking over at her Queen and then back at the bowl. The liquid was calm and quiet. Orme placed her hands on each side of the bowl, closed her old grey eyes and muttered some spellbound words. The black liquid started to tremble as ripples waved through it. The Ice Queen turned to see what Orme was doing.

"What do you see?" she barked.

"The only image we have been presented with, is a lone shadow in a grey cloak... with a golden locket," said Orme as she stared at the picture. Her grey eyes stared at the image until the picture faded back into nothing. The Ice Queen was now becoming frustrated and marched back to the old witch, her long white dress swished behind her, leaving flakes of ice behind her.

"How is this helping me? Who was in the picture, a friend or an enemy?"

"There was no image of the face nor was there sign of ill intent," said Orme "but the golden locket, I'm sure I recognised it." The Ice Queen put her hand on her hip and sighed with annoyance. Her cold blue eyes looked almost white as she became more aggravated. Her blood red hair hissed around her body as if it were coming to life.

"Orme, find whoever it is and bring them to me! Whatever the intent, good or ill, I need to know!" The old witch nodded, picked up the Crystal bowl and slowly walked out of the main hall back down to her chamber. She had a confused expression on her face, she knew she had seen the golden locket or one very similar to it before.

The Ice Queen stared out into the darkness. She knew her guards, watch towers and spies would soon inform her of any strangers or threat. However, she remained restless and paced angrily on the balcony, a thick layer of ice forming beneath her crystal shoes.

Back in her chamber, the old witch climbed down the slime covered green stone steps into her den. She'd practiced her magic from this dingy den for hundreds of years. No natural light could penetrate the stone walls which encased the room. Piled high on shelves were ancient books of magic. There were various sized jars of mysterious magical ingredients of various colours, some living, some growing and some dead. A cauldron simmered over a low fire and occasional curls of smoke would creep up the chimney to the outside world. It was here in this room where Orme had made and conducted the spell on the mountains, neither side to ever cross into the other without pain or misfortune. She knew it was enduring and the Ice Queen need not worry.

She placed the Crystal bowl on a stone mantle and straightened her cloak. Her old bony hands groped around in a wooden cabinet for an envelope which contained a small golden leaf. She gently broke a section of the leaf off and admired how is shone brightly in the candle light. The golden leaf was extremely fine and so thin you could almost see through it. Orme held it up and its reflection lit up her grey eyes, a small smile crept onto her haggard face.

"It's been a long time my old friend," she muttered as she hobbled over to her cauldron. She crushed the golden leaf in her hand and dropped it into the steaming waters below. The water bubbled with red and orange flashes as the leaf scattered over it. "With Ordram's Leaf, show me now, the wearer of locket, golden and proud." The old witch stood back as flames spilled over the cauldron and danced into the centre of the room. The flames flickered around each other, Orme watched as they slowly formed a portrait. An image appeared in the flames of a shadowy figure in a grey cloak. "Show me closer, show me a face, give me a name..." She peered into the flames waiting for them to tell her who was wearing the golden locket. With a bright flash, the flames jumped back into the cauldron and the room went dark.

Orme crept over to the fireplace and looked into the dark waters of the cauldron, the golden fragments of leaf were shimmering as if untouched on the surface of the still water. It was becoming clear to Orme that something was blocking her from seeing what she wanted to see. She frowned with irritation as she stared into her cauldron. It was only a few moments later when she saw the golden fragments forming into the shape of the golden locket. With no clear answer to her question, she was not sure what this could mean. Usually when performing spells and magic she would be given answers, not puzzles.

Orme slowly made her way out of the den, up the cold stairs and into her chamber. She poked the fire back to life before sitting back in an old rocking chair, not knowing whether it was herself or the chair which creaked. Orme had lived in the Dark Castle for hundreds of years and supported previous Kings and Queens with their rule over Cragfeld. It was only when the Ice Queen took the throne that Orme felt she could use her powers to their full strength. The Ice Queen had a cold heart and wanted to be in control of everything, nothing would happen without her knowing. The old witch knew she had a compatible union, they were as cruel as each other. To cast a spell and brainwash the people of Cragfeld had been a successful collaboration of the two. The people would feel as if they were living quite happily in Cragfeld and never question anything the Ice Queen did. It was as if they were in their own bubble and nothing could burst it.

As she sat rocking in the chair and staring into the fire, Orme tried to remember where she had seen the golden locket before. Her brow furrowed and the wrinkles around her eyes creased deeper.

Way up in the mountain now far above the craggy border, Rose and her two companions took a rest. It seemed incredibly quiet to Rose as she was used to the noises of the people far below in the villages. The two Grocklings heard a crackling sound not too far away from them as if other animals were grazing or wandering close by. The light from the moon helped Rose slightly to see where she was going and to follow her friends as best she could.

"Maybe we should carry on," said Furdon "We're not too far away and don't want to meet anything untoward, Silver-tips and the like. I'm not sure how they'd react to seeing a human."

"What's a Silvertip?" asked Rose, having never heard the name before.

"They're not the nicest creatures to meet on a dark night," said Fiddy, hiding behind Rose's leg "They're snarling, drooling, growling…nasty, angry beasts."

"Ok Fiddy, that's quite enough," said Furdon "Sorry about him Miss Rose, he had a run in with a Silvertip a few weeks ago, quite a rough encounter wasn't it?"

"Oh yes, it was awful," said Fiddy "I can still see it now, it's breath was like rotten meat. Large, aggressive hounds, much bigger than you could imagine, standing twice your height. They have white tips on the ends of their ears, which actually help us to see them when it's dark."

"Yes, maybe we should hurry," said Rose, not wanting to meet the creature that Fiddy had just described. She started to move up the mountain with a nervous sideways motion, "You say we're nearly there?"

Fiddy and Furdon did not move and stared at Rose. Rose didn't realise she was idling her way up into the path of a Silvertip which had sniffed them out and crept up on them. Rose saw the expression on the Grockling's faces and could tell something was not right. She could feel the heat coming off the animal's body, she could smell the stench of rotten meat as its breathing got louder. Rose slowly turned to face the Silvertip, a large silhouette in the moonlight loomed in front of her. It was too late to hide or run. The Grocklings stood motionless, all they could do was watch. The Silvertip lowered its head to have a good look at Rose. She saw its large eyes scanning her and it started sniffing around her, its teeth glinting in the light. Rose stood motionless not daring to blink or even breathe, she could feel her heart pounding hard and fast. The Silvertip growled softly, a deep gurgling sound rumbled from its belly, it was unsure of what it had come across. It nudged her with its nose and pushed her back a step. It nudged her again, this time it was more of a nuzzle against her arm than a push. Fiddy and Furdon had never seen this before and thus did not know how to advise Rose to get out of the situation when she mouthed 'What do I do?' to them. She did not hear any anger growling from the beast. She slowly raised her arm and put it out to touch the animal on its neck. The two Grocklings were nervous, they knew their new friend had not encountered a creature like this before, yet they could not believe how calm she seemed. The Silvertip did not seem startled as Rose gently stroked its thick wiry fur. Rose turned to her friends and shot them a look of disbelief as they stood wide eyed and speechless. A haunting howl echoed from the other side of the mountains and the Silvertip raised its head, as if it was being called upon. It nuzzled Rose again before raising its head and letting out a deep blood churning howl. It then turned and leaped up the mountain, its huge body disappearing in the darkness. Neither Rose or the Grocklings knew what to say or think and stood motionless for a few moments.

"Well I never," said Furdon eventually "Never in all my days have I seen a Silvertip do that." Rose smiled, mostly with relief that she had encountered a Silvertip and still had all of her fingers and limbs intact.

"So you can see me from a mile away but not that great thing stood right in front of you?" she laughed "I don't know what you were scared of Fiddy, they seem lovely creatures to me, I may get one as a pet one day." Fiddy blushed as his friend teased him, his encounter had been a lot more frightening. They began to walk again, up the mountain and into the rocky cliffs.

CHAPTER TWO

The two Grocklings took Rose by the hand and showed her the way along the cliff face, on a narrow ledge with a sheer drop below. Rose was a lot bigger than the Grocklings so had to balance and step carefully on her toes, holding on to whatever rock she could. She did not like this one bit and had to lean in as close to the mountain side as she could, one slip of her foot would mean a long fall down the cliff. Her cloak was wafting in the wind which was whistling down the mountain, it caused her to wobble occasionally and she felt her heart jump into her mouth. Her palms felt sweaty but she had to try and focus on getting to the end and looking anywhere but down. From time to time she felt as if something was flying passed her, like a flap of giant wings close by. She did not dare turn around in case she lost her grip so she convinced herself that it was her cloak wafting in the wind. The winged wardens from the mountain tops were doing their patrols over the mountain, fortunately they did not notice Rose as they flew by. Eventually they came across what appeared to be a cave in the side of the cliff face. Furdon lit his torch and placed it on a hook on the wall of the cave. Rose was relieved to get there and end the tedious balancing act. At first Rose did not think anything of where she was and took a seat on a boulder to get her breath back and calm herself after that unnerving ordeal. It was only when she took a proper look around that she saw she was in what we would refer to as a porch. It was a place for leaving hats, handkerchiefs and anything one may have collected on the nights patrol before entering the main house. Rose pulled back the hood of her cloak and shook her hair free, the light curls bounced with freedom around her face which was flushed pink from the walk.

"This is where we live," said Fiddy, excitedly jumping onto Rose's lap. "Well not exactly here, once we're through the next doorway, that's where we live." Rose looked around the room but couldn't see the doorway that Fiddy had mentioned.

"Is it a secret doorway?" she smiled, "I don't mean to be rude but I can't see anything but a cave wall."

"Which is exactly how it's supposed to look," said Furdon "We don't want all and sundry coming to visit uninvited. Please look more closely, have a wander round and see what you think, see if you can find the doorway."

Fiddy jumped off Rose's lap and walked around the cave with her, giving her clues to whether she was growing hotter or colder at finding the doorway. After a few minutes Fiddy made it clear that Rose was boiling hot and could not get any closer. Rose ran her hands over the wall and examined the stone but couldn't see anything other than rock, there were no ledges or handles to show any sign of where to go. Frustrated she couldn't find anything she sat on a boulder, at which point Fiddy was about to burst with eagerness as he was still playing the game. He gave her a clue and pointed at what she was sitting on. Rose stood up and looked at the boulder, a very plain and normal looking boulder.

"That's the doorway?"

"No," said Furdon "That's the camouflage, the doorway is under the boulder."

"But how do you shift the boulder, it must weigh a ton?"

Furdon took his torch off the hook on the wall and gave it to Fiddy to hold. Furdon then twisted and turned the hook on the wall around full circle. There was a soft rumbling sound as the boulder was pulled on some hidden mechanism out of the way. Underneath the boulder was a small round wooden door which looked like a trapdoor. Rose was amazed and she had never expected to see anything like it in the rather sparse cave.

"Are you expecting me to fit through that doorway?" asked Rose, knowing her human body would not fit through a hole designed for a Grockling.

"Of course you'll fit Miss Rose," smiled Furdon, as he pulled the door up and open.

Fiddy led the way and jumped through the hole and lit a torch in the tunnel below so Rose could see where she was going. Rose place one foot down the hole, knowing full well that she would get stuck if she attempted both legs. Furdon could see the doubt in her eyes.

"Do not worry," he said reassuringly "Close your eyes, count to three and cough, then you will be through." Rose had not heard anything so silly in all her life but the Grocklings had got her this far, so she believed she should give it a go. With only her feet down the hole she closed her eyes and hesitantly started counting.

"One… two… three… cough."

She opened her eyes and found herself laid on the floor of the tunnel beneath the doorway. Rose could not believe it, 'How did that happen?' she wondered, looking at Fiddy wide eyed. Fiddy smiled at her and Furdon made sure she was Ok before joining his two companions in the tunnel and closing the doorway behind him. There was a grinding sound as the boulder shifted back into place over the hole.

The two Grocklings could stand tall and walk normally down the tunnel but Rose had to crawl on her hands and knees. It was not a dirty tunnel as dried grass reeds covered the floor like a carpet. Rose was beginning to feel slightly claustrophobic as she shuffled along the tunnel as it felt close around her, she was used to being outdoors, not underground.

"I heard the Ice Queen has a few Silvertips in the Dark Castle," said Furdon, making conversation, "To guard her secrets from and scare off intruders. Is this true?"

"I wouldn't know," said Rose "It was a long time ago since I was in the Dark Castle. Anyway, the spell cast upon the people of Cragfeld has prevented them from intruding on the business of the Dark Castle since she took the throne."

The three friends continued along the stone tunnel, getting deeper under the surface of the mountain. Furdon's torch was the only light they had until they neared the end of the narrow tunnel. Rose felt she had more space around her shoulders and was able to move a lot easier. She could see a dim light glowing ahead of them as if they were approaching the main cavern. Furdon stopped at the end of the tunnel, placed his torch in a socket on the wall and helped Rose scramble down a few rocky steps. She was relieved to be able to stand tall again. Guided by her new friends, she followed them through a doorway which had been carved out of the stone. In front of her was a vast cavern with steps and walkways crisscrossing overhead and down below. The cavern was glowing with fire lanterns which were dotted around the paths and stairways. Rose was amazed at the size of their home, it looked almost the same size as the Dark Castle. Despite having stone walls and no natural light, the cavern did not feel cold or unwelcoming. There was a warm feeling in the air. Hundreds of Grocklings lived here. When Rose stepped into the cavern, the chit chat of voices went silent as all the Grocklings stood amazed at what they saw before them.

"Come with us," said Furdon "We want you to meet the rest of our troop."

As Rose followed Furdon, she had Fiddy at her side reassuringly holding her hand. As the word spread about the visitor, more and more Grocklings appeared in doorways and on ledges to look upon Rose with wide eyes of surprise. Some started to follow her down the steps which spiralled down the outside wall to the heart of the cavern. Others bowed or curtseyed as she passed by. Rose did not know what to make of their reaction so smiled politely as she began to feel nervous and very outnumbered. Most of the Grocklings were wearing black coats like Fiddy and Furdon, though there were a few wearing blue jackets and others wearing brown. The Grocklings watched Rose in wonder and a murmur of curious voices started to follow her.

"Now, now, settle down," said Furdon to his friends as they reached the bottom of the stairs, "There's no need to be rude or stare, this is Miss Rose."

At this point, several Grocklings were jumping around excitedly whilst others wanted to get close and touch her. Furdon invited Rose to take a seat on a carpet of grass reeds and told the others to give her some space. She crouched down and sat with her legs crossed under her, with her grey cloak loosely draped around her shoulders. There was a small group of Grocklings perched on a step above them, looking down on what was happening. This small group were wearing burgundy jackets and did not look particularly impressed at a human being in their home. They did not smile or welcome her but were sitting twitching their tails at the upheaval and muttering amongst themselves. Rose however could not help but smile, she could never have imagined she would have been doing this when she woke up earlier.

"Fiddy, go and get Frithad and Eady… Tell them we have a long overdue visitor," ordered Furdon as he took a seat next to Rose.

A few minutes later the excited voices settled down and went quiet as Fiddy returned to the group with Frithad and

Eady, the apparent leaders of the Grockling troop. Rose turned to see who they were, expecting to see two larger and more authoritative figures. Instead, out from the dimly lit doorway at the base of the stone staircase appeared two very regular looking Grocklings, the only difference being that they wore long orange jackets which were down to the floor and dragged slightly as they walked. The troop parted to clear a pathway for Frithad and Eady to make their way to the front of the crowd. They walked up to Rose and swished their tails as they looked her over. Their faces were quite stern while they whispered something between themselves. They then turned to Rose and smiled kindly at her before turning to face the hundreds of Grocklings who were now gathered around.

"It's been too long since we've had the pleasure of human company," bellowed Frithad "and so, we must make this one welcome amongst us."

"She's called Rose," whispered Fiddy.

"Oh right, yes of course," said Frithad "Rose, make Rose welcome amongst us. I'm sure you'll each get to greet her but now, please go back to your burrows whilst Eady and I get her settled."

"Settled?" said Rose in a low voice to Furdon, "I didn't think I was stopping for long?"

"At least for the night Miss Rose," replied Furdon "It's too dark outside now, we don't want to put you in unnecessary danger. We'll take you back down the mountain at sunrise, if you wish?"

Rose was not best pleased as she had to go and help in the bakery in her village at dawn. Even though it was hard work and she did not like her boss, she never liked to let anyone down. However, she had agreed to meet the Grockling troop and was here now so decided to make the most of it. Besides, the walk up had taken a few hours and she needed a rest before going back down.

Eady approached Rose and did a small curtsey in front of her. Rose could see she was the lead female of the troop and looked older than the others and had a more elegant way about her. Her feline features were delicate and her fur was glossy with a little silver at the edges. Frithad was the male leader and had silver grey fur and a long, thick fluffy tail which twitched inquisitively and he and Eady got acquainted with their guest. Fiddy sat as close to Rose as he could, he had made good friends with her on the walk and did not want to go back to his burrow. Furdon stood tall on the other side of Rose, awaiting the moment when he could proudly tell his story of finding this lone stray human.

"It is a pleasure to meet you Rose," said Eady "As you know, our kind have been forbidden from communicating with your kind so this is a truly wonderful moment to which I never thought I'd see again."

"Here, here," said Frithad jovially "Can we get something for the young lady to eat and drink! You must be ravenous after the long walk?"

"Erm yes, Sir, I am," said Rose. Frithad laughed and his entire belly shook, he wasn't as lean as the rest of his troop.

"Sir?" he laughed "No need for such formality, call me Frithad, everyone else does." A young Grockling in a brown jacket appeared next to Rose with a basket of food. There was fresh bread, cheese, fruits and berries. Rose was pleasantly surprised as she was not sure what to expect, she thought Grocklings may have had a rather different diet compared to what she usually ate.

"Thank you," she said, taking a piece of soft bread.

"We've been waiting for you for a long time," said Eady "And as you can tell we're all thrilled to see you at last."

"It was only a few days ago when Furdon and Fiddy saw me though? That's not too long." Eady looked at Frithad and then back to Rose, slightly perplexed.

"Rose, we've been waiting for you for years, not days."

"I beg your pardon?" Rose was confused "You must be mistaking me with someone else."

"Not at all," continued Eady "Only when the timing was right and you were ready to meet us, then you would be brought to us." Rose paused and looked at Furdon who smiled at her and nodded his head. She then looked at Fiddy who was about to pinch a piece of cheese from the basket when he saw her look at him, he gave a cheeky smile and snuggled up to her.

"It is as Eady says" said Furdon "Though we only saw you a few days ago, we had to wait and see if you were the right one before inviting you here. Since the Ice Queen took her throne, many humans would have attacked us. But you didn't."

"Why would I have attacked you? You hadn't caused me any harm or threat."

"The Ice Queen would kill us herself if her magic could reach us... as it can't, she'd use humans as her tool to get the job done," sighed Frithad.

"Why would she kill you? You live in the mountains and have nothing to do with her."

"It's not that simple," said Eady "We have something hidden deep in our mountain which when used by the right person could bring a great threat to her throne."

Rose looked astonished and thought they were joking so started to laugh. It was funny how the Grocklings were thinking she was the human they had been looking for to end the reign of the Ice Queen. When she looked around her, none of her friends were laughing with her and were in fact frowning that she was not taking them seriously. Rose felt as if she had been tricked into coming to meet the Grocklings and did not like that one bit. She got to her feet and would have stormed off one way or another but did not know where she was and would probably get lost. Frithad and Eady were concerned at her reaction, thinking she would be more helpful.

"Do you not want to Ice Queen to be defeated?" asked Frithad.

"Of course I do," scowled Rose as she paced around "She has damaged the island and the people of Cragfeld with her selfish control but who am I to walk into the Dark Castle and…"

"You wouldn't be going straight to the Dark Castle," said Frithad. Rose turned to look at him, her blue eyes quite emotional as it was dawning on her that it was all very serious. Eady took Rose's hand in a soft but serious way.

"Please, follow us Rose," she said "We'll show you why you're here."

Fiddy took her other hand and the five of them walked towards a doorway where some very steep stairs spiralled down even deeper into the mountain. As that moment the mountain groaned, Rose had never heard such a load noise as it bellowed through the rock. Undisturbed, Frithad and Eady led the way as Rose tentatively followed them with Fiddy and Furdon close behind. The steps felt cold and looked wet, though were not slippery. There was the sound of dripping water echoing up the stairs from far below. They entered a small chamber with a stone walled well in the centre.

"Did you know the Ice Queen used to go by the name of Mordisan and she had a sister?" asked Frithad "Yes, indeed. Rika should've had the throne but Mordisan was very jealous and wanted Cragfeld all to herself. She took her sister into the tall tower of the Dark Castle and tricked her into sipping a magic potion. As soon as the potion started flowing through her veins, Mordisan cast a spell so cruel… she watched as Rika slowly became encased in ice, frozen and forgotten."

"And from that day," said Eady "Mordisan's cold heart froze solid and she became known as the Ice Queen. She's no longer capable of feeling anything but evil, she lives off it, thrives off it. Which is why the old witch is her ideal partner, full of dark magic so powerful that the two combined are a force to be reckoned with."

"I didn't know this," said Rose, her voice soft and sad "How could she do that to her own sister?"

"I suppose you were told she's a good Queen and Cragfeld has flourished under her rule?"

"That is what the elders have told us…" said Rose "But the Ice Queen has a spell on her people, they believe what she tells them and they never question her."

"Yet, you do? Don't you find that interesting? She can't get to you?"

"I thought she was punishing me in her own way, keeping me isolated and lonely with no friends." There was a sniffling noise as Fiddy once again let his emotions get the better of him, Furdon sternly handed him a handkerchief to dry his eyes.

"Her powers may have influenced you when you were young," continued Eady "But as you got older and stronger, they seem to fade."

"I don't understand," said Rose "Why do you think I can help you, I'm sure you have mistaken me for someone else, I'm not a warrior, nor do I have any magical tricks up my sleeve." Frithad took hold of Rose's hand and she bent down so he could look her deep in the eye, almost into her soul.

"Rose, we each have a warrior inside of us, it's only when we need to be really brave do they show themselves. Take a look down the well and tell us what you see."

Rose crept cautiously over to the well. The low walls only came up to her knees but they surrounded a hole in the cave floor, which a human could easily fall down if they were not careful. A grey mist circled the surface of the hole like a whirlpool and Rose found herself staring hypnotically into it. The Grocklings looked on as the mist in the pool changed from grey to purple and lit the room with a lilac glow. Rose crouched on her knees and placed her hands on the side of the well to steady herself as the mist cleared and there was nothing but blackness falling deeper into the mountain. Rose was about to turn to Frithad and ask what she was supposed to be looking for when a white light filled the well. Out of this light, shadows started to form and a picture developed. They saw a determined woman with fight in her eyes and pure light within her, facing up to the Ice Queen. The woman was strong and had fire in her belly and an army behind her. The last thing they saw as the image started to fade was the golden outline of a leaf resting upon the woman's neck. As the image faded but lingered, Rose stood and turned to her friends who were all as taken aback as she was.

"I've never seen the image so clear," said Frithad.

"Which means time is getting near, it's time to prepare," said Eady.

"What do you mean?" Rose was becoming frustrated "Will somebody please tell me who that woman in the picture is and what's going on?"

"That woman," said Eady "Is you...!" Rose turned back and looked closely at the faded picture, trying to recognise something which could be true about it. "It is you my dear but this is showing what is yet to come, not what has been."

"That could be anyone, you can't be certain it is me. Besides, she looks older and stronger than me," said Rose.

"Didn't you see the golden leaf?" asked Frithad, who was becoming annoyed at Rose's disbelief "the golden leaf around her neck?" Rose looked into the eyes of each of the Grocklings and then reached inside her cloak and pulled out the golden locket which hung around her neck. Her new friends all stood wide eyed and in wonder.

"Oh my," said Eady in a soft voice "Oh dear Rose, may I look at it more closely?" Rose leaned forward so they could each look at the locket, "It was my mother's, I never knew her but the people who raised me said it belonged to her. I've never been able to open it but I've never taken it off."

Over the years the locket had lost its lustre and shine. The oval shape sat comfortably between Rose's collarbones and had a fine chain looped around her neck. Eady took a handkerchief out of Frithad's pocket and gently rubbed the surface of the locket to clean it up. With each stroke the locket became spotless and an engraving became apparent. A fine etching of a leaf with seven points had been swirled beautifully onto the locket. Eady and Frithad smiled, knowing Rose was definitely the one they had been waiting for.

"The locket can't be opened again until it reaches Ordram," said Frithad "It's your task Rose, to travel to Ordram."

"What's... where's Ordram?" asked Rose "There isn't anyone or anywhere on Cragfeld with that name and beyond Cragfeld there's nothing but endless ocean."

"That's what you have been told," said Frithad "And that's not the truth. There are many lands beyond Cragfeld my dear and you'll be seeing things you could've only dreamed of."

At this point Rose's eyes lit up, she always knew there was more beyond the mountains than she had been told. Now she was starting to believe the Grocklings were telling the truth. She could not believe that now, all of her questions might be answered. She always wanted to see what lay beyond the mountains.

"Ordram's a magical place," said Eady excitedly "Ordram's a magical tree. When you reach him you must get one of his leaves for this locket. Only his power and magic is strong enough to bring the Ice Queen to her knees, end her reign and return Cragfeld back to how it was."

"While you're gone we'll get everything ready for your return. Don't be scared dear, you'll not be doing this alone. When the time comes, we'll be by your side," said Frithad proudly. Rose's sense of adventure was stirring and she was coming round to the idea of exploring lands far away from

Cragfeld. She did not like the idea of fighting the Ice Queen but she would cross that bridge when she got to it. All she could think of now was finding Ordram and seeing what worlds awaited her outside this island she'd never left.

"When am I to go?" she asked, feeling quite excited now and raring to go. Eady's face filled with joy at her acceptance of the task.

"You must rest now," said Eady "And at sunrise you'll start the journey. It isn't going to be easy and you'll come across places and creatures both good and bad." The four Grocklings and Rose made their way back up the steps to the main cavern. Fiddy and Furdon showed Rose where she could sleep and they fetched her some blankets. Frithad and Eady wished her a good sleep and would see her in a few hours.

Rose could not believe what had just happened. She always had a feeling there was more to her life than mundanely helping in a bakery. Now she felt as if her spirit had been woken and she started to imagine what lay ahead. Of course she was quite scared too, leaving the place she knew for a place she never knew existed. What a day she had. Fiddy and Furdon did not want to leave her so sat either side of her until she went to sleep.

Two of the burgundy coated Grocklings had been waiting for the others to reappear in the main cavern and when it was quiet they crept down to them. Fiddy and Furdon stood to greet them but their manners were lost on these individuals.

"So she's the one then, eh?" said the bigger and stronger looking of the two, "The one we're supposed to help? She hasn't a clue about Ordram has she?!"

"Yet we're to join her?" snarled the other, "No chance!"

"Yes, she's the one," said Furdon "And you will respect the orders from Frithad and help her. By helping her, you're helping our troop and every other creature on this cursed island."

"Oh right," said the first "For the greater good and all that? (hiss) We've been trained to fight with warriors, we've earned our burgundy jackets... and now we're expected to go with this girl."

"Yes, yes you are!" said Furdon sternly."

"Well if you or Frithad thinks that's going to happen, then you'll have to think again. I've spoken with my fellow fighters... to go with her, who has never fought a battle in her life would be putting ourselves in danger and that's something we're not prepared to do."

"Listen you brute," said Furdon, now becoming angry "if you don't help her, then you'll put her and this entire mission in danger... and it will have all been for nothing."

"Yeah, yeah, whatever!" they hissed and went back to their pack. Furdon sat back down next to Rose and Fiddy went to sit next to him.

"What now?" asked Fiddy "They knew they were trained to fight and protect whoever was chosen for this task. Nobody knows what she could face on her own."

"I know Fiddy, I know." With worried minds they tried to get some rest.

Whist the rest of the Lowlands and villages of Cragfeld were sleeping and the mountain was rumbling, the Ice Queen could not settle. The old witch was still in her chamber conducting spells and stirring up magic. The Ice Queen paced across the landing which looked down on her throne. The throne was once a majestic and beautiful creation which now sat under a layer of thick deadly black ice. No amount of heat could melt the ice or have any effect on the Ice Queen herself. Her powers were stronger than anything humankind could throw at her. As she paced, her gown trailed after her and left snowflakes sparkling around her tall elegant frame.

"What's stirring?" she muttered to herself "It must be those damn Grocklings, it must be! If something is amiss which I can't see, it must be under the mountain, damn them!"

She turned quickly and her blood red hair tumbled over her shoulders as she marched up the ice steps to the tallest tower. The ice under her feet would make the rest of us fall but it was her creation and it moved with her, as she directed it to. She almost floated up the steps to the tallest tower to her sister's frozen tomb… she rarely came to this place as it reminded her of all the things she hated.

Everybody had loved Rika and praised her kindness, never noticing Mordisan in the shadows. The Kings and Queens, Lords and Ladies had all of their attention on Rika whilst Mordisan slipped into the darkness to perfect her craft and strengthen the powers inside her. Mordisan was only noticed by one person, the old witch. At seeing the darkness within Mordisan's heart, Orme took her under her wing to teach her and grow her strong. Between them, over many years of practicing long forgotten dark magic, they rose up together and took everything they wanted. Kings and Queens were banished never to return to Cragfeld and threatened that if they tried to take it back, Rika would feel unimaginable pain for all eternity. Nobody wanted Rika to suffer so instead they stayed away, leaving her frozen at the hands of her sister.

Mordisan had an anger within her which she used to fuel the powerful magic. As she approached the ice chamber where her sister lay, she glared at it with malice. She raised her arms, took an intake of cold air and pushed a wave of power towards the wall and melted a doorway through the thick wall of ice. She stared through the doorway for a few moments before stepping hesitantly forward, knowing seeing Rika again would anger her even more. The room of ice was bare apart from the table on which stood the block of ice around her sister. The Ice Queen slowly stepped towards the table and with a frozen stare glared at Rika. Mordisan did not want to see her sister resting peacefully and had left her in the position in which she had been frozen;

her sad eyes crying out for help and her arms reaching out to her sister to stop what she was doing to her. It reminded the Ice Queen of the hatred she had to carry which had been necessary for her to get and keep the throne.

"The only reason I keep you here, sister," she hissed "It's not because I want to, it's because I have to. Your face reminds me of all the pain it took to get me what I wanted. Your blue eyes looking at me with a goodness which I've never had or wanted to have. You always thought you were better than me didn't you? Look at you now, look where being good got you! The people of Cragfeld don't remember you, any writings of you have been destroyed and let's face it, nobody wants you back. For one hundred and fifty years you've stood there, frozen in time while the world around you forgets you. It's me who'll be remembered." The Ice Queen smiled as her tormenting comments flowed from her lips like poison. "No, dear, dear sister, you're stuck here with me. Kings and Queens far away from Cragfeld may talk of you as if you were once something special, then again, probably not. You were nothing compared to me. My powers are stronger than you could have ever thought and with Orme at my side, Cragfeld will remain mine for thousands more years. Which is why I haven't killed you sister – You can watch me, like I watched you take the light for all those years. Even your handsome Prince Vecter hasn't tried to save you, you'll just be a distant memory to him now. Still, he mustn't have loved you as much as he said, where was he when you needed him? So sad, little Princess lost and forgotten, forever!"

The Ice Queen placed one hand on the ice coffin which encased Rika, it crackled under her touch. She looked into her sister's sad pathetic eyes and smiled with hatred at her. She turned and walked out of the frozen chamber, laughing to herself as she thought about how people shouldn't have ignored her and had paid the price for doing so. Rika's body was not dead, she lay frozen in an eternal slumber. The Ice Queen summoned a ball of magic in her hand and threw it in the doorway to refreeze the chamber solid. A howl from a Silvertip echoed down the mountain like a haunting cry of times long forgotten.

The Ice Queen left the frozen chamber behind and wound her way back down the spiral stairway to the main hall. A gust of ice wind whistled through the open windows and twirled around the room as if doing a dance for the Queen. She stamped her foot and all of the windows slammed shut, the whistle of the wind was locked out. Orme was waiting behind a tall stone pillar watching as Mordisan returned from the tower.

"What are you doing Orme, you know I know you're there, so why hide?"

"You're restless and disturbed my Queen, as am I. This night leaves me wide awake."

"Did you find out who the lone stranger in grey could be? Or indeed anything about the locket?"

"I did not," sighed the old witch "There are strong powers in force preventing me from seeing what I have asked."

"Strong powers?" the Ice Queen laughed, "Compared to ours, nothing is as strong as the two of us united. Besides, my watch towers and guards would surely alert me to any lone grey figures. No human would reach the craggy border without my knowledge and even if they do make it then they wouldn't survive. The Grocklings are up to something, it is the only explanation I can feel that's causing unrest. They're not a threat, they're just a parasite I've had to get used to." The old witch left the Ice Queen brooding and hobbled back down the corridor into the murky shadows.

Rose had soon drifted off to sleep, the climb up the mountain had exhausted her. After a short deep sleep she woke wondering where she was, as if the day before had been a dream. She looked around her and saw Fiddy to her left and Furdon to her right, realising it had not been a dream after all. The cavern around her was dimly lit and Rose could just see outlines and silhouettes of stairs and walkways above her. She felt as if she was being watched but could not see anything in the gloom so pulled the blanket over her head and began going over everything Eady and Frithad had told her. As much as she wanted an adventure she did not want to embark on such a demanding journey. Rose never felt she had fitted in but right at this moment she would have loved to have been snuggled up in her own bed. She was in a place she never knew existed and would have trouble finding her way home without Fiddy or Furdon by her side. She closed her eyes and let her mind drift to the rocky ledge where she had found comfort being on her own. The Grocklings had found her, they believe for a purpose and she went willingly with them up the mountain. And what of the golden locket, a gift from her mother – how could this be relevant to anything? There were no obvious answers but she knew life on Cragfeld would be the same thing day in and day out without any change or excitement. By journeying to Ordram at least she would have the adventure she had always thought about.

"Miss Rose, are you awake?" said Fiddy's small voice in a whisper over her shoulder.

"Yes Fiddy, I am."

"Are you hiding under there?" he said lifting up the blanket and laying next to her underneath it.

"Yes, I felt as if too many eyes were looking at me so I covered up."

"There are no eyes looking at you, apart from mine Rose, trust me, I can see in the dark like you can see in the day."

"I know, I just got that feeling. What are you doing awake anyway?"

"If you don't mind me asking, can I come with you when

you leave tomorrow? I'll not be a nuisance I promise. I know we've only known each other a few hours but you're my friend and I want to come, if you'll have me?" Rose looked into Fiddy's big green eyes and smiled.

"How can I refuse?" she said. She was actually rather relieved as the thought of going to strange places by herself was quite scary. At least with Fiddy by her side she would have trustworthy company.

"Can I come too?" whispered another voice, Furdon lifted up the blanket and joined Rose and Fiddy under it. "I think we got you this far, it's only right we both come with you? We may only be small but we've sharp eyes and are quick on our feet."

"Sharp eyes? You mean like when you didn't see that great Silvertip creeping up on you?" she teased.

"Well, apart from that," he blushed "That'll never happen again, we promise."

"We promise," repeated Fiddy sincerely. Rose smiled and put her arms around her friends feeling grateful to have two good friends by her side.

"Of course, I'd be honoured to have you both come with me." They snuggled under the blanket and talked in low voices about the events of the last few hours. Rose could not have seen any of this coming and now, with good friends by her side was feeling ready for whatever lay ahead of her.

As Rose drifted between wake and sleep, her imagination was conjuring all sorts of scenarios she would face. She could hear a strange but familiar voice talking in a mumble to her as sleep washed over her. Fiddy nuzzled up next to her, equally as excited at what lay ahead. He knew he had met Rose for a reason, more than finding her and bringing her to the cavern to meet the troop. Fiddy was a lot more excited about the adventure than Furdon who was a lot more serious, knowing that it was not going to be an easy task ahead.

CHAPTER THREE

The following morning Rose was shaken awake by Fiddy and Furdon, her eyes were bleary through disturbed and restless sleep. Several other Grocklings were running around preparing a breakfast for Rose and packing a few goodies into a bag for her journey. Rose was escorted by a couple of female Grocklings to a smaller cave where she could wash in the waterfalls. It felt good to have the cold clean water wash over her skin, she felt reinvigorated and wide awake. Fresh clothes had been left for her in a dry alcove near the door and surprisingly they fitted her perfectly. She flung her cloak around her and made her way back to the main cavern.

"Breakfast Rose?" asked Fiddy as he held out a plate of delicious food for her. There was fresh bread, soft boiled eggs, sweet blueberry muffins and crunchy oat biscuits.

"Oh goodness," she said, her face lighting up.

Frithad and Eady were already seated on the blanket, eating breakfast and talking amongst themselves. Fiddy and Furdon sat next to Rose as she crouched down and began tucking into the breakfast treats laid out in front of her. She did not realise how hungry she was until she started eating the delicious fare.

"How are you feeling this morning?" asked Frithad as he scoffed on a biscuit "We hope you slept well and were comfortable?"

"Oh yes, thank you," Rose had actually had a troubled sleep but did not want to be rude to her hosts, it was not their fault her mind was buzzing and she could not get comfortable.

"That's good," said Eady gently "You'll need plenty of energy, especially for the next couple of days. It'll take that long to get out from under the mountain."

"Under the mountain?" Rose was surprised "Surely we go up and over the mountain?"

"It'd be too dangerous," smiled Eady "We can't be certain either way if the Ice Queen knows you're here or not, we don't want to risk it anyway. If you go out and up the mountain, her spies will see you and the watch towers will send out their winged wardens who'll grab you and take you to the Dark Castle. If you go under the mountain, she'll not know anything, not until you're away from Cragfeld where her magic can't touch you."

"Going under the mountain has its dangers too," said Frithad "Which is why you'll not be going alone." He whispered to one of the Grocklings in a brown jacket to call the Fighters to the meeting. Six Grocklings wearing burgundy jackets made their way down to the cavern floor and stood tall and proud in front of Frithad.

"These are our Fighters who've been trained to deal with most hazards you may face. They've been waiting for this moment…"

"Frithad…" interrupted the large Grockling who'd spoken with Furdon the night before "We've been trained to fight and defend warriors and Kings, not, if you beg my pardon, a young girl who hasn't a clue why she's here. We've agreed as a group, this mission is not ours."

"What's the difference?" scowled Frithad "She's the chosen one and you've been trained to help the chosen one… whoever it may be!" Rose watched on as the two Grocklings shared heated words.

"If they don't want to come with me, there's no point forcing them," said Rose, in a soft tone "I don't know where I'm going but I won't be going alone." Frithad and Eady looked at each other uneasily. "My two friends Furdon and Fiddy have already volunteered to join me and I'd be privileged to have them by my side."

"But they've had no training…?" said Frithad, leaning forward, disappointed at his Fighters. He sighed heavily "But, I suppose… and if they have already volunteered…?"

"It is fine," said Eady "You've made friends and have a close bond already. If Fiddy and Furdon swear to protect you with all they have, then who are we to stand in their way?" Fiddy and Furdon looked at each other and smiled, trying not to jump up with joy.

"We must pack you up properly with food and weapons," said Frithad, clicking his fingers and setting a few Grocklings on this task.

"Weapons?" asked Rose "What kind of weapons, what will I need them for?"

"All sorts of weapons for all sorts of occasions," smiled Frithad "Better safe than sorry."

As breakfast came to an end, Grocklings in brown jackets cleared everything away. Then appeared the Grocklings in blue jackets with bags, parcels and weapons which Rose didn't recognise but thought looked quite small. Rose was loaded up with one bag and the rest was handed to Fiddy and Furdon.

"Right then," said Frithad "There's no time like the present and we have to say goodbye sooner or later." He paused and smiled at Rose "But we'll see you again, in no time at all." He reached up to shake her hand and wish her well. Eady however gave Rose a warm hug.

"Be careful won't you Rose, only trust those you know."

The rest of the Grockling troop had gathered to say goodbye to Rose, Furdon and Fiddy and wave them off as they made their way to the doorway and down the staircase to the well. The Fighters did not make eye contact with them as they left, feeling slightly ashamed at their behaviour but not backing down from their decision. As they reached the well, the grey mist was swirling over it like it did the night before.

"How will I know I'm going the right way?" asked Rose.

"You'll know," said Frithad "There'll be help when you get out of the mountain and Ordram will sense your arrival and show you the way."

"We are so proud," said Eady, a tear building in her eyes "Thank you Furdon and Fiddy, good luck, we will be ready for your return." Rose looked around her, for a doorway or staircase.

"Which way do we go?" she asked.

"The only way out is through the well," said Frithad, pointing to the swirling surface over the well.

"But that's a deep hole," said Rose "I saw last night it falls deep and dark into nothingness."

"It is what you need it to be," smiled Eady reassuringly "You have to trust it."

"You mean you expect us to jump in there?" doubted Rose.

"Yes, it's the only way."

Rose looked at Fiddy and Furdon, who were looking back at her with disbelief and thinking it was going to be a painful landing.

"Well, I say we go for it," said Fiddy "We just have to take the leap together." Rose smiled at his brave attempt to rally them together.

"Ok," said Rose as some of Fiddy's energy was contagious "Let's hold hands and all go together?" The three friends held hands and peered into the swirling mist. Feelings of nervous excitement at not knowing what was on the other side rushed through their veins. "I'll count to three and on four we go. Hold my hands tight and don't let go." Her friends looked up at her with their trusting green eyes and nodded. "Ok then… here we go… one… two… three… go." With that the three friends jumped down the well and vanished through the grey mist. Frithad and Eady looked at each other and then stared back at the hole, there was nothing they could do now but wait.

Rose could feel cold air rushing passed her face as they fell. Grasping her hands tight were Furdon on Fiddy who could see nothing but blackness beneath their feet. Flashes of colour exploded in front of Rose's eyes, not on the walls of the well but as if bubbles were bursting and the rainbow of colours splashed around her. She found herself forgetting she was falling as she was mesmerised at the display. It seemed as if they were falling for an age. Down below them Furdon could see a grey mist swirling as they quickly approached it. They hit the mist at high speed but it acted as a cushion to their landing as they slowly sunk through it. They couldn't see or hear anything while they were sinking through this thick fluffy cloud. They kept hold of each other, not knowing how long they could be here or even what awaited them at the other side. Rose closed her eyes and waited. Eventually she felt a draft on her feet, which worked its way up her legs as they slowly reached the end of the fall and came through the other side of the mist.

They were gently dropped into what seemed to be a dark tunnel. It felt damp and there was a smell of earth and soil around them. They did not want to let go of each other until they were positive they were all safe and in the same place. Between the Grocklings, they kept hold of Rose but with their free hands rummaged through a rucksack for a lantern. After quite a bit of fumbling around they managed to get one going. Only on seeing each other did they let go of each other's hands.

"Wow, what did you think of the light show?" asked Rose.

"What a light show?" said Furdon "I saw multi-coloured

toadstools and dancing fairies on my fall!"

"Really, how incredible. What did you see Fiddy?"

"Golden leaves and dragonflies…" said Fiddy with a puzzled expression.

"How very strange," Rose smiled "But at least we made it to… wherever we are."

They looked around as Rose got to her feet and was able to stand tall in the tunnel. Above them was the other end of the well which still had grey mist circling in a whirlpool just as at the other end. They were at the dead end of a tunnel with only one direction open to go. Apart from the sound of them talking, it was otherwise quiet and still. The tunnels didn't look as if they'd been used for a while, with layers of dust and soil but no trace of previous footsteps. Having decided to share one lantern between them they slowly walked along the dark path. On either side of them was a rocky soily wall which wrapped around them like a tube looking as if it hadn't been touched for years. It wasn't long until the path split. The left tunnel appeared exactly the same as the one on the right.

"What now?" asked Fiddy as he gazed left and right, hoping for some kind of sign.

Out of the darkness came a rumbling noise, almost right above their heads. Pebbles and dirt were shaken from the roof of the tunnel and dropped around where the three of them were standing. When the rumbling faded and there was a hiss coming from behind them and a cha-cha-cha-hiss rattle in the shadows.

"Does anyone know what the heck that was?" asked Rose, turning to see if there was anything behind them. Nothing was there but the dark empty tunnel.

"No," said Furdon "But I believe we've been dropped into Boven, a tangled maze woven into the mountain."

Before Furdon could finish there was another rumble which sounded to be getting closer. All of a sudden the rock and soil of the tunnel to the right of them began to crumble and shift. There was something moving the earth and before they knew what was happening the tunnel to the right had been completely blocked off. The rumbling died down and there was a hissing noise in front of them, a rattle of cha-cha-cha-cha-cha-hiss from the other side of the tunnel wall.

"I say we make a dash for it," said Fiddy.

"Me too," agreed Rose with a slight tremble in her voice.

They started going as fast as they could down the tunnel, with the little lantern they had it did not light far. They could hear the rumbling in the earth around them, not sure if it was coming from above, below, or either side. They kept moving until they came to a dead end. Cha-cha-cha-cha-cha-hisss could be heard close by, whatever was in the maze with them knew they were there and was following them. There was a deathly silence for a few moments before the tunnel walls started to crumble and the earth was being shifted and packed tight again. Rose saw a flicker of something silver and scaly as the earth moved around them, they each held onto each other as the tunnels were shaking around them. Then silence. Rose lifted the lantern which revealed they were no longer in a dead end. The tunnel behind them from which they had came was now blocked off and there was a choice of three tunnels in front of them.

"Whatever it is that's doing that, is playing with us like a toy," said Rose. The fear had now turned to anger as they were being mocked. "Tunnels are being remade and re-shaped as we go, we'll never find our way back."

"Miss Rose," said Furdon "The Boven maze is intended to confuse travellers who pass through it, no journey will ever be the same as another because the maze is always being reformed by the three Sneckaluses which live in it."

"And a Sneckalus is…?"

"It has the tail of a rattle snake which helps push it through the tunnels, its front legs help it speed along and it has huge paws which effortlessly shift dirt. They are blind but sense vibration around them and can smell fear."

"Don't they sound a treat!" said Rose sarcastically "So if the tunnels keep moving, how are we going to find our way out of this place?"

"It depends how much fun the Sneckaluses are having with us, if they soon get bored with us then they will guide us out. If they want to keep us longer then they will… so I've heard anyway. Never been here myself."

"Any ideas how we could make them bored of us…"

The earth started to shudder again so the three friends made a dash for it down the middle tunnel which had just been carved out before their eyes. As they were running they could hear a Sneckalus, or maybe all three following them until they reached a fork in the path.

"Which way?" said Rose, slightly out of breath.

"It doesn't matter," said Furdon.

"What do you mean it doesn't matter?"

"We are toys in their maze. The only way they will get bored of us is if we act as if we know where we are going. Walk confidently and assert power with every step. If they smell fear then they can play with us until we give up, stop moving…"

"Right, I see what you're saying," said Rose boldly "Let's keep moving until we are let out of here, any direction and every direction… as long as they run out of steam before we do."

Fiddy and Furdon agreed with Rose and with one either side of her walked forward and down the tunnel on the left. Rose held the lantern to show them the way, until a Sneckalus powered in front of them to block the way and forge a new choice of tunnels. Each time Rose confidently strode, thinking they were probably making no progress and going round in circles but that was not the aim of the game. Whenever a Sneckalus charged in front of them, another would blast the tunnel behind them so there was no going back. Constantly around them they could hear the tails rattling cha-cha-cha-cha-cha-hisss, cha-cha-cha-cha-cha, cha cha-hisss. Tunnel after tunnel, turn after turn, they kept walking as if they knew exactly where they were going. The noise and amount of rumbling in the mountainside around them seemed to quieten down somewhat, as if one or maybe two of the Sneckaluses were getting bored with these three. Maybe they had picked up vibrations in another part of the maze and found someone or something else to tease and play with. Rose and the two Grocklings still had company and were determined not to be the first to give in. If they had one Sneckalus on their tale they would still have to keep going.

"Why don't you two get on my shoulders?" suggested Rose "There will be fewer vibrations for these creatures to follow and you can have a rest at the same time."

Fiddy did not hesitate and while Rose strode along, he jumped up her cloak and onto her shoulder. Furdon knew it made good sense and hopped up to her other shoulder. With fewer vibrations the Sneckalus thought there were fewer things to play with in the tunnel below. The rattle of a tail still followed them, though they could not be sure whether it was one or two. The rattle was all around them but some-how seemed further away and not right next to them as it had felt before.

After walking around the Boven maze for hours, Rose was becoming bored of the game. Fiddy tried to distract her by telling her stories, whilst Furdon fished around the rucksacks and provided a few snacks to keep her going. By now there was only one Sneckalus burrowing around them, there was only one rattle and it was either slightly in front of them or slightly behind them at any one time. Fiddy and Furdon took it in turns to hold the lantern as Rose's arm was getting tired too. With a loud thundering noise the Sneckalus powerfully broke through the tunnel in front of them, it moved at such speed Rose only caught a glimpse of its tail as it moved. Then all was quiet, shaking of earth around them eased and the cha-cha-cha-cha-cha-hisss faded as it went away.

"You did it Miss Rose," cheered Fiddy, hopping up and down on her shoulder.

"Well done," said Furdon "Listen, silence… we've been left alone at last."

"Huh?" murmured Rose, who had gone into a trance-like state through boredom of walking through the dark monotonous tunnels. Furdon took the lantern and jumped down to investigate the layout of the final tunnel.

"We must only have a few hundred metres to go and we will be out of the maze, come on, let's go." Furdon had a light in his eyes which inspired the other two to follow him, almost running.

At the end of the tunnel they could see a glow of orange light. Rose would have loved to see daylight but knew it was not to be. As they slowed their pace and reached the end of the tunnel, they found themselves looking upon a vast well lit opening in the rock. It was narrow but deep and had a waterfall pouring out from a small drop below their feet, right down to the bottom, where their eyes couldn't see. The orange glow was being emitted from a single globe of light which seemed to float freely around the waterfall.

"Can either of you see a path or a way out?" asked Rose, gazing down at the waterfall until she felt dizzy.

"I can't see anything," said Furdon "The sides of the rock are sheer and smooth, no path though."

The orange globe floated slowly over to them like a giant seamless balloon. There was a light coming from its core. As it got closer to them, it dropped slightly so that it's upper surface was the same level as the floor of the tunnel. The globes shape softened and appeared more like an oval cushion of air.

"Are you getting on then or just going to stare all day?"

said a fairly harsh voice from inside the structure.

Taken aback and with no other option Rose stepped onto the strange floating balloon and the two Grocklings jumped after her. The balloon slowly descended down the side of the waterfall which drenched the three travellers. Furdon looked bewildered and poked the surface of the balloon trying to work out what it could be. The structure started to wobble and it sounded like it was giggling, Furdon must have tickled it. In turn Rose and Fiddy started to chuckle as Furdon promptly composed himself and stopped poking around. When they had floated to the bottom of the waterfall, the orange balloon reshaped itself again to form steps for the three passengers to safely disembark.

"Thank you for using this service, please have a safe onward journey," said the voice inside the globe as it lifted itself off the floor and slowly floated back up the waterfall. Rose watched in amazement. With nobody knowing what to say, they looked at each other in disbelief at what had just happened.

They stood under the waterfall trying to see where they were to go now. At the back of the waterfall was a dry ledge which looked a little like a pathway but it was not clear. Rose took the lead and her friends were right behind her. The pathway gradually spiralled up to a doorway with a stone arch in the rock.

"Come in, come in, stop making the place look untidy," said a male voice from the other side of the doorway.

They did as they were told and followed the direction of the voice. There standing in a cluttered cave was an elderly looking man in a long orange cloak which seemed to be covered in scorch marks. Inside the cave were shelves piled high with clutter, glass bottles full of strange looking liquids, trinkets, and wooden cabinets bursting at the hinges with books and papers. The elderly chap was hurriedly marching around picking things up, putting things down and generally just shifting things from one place to another with no real meaning. A white cat hissed when it saw the Grocklings, not sure what to make of them. There was a stone sink carved into the back of the cave in which fish occasionally jumped up out of and then dived back in. The stone sink did not actually have a bottom so any water life that wanted to drop in could do so. The sound of the waterfall echoed around the room the three friends talked in whispers as they walked in.

"Have you never been told whispering is rude?" said the old man as he huffed across the room from pillar to post. "Do sit down, stop making the place look untidy."

Rose looked around to see where they could sit amongst the clutter. She saw a wooden stool near the fireplace and made her way over to it and told the Grocklings to sit on her shoulders out of the way. The white cat came over to Rose and rubbed against her legs before going to sit on a cushion and stare suspiciously at her companions. The old man continued to rattle around, clinking glasses as he knocked them around. He then stopped, turned to look at Rose and stared at her for a while.

"Have you ever been told it's rude to stare?" said Rose, in the same way he seemed to communicate.

The old man started laughing and made his way over to sit with Rose. He threw a load of papers off a wooden cabinet and perched upon it dangling his skinny pale legs. Rose could see his glasses were broken and had been bodged back together with whatever he could find. White tufty eyebrows sprouted wildly above his old eyes and wisps of white hair could be seen under the hood of his orange cloak.

"So young lady, you are the one?" he finally said, looking her up and down "You're a lot younger than I was expecting but still... I can't be one to comment on age now can I? hmmm! No, no, no, not at all. I have been waiting for you, haven't you been told it's rude to keep an old wizard waiting. I have a busy schedule and can't be sitting around for you all day."

"We do apologise," said Furdon "The Sneckaluses held us for longer than expected."

"Did they indeed," wheezed the old man "You must've entertained them for a while. Still, they have nothing better to do with their time than chase around that maze all day, they will have enjoyed the excitement… for a while anyway. Good to see they got bored before you did, otherwise you wouldn't be here would you!" He paused for a moment and then looked back at Rose, "Have I met you before?"

"Erm, no Sir," she said.

"Call me Bolstone," he said gruffly.

"Erm, pleased to meet you Bolstone, my name is Rose and these are my friends Furdon and Fiddy." said Rose, bowing her head slightly with respect, hoping it would appease him.

"I know who you are," said Bolstone in a slow soft voice "You are the one who's going to save Cragfeld from the Ice Queen. I can see it in your eyes you don't believe it… but that is how it is. You'll feel like you have a fire inside you when the time comes." The white cat moved to sit on the edge of the sink and teased each fish which decided to pop up out of the water. There was a tremble around them in the mountain as it shifted.

"Bolstone, if you don't mind," said Rose "Please can you tell us more about our journey to Ordram? We haven't been given a map, let alone any information about getting there. We were told we'd be guided along the way…"

"And so you shall be guided along the way," said Bolstone "Each person you meet at every stage of your journey will help you or hinder you… but even I can't foresee which direction you'll take. There are hundreds of different options you could take but Ordram will have a magnetic pull on you and you'll know you're going the right way." Bolstone got up and started rearranging things again. "Would you like some tea?" he offered eventually.

"That'd be lovely, thank you," said Rose. Fiddy and Furdon didn't care for tea and hoped for something a little more milky but didn't dare seem disrespectful to the old wizard.

Bolstone stumbled around the kitchen, or what they guessed to be the kitchen under all of the chaos. With a rattle of pots and chinking of cups he hobbled back carrying a tray of tea and cakes. Fiddy didn't look happy but a swift jab in the ribs from Furdon reminded him of his manners.

"I could do with a table and a few more chairs couldn't I?" he said, snapping his fingers. From under a clutter of papers appeared a table which shook itself clean and stood proudly in front of Bolstone and his guests. Moments later an arm-chair heaved itself free from against the wall and almost coughed as it blew the dust off itself and stood in front of the wizard. "I don't know what you are suggesting, you're clean enough," he muttered at the chair as he took a seat.

The old wizard had the tea tray on his lap and poured out a cup for each of his guests. Rose was given a cup of sweet milky tea. As the wizard poured out a cup for Fiddy, he saw it wasn't tea, rather a luxurious creamy milk with a dusting of chocolate. When it came to Furdon, it wasn't tea or creamy milk but out poured a thick creamy ale… Furdon's favourite. By this time they were highly intrigued about what would come out of the teapot for the old wizard. They waited in anticipation as Bolstone slowly lifted the handle, into his teacup was a hot orange liquid which smelled a lot like whiskey but none of them wanted to comment. His white cat came over and pawed at Bolstone who tipped some liquid onto a saucer, the ideal treat for a cat was indeed milk. They each sipped on their drink of choice, a warming sensation melted through them.

"Tell me, young lady," said the wizard after a couple of minutes "Have you ever met the Ice Queen? I myself have only seen her a couple of times, I haven't been to Cragfeld for many, many years."

"I met her once when I was a younger," said Rose "My friend and I were summoned to the Dark Castle when we'd been thinking of crossing the border into the mountains."

"Indeed," he wheezed and then coughed to clear his throat "And let me guess she turned your friend into one of her mindless flock?" Rose nodded. "But you remained you?" Again Rose nodded. "Interesting indeed." The old man looked over his glasses at his guests. "I've never had a pleasant encounter with the woman and I can't say seeing her again is on my top ten list of things I need to do before I get any older. Does she still have that old witch at her side?" Rose nodded once more. Bolstone got up and sighed as he straightened his back. "She's a nasty piece of work, we were in the same class at school you know, she was always going off on her own to practice black magic. Now look at her, she's exactly where she wanted to be – with a cruel Queen at her side."

"It is said that between them, their magic and powers can't be defeated," said Rose.

"Is that so? Well that depends who has tried. Her watch towers and guards can see any threat approaching for hundreds of miles and if anyone does make it to Cragfeld, she soon snatches them up. They don't stand a chance against her. For the weaker minded she casts a spell on them to forget where they came from and sends them out into the villages, praising how wonderful she is – it's like she has frozen their minds."

"And what about the ones with a stronger mind, what happens to those?" said Fiddy, not sure if he actually wanted to hear the answer.

"She casts a whirlwind of ice and air around them, encasing them in a sparkling crystal before shrinking them and hanging them from the chandelier in the main hall of the

Dark Castle. Poor blighters stuck there." He shook his head and a frown furrowed his brow. Fiddy made a gulping sound as he swallowed his beverage and started nervously twirling a ringlet of Rose's hair between his fingers. The old man began shifting stuff around again.

"Don't you know it's rude to keep an old man from his work?" he muttered.

"But aren't you going to help us?" asked Rose "Isn't that why we are here?"

"Help you? Help you? Whatever gave you that idea?" he frowned "What do you need me for?" The Grocklings looked at each other and then at Rose, all quite as confused as each other. Rose felt quite miffed and frustrated with the old wizard.

"It was you who invited us in here?" she snapped "If we knew it was just for a chat then we wouldn't have wasted our time!"

Bolstone turned around and looked over his glasses at her. He had a glint in his eye and started to smile. Rose got to her feet and straightened herself, looking taller and feeling as though she could assert herself better.

"See, there's a spark inside you young Rose, a spark that you haven't fired up to its full potential. That day will come, that day will come."

"Spark or no spark, my friends and I need to know how to get out of this miserable mountain. Are you going to help us or not?"

"Have you never been told it's rude to speak to an old man like that?" he continued rummaging through the piles of rubbish, bottles, books and paper on the side.

"And don't you know it's rude to treat your guests this way?"

The old man laughed a wheezy laugh and made his way back to the armchair where he fell back into it and encouraged Rose to sit back down.

"I like you young lady, you have courage and a healthy spirit flowing through you, don't lose that." The room felt quiet, outside the thunder from the waterfall pounded around them. A small blue fish jumped up in the sink, saw the white cat ready to claw at it and quickly dove back in with a plop. "Now what can I do for you? I can help you out of this mountain can't I? Yes, yes, I can do that."

Rose rolled her eyes with frustration at Furdon as they seemed to have been in this cave far longer than necessary. Furdon knew how she felt but also knew some things could not be rushed. Fiddy slipped down onto Rose's lap feeling quite bored and waiting for something to happen. Bolstone got to his feet once again and politely asked a wooden cabinet to open its heavy oak drawer. Upon request it did so and Bolstone searched around, appearing to fall deeper and deeper into the cabinet as he hunted around. With only his skinny ankles sticking out from the drawer, Rose thought he was about to vanish into it completely. Deep within the cabinet came a cheer, as Bolstone eventually found what he was looking for. Out of the drawer reappeared his ankles, knees and bottom, until he was able to lift the rest of himself out. He brushed off his old orange cloak and straightened out his hood and glasses. In his hand was a little red book with a leather cover and musty brown pages.

"I knew it was in there somewhere," he said, looking very pleased with himself as he flicked through the pages "if I can find the right page, then we can get you out of here."

"But don't you know the way Bolstone?" asked Fiddy.

"No, no, no! It's years and years and years and years since I left this cave. I'm better in here, can't be doing with that lot out there. Nothing but trouble makers getting up to mischief. No, no, no! I'm much better in here." Rose was beginning to wonder what was waiting for them when they got outside. Bolstone was not making it sound a pleasant place.

"Who are the trouble makers exactly?"

"Oh you'll see," he said "They might be nice to you but they like to play tricks on me. I give as good as I get mind you and keep them entertained but I'm getting too old for their energetic games. Pixies are naughty and Fairies can be just as bad if they want to be, just watch out for them both."

"Really? Pixies and Fairies? I've never met any before!" said Rose, unable to hide the excitement in her voice.

"You're not missing much," said Bolstone, as he found the right page in the book. "Still, you're quite a way off from where they live but you'll have to go through their patch at some point or other on your journey, no matter which way you choose to go."

"Which way would you suggest we go?" asked Rose as she tried to peer at the page in the book without being caught out.

"Let's see," he muttered "You could go through Featherly and Whitesand, or Drakenstop and White Acre, or then there's Hazy View and White River... you'll end up in Teardrop Glen which ever path you take."

"And after Teardrop Glen?" she asked.

"That's as far as my map shows," he said "But don't worry, you'll find your way."

"Well, I don't suppose it matters which way we go if all the paths lead to Teardrop Glen?" suggested Rose, looking at Furdon and Fiddy for some input.

"No, I don't suppose it does," said Furdon "But which is the least dangerous path?"

"Good question," said Fiddy "Which path is less dangerous?"

"None of them are entirely safe," said Bolstone "It depends what mood the Ogres and such bullies are in as you pass through their lands."

"Ok," said Rose "Then I say we set off and see where we end up if they are all much the same."

"If that is what you wish," said Bolstone "And if that is the case then it is time we said our goodbyes. Don't you know it's rude to keep an old man from his chores," he chuckled beneath his white fuzzy beard.

Rose let a smile slip onto her face, she was getting used to Bolstone's humour and character now and was feeling relieved he would help them get out of the mountain so they could get on their way. She was looking forward to meeting Fairies and Pixies, even after what the old wizard had said about them. More than anything she was looking forward to getting out into some daylight as she was growing tired of the darkness of the mountain.

Bolstone walked over to the cave entrance and waved his hand at the others to follow him. They walked in single file down the ledge to the base of the waterfall where water was crashing into a large pool.

"That's the way out," said Bolstone, pointing into the pool of water "It's best if you jump from a height, otherwise you could end up in the swamps at the other side, which aren't pleasant at all, no, no, not at all pleasant." He reached into his pocket and pulled out four orange marbles. "Take these with you, one each to get you through to the other side and the fourth I'd like you to give to the old witch when you see her, tell her it's a gift from an old friend." Rose looked puzzled at him wanting to give Orme a gift, she took it and put it in her pocket. They each took an orange marble and looked for a place where they could jump in. Bolstone smiled and slowly made his way back along the ledge.

"Are we going to see you again?" Rose called after him.

"Maybe yes, maybe no, probably yes, probably no," he called back and waved.

"Thank you," she shouted as he vanished out of sight. There they stood, each holding an orange marble. They took hold of each other and looked into the frothing pool of white water.

"I've got a feeling of déjà vu," said Fiddy "The three of us about to jump into a pool and into whatever is on the other side."

"I was thinking the same thing," said Furdon "But looking around us, there's no other way out and so we must trust him. Even though he was a bit strange."

"No need to be rude," laughed Rose.

"Are you going to count us in again Rose?" asked Fiddy.

"Yes, are you ready? Ok then, one… two… three… go!"

Holding each other's hands they jumped into the water and vanished out of sight. Bolstone reappeared from around the corner with a proud look in his eyes as he looked into the pool, 'Of course, you'll see me again young lady,' he muttered to himself.

CHAPTER FOUR

Unbeknownst to Rose or the Grocklings, as they tussled through the water, a shock wave had pulsed around them as they jumped into the pool and it shook Cragfeld mountains like an earthquake. The tremor vibrated through the mountain and rattled through the Grocklings cavern, up to the surface where stone and rock tumbled down to the valley below. Howls from the Silvertips could be heard piercing the night with a haunting wail as they ran up the mountain to avoid the shower of stones. The fires of the watch towers flickered as gusts of wind whipped around and picked up speed at the highest points. The winged wardens with their black bat-like wings were shaken into the air, not knowing what was happening around them. They had seen no threat from the ocean and no wandering souls from Cragfeld in the mountains.

The old witch was in her chamber as the Dark Castle shook around her. Spell books and potions shuddered across the den and the cauldron in the hearth rocked on its belly. The Ice Queen stood in the main hall felt the ground beneath her feet trembling as the shock wave pushed itself through the walls of the Dark Castle. The chandelier above her head rattled as each droplet shook and bumped into each other. Her captives inside each chandelier droplet were knocked from side to side until the tremor subsided. The Ice Queen lifted her arms above her head and summoned a sphere of ice between her hands, she threw it onto the floor. A thick layer of ice quickly spread around the walls, floors and ceilings of the Dark Castle like a strong impenetrable cement holding everything in place. She looked up at the chandelier which was still swaying about, with one cold glance it froze in the air and everything was quiet again. The Ice Queen looked out of her balcony wondering what damage and harm had been done to her people. Unbelievably the villages were untouched and the people were sound asleep in their beds, without a clue of the powerful tremble that had just surrounded them.

"Orme!" she yelled.

Her voice ran through the hallways until it reached the old witch's den and grabbed the old witch by her cloak, dragging her to the main hall where the Ice Queen had a furious red glow. Her hair was serpent-like with anger as it hissed around her shoulders. Orme was not scared of Mordisan, they each knew how strong the other was but Orme knew more dark magic to put her in her place if she ever got too much.

"What was that?!" barked the Ice Queen "Surely you could have seen this, we could have seen this?"

"It is a quake from under the mountain my Queen, from a place we can't see."

"Well surely we could have seen Cragfeld being pounded by rock fall or the Dark Castle shaking around us?"

"The people are safe my Queen, the wave washed over them and left them untouched."

"Yes I can see that for myself you old goat! I want to know why this didn't appear when we looked into the Crystal bowl." From above them they heard a muffled laughter as the captives in the chandelier began to mock the Ice Queen and the old witch. With one look and her eyes glowing silver with venom she dropped the temperature of the droplets of crystal until they were so cold that nobody was laughing from inside.

"How dare you mock me!" she said to the prisoners "Think yourselves lucky I haven't dropped and smashed you each into a thousand tiny pieces."

"There will always be powerful magic beyond our reach," said Orme "But between us, our power is stronger than theirs, so there's little to worry about my Queen. They're practicing in their world and we're feeling the after effects, just as they feel ours when we've been using the dark forces."

"I suppose," shrugged the Ice Queen, hardly satisfied with the answer. "I feel there's something at work Orme, something that is trying to catch us off guard."

"Then don't let it, think now and prepare for the worst. Be ready for whatever comes your way, if ever it comes."

The Ice Queen looked at Orme and smiled as poisonous thoughts started flowing through her mind. They would summon and create a force which nothing could penetrate, an army so strong and unyielding that caused any enemy to die of fear upon seeing such death-filled creatures. Creatures which would not fall at the hands of humankind, creatures of magic and sorcery.

"We have work to do," she snarled.

Rose coughed and spluttered as she found herself being washed up at the edge of a freshwater pool. In her left hand was her orange marble and in her right hand was a rather displeased looking Furdon who had Fiddy grasping his tail.

"Ok Fiddy you can let go now, we made it," he said trying to free himself "We Grocklings don't like water Miss Rose, never mind jumping into it and been tumbled around like feathers in a storm."

"I can't say I enjoyed it much myself," she said standing up and trying to shake the water out of her clothes and boots.

Fiddy spat out a mouthful of water and looked extremely sorry for himself with his ears drooped low as he tried to get himself together. "At least we made it out of the mountain, it's good to see day light and feel fresh air on our faces."

They each popped their orange marbles into their pockets and had a look around to see what was what. At the far end of the pool where they had washed up was a small waterfall, flowing slowly and taking its time splashing bubbles and sending ripples out as far as it could reach. Above the waterfall was a tall vertical cliff which disappeared into clouds. Surrounding the pool and waterfall were rocks and boulders with a few little trees and bushes dotted around. Rose climbed up the boulders and could see they were close to the top of a mountain which looked down over a lush green valley of trees and meadows. The sun felt warm so Rose took off her grey cloak and packed it away. She was feeling better to be outside and feel the clean air on her skin.

"What do you reckon? Up the mountain or down the valley?" she said. When Furdon turned to look at her he saw an old wooden post sticking out from between the rocks.

"Was that there a minute ago or has it just sprouted from the ground?" he said pointing to the wooden post.

"I don't think it was" said Fiddy "But I was squeezing water out of my tail so can't be sure."

Rose cautiously approached the wooden post and noticed there was an arrow on it pointing 'this way'. As soon as Furdon and Fiddy had dried off satisfactorily they approached the sign for closer inspection.

"I guess we are to follow it 'this way'" said Furdon shrugging his shoulders.

"I suppose so," said Rose "It's not like we have any other clues is it?"

They each returned to the edge of the pool to collect their bags. While their backs were turned the wooden signpost spun around on the spot. When Rose twisted back and saw this, it was pointing in another direction and read 'that way'. With Fiddy and Furdon either side of her they returned to the wooden post and started to poke it and see if it would spin again. No matter how hard they shoved it, it wouldn't budge.

"Maybe it's that way instead?" suggested Fiddy, looking to where the arrow was now pointing, down a narrow shingle path.

"I don't know," said Rose "I think someone is playing with us. I think we should ignore the signpost and follow our gut feeling… and my gut feeling is telling me to go down the valley to the green meadows rather than the tangle of rocks over that way." Just then the signpost spun around again and pointed to the pool of water and read 'another way'. "Look at it anyway, it must be broken, we just came from there!"

"Broken piece of old rubbish," said Fiddy, kicking it as he walked by. There was a cracking sound from within the post and out from its side sprouted a leg which kicked Fiddy back. Amazed, they all stood there and stared at it. It spun round on the spot and then shot back into the ground, disappearing as quickly as it had appeared.

"This is a very strange place," said Rose "I don't know about you two but I have a funny feeling we're being watched." Furdon and Fiddy looked around and scanned every rock and bush in sight but could not see anything looking back at them.

"Come on then," said Furdon, hitching his bag over his shoulder "Let's get moving one way or the other. I don't like the feel of this place."

They scrambled over the boulders and slowly made their way over the rocks to take the path to the right. They could feel something vibrating underfoot and held onto each other and the rocks around them to keep balance. A few loose boulders started to roll as if they had minds of their own, gathering themselves in a pile in front of Rose blocking any way through to the path to the right.

"Apparently it's not this way," said Fiddy, turning back to go the other way.

"I'm not liking this place at all," said Furdon "I wonder where we could be?"

They turned away from the pile of boulders which had blocked their path and stumbled their way back over the rocks to start again and try the other path. A breeze made its way up the mountain which felt cool and refreshing as it passed by. It ruffled its way through the small bushes which were dotted around the mountain side. Yet long after the breeze had left them, the bushes were still shaking and dancing as if the breeze still tickled them.

"The trees and bushes are watching us, I can feel it," said Furdon, looking suspiciously at each one.

A little bush nearby shook its delicate green leaves and pulled itself out of the ground. Using its roots it pulled itself over the rocks and boulders like an octopus and replanted itself in front of the three bewildered looking friends. It shook its leaves as if it were making itself presentable and then lowered its branches in a bowing motion. Rose automatically curtseyed back and nudged her friends to bow to show some respect. The little bush almost pointed down the path which they intended to travel and shuddered its leaves. Instead it pointed out a third route which none of them had seen, straight down the mountain side. There were some narrow steps carved into the mountain side, the little bush pointed to these and made a nodding motion with its branches towards them. Fiddy curiously went up to the little bush for a closer look but as soon as he was in reach, it flicked him with a leaf and slapped his face. In shock, Fiddy leapt back and up onto Rose's shoulder where she could not help but laugh at him.

Furdon lead the way down the steep mountain side. Rose turned to thank the little bush for its help, which bowed proudly and nestled itself comfortably between boulders. The two Grocklings were used to scrambling around mountains and found it easy going. Rose however was not finding it as simple and was almost sliding her way towards the stone steps rather than carefully climbing down. Furdon was first to reach the steps while Fiddy made sure Rose was okay. There was a flat stone ledge at the top of the steps where they each composed themselves and took in their surroundings.

"Look here," said Furdon "This chunk of rock has Hazy View carved into it."

"At least we now have an idea where we are," said Rose "Do you think that is White River down there?"

"I think so, though I'm only going from what Bolstone told us," said Furdon.

The view from where they were sitting was, in Rose's eyes, stunning. She had never seen any other views other than those over Cragfeld which were grey and dull compared to this. The bright sunlight beamed over everything in sight, from the river and forest below, over the mountain-side and as far as the eye could see. What Rose presumed to be large birds circled in the sky above them. Other smaller birds flew passed them as if racing each other down the valley. The sound of the river thrashing far below was the only noise they recognised. There were shrieks and roars echoing around which none of them particularly liked the sound of and did not have a clue what creatures would make such noises. The air was warm and clean, with a scent of pine wafting up from the forest.

"It seems to be a long way down doesn't it?" said Rose "You go first Furdon, you're quicker than me and can check what is beneath us as we go. Fiddy, I'll go in the middle and then you follow behind making sure everything is safe above us."

The steps were almost a vertical drop which Rose used

more like a ladder to make her way down. There was very little space for her to balance her toes and not many places for her to hold onto with her bare fingers, which did not take long to feel sore. Furdon felt quite relaxed and was humming a tune, Rose found this helped to calm her nerves as she cautiously eased herself down after him. Her finger tips were almost red raw as she tried to grip each of the narrow stone steps. Fiddy watched on and encouraged Rose. A shriek from high above them in the sky helped them to pick up their pace slightly. Even with incredible eyesight, Fiddy could not see what was soaring above them.

"Nearly there," shouted Furdon "Only a few more steps to go."

"I counted eight hundred and twenty steps," said Fiddy confidently "How many did you get?"

"I wasn't counting," smiled Rose "That was not easy." Her fingers and hands were grazed and sore.

Furdon helped Rose down the last few steps, then whispered to Fiddy "I got eight hundred and thirty five." Fiddy liked things to be certain and wanted to go and recount the steps but was quickly discouraged from this as Furdon reminded him they were there to work, not play. Fiddy kicked the dirt childishly and plonked himself down. Before he could start to sulk there was the sound of something crashing through the forest on the other side of the river. He jumped to his feet, hid behind Rose's leg and stared into the forest, looking for any signs of movement.

"What the blazes do you think that could be?" said Rose "Whatever it is it sounds huge!" There was a crackling noise as the trees were being shoved around and trodden on by something which remained out of sight.

"I suggest we wait here until whatever it is has settled down," said Furdon "At least that way we have this wide stretch of fast flowing river between us and… it."

"What if it crosses the bridge?" whispered Fiddy.

"What bridge?" asked Furdon.

"That bridge over there, up river," Fiddy pointed to a rather rickety wooden bridge.

"Just keep still and quiet," bossed Furdon, sitting back at the bottom of the steps, where Rose and Fiddy joined him. Rose fished around in her bag and dug out her grey cloak which was camouflaged against the rocks for them all to hide under until the noise has quietened down.

The crackling and thrashing noise seemed to be getting closer in the forest just over the river. Rose peeked over the top of her cloak just as two Ogres smashed their way into the clearing on the other side of the river. Her eyes were wide and her mouth dropped open, she had never seen such things. They were almost as tall as the trees, had dirty looking leathery skin and thick black hair crowning their large heads. They looked strong and powerful, each of them was carrying a large wooden club which they swung at each other when they shouted and grunted at each other. They were barefoot as they stormed about grumbling angrily at each other causing the earth beneath their feet to tremble. Fiddy and Furdon had a quick look but soon shot back behind the safety of the grey cloak when they saw it was Ogres. They were obviously having an argument about something and were each as mad as the other. Fortunately they were too involved in their own squabble to notice anything else around them. Their deep voices boomed at each other as they turned and headed back into the forest and out of sight.

"Ogres!" sighed Furdon "Thank goodness they didn't look over this way or catch our scent."

"Why? What would they want with us?" asked Rose naively.

"Have you never read about them or been told stories?"

"No, all books and stories were destroyed when the Ice Queen took her throne. She even erased them from the minds of the village elders. What's an Ogre, apart from a huge lump of muscle with anger issues?"

"They aren't clever and simply rely on their size to get their way. Grocklings are safe and of no interest to them… but you unfortunately, would appeal to them as a light snack!"

"What! They eat people?"

"Yes, I'm afraid so…"

"That's horrible," she said with disgust. "How do we avoid bumping into them and stay out of their way?"

"We should try and stay downwind from them but it could be risky, with them moving around so much and the wind could change in their favour. They do not like water so let's stay close to the river." Rose decided she would rather keep her grey cloak handy in case they needed to hide again so she clipped it around her neck and lifted her bag onto her shoulder. They clambered over the slippery stones at the side of the river to the rickety old bridge.

"It doesn't look very stable," she hesitated "You two will be able to scamper across but it looks about ready to give way if anything heavier tries to cross, and the river looks cold and quick."

Fiddy sprang across the bridge barely touching it. Furdon did the same. They waited at the other side and watched as Rose took tentative steps as the wood creaked beneath her. There were missing planks which made it more difficult for her to negotiate and the water gushing not far below was intimidating and making her dizzy. She clung to each wobbly post, slowly stepping her way across as her friends encouraged and cheered her on. When she reached half way there was a wide stretch where the bulk of the bridge had been swept away and had only stayed together with one desperately thin beam. The aged wood was slippery and smooth so she found it difficult to balance, she took it one step at a time. She lowered herself down to crawl across, trying her best to overcome the dizziness. She could hear Furdon and Fiddy calling to her and she did not dare lose focus causing her to slip into the river below. Within a few metres of the riverbank she looked up to see her friends, no longer cheering her on but encouraging her to go back. She lifted her eyes and saw one of the Ogres had come back and was watching as she edged closer to be within its grasp. Colour washed from her face as the Ogre stood as close as he could to the river without getting his toes wet ready to lunge his arm forward and grab her. She felt the draft waft her hair off her face as his giant hand only just missed her, she started to shuffle back. Fiddy dashed onto the bridge and over her shoulder to encourage her back while Furdon tried to distract the Ogres attention by climbing up him and poking and prodding him around his ears and face. The Ogre was irritated by Furdon but was not distracted from Rose sitting in the middle of the bridge. The other Ogre had stolen his breakfast so he was hungry and wanted a meal he did not have to fight for. Rose was scared and did not know what to do, the flimsy beam beneath her was creaking as she tried to reverse as fast as she could. The Ogre was becoming frustrated, firstly because he was so close to getting hold of Rose and secondly because Furdon was poking and prodding him. The Ogre was trying to avoid the water but was leaning so far into it his foot slipped as he lunged forward. He crashed onto the bridge, destroying what was left of it. Furdon clung on for dear life as the cold water washed over the Ogre who quickly found his feet and back to the side of the river. Furdon perched on the Ogre's shoulder and looked heartbrokenly into the river as what was left of the bridge was washed away, with no sight of Fiddy or Rose. The Ogre grunted as he stood tall and threw his heavy wooden club on the ground, causing a dent in the grass around it. Furdon was quietly sitting on the Ogre's shoulder who had such thick skin he couldn't feel him.

Furdon felt a tap on his shoulder as Fiddy who, at the last second had leapt onto the Ogre as he plunged into the river.

"Where's Rose?" asked Furdon, he was scared and nervous not knowing if she had been swept down the river or crushed under the weight of this blundering idiot.

"I don't know," said Fiddy softly "The last thing I saw was a giant hand reaching towards us."

The Ogre however did not seem sad or worried as he grabbed his club again and stormed back into the forest. He had the club in one hand but the other hand close to his chest. Fiddy clung to the Ogre and peered over his shoulder and down the thudding body of this beastly character. The ghastly breath huffed from his lungs as he marched angrily deeper into the forest. In the Ogre's hand, Fiddy could see two legs sticking out from between the fat grubby fingers.

"He's got Rose!" squeaked Fiddy as he crept back to where Furdon was sitting looking lost.

"And how do you suppose we get her back?"

"Where there's a will there's a way, that's what you're always telling me… and I'm not going to let this stinking Ogre be the last thing our Rose sees!"

The Ogre strode with speed to a clearing where he looked around him to make sure he was alone before opening his hand. Rose was sitting scowling at him. Out of the corner of her eye she glimpsed the Grocklings who had hitched a ride on the Ogre's shoulder, she tried not to look at them as she did not want to give their presence away. Fiddy however was jumping up and down waving to her until Furdon pulled him back and told him to sit quietly until they knew what the Ogre had planned. Ogres would either eat their meal straight away or hoard it in a cave to eat later. Either way, the Grocklings had to find another place to hide.

When they jumped down, they landed with a crunch onto the ground. The Ogre heard this noise and thought it was his friend coming to see what he had found but when he turned around he saw nothing and sat down, staring at Rose. It did not take long for Fiddy to realise they were standing amongst a blanket of bones, bones from previous snacks and meals the Ogre had found. There was a stench of rotting meat in the air which made the Grocklings nauseous as they tiptoed over the bones and up a tree out of the way.

"Humph," grunted the Ogre, frowning at Rose "Not really sure what to do with you now."

"Put me down and let me go!" she grumbled.

"And why would I do that, I'm starving."

"You don't look starving!" She looked him up and down.

"What you tryin' to say?" His voice was slow and deep.

"Just that you look well fed and don't really need any more to eat, do you?"

"You sayin' I'm fat," he frowned, looking down at his belly.

"Well, not quite," Rose realised she didn't want to upset him too much as he might just eat her as comfort food.

"Don't think I likes you!"

"I don't think I like you either!"

As she stood in his hand she felt more angry than scared as she gazed upon this huge Ogre. His big black bushy eyebrows twitched and his bloodshot brown eyes stared right back at her. The stubble on his chin was coarse like stumps of wire protruding from his face. His breath left little to be desired from the reek of rotten meat that was wedged between his chipped and crooked teeth. She stood in his hand for a few moments and looked around her at the mess of bones on the floor and inhaled the stench in the air.

"You know there are better things you can do with your time than chase after food and pick fights with your friend…"

"Humph," he mumbled "He's not friend, he steal my food."

"Well maybe you're a better hunter than he is," she said

trying to appeal to his ego "And maybe every now and then you shouldn't rise to his challenge... and tidy up around here instead." The Ogre looked around at the bones scattered around the clearing and spreading their way into the surrounding tree line.

"Humph... I think you a mean person."

"Likewise," frowned Rose, her arms crossed firmly in front of her "And I actually think you're a bit of a bully."

"Huh? I not a bully," he frowned at her.

"Yes you are," said Rose, feeling brave "You tried to scare me, a tiny person who is the size of your thumb and then kidnap me, bringing me to this tip you call home. Tell me how that is not bullying?"

"Er... but I hungry," he said.

It was becoming apparent to the Grocklings that the Ogre in front of them was neither clever, hungry or too angry otherwise it would've eaten Rose on the spot without hesitation.

"Now, are you going to tell me your name and put me down?"

"No, why would I do that?" He boomed.

"My name is Rose and I'd like to get down, your hand's hot and clammy."

"Me Zwodder," he said at last, lowering his hand to the floor "Don't run off," he raised his club threateningly.

"I won't," she said firmly "Are you going to clear an area for me to sit then or must I tread amongst this clutter." Zwodder put his club down and swept some bones to one side before Rose stepped off his hand into the cleared space.

"You smell funny," said Zwodder.

"You don't smell too good yourself."

Zwodder smiled at her, he was actually enjoying playing with his food for a change instead of having to fight over it. As Rose was standing looking around her, the Ogre caught a glimpse of the golden locket under her cloak.

"Oooh shiny, pretty," he grinned pointing to her locket.

"Yes, it was a gift from my mother."

"I want."

"You can't have it."

"I want it."

"It's mine and you can't have it."

Zwodder got to his feet and strode around in a huff. He wanted the golden locket and had forgotten he had taken Rose as a snack to enjoy on his own.

The Grocklings were sitting up the tree wondering how they could get Rose away from the Ogre so they could continue their journey. Rose was wondering the same thing herself. She was quickly able to see that Zwodder was quite simple and easily distracted. She had to try to bargain with him to let her go. He seemed keen on the golden locket but she couldn't bargain that for her freedom and she could not think of anything else he might want. She sat on the floor and pulled her knees close to her chest while she tried to get ideas together. Zwodder went to sit next to her, neither of them saying anything for a while. The Grocklings got comfortable, there was nothing they could do yet and had to wait patiently for Rose to make her move. Zwodder stood up, stretching his arms up into the tree tops and nearly knocking Furdon from the branch he had found and got comfortable on. The Ogre began scratching around the clearing, occasionally glancing back at Rose. He wanted the golden locket.

"Now what are you staring at?" she said.

"Wonder how best to eat you," he grumbled "That would get me a gold locket. Maybe boil you, or roast you... maybe you taste better raw? But no, you smell funny, might taste nasty." He flicked a few of the scattered bones around while he decided how best cook her. A few skulls rolled past Rose's feet, she closed her eyes and pulled her feet in closer to her.

Rose was gently rocking back and forth when she felt a burning sensation in her pocket. She slowly lowered her hand into her pocket as not to catch Zwodder's attention, she could feel the round marble which Bolstone had given her. The heat became too much and she had to take it out of her pocket. The orange marble was glowing and it caught Zwodder's eye.

"Oooh, I want," he said admiring the glowing marble which looked gold in the light.

"You want this?"

"Yes, mine, I want."

"You want this of mine… and I want you to let me go."

"Give, I want," said the Ogre becoming hypnotised by the marble.

"I'll give it to you, if you let me go."

"Yes, I want it, give."

"Promise you and your friend will leave me alone."

"Yes, yes, give it."

"Promise me…"

"I promise."

Rose lifted the glowing marble up to Zwodder who was mesmerised by it. He took it in his hand and it instantly grew to the same size as the tip of his thumb. Zwodder watched the colours of fire and gold swirl around inside the now giant marble. Fiddy and Furdon were now fully alert, watching the show unfold before them. They saw Rose had found a way to get free and the Ogre did not seem to care, he had got something new to keep him occupied.

Whilst Zwodder looked in wonder upon his new toy, Rose slowly crept away and tiptoed through the bones and into the forest. Above her head her friends jumped through the tree tops from branch to branch and were relieved to be reunited with Rose. Fiddy jumped up all over her, spiralling around her like a pole. Furdon smiled, his big green eyes blinked up at Rose, not quite believing how she managed to get away.

"What happened down there?" asked Furdon as they hastily put distance between themselves and the Ogre.

"The marble in my pocket, I don't know what happened but it gradually got hotter and hotter until I had to take it out."

"Thank goodness for that," cheered Fiddy.

"Bolstone must've seen you somehow?" Suggested Furdon as he reached into his own pocket and pulled out his marble. Fiddy and Rose wrapped their hands around Furdon's hand which held the marble and they whispered 'Thank you Bolstone'.

"An old man has better things to do than distract a stupid Ogre. Keep your eyes open and your wits about you," came a muffled voice from the marble which flashed blue and then back to orange. Furdon put the marble back into his pocket and the three of them dashed as quickly and quietly as they could through the forest.

As they got deeper into the forest the trees grew thicker and light grew thinner. It felt dark as they stepped over undergrowth which they found tangled itself around their feet and hindered their progress. It grew almost as tall as the Grocklings who found it easier to hitch a ride on Rose's shoulders than fight their way through it. She was getting used to them doing this but did not mind as they were not heavy and she could hardly feel them. Only when she wobbled and almost lost balance would a thick black tail or two swish in front of her face as they steadied themselves.

"This can't be the right way surely?" she muttered, lifting her legs to almost hip height to get over some of the under-growth. "We were told Ordram would guide us… I'm going to be honest… I don't feel guided, just completely lost. Every way I turn in this place looks exactly the same in every direction. I have no idea if we're getting deeper into this mess or going around in circles." She stomped around with frustration.

"The main thing was getting away from the Ogre and his friend," said Furdon "Not knowing where the other one was we didn't really focus on the direction we took."

"Plus we didn't know where we were anyway, that Ogre carried us a long way," said Fiddy.

"I thought we were going to stay by the river?" said Rose, feeling frustrated "What happened to that plan?"

"There's no point getting stroppy Miss Rose," said Furdon "We're in this together so let's not take our irritations out on each other."

"What do you suggest we do then, Mr Logical!"

"Stop, take a breath and think with clarity."

"Easier said than done," she said, taking a few deep breaths and trying to calm down. She was feeling quite panicky, she had never been lost before as the Ice Queen had prevented people wandering off into the unknown. She did not like it and she wanted it to stop. She wanted to get out of the forest and into daylight again.

Fiddy stared up into the tree tops to see if any light from above was penetrating the thick canopy. There was a small speckle of light in the tree tops behind them so Fiddy suggested they aim towards that in the hope the forest would start to thin out again. Rose ploughed on through the bushes and brambles, it was exhausting work and the tangle around her feet was holding her back. It was as if every time her foot touched the ground a vine would purposefully tether around her ankle

Rose paused to get her breath back and could feels the vines looping around her ankles. She was tired and felt her energy draining as her muscles strained with every step.

"Are we getting anywhere, what can you see?" she panted.

"Erm, what's that Miss Rose, is it a bramble spiralling up your leg?"

As they looked down, a thick gnarly looking vine quickly

twisted up around Rose's waist and before they could cut it away it pulled her down with a sharp tug into the undergrowth. She landed with a bump and after a second or two she felt a jolt as she was dragged under the bushes. She grabbed her friends, one in each hand and they bounced and thudded uncomfortably after her. She pulled her friends towards her so they were nestled on her tummy and she curled herself around them as much as she could to protect them from the tearing undergrowth which thrashed around them as they were pulled along.

After a few minutes she was flung into the air and landed on a grassy knoll in the middle of an opening in the trees. She had no clue what just happened but was quite relieved to get out of the darkness of the forest and see daylight beaming down on her. The sun shone in her eyes and dazzled her. The two Grocklings appeared from under her cloak looking rather traumatized.

From out of the trees stepped a lizard of monstrous proportions. It stood as tall as Rose could reach and its scales shimmered blues and greens in the light. With amber coloured eyes it watched Rose and her friends as they got to their feet. Rose saw ridges down the lizards back leading to a long powerful tail which was swaying from side to side. She soon realised it was the lizards tail and not a vine which had grabbed hold of her and dragged her to this place. The lizards purple tongue occasionally flicked the air as it weighed up the three characters who were trying to do the same thing about it. As the lizard stepped out from the trees and onto the grassy verge, Rose and the Grocklings found themselves edging backwards out of its way. The lizard hissed menacingly and lay down in front of them, its sharp talon like claws resting on the ground. The lizard whipped its long tail around them and into the air before pulling it back, the sharp end crashed down in front of them and shook the ground beneath them.

From behind them came a rattling noise as if someone was unlocking a door. They looked around them but saw no building and they quickly turned back to the lizard which was still watching their every move. The rattling noise came again and the three friends now did not know where to look. From the top of the grassy knoll close to where they were standing, the rattling was now a lot louder and there was a creaking of rusty hinges as a trapdoor opened outwards, covered in grass and perfectly hidden. The lizard stood up and stepped back slightly, looking strong and proud. Out of the trapdoor stepped a young man who stood tall in front of them. He appeared to be a man of the forest, with weapons fastened to his belt and a fearless glint in his eye. His dark hair hung untidily round his face but his brown eyes were bright and looked upon the three of them with speculation.

"Thank you Hildfall," said the man who spoke in a soft deep voice to the lizard "You've done well. Until I call you again, you can go back to Drakenstop." The lizard bowed and hissed loudly before whipping its tail around and then vanished into the forest and out of sight. "You three however appear to have got yourselves a little lost. Come inside, out of the forest."

He held the trapdoor open as Rose and the two Grocklings cautiously stepped over to him. They looked at each other, then at the young man before peering into what was below the trapdoor. They were tired of the forest so any break from it was welcome but they did not know who this man was and they could get themselves into even more bother. They saw no alternative so stepped down the ladder into the secret hideaway, followed by the young man who closed and locked the door behind him.

CHAPTER FIVE

Beneath the trapdoor in the grassy knoll was an underground corridor. It was clean, tidy and well-furnished and you could have been mistaken for thinking you were wandering the halls of a castle. Lamps were placed at even intervals along the walls. The young man guided them through the passageways at a fairly hasty pace.

"You three were in somewhat of a pickle out there, weren't you?" he smiled at Rose who appeared embarrassed at her clumsiness. "Don't worry, you're not the first and you certainly won't be the last."

"We were running away from an Ogre," she said "And, well… we lost our bearings."

"An Ogre, eh? You did well to get away from him."

"Where are you taking us?" asked Furdon, who was becoming very protective over Rose.

"Aren't you hungry?" asked the young man "I can offer you food and a rest before you go to where you're going."

They arrived in a large room with a round stone floor and a table in front of a low warm fire. The room had a domed ceiling from which lanterns glowed dimly. Large thick rugs spun from fine silk were spread randomly around the floor which felt luxurious underfoot for the Grocklings compared to the roughness of the forest. Upon the table there were four place settings with ruby red goblets filled with a hearty red wine. The three friends were encouraged to sit down and make themselves comfortable whilst the young man went to get them something to eat. Whilst he was gone, Fiddy picked up the goblet and did not like the look or smell of what was inside. Rose on the other hand took a sip of the red wine and smiled contently as it warmed through her. A few moments later the young man retuned carrying a tray of thinly sliced cured meats and a selection of cheeses in one hand and a tray of cakes and biscuits in the other. He placed these down on the table and fetched a jug of water and put it in the middle of the table.

"My name is Troostan, welcome to my home."

"I'm Rose and these are my two friends Furdon and Fiddy."

"It's a pleasure to meet you. I've heard so much about Grocklings but have never had the pleasure to meet one. I've heard you're fine and courageous?" The Grocklings blushed and began to warm to the wild-looking man who encouraged them to eat and drink while they chatted.

"How did you know we were in the forest?" asked Fiddy "And why did you think we were lost?"

"I didn't think you were lost, you were lost," said Troostan "I was watching you getting tangled up and going round in circles for quite some time. When it was clear you weren't going to walk in a straight line I thought we'd better get you out of there."

"We?" asked Furdon as he nibbled on a sweet oat biscuit.

"Yes, Hildfall and I."

"Oh right, the lizard."

"Don't call him a lizard, especially to his face. He won't take that at all well and the last thing you want to do is upset him. No, Hildfall is a juvenile dragon who I've known since he was a hatchling. The other dragons on Drakenstop are wild and won't come down to the forest. Hildfall however has been a loyal friend and has helped me out of a few awkward situations."

"Like what?" asked Fiddy intrigued.

"Well, like your friend Rose here, I too was also in the hands of an Ogre. This is going back a few years mind you. Just before the stinking Ogre was about to throw me into his cooking pot and turn me into stew, Hildfall thwacked him with his tail. The Ogre dropped me to see what was happening and because he was so slow and clumsy on his feet, Hildfall grabbed me with his tail and took me into the forest away from the Ogre and his cooking pot."

"… And this is your home, you live here underground?" asked Rose as she gazed around the room.

"You say that as if there's something wrong with it?"

"No, not at all…"

"Isn't my home up to your fine standards?"

"No, really it's lovely."

"Good…!" he frowned "And yes, I've lived here since I came to the forest many years ago. I can hunt, eat well, and live in safety. Nothing from above can bother me as they can't track me underground."

"You live here alone?" asked Rose, worried he might bite her head off again.

"Yes," his brown eyes looked at Rose, lingered for a moment and then he took a sip of wine.

"We live under the ground," interrupted Fiddy "Though not like you, we live in a huge cavern in the mountain and there are hundreds of us."

"That's nice," said Troostan "Then you're more used to having company than I am."

"I'm sorry, have I said something to upset you?" Rose asked.

"No… it's as I say, I'm not used to having anyone else in my home."

"So… why did you bring us here, you didn't have to you know."

"I know. But if I hadn't then you'd still be wandering in circles out there and I couldn't sit and watch. I've been brought up better than that, especially as you are a young lady in a country you've never been to before."

"How do you know that?" her eyes moved quickly over him "How do you know we are new to this place?"

"For a start no human in their right mind who knew this land would wander around Ogre territory. Which reminds me, how did you escape him without a dragon on your side." Fiddy was about to blurt out the marble story but Rose beat him to answering.

"It was luck," said Rose "Luck and good friends in the tree tops who helped me."

"Really, is that so?" said Troostan with a tone of suspicion.

Even though Troostan had a rather rough hosting technique they didn't feel as if they had to rush or get out of his way. Fiddy and Furdon filled their bellies with the delicious food and washed it down with the crisp clean water. Rose sipped the wine and slowly her appetite returned and she nibbled on cheese and biscuits. She was feeling as if she had her guard up slightly towards him but only because he had been quite sharp towards her.

"So, why were you wandering around the forest unguided?" asked Troostan eventually "It's dangerous out there and the last place you'd wish to be, especially come nightfall."

"We are on our way to Ordram," Fiddy blurted out.

"Fiddy, hush," whispered Furdon "We don't want all and sundry knowing our business."

"I'm not all and sundry Furdon," said Troostan "These lands are full of untrustworthy creatures but woodsmen aren't some of them. Others would trick you, torment you, use you and try to eat you but that's not our kind of thing. We'd much rather keeps ourselves to ourselves but help those who are lost when needs be." He filled his goblet with more wine and looked at his three guests, "Why are you on your way to Ordram? It is a long way from here."

"We've made it this far from Cragfeld," said Rose proudly.

"Ahhh Cragfeld," he sighed.

"Do you know it?"

"Of course I do, the island of the Ice Queen. The island where people breathe but don't live, trapped in an empty existence."

"Sounds about right," sighed Fiddy.

"That's my homeland," defended Rose "The Ice Queen has killed it, not the people."

"Oh Mordisan, the Ice Queen…" said Troostan staring into the embers of the fire as if thinking back through his mind.

"Have you met her?" asked Rose, the wine and the fire were mellowing her and her snappy tiredness drained away.

"I had the displeasure of meeting her many years ago before she conjured dark magic over Cragfeld. She was cold-hearted long before she got all this power… I know it sounds awful but at least if she has Cragfeld then she'll stay put and we all know where she is."

"That's hardly fair! To sacrifice all those innocent people to her…?" scowled Rose.

"Why weren't you one of them?" he asked "Why didn't she trap you too?"

"I don't know, lucky escape."

"You seem to have a few of those," he smiled. Rose couldn't help but agree and smiled back at the wild woodsman who had a kind heart underneath his rough exterior.

Fiddy grabbed a soft cushion and moved closer to the fire, where he plumped it up and lay down. His stomach was full and he felt relaxed for the first time since he left his cavern in the mountain. He soon felt drowsy and fell asleep, snoring daintily. Furdon too looked tired but was reluctant to leave Rose with this young man. Rose could see his eyes were heavy and reassured him that she would wake him if he was needed. He too plumped a cushion and buried his head in it and fell asleep. Rose and Troostan moved over to the fire and sank into a couple of armchairs.

"You have a long enough journey ahead of you, why don't you stay here and get some rest? It would be foolish to leave before nightfall anyway and I truly wouldn't want you to be wandering out there in the dark. Then tomorrow you can leave at first light, I will walk with you some of the way."

Rose was grateful for his kind offer which she accepted. She looked at her two little friends who were sound asleep, she did not want to disturb them. It had been a long day for all of them and if they were in the home of Troostan then they were safe and out of harm's way, for a while anyway.

Troostan was interested in getting to know Rose a little better and they each seemed less defensive as the evening drew on. The fire was warm and they spoke a little more freely as they began to relax in each other's company. He could see she was loyal to her friends and had a fiery spirit but he was curious as to what she was doing and why she was on her way to Ordram.

"Do you have any weapons in those bags you carry?" he asked.

"Not what I would call weapons," she smiled "More like tools which the Grocklings gave us to help us on our way. Why do you ask?"

"You're going to need something to defend yourself. If you allow me, I can give you something tomorrow before you go?"

"Thank you, I'd appreciate that," she took another sip of wine and got comfortable in the chair.

"Rose, what are you staring at me for?"

"Forgive me, I've not seen a free-thinking man for a long time. You have light and warmth in your eyes, I've not seen it before… the people who I grew up amongst have cloudy eyes and are spellbound. Your eyes show that you've seen many things and been to different lands." He moved his hair from out of his eye and winked at her, making her laugh. It had been a long time since she laughed and it felt good, her face glowed and her eyes lit up.

"Why are you going to Ordram?" he asked.

"I don't know but I'll find out when I get there. But this locket apparently has something to do with it." Troostan looked at the locket and then at Rose. A furrow made its way across his brow and he stared into the hot coals of the fire again.

"I recognise that," he said finally "Though it is a long time since I've seen it, if in fact it's the same one."

"What are you on about? My mother gave me this?"

"Where's your mother now?"

"I never knew her... I'm an orphan."

"Oh... sorry, I didn't mean to..."

"It's Ok," she sighed looking down upon the locket "I've never been able to open it and from what I've been told won't be able to open it until I get to Ordram."

"This I know is true. I don't know where your mother found it but it was made by Ordram so only he can open it once it has sealed shut. You must be trusted to carry that with you, keep it safe."

"I intend to."

Troostan had seen the golden locket before and recognised the leaf engraved upon it. Ordram only gave these lockets to Queens and Princesses so he was flummoxed as to how Rose's mother had got hold of it. He thought maybe she worked in a Palace and had found it or been given it. This detail was not his concern. He knew it was valuable, which made the person wearing it valuable and he had to do all he could to help her. His territory did not stretch far but he would keep her safe as long as she was in it.

Troostan could see Rose was becoming tired so showed her over to a bed at the edge of the room. The bedding was finely woven out of the purest silk. She wrapped herself up and felt warm and safe. Troostan refilled his goblet with wine and went to sit back in his armchair to gaze into the orange red embers of the fire.

The Ice Queen and Orme worked through the night and all the next day conjuring spells and concocting magic they had never had to use before. They were creating a fighting force to defend Cragfeld from whatever came over the mountain. Creatures who had no fear of death because they would not fall at the hands of a human. In the Ice Queen's spell room, words were being muttered in ancient languages to summon the vile venom they needed.

"Orme we need human blood," she growled "We need human blood so our friends here are immune to them."

"Yes, my Queen," hissed the old witch from under her cloak "I shall gather from the land and you can drain them as you wish."

In a waft of black smoke the old witch vanished into the villages of Cragfeld to capture some humans for their blood. The people of Cragfeld carried on their lives not knowing they were under a spell and believed everything to be a normal life. Farmers farmed, bakers baked and drinkers drank. To each villager nothing felt odd and they believed they were protected by the Ice Queen, when it was in fact the complete opposite. The Ice Queen would use her people to experiment her magic on, sometimes cruel and torturous spells, some more agonising and painful than others, either way the ending result was not a good one for the victim. Of course in normal circumstances family and friends would miss the person, not in Cragfeld, the Ice Queen would cast a new stronger spell on the family and friends to make them forget that the missing person ever existed. Orme had her pick for blood supply and found easy targets hanging around outside the village pubs, the drunker they were, the easier they fell. Strong looking men would go to the pub after a hard day's labouring in the fields for a few drinks to unwind before going home. If there was beer in their system they generally lacked focus and did not think clearly. Orme wafted quietly down from the Dark Castle in a cloud of black smoke. She'd appear to them as a young beautiful woman who had a soft sensual and hypnotic voice. The men would be drawn to her like moths to a flame. As soon as they were in reach, she gave each of them a poisonous kiss and they would vanish from before her in a cloud of grey smoke. Orme had sent each of her victims straight to the Dark Castle where the Ice Queen was waiting. The old witch had tricked and kissed a dozen strong men before going back to the castle to continue her work with the Ice Queen to perfect the spell.

"With every drop of human blood we can bring life to the veins of our creations," growled the Ice Queen, looking pleased with herself. She turned to look at each of the men strung up in front of her with ropes made of ice and magic which could not be untied.

"We can get many, many drops of blood from this lot," the old witch hissed as she mocked and poked them with her bony fingers.

The Ice Queen took a large intake of breath and blew out of her body hundreds of ice crystals which landed under the row of men who were dangling a few inches above the floor. Each crystal represented one dreadful creature that would fight in her army.

"Orme my dear, would you like the honour of casting the spell while I drain the blood from these generous donors?"

"It would be my pleasure," the old witch gleamed and began to mutter words never spoken for thousands of years, in a tongue very few had an understanding of.

The Ice Queen walked around her captives with long purposeful strides and looked each one up and down thoroughly. The old witch had cursed the men as she kissed them, sending them into a state of slumber, they were unaware of where they were and what was about to happen to them. From her belt, the Ice Queen took in her hand a dagger of ice that was sharper than any blade. The ice dagger glowed blue as she gazed upon its beauty. She took pleasure from this, her frozen heart strengthened with the more pain she caused. Fortunately for these men they were too numb to feel the blade slicing through their veins. The Ice Queen chose to cut through the forearm of each man so she could watch the blood trickle down the hands and fingers and onto her crystals below… drip, drip, drip. From the twelve men, hundreds of drops of blood were falling onto the ice crystals which began to absorb the blood and turned red.

"I think that's enough now my Queen," said Orme who never liked to kill the victims. She preferred to spare their lives as they might come in useful again one day. The Ice Queen had no such regard and laughed at Orme's comment. "But my Queen, these are strong men, we might need their blood another time."

"Urgh, you're such a spoil-sport sometimes," snapped Mordisan "But I suppose you're right, no point wasting their strength. I will put them to better use soon but for now, I will keep them captive with the rest of them and add them to the crystals in my chandeliers." Her eyes flashed red as she wiped over each man's bleeding forearm with her thumb. The wounds instantly healed over and no more blood was lost. She licked their blood off her fingers with pleasure and could taste their vitality slide down her throat. She summoned fire and ice in a ball which spun over the captured men and burst over them like lava. The men began to squirm and wriggle, no curse from the old witch could help them or hide them from this. A whirlwind spun quickly around each man, shrinking them and capturing them inside new crystals which were added to the chandelier in the main hall.

Orme and Mordisan shared an evil smile as they fixed their attention to the blood soaked and spellbound ice crystals on the floor before them. After a few seconds the magic began to show it was working, as each crystal developed and grew into a large silver egg, hundreds of which lay before them.

"Ahhh it's working," said the old witch with satisfaction.

"These eggs must be kept safe," ordered the Ice Queen as she walked around the nest. Within each egg was an evil creature which would follow her command and have deadly venom coursing through its veins. They would grow strong under her watchful eye, ready for the day they would be unleashed and defend the Ice Queen and the Dark Castle.

Bolstone was taking a nap in his chair and had his legs stretched out in front of him. His white cat Alfred was sitting on a pile of books which were balanced precariously at the edge of a table, his slender tail flicking back and forth. The old wizard woke with a jump, startling the cat and making him shoot into the air, sending books and papers flying everywhere.

"What, hmmm, er what?" muttered Bolstone "Alfred look at this mess you've made." Papers were floating round him like confetti. He looked at Alfred disapprovingly at the mess he'd made but the cat hissed as it wasn't his fault and went to sit next to the bottomless sink and watch the fish swimming around.

"Oh yes…" said Bolstone "I remember now, what a horrible dream for an old man to have. No need for such dreams and it is rude to send such visions to an old man."

He pottered over to his kitchen and made himself a pot of tea. He used a mixture of orange, green and black leaves, crushing them up and adding hot water to the little blue teapot. The mixture swirled in a whirlpool like a rainbow and stirred up a terrific aroma of strawberries and caramel. Bolstone placed a little cup on a tray and carried it along with the teapot over to his armchair where he poured it out and enjoyed every delicious sip of his fabulous concoction. When he was finished, he looked into the bottom of his cup at the tea leaves which were stuck to the sides in a random position. To you and me they looked random but to the old wizard he saw a picture that disturbed him to his core.

"Oh, no, no, no. This won't do, this won't do at all. I must tell Frithad of this news." he said placing the teacup back on the tray and placing his head pensively into his hands. For in the tea leaves he had confirmed what he had seen in his dream to be true. He heard the words of the old witch as she chanted the ancient spell, an ancient spell to which few people had heard... but Bolstone was one of the few. He recognised it immediately. Upon hearing the words and seeing images of blood soaked crystals he knew the Ice Queen was conjuring up something dark and toxic.

"Alfred, you keep an eye on the place. I'll not be gone long but I must tell Frithad what I've seen. Oh but look at the state of me, I can't go looking like this, I must change." In a swirl of smoke the old wizard wrapped himself inside an orange cloud which hovered a few feet off the floor. Alfred simply stared at the old man, twitched his tail and continued watching the fish below hoping they would start jumping up soon. Alfred was used to the old wizard and his funny little ways so he ignored him most of the time.

The old man floated out of his cluttered cave and up the side of the waterfall, trying to avoid the mist and spray as best he could. He reached the entrance to the Boven maze and stared into the dark tunnel before him. A frown appeared on his brow as he did not like the Sneckaluses and would try and avoid getting their attention. He gave a little tap within the orange cloud and he promptly shrank to about a quarter of his usual size. With this he could float through the tunnels without causing a sound or vibration and avoid catching the attention of the Sneckaluses. It was dark but he gave off an orange glow which lit up just enough of the maze around him to make out the tunnel walls and new offshoots where the Sneckaluses had been busy. The tunnels of the maze were never the same but the old wizard was guided by the temperature of the tunnels, as they were slightly warmer at the top of the maze, where the well into the Grocklings cavern could be found.

Bolstone saw the dim grey light ahead so knew he had made it without a single Sneckalus sensing his presence. Not that they could harm a wizard, it was simply that he found them vile and ugly. Bolstone looked up the well and nodded his head so the cloud he was in would lift him up. The well had flashes of colour bursting around the walls but Bolstone ignored this until he reached the top and popped up through the well and into the Grocklings cavern.

"Ahem…" he called, surprised nobody was there to greet him "Ahem…" he coughed a little louder. A few moments later, Frithad and Eady hurried down the steps out of the main cavern to see who had come up through the well. They were accompanied by two Fighter Grocklings who made sure it was safe before scrambling down.

"Good grief," cheered Frithad "Bolstone my old friend, it's been too long. My, my it's good to see you."

"Likewise," smiled Bolstone, still hovering above the well in his swirling cloud of orange magic.

"Won't you come in?" said Eady.

"No, no, not stopping."

"Then how can we help you?" asked Frithad, still beaming at seeing his friend.

"As you are aware," said Bolstone "A young lady by the name of Rose and two of your kind came to see me."

"Oh yes," said Eady excitedly "They made it through the Boven maze then, Oh that's good to hear."

"Yes, yes, yes they made it through the maze. They're now somewhere in Ordraskop, on their way to Ordram but have got stuck in Grimdell Forest… having had a close call with an Ogre, hmmm yes."

"Oh dear," said Eady beginning to worry "Are they Ok?"

"Yes, yes, yes they're fine," grumbled the old wizard "But they're not the reason for my visit to you now." Frithad and Eady looked at each other and then back to Bolstone, it could not be good news. "I've seen and heard something very grave indeed. Orme and Mordisan haven't been able to see Rose making her way from Cragfeld and into Ordraskop which has unnerved them… they know something is amiss. They know greater powers are at work and are preparing for a battle which might or might not come. They can't see what's happening and are planning for the worst, oh yes, yes, the worst." The Grocklings grew worried and fear washed over their faces. "Mordisan with the help of the old witch is summoning dark magic that hasn't been used for thousands of years to create a fearless army of creatures which will defend the Dark Castle and the Ice Queen."

"Oh dear, oh dear," said Frithad "What can we do?"

"Not a great deal for now," said Bolstone "But you should be prepared for whatever might happen and do whatever you must to protect yourselves. I will help, when the time comes, I will help you."

"Thank you Bolstone, for telling us what she's up to," said Frithad "We will prepare ourselves and await your next visit."

"Good, good," said Bolstone "But for now be at ease, Rose is safe and making good progress." Frithad and Eady were relieved. "I must go now my dear friends, things to do, you know how it is."

"Yes, of course," smiled Eady.

"Cheerio my friends," grinned Bolstone.

And with a little wave he disappeared down the well. He

negotiated the Boven maze and was back in his cave before Alfred had had time to enjoy the peace and calm.

Having dozed off in his chair, Troostan woke early to see Rose and the two Grocklings were still sleeping. He got up and stretched out and tried to click out the crick in his neck. Furdon heard movement and woke to see Troostan walking over to Rose and crouching in front of her. Before he woke her, Troostan looked at Rose and smiled at her bravery. Rose's hair had fallen over her eyes, which Troostan gently pushed one side so he could admire her beauty as she slept.

"What are you doing?" whispered Furdon, making Troostan jump slightly.

"It's time to prepare," said Troostan "It's best, safer to set off at sunrise…"

Furdon got up and pulled the cushion out from under Fiddy who rolled onto the floor and continued to snooze. Furdon gave him a swift kick and Fiddy woke, wondering where he was and why his friend was kicking him. Rose rolled onto her back and Fiddy leaped onto her tummy and jumped up and down to wake her up.

"Fiddy, is that really necessary?" she said, her voice soft and sleepy.

"Yes, time to get up," said Troostan. Rose opened her eyes not realising how close Troostan was, which startled her and she woke quickly. He smiled at her and shuffled back a little, "Is that better?" he said. Rose smiled and rubbed her eyes, Fiddy and Furdon now stood next to Troostan waiting for Rose to get up.

"What time is it?" she yawned.

"Close to daybreak," said Troostan "I want to make sure you're prepared and armed adequately before we leave."

"We…?" questioned Furdon.

"Yes, Furdon," confirmed Rose "Troostan's kindly offered to escort us to the edge of his territory." Furdon felt they were managing well enough without any help of a scruffy woodsman.

They got up and had a wash while Troostan prepared a light breakfast for them. After overeating the night before, Fiddy didn't feel hungry but couldn't resist bacon, eggs and sausages when they smelled so delicious. They chatted like old friends over breakfast.

"Troostan, can you please tell us where we are exactly?" asked Rose "We landed into this new world through a waterfall and don't actually have a clue where we are."

"Apart from White River and Hazy View," corrected Fiddy, remembering back to the stairway carved into the mountain.

"You don't know where you are?" laughed Troostan "No wonder you were lost. You are currently sitting having breakfast in my home which sits under Grimdell Forest."

"And Grimdell Forest is in…?"

"Ordraskop, the world of Ordram."

"Oh, right, that's good then, we must be on the right path?"

"Yes, but not if you keep going the way you are…You make too much noise, you're bound to catch the attention of things a lot worse than Ogres. Try and keep your voices soft and your footsteps gentle in the future." Rose blushed, she didn't like the thought of being a loud blundering mess.

After breakfast, Troostan lead them down a long corridor at the end of which were two large wooden doors. Behind one door there was a loud humming buzzing sound, he said there was a colony of giant bees which had made themselves at home. He let them stay in exchange for the occasional bowl of honey. Behind the other door was, as Troostan described it, his stable.

The door appeared to be jammed shut. Troostan took a knife from his belt and pushed against the door and cut at what was keeping in shut. When they eventually entered the room, Rose was expecting to see elegant horses in a stable block, what she actually saw left her wide eyed and nervous. Two huge spiders were sitting at opposite ends of a long room with webs and threads hanging from beam to beam. Troostan saw Rose's face and he laughed at her as he introduced them to each other.

"Rose, Furdon and Fiddy, I'd like you to meet Spinbra and Betula."

"Erm, Ok, nice to meet you two too," she said eventually "They're huge, I've never seen…"

"I know," said Troostan proudly "You don't get these in Cragfeld do you!"

Fiddy and Furdon shook their heads and clung onto each other, thinking they were the perfect size for these huge spiders to snack on.

"Are they dangerous?" asked Rose, not wanting to take her eyes off them in case they pounced.

"Not to you Rose, or indeed your friends. They're well fed on other things and have no interest in pure bloods. It is Spinbra that wove the bedding you slept in last night and the rugs which lay upon the floor. Betula is my hunting spider, he's strong and has a painful bite to anything that gets in our way or causes us bother." Rose looked closely and could see Spinbra spinning and weaving her silk into strong and beautiful things. Betula made no movement and was quietly awaiting his masters command to go hunting. "I've asked Spinbra to make you some nets and rope which you will take with you. Along with these, a long sharp dagger for each of you." Rose looked at the blade which appeared far too big for her but on taking hold of it, it barely weighed anything in her hand.

"Thank you," she said "That's very kind."

"It's the least I can do to help you, after all I can only take you so far, not all the way. It's nearly sunrise so we'd better ready ourselves to go. There are three ways out of my home into Grimdell but I don't recommend going out the same way you came in, too many eyes would've seen you."

"We'll go whichever way you suggest," interrupted Furdon, "The safest preferably."

Troostan rattled a chain on the wall which called to Betula to go hunting. The great spider, dark brown in colour shifted one leg at a time and raised its body from the corner in which he had been sitting. Betula crept down the wall and along the tunnel where he stopped next to Troostan. Rose couldn't believe her eyes. Betula's skin was like a tough armour which protected every inch of his huge body. He had huge black pincers at the front of his head which would effortlessly be able to slice a person in half.

"He's incredible," said Rose "May I touch him?"

"Of course, he likes his underside being tickled," said Troostan.

Rose leaned over to Betula and rested her hand on his body and stroked up and down on his strong body. His armour shell was cold but Betula sensed her touched and moved closer to her for a bit more attention. Rose smiled and enjoyed being so close to such a magnificent creature.

"He's stunning," she admired. Fiddy and Furdon didn't want to miss out so copied Rose as she stroked Betula's side. The touch of the Grocklings was a lot softer and seemed to tickle the spider making him stomp one of his front legs on the ground to show he liked it.

"I'm glad he likes you," said Troostan "Because he is our ride out of here!"

"What, we're going to ride him?" she said in shock "Surely he can't take all of our weight, we might fall."

"You won't fall, trust me. He's strong and will barely know you're on board."

Troostan put his knee out and indicated to Rose to use him as a stepping stone onto Betula. She took Troostan's hand and cautiously put her other hand on Betula's side. Troostan gave her a push and before she knew it she was sitting at the front of this wonderful spider's body. Troostan threw some rope over to her, rope which Spinbra had made, he told her to fasten it round her waist and then round a hooked piece of Betula's armour. Fiddy was looking on in amazement. Troostan then climbed up and sat next to Rose. The two Grocklings then scampered up and tied themselves on. Rose thanked Spinbra for the ropes and nets which were packed in their bags. They were ready to go.

Betula lifted his body up away from the floor and each of his legs stepped in a smooth motion and they felt as if they were gliding along. There was an opening in the wall at the end of the tunnel where Betula squeezed his legs up to his body to get through. With a vertical drop, Rose and her friends clung onto the spider's armour as they descended into the darkness. Spinbra's rope was strong and had fastened them securely so they wouldn't fall. There was a cool draft coming from far below them. All they could hear was the pattering of Betula's feet as he negotiated his way down.

When they reached the bottom of the steep climb, the floor levelled out for a short way. Betula reared up and used two of his front legs to kick a door outwards and open. There before them was a breathtaking view of mountains dusted with pure white snow. The early morning sun shone a soft pink light onto the snow, making it look even more wondrous. The door from which they came was on a cliff face and was hidden well, only Betula and Troostan knew where to find it and only the strong legs of this spider would be able to endure the climb to get to it. Rose turned to Fiddy and Furdon who were staring over this land in awe. Beneath them was a wooded valley from which they could hear the sound of a river trickling as it was winding its way along.

CHAPTER SIX

Rose held on tight as Betula swung his body out onto the cliff face and kicked closed the door to Troostan's home. Fiddy was holding on for dear life as they descended head first into the valley. Troostan told Rose to lean back and enjoy the ride. Furdon had nestled himself between Troostan and Rose so he could not see or hear anything until they had safely reached the bottom.

As they moved along the forest floor Rose became aware of how quiet it was, especially with Fiddy being silent for a change. Betula hardly made a sound as each of his powerful legs and feet gently touched the ground beneath them. She now realised that she must have sounded incredibly loud and clumsy as she stumbled around the forest floor only the day before.

Troostan did not have reins or any way of controlling Betula. There was no point trying to control something that could free itself at anytime. It was more of a bond of friendship and respect for each other that connected the two and as long as Troostan asked nicely then Betula would oblige. Troostan had asked for Rose and her friends to be taken to the edge of his land as safely and as quietly as possible and Betula seemed happy to do this.

Even though the forest seemed quiet and calm in the early morning light, Fiddy was not convinced that they were out there alone. Rose and Troostan were looking forwards in the direction they were moving but when something caught Fiddy's eye both he and Furdon turned around and looked behind them. Of course the spider was well aware of where it was and what was around them, his eight shiny black eyes did not miss anything. Betula knew there was nothing to worry about but Fiddy was doubtful as leaves rattled and branches in surrounding trees shook from time to time. Troostan turned to see Fiddy and Furdon looking into the forest in search of any movement.

"You can look as much as you like my little friends, you won't see anything."

"But there's something, or some things in the trees following us."

"I know," said Troostan "And Betula knows so don't worry your little selves."

"But why can't we see anything?" asked Furdon.

"Because they don't want you to see them. They are just as curious about you as you are of them."

"What are they?" asked Furdon.

"They're Tree Pixies. They can be a nuisance later in the day when the sun sets but right now, they're just being nosey as to who I have with me."

"How many types of Pixies are there?" asked Rose, casting her eyes into the trees to see if she could catch a glimpse of them.

"Well let me see," said Troostan, sitting up straight "There are Tree Pixies of course, Water Pixies and Forest Pixies. Each as troublesome as each other, liking to play tricks and games on anyone they think will fall for their mischief."

"I don't think I like the sound of them," said Rose "I don't like being teased."

"Nor do we," chirped Furdon and Fiddy.

"Nor does anyone I should not imagine," laughed Troostan "The best thing is to ignore them, they hate to be ignored.

They like to wind you up and be the centre of attention so if you pretend they're not there, like Betula is doing right now then they will get bored and go away."

"So Fiddy and Furdon should turn to face the front and ignore them?"

"I think it best," smiled Troostan as he looked straight ahead.

Betula came to a deep ravine in the forest floor which dropped far beneath them and was a wide as the trees were tall. His shiny black eyes twinkled as he looked around them as he thought of the easiest way of getting across. He did think about throwing a thread of silk over, which would have been fine if he didn't have passengers. Again he could have jumped across but did not want to scare them. So he rested his back four legs on the ground and reared up, Troostan told them all to hang on. With one powerful kick he knocked a tree down which cracked and fell, landing across the ravine like a bridge.

"I did say as quietly as possible," teased Troostan, rubbing the spider's leg for reassurance.

Betula tested the bridge to make sure it did not wobble too much before gently balancing his great body upon it. While he calmly and confidently stepped along the bridge, his passengers looked down the ravine which made them dizzy. It would be a long fall if they slipped. Yet far down the ravine they could see a fast flowing river, above it swooped Water Dragons playing in the rapids. When Betula had his front four legs on the ground at the other side of the ravine, he used his back legs to knock the tree down into the gorge.

"Why did he do that?" asked Rose "Surely you need that for getting back?"

"We will go another way," said Troostan "We don't want to make it easy for anything to follow us do we?"

"No, I suppose not," said Rose, wondering what exactly he could mean and who could have been following them.

"We're nearing the end of my territory," said Troostan "So we'll have to leave you shortly."

"Oh really, that's a shame," said Rose shyly.

"Oh can't you take us to Ordram?" whined Fiddy.

"I'm afraid not young sir," smiled Troostan "But try to keep quiet and observant and you should fare better." Betula lowered his belly to the floor and tilted to one side so his passengers could untie their ropes and slide off his back. He then turned and waited for Troostan as he was saying goodbye.

"We'll see you again won't we?" asked Fiddy, though Rose actually wanted to know the answer to that question more than Fiddy. She had taken a shine to Troostan and would miss his company.

"Who knows," said Troostan "Maybe I'll visit Ordram one day, or even venture to Cragfeld."

"You'd be more than welcome," smiled Rose "As long as the Ice Queen didn't see you and turn you into one of her mindless flock."

"Yes, that's true, maybe not then eh?"

Troostan shook the hands of Furdon and Fiddy, wishing them luck and to look after Rose. They promised to do their best as always. Troostan turned to Rose and took her hand, smiled from beneath his scruffy hair and pulled her close for a hug. Rose was not quite prepared for that, she had not been hugged for a long time… it felt good and she hugged him back. He wished her well and climbed back onto Betula who politely bowed his body low before turning and scuttling into the forest.

"I think he liked you Rose," teased Fiddy.

"Don't be silly," she blushed.

"Come on," said Furdon "Let's not distract ourselves from where we are. Troostan kindly brought us a long way… which would have probably taken us two or three days to negotiate that forest. The Pixies could have been an unwanted distraction as we walked and rested so it's a good thing we're here... the other side of Grimdell Forest it seems."

Behind them stood the tall forest which stretched for miles. In front of them were sloping hills and meadows with a deep ravine to the left. On either side of them were mountains which now looked lilac rather than pink as the sunshine hit the snowy peaks.

All of a sudden, out of the ground popped a wooden signpost which looked a lot like the one they had first seen as they came into Ordraskop. Upon it was the carved arrow which spun around and read 'this way'.

"Oh not you again," moaned Fiddy "If you're going to be as useless as last time we met, you might as well go away." The signpost spun round on the spot again and this time pointed into the forest 'that way'.

"Right, yes it's the same one," said Furdon "I say we head down this meadow, stay away from the ravine and only go into the mountains if we have to."

"That sounds a good plan to me," said Rose. The signpost spinning around again and pointing 'another way'. Fiddy had not learnt his lesson from last time and gave it a kick as he walked by. The signpost crackled and creaked as an arm appeared and its body bent forward, giving Fiddy a slap on his back. It was a strong slap as Fiddy ended up face first in the grass. They all turned to glare at the signpost, where it got the hint that it was not wanted around and shot back into the ground.

"I really hope that thing doesn't keep popping up," said Fiddy, wiping his face and jacket clean.

"Me too," said Furdon "Neither use nor ornament."

"Ignore it," said Rose "Come on, let's get out of here. I say follow the line of that stone wall to the right, it looks to be a well-worn path." Rose lifted her bag up onto her shoulder and double checked her golden locket was safely tucked out of sight.

The early morning sun already felt warm as they walked in the long grass over to the stone wall. This stone wall was a lot taller than it first appeared, at least three or even four times the height of Rose. They couldn't understand why it was there or the reason it had to be so tall. Maybe there was something on one side of the wall that is not welcome on the other. They agreed that to stay close to the wall so they could remain less obvious to any onlookers. On the tops of the mountains they could see dragons swooping from peak to peak with bursts of flame occasionally shooting from their mouths.

"Drakenstop doesn't look very inviting does it," said Fiddy "Dragons seem to be angry creatures and I hope not to meet one."

"You've already met one," corrected Furdon "Hildfall, remember."

"Oh yes but he wasn't a fully-grown dragon and didn't have wings or a fire-breathing mouth."

"I'm sure he will when he's fully grown," said Furdon.

"Yes, well, I still don't wish to meet one," he whined. Rose chuckled to herself as her friends chatted between themselves.

Halfway along the wall they came to a gap in the stones. Not as tall as the wall but about as tall as Rose and narrow enough to fit a person through. The wall was a lot thicker than they first thought too, as it looked like a short tunnel running through to the other side.

"What do you think," said Rose "Should we go to the other side?"

"No, I think not Miss Rose," said Furdon "Troostan is on this side of the wall, we don't know what's on that side of the wall."

"Agreed," said Fiddy.

Rose peered through the gap in the wall to see if she could

see anything on the other side. She was astonished by something, she stepped back when she saw what appeared to be herself looking back at her.

"What is it Rose?" asked Furdon, peering through the wall to see nothing but an empty tunnel "What did you see?"

"I saw... myself," said Rose, feeling shocked "I saw myself at the other side of the wall looking to see what was at this side of the wall."

"That's impossible," said Fiddy "You're here, not there, how can you be in two places at once?"

"Maybe it was a mirror or an optical illusion?" suggested Furdon to try and put her mind at ease even though he saw nothing of Rose or himself at the other side.

"No, it was as clear as you two standing in front of me now."

"Have another look, just to double check," said Furdon. Rose stepped back to the gap in the wall and looked through to the other side. This time she saw herself smiling and waving down the tunnel before turning to run away.

"Well, I... er," she mumbled.

"You, er what?" asked Furdon.

"I saw myself again but this time smiled and waved at me before running away." The Grocklings looked at each other with slight concern about Rose, was she seeing things? Even Fiddy then checked and had a look down the gap in the wall but could not see anything.

"As strange as this is," said Furdon "I don't think we should let it distract us. We should stay on this side of the wall and keep walking until we get to the end. Things might make more sense when we get to the other end." Though he sounded as if he was trying to convince himself more than Rose.

They continued down the pathway at the side of the wall. Rose was distracted by what had just happened, while Fiddy and Furdon were chatting to each other about the unusual things they saw. From multicoloured toadstools sprouting from the wall, to flowers which bowed their heads as they walked by. Loose rocks would rearrange themselves along the wall and would turn to look at the three travellers below them.

"Do you ever get that feeling you're being watched and whispered about?" asked Rose.

"Since coming to Ordraskop, all the time," said Furdon "Why, are you sensing it strongly now?"

"Yes!" Rose looked straight at the wall and took a few steps back. Fiddy and Furdon did the same thing.

From amongst the rocks which made up the wall, eyes began to appear and look back at them. Several pairs of grey dry eyes which blended into the stone walls were open and looking at each other. These eyes belonged to the wall, there were no heads or bodies to which they belonged but they were simply watching the passersby and talking to each other as spectators.

"How very peculiar," said Furdon.

"They probably think the same about us Furdon," said Rose.

"What do you suppose they are?" asked Fiddy.

"Who knows," said Rose "There are eyes watching us from all over the place. Don't you find it tedious and exhausting!"

"Yes," said Furdon "But we're on our own journey and it's none of their business, they can stare as much they like."

"I know," sighed Rose as she looked at the grey stone eyes blinking at her, "I'm just getting sick of the feeling that everyone and everything knows we're here and are talking about us."

Fiddy took her hand and encouraged Furdon to take the other side. They walked hand in hand, knowing they were being watched and talked about with every step. The sun was shining on the other side of the wall so they were walking in the cool of the shade down the wall. It must have been midday by the time they neared the end.

At the end of the wall was a rickety wooden gate which was guarded by a rickety wooden man. He was leaning against the gate having a nap and blended perfectly into his background. So much so, the friends only knew he was there because he was snoring. The wooden man was made up of planks, sticks, and other pieces of wood which had randomly been collected from the forest. If he broke his arm or leg then he would have to find another suitable branch to make a new one. His head had come from the thick branch of a knotted and gnarly tree. The wooden gate he guarded was just as thrown together as he was.

"Excuse me," said Rose softly, so not to startle him "Excuse me, can you help us." The wooden man showed no sign of hearing anything and carried on snoring. Furdon then had a go.

"Hello, sir, can you help us…. can you hear us?!" he joked.

Fiddy went up to the rickety wooden man and gave him a swift kick with his foot.

"What no, not you again," said the wooden man as he got up from his nap. "That's the third time you've kicked me and I'm growing tired of it."

"How can that be?" queried Rose "This is the first time we've met you."

"Is it? Think again my dear," said the wooden man "This is the first time you've seen me in my true form. Your little friend kicked me not long ago at the edge of Grimdell Forest, and then a couple of days ago at the pool above Hazy View."

"What? You mean you're the wooden signpost…"

"Who doesn't know his left from his right," interrupted Fiddy.

"I do know my left from my right. What is clear is that you don't have any manners for people trying to help you… I may have lost my bearings a couple of times but I was trying to help you get here."

"And we managed it fine," grumbled Fiddy.

"Calm down Fiddy," said Rose "We're here now and this gentleman was obviously trying to get us here, in his own special way. Why did you appear as a signpost and not as yourself?"

"Oh it's easier to travel lightly," he said "My name is Haroud."

"Harold?" asked Furdon.

"No, Haroud, are you deaf?"

"No," said Furdon, taken aback by his lack of manners.

"Do you happen to know Bolstone?" asked Rose, thinking the two were similar in character, blunt in their manner which would appear rude to most people.

"Bolstone… Bolstone… hmmm, the name rings a bell," he muttered. "Ah yes, the old wizard. How is he? I knew him well, he used to visit often. Not seen him for a long, long while though. He's stopped visiting, why's he stopped visiting?"

"Something to do with the Pixies being a torment," said Rose.

"Oh yes, well in that case I don't blame him. They can be irritating little blighters you know, have you met any yet?"

"Not yet," said Rose "But I'm sure we will before our journey's over."

"Ahh yes, your journey," sighed Haroud "I've been waiting for you, what have you been wasting your time doing, I was about to grow roots standing here waiting for you!"

"To be fair on us, we didn't know you were waiting… and we had a little problem in Grimdell Forest."

"Yes, that's true," he agreed "But now you're here, I can help you… Through this gate is a path down to the valley. In this valley are flowers you've never seen before, huge great things, seem to attract Water Dragons mind you."

"Water Dragons!" Fiddy's eyes widened with fear. "I don't want to meet a dragon."

"Don't you worry your little self," said Haroud. "Water dragons are more playful than harmful compared to their mountain cousins." Fiddy was not convinced and hid under Rose's cloak. "Er, now, where was I...?"

"The valley of flowers..." intervened Furdon.

"Oh yes, of course. Now once you get down the valley, you must navigate through the stems and foliage. The flowers seem to get bigger the further you go and closer to the mountains. Be careful what you say to each other down there, those flowers can hear you and are very jealous of each other, always comparing blooms and displays. And, well, er that's all I can tell you."

"And what happens when we get to the other side?!" asked Rose.

"Are you deaf too," huffed Haroud. "That's all I can tell you! Dear me! Come now, we don't have time to dilly dally and chat all day. You're not the only ones who have things to do and places to be."

Haroud turned to the rickety old gate that looked as if it would fall apart as soon as he touched it. Tufts of grass had grown around the bottom and moss had wrapped around the hinges. Furdon was first through the gate, followed by Rose. Fiddy lagged at the back eyeing Haroud as he shuffled by, both wondering if the other was going to give one last kick. Neither did and Haroud shut the gate behind them.

"Thank you for your help," said Rose. Haroud waved his branch and twiggy fingers before sitting back against the wooden gate post and dozing back to sleep in the warm midday sun.

"Not the friendliest bunch are they, here in Ordraskop?" said Furdon.

"Not really," agreed Fiddy.

"But at least we're being helped in one way or another," said Rose.

They stood at the top of a hill looking down into the valley where in the bottom they could see huge flowers swaying back and forth. This was definitely the most lush part of Ordraskop they had come to, grass was vibrantly green, trees and bushes carried large leaves which were as long as Rose was tall. Smaller flowers around them turned to see who was here, opening and closing as the three friends walked by. There was a sweet aroma dancing through the air but it smelled more like sweets and candyfloss than flowers. As they wandered down the overgrown path they felt as if they had shrunk rather than the flowers were big. Huge water droplets would, every now and then drip from the leaves and petals above, crashing to the ground and almost drenching the three friends if they didn't move in time. As they reached the valley bottom and arrived under the canopy of flowers, it felt cool and dry out of the sun. Birdlife flew from stem to stem but paid no attention to the three new arrivals. What they presumed were Water Dragons flew above the canopy occasionally jumping from flower the flower causing the petal ceiling above to shake..

"Wow!" gasped Rose "Have you ever seen anything like this before? It's magnificent." Both Grocklings shook their heads, as they took in the beauty around them. Everything seemed to be calm and tranquil. Rose felt she could relax a bit with no obvious threats from Ogres and such.

They walked for hours under the canopy not talking about anything in particular, more chit chat and getting to know each other better. The plant life around their feet would turn as they walked by but as soon as they had gone, would turn back to carry on as they were. Insect life appeared to be getting bigger too, the further they went. Deep humming and buzzing could be heard all around them as bees buzzed far above their heads. It was of course Fiddy who had to disturb

115

the peace and pass comment on one flower being brighter or having more unusual petals than the others.

"Fiddy," said Rose in stern tone "Don't you remember what Haroud said, these flowers get very jealous of each other. The last thing we should do is compare them against each other."

"I was only passing comment," said Fiddy, looking sorry and hiding under her cloak again.

"Please be careful, we don't want to cause trouble do we?"

"I know," agreed Fiddy "I'm sorry, but you can't help notice these things."

"Fiddy, be quiet," scolded Furdon. The flowers around them were beginning to notice the three strangers and listen to what they were saying. They began to sway and swish around Rose and the Grocklings.

"I can't help admiring the lovely colours," chirped Fiddy "When you live in a mountain on Cragfeld, everything is so dull and grey compared to this. I love the colour of that turquoise one over there."

"Yes, I know that but there's no need to say anything about any of them, you're upsetting them… look." The heads of the flowers were tilting downwards trying to see what was whispering beneath.

The large thick stems of the flowers around them began to bend and a gap in the flower heads above allowed sunlight to beam down. As they looked up they could see a large bee hovering above the gap before it dropped down through the flowers to see who was disturbing the tranquillity. The bee itself was a scary looking thing, well they are quite scary at their normal size in the human world but these were similar in size to a cow. They were dressed proudly in an orangey yellow and black-striped jacket, from which their sail like wings hummed. The bee landed on a nearby leaf and looked at Rose and her companions. From off its back climbed a small slim lady dressed in matching attire to the bee. She was similar in height to the Grocklings, who until this point were thinking they were the smallest things in Ordraskop. The lady wore a small top hat, it was perfectly placed upon her tawny hair which was tied back neatly into a bun. She had large brown eyes and a delicate chin which framed small red pouted lips. In her hand she carried what looked like a riding crop which she use to control her bee. She did not looked pleased to see them at all.

"Who are you and what do you think you're doing?" she grumbled with a slight buzz in the back of her throat. "I'm trying to collect pollen up there and whatever you're saying to upset my girls is making it very hard work." The bee buzzed in agreement.

"Oh, we're sorry," said Rose, elbowing Fiddy with disapproval. "We're new to the area and haven't seen such wonderful flowers before."

"Which I can understand, I have a fine collection," she said "But why would you compare them against one another. Each is as beautiful as the next because they're all different. The blue rose for example can't be compared to the red daisy because they are two completely different flowers. Just as you, whatever you are, don't look the same but I'm sure underneath your stupidity you have different qualities all as valuable as each other."

"Yes, we didn't mean to cause any offence to anyone," back-pedalled Rose. "We are so very sorry."

"Yes, so sorry," said Fiddy, coming out from behind Rose's leg. Furdon rolled his eyes at him.

"We're from Cragfeld, my name is Rose and these are my very good friends Furdon and Fiddy."

"Good friends or stupid friends?" the little lady questioned "My name is Midge and my bee here is Blaze." Midge drew the riding crop in her hand and blew into one end like a flute. A soft melody bubbled its way into the air and up to the flowers above. A few seconds later another giant bee appeared and flew down to sit next to Blaze.

"This is Burn," said Midge "And he will carry you up so you can apologise to my flowers directly. They soon get upset which effects the quality of the pollen and ultimately the honey made from said pollen. The last thing I want is poor grade honey just because a few idiots couldn't keep quiet." Midge approached Burn and prepared him for his passengers. "Come now, Rose first and then you two can sit on her lap, we don't want anyone falling off do we?!" Midge was quite scary for such a small lady, her voice was stern and authoritative.

Rose climbed up onto Burn and had one leg dangling either side of his thorax and just in front of his wings. Fiddy and Furdon then jumped up onto Rose's lap where they held onto her tightly. With a deep rumbling sound, Burn took flight up from the valley floor through the canopy of coloured petals. Close behind them Midge followed on Blaze. They hovered above the flower which had vibrant red, yellow, and purple petals. Fiddy could now see each flowers was indeed different and none were exactly the same. In the centre of each flower lay bundles of golden pollen which would indeed make some fine tasting honey.

"Go on then…" barked Midge, "Say you're sorry and we will drop you back down." Fiddy popped his head up and looked down nervously.

"I'm sorry," he squeaked "You are all beautiful, equally beautiful as each other." The flowers below appeared to relax again and sway calmly, rather than looking tense and closing their petals as before. The gap in the flowers however, had closed and the bee would not be dropping his passengers back on the valley floor.

"I thought you said you'd drop us back down?" Rose asked Midge.

"Oh I did… I just didn't say where," Midge smiled insincerely and had a nasty glint in her dark eyes. "You wander into this valley, cause upset and affect my pollen supply... a quick apology won't make it up to me. Burn, take them to the Spiralilus and let her take care of them... I have work to do."

With that, Midge steered Blaze away and they flew back down the valley to continue collecting pollen from the mosaic of flowers she watched over. Burn on the other hand lifted up and flew slowly up the valley.

"Why Fiddy, why couldn't you just keep quiet?" hissed Furdon.

"Look there's no point starting an argument," said Rose "What's done is done, and on the bright side we're having a lift up the valley and are going the right way."

"I said I'm sorry," said Fiddy "How was I to know Midge would get this disgruntled at us." He snuggled closer to Rose, where she put her arm around him to reassure him it was okay and she wasn't mad with him.

Below, amongst the carpet of coloured flowers they saw a large red flower which looked different to the rest. Five dark red petals were closely connected to each other and there was a white line which appeared to circle its way to the centre of the flower. Burn hovered over this flower for a few seconds before tipping his body so the three of them fell from his back and into the centre of the flower below. They landed surprisingly softly in a thick yellow syrup which glooped around them and was sticky to touch. The petals now looked like a steep wall which they would not be able to climb.

"Welcome to Spiralilus," said Furdon sarcastically, trying to wipe the syrup off his hands.

"What do you suppose Spiralilus is?" asked Rose.

"So far, not as nice a place as the valley floor!"

"More to the point, how do we get out of here?" said Fiddy, also trying to clean off the syrup from his hands and coat. His tail was dripping in the stuff, which did not please him at all.

They could now see that the white line, was actually hundreds of steps spiralling from the centre of the flower. Rose told her friends to climb onto her shoulders out the sticky syrup and she walked over to the bottom of the steps ready to start climbing.

"And where do you think you're going?" came a hard female voice. They turned to see a slimy grub sitting in the middle of the syrup from which they had just got out of. She was bathing in the slime, swishing her body around with pleasure and letting it run over every inch of her. She was a chubby looking grub who wallowed around all day with nothing better to do, until these three were off loaded into her domain. There was nothing nice about this ugly creature who would be able to eat them for lunch if they failed to answer her questions.

"We're leaving," said Rose, she placed on foot on the first step but slipped off straight away.

"Aa-ha, not as easy as you first thought is it?" said the disgusting creature. "And why would I make it easy for my lunch just to walk away from me, I haven't eaten for hours and am starving." Rose exchanged glances of 'what now!' with her friends and lowered her leg back to the floor.

"We're not your lunch," glared Rose "We've been dumped here by accident and would like to leave now… We are on our way to… elsewhere!"

"Really," gurgled the slimy grub "You think you're here by accident? That is incredibly naïve of you. Nobody ends up here in my company by accident." She glared at them, leaning her body forward to get a better look, slime dripping from her back into the pool of syrup below. "Where would you rather be than here with me anyway, everybody enjoys time with me. I'm Lilus and you're in my home, why don't you get comfortable?"

"As we said, we're expected elsewhere and can't spend it

here with you, as nice as you may be."

"Ahhh flattery will not get you anywhere," gurgled Lilus "The only thing that will get you anywhere is by answering five questions correctly. I think that will be a doubtful ask of you so you might as well sit down and relax and let me start digesting you. Please take a dip in this lovely pool, it will tenderize you wonderfully."

Rose looked at her friends who simultaneously tried to squeeze as much of the syrup from their tails as they could, whispering to Rose to try and come up with a plan to get them out of there. Rose told them to be patient and maybe the five questions would not be too difficult. With one correct question they could access one flight of steps, if they got it wrong they would slide back down into the syrupy stomach of the Spiralilus in the company of Lilus.

"Ask us the questions," demanded Rose confidently. With such confidence in fact that Lilus was taken aback. Lilus was used to her captives falling at the first hurdle so only had one question ready. She would have to come up with four more if they got the first one right. She was quietly confident she would be having lunch before too long.

"As you wish," she drooled "Question one, how much pollen does a bee take from the Spiralilus flower?"

Rose didn't hesitate with her answer "None."

"Correct," said Lilus disappointedly.

"How did you know that?" asked Fiddy.

"Easy, look around you, there's no pollen." Fiddy and Furdon had been less observant.

"Hmmm, well done," slobbered Lilus "You may take the first flight of stairs."

Rose placed her foot on the first step which she expected to be slippery but was now as dry as a bone. She balanced her way up the first flight of stairs with her friends perching on each shoulder. At the top of the flight of stairs was a gate, she had to get the next question right to get through the gate and up the next set steps. If she got it wrong then she would slide back down to the beginning.

"Question two." Lilus had to try and think of something, "How many steps spiral from the bottom to the top of my Spiralilus?"

Rose looked around her and called "Three hundred and fifty six."

"Correct," said Lilus beginning to feel angry and frustrated.

"How did you know that?" whispered Fiddy.

"I didn't, it was a guess," smiled Rose. The little white gate opened and Rose marched up the next lot of steps.

"Question three, what colour is my hat?"

"You're not wearing a hat!"

"Wrong, I asked for the colour... so down you come." Rose slid back down one flight of stairs.

"That was a trick question," she snapped.

"A trick? A trick? Would I be so tricky?" laughed Lilus, satisfied with her doing. "Question four, name a bee who flies over this valley regularly? If you can name two, unlikely, then you can take two sets of steps."

"Blaze and Burn," shouted Rose. The steps in front of her reformed and she scrambled up the two flight of stairs as quickly as she could. The closer to the top of the petals, the narrower the steps became. The petal walls were smooth and had nothing for her to hold on to.

"How did you know that?" said Lilus as she gurgled and sploshed around.

"How did you think we got here?" laughed Rose.

"Don't you dare laugh at me," said Lilus, writhing in frustration both at Rose's quick thinking and at her own foolishness of such a simple question. "Question five, how hungry am I?"

"You're starving!" answered Rose, who could see Lilus was beginning to trip herself up and the more angry she got, the less thought out her questions would be. The next gate in front of Rose dropped down so she could tip toe her way up.

"Almost there Miss Rose," encouraged Furdon "One more to go." Rose and Fiddy smiled.

"Be prepared for a long fall my dear," Lilus writhed and gurgled in the sticky pool far below "Question six, how do you expect to climb out of here with no steps?" The final set of steps began to slowly sink into the petal walls.

"Drat!" said Rose "Any ideas?"

"You keep her busy Rose," said Fiddy "I think Spinbra's rope might just be what we need." He fumbled in the bags and got hold of the fine strong rope. He made sure they were all tied together before he swung it around their heads and threw it to the top of the petal. The thread was so fine that Lilus could not see what they were doing.

"I'm waiting," called the slimy creature feeling pleased with herself. "I told you it was a long way down, it would've been so much easier if you'd just sat down next to me and... let me win."

"You seem used to getting your own way all of the time," shouted Rose, watching the syrup below swish around Lilus's squidgy body. "How does it feel to lose?"

"My dear, can't you see I've not lost. With no way out you only have one way to go and that's down." As Lilus spoke, the steps from under Rose's feet began to tilt together into a slippery slide, where Rose was expected to fall, spiralling back down to where Lilus was waiting. The rope of silken web held them tight and it took their weight. Lilus squinted her grubby eyes, confused at how they were still up there when they should have dropped to her dinner table.

"Now what?" said Fiddy.

"I thought this was your plan" said Furdon. "Please tell me this wasn't all you'd got? And you'd thought about how we'd get out after dangling around?"

"Er, well it's better than sliding back down to her!"

"It's okay," said Rose. "Fiddy, you've done brilliantly. I

can use the rope against the side of the petal, which isn't that steep now we're near the top and I can pull us out." Rose turned to face the red petal wall and rested her feet against the side of the flower. She composed herself and summoned strength in her arm to pull herself up the rope. There was no grip under her feet which made it almost impossible to get anywhere.

"Well done Rose," cheered Fiddy "You can do it."

"I'm not sure I can," said Rose, "I can't get any hold underfoot."

"I know this is going to sound difficult and you're already tired," said Furdon "But can you pull yourself up with just your arms? Fiddy and I will climb up ahead of you which is already less weight on your shoulders."

"I don't know Furdon… but I'll never know unless I try will I?"

"That's the spirit," he smiled. Both he and Fiddy pulled themselves up the rope to the top of the petal and waited for Rose to do the same. She groaned as she heaved herself up, her muscles straining at never being used like this before.

"Come on Rose, you can do it," shouted Fiddy.

Rose inched her way up the rope but before she had got far, the flower of the Spiralilus began to close. Lilus was determined to get her meal and if she had to crush her prey then she would.

"Quickly Miss Rose," called Furdon, who between him and Fiddy tried pulling the rope up.

A joint effort made a slight difference but the petals were closing quicker than she was climbing. They were each using all their efforts to get Rose out and could hear Lilus laughing far below. The flower was closing tighter and the three friends were panicking, pulling the rope with all their might.

Rose looked up and into the eyes of her friends who were not giving up on her. Rose saw a shadow pass above them but before she could draw breath to warn her friends, a Dragon swooped in and grabbed Fiddy and Furdon with its back legs. Fiddy had fastened the three friends together and Rose was dragged up the side of the Spiralilus as it was about to close around her. Lilus could be heard screaming at her defeat. Rose dangled by the thread of rope as the Dragon flew higher with Fiddy and Furdon screaming and wriggling in its claws.

CHAPTER SEVEN

The Dragon lifted higher and circled over the valley of flowers with Fiddy and Furdon in its grasp. There was nothing they could do with giant talons wrapped around them like a steel cage. All they could do was look down as Rose dangled from the thin thread of spiders web. It was tied tightly around her waist and she clung on with both hands. Rose looked up at her friends to see if they were both Ok, under the circumstances. The wind whistled around them and they could hear nothing but the beating of Dragons wings and the rumble from its chest just before it bellowed a roar.

"I don't suppose this is a Water Dragon?" asked Fiddy hopefully. Furdon smiled and shrugged his shoulders, not knowing one kind of Dragon from another.

Below them they could see they were getting further away from Grimdell Forest and the tall wall leading to the valley of flowers. They were climbing higher and the air was feeling a lot cooler.

The Dragon roared as it came in to land at the top of a mountain, hovering while it gently placed Rose to the floor before letting go of the Grocklings and then thudding itself to a halt. Fiddy and Furdon ran over to Rose as she stumbled to her feet and they made sure they were all okay and un-injured. The Dragon cast its amber eyes over them and let out a loud shrill call.

"In answer to your earlier question, Fiddy, no I don't think this is a Water Dragon," said Furdon "It must've seen us two perched on that flower as an easy catch."

"Don't say that," said Fiddy, holding onto Rose's cloak for comfort.

The mountain top was cold and snow swirled from peak to peak. The ledge on which they had landed was in front of a deep dark cave. The grey rocks around them shuddered from time to time when a rumbling sound came from deep within the cave. They could not see far into the darkness but they knew this was the Dragons lair and there might be more than one living here. The Dragon who had brought them to this place roared into the cave and then lay down just inside the opening, as if his job was done for now. He rested his body on the floor and lay his head down but he didn't take his eyes off the three strange looking things in front of him. He had a reddish tinge to his otherwise grey scaly skin and a powerful tail which he whipped back and forth, each time almost hitting the friends who stood huddled together not daring to move.

The mountain vibrated under their feet and a deep gurgling growl came from within the cave. The Grocklings had better vision that Rose as they were used to wandering through dark caves and caverns. They could see a Dragon of monstrous proportions edging its way out of the cave and closer to the light. Rose could see her friends becoming nervous as they pulled on her cloak for comfort, Fiddy hiding behind her leg as usual and Furdon ready to defend Rose against this beast. As it edged closer towards them, Rose could see a shadow forming in the darkness of the cave. As it got closer to the light, Rose too was terrified at its size. They were in its lair with no way of getting away. They could not back away as there was a vertical drop down off the mountain and they were pinned in by numerous dragons who were clambering closer to see what had been brought to the den. There were Dragons of all sizes, some with red tinges, others with blue or green but they were all as equally as strong and as fast as each other. The Dragon from inside the mountain appeared in the mouth of the cave. It was walking on all fours, scraping its claws on the floor as it moved. This Dragon wasn't tinged with colour but was jet black and shimmered like oil in the light. Its scales were thick and strong like a million shields protecting its body. From under a heavy brow were two grey black lidless eyes. Swirls of smoke twisted out of its mouth and nostrils with each breath. The Dragon reared up and let out an almighty roar which blasted out of its lungs along with a flame of intense heat. Rose could see its jaws were powerful and lined with long sharp teeth. This huge Dragon looked at the three terrified strangers and growled as it lowered itself back onto all four strong intimidating legs. With a quick flick and a huge cracking sound the Dragon hit its tail on the floor right in front of them.

"Alright now that's quite enough," said a voice from the back of the cave "There's no need to overdo it is there?" Out of the darkness came a voice and a figure they recognised, it was Bolstone dressed in a long black cloak which had an orange lining which flashed as he walked.

"Bolstone!" they all said at once, with relief at seeing a familiar face.

"Yes, yes, it's me. Don't you know its rude to drag an old man out in weather like this?" he teased. "Well you do know how to get yourselves in some bother don't you? Sorry about the Dragon rescue service but it was the quickest safest way to get you off that wretched Spiralilus." He walked over and greeted them enthusiastically. "Don't worry about this lot, they put on a good show though don't they. Go on now, shoo, shoo the lot of you... apart from you of course," he said to the big black Dragon still grumbling in the mouth of the cave.

"You mean, you're friends with the Dragons?" asked Fiddy nervously.

"Of course, been friends for a long time, never have a Dragon as an enemy that's the best advice anyone could give you. This fine Dragon is Blackfall, he's the King of Dragons on Drakenstop and we go back many, many years." Blackfall sighed in agreement as wisps of smoke danced around his teeth. "Seen each other through thick and thin, good times and bad, haven't we old chum? Yes, yes, so anyway, I'm here to talk about you... you have made it to Drakenstop, welcome, welcome."

"It's not been the smoothest journey," said Furdon, the Dragon who carried them lay nearby and thrashed its tail at his comment. "No, no the ride with you was fine, I meant the journey as a whole since we left Cragfeld." The Dragon acknowledged his comment, he did not want any complaints about his flying skills.

"I can see that for myself," laughed Bolstone "But what doesn't kill you makes you stronger, isn't that how the saying goes? That Ogre was a fool and only needed distracting with something unusual... But the Spiralilus are notoriously difficult to get out of once they have their sights on you."

"You mean there are more of them?!" said Rose.

"Oh yes my dear, quite a few, where there are flowers they usually pop up. But enough about them. Like I said, terribly sorry about an abrupt introduction to Blackfall and the rest of the Dragons but it was the quickest way to get you out of there. You're making progress, slow progress... but slow progress is better than no progress...!"

"It feels as if we are taking forever," said Rose "Going round in circles, getting caught up in things which delay us more and more."

"And isn't that part of the fun?" cheered the old wizard

"Yes you're on a serious journey but have a little fun along the way. I've not become the old man I am today without a little fun you know… Don't be so scared of things, they can feel it. Fight fire with fire and let them doubt themselves. Much more fun than it sounds believe me, er um, yes."

"Easier said than done when you're about to be digested in a Spiralilus," said Rose "is that why you're here, because we were in trouble again?"

"No, no, no, not at all…" grumbled Bolstone from under his bushy eyebrows. "I'm here on my own business, don't ask me what… it's rude to ask an old man about his business." Bolstone did not want to worry Rose about what the Ice Queen and Orme were up to, they would find out soon enough.

"It's good to see you though," interrupted Furdon "We thought Blackfall or one of his friends was about to turn us into toast."

"He could've done, yes, yes, very easily if he wanted to," said Bolstone as he wandered over to Blackfall, perching on a talon as if it were a bench. "Had he not known you knew me then you would've found yourselves in another mess wouldn't you?" A flash of red flickered in the Dragon's eyes.

"We're grateful for your help," said Rose.

"Next time don't leave it so late to call me!"

"Call you?" asked Rose, wondering what he meant.

"Yes, you heard me, you called me… well actually it was Fiddy who called me. Have you forgotten about the marbles I gave you. It's very rude to forget a present from an old man you know. You, Rose called me when you were struggling with the Ogre, Fiddy called me when he was struggling with the Spiralilus. Be careful from now on as only Furdon can call me again. But whatever you do, don't use the marble intended for Orme, no no, no, don't do that." Fiddy looked baffled as he didn't think he'd called for help and felt in his pocket – he couldn't feel the marble, it was gone.

"Hey, my marble's gone," he cried, flapping his pockets inside out.

"Of course it's gone," laughed Bolstone "You've used it, you can only use it once." Fiddy was disappointed at the sudden realisation.

"If you don't mind Bolstone," said Rose "Are you going to help us down from here and back onto our path to Ordram? It is after all rude to keep an old man from his business."

"Quite right too my dear, quite right," said Bolstone, jumping down off Blackfall's claw. "From the other side of the mountain you can see Ordram glittering on the horizon, did you know that? Hmmm? So you know which way to go. I'll have one of Blackfall's chums guide you round the mountain to the path, you can find your way from there."

"Thank you," called Rose as Bolstone turned to head back into the cave.

"Carry on, carry on, doing splendid, yes indeed," shouted Bolstone.

"See you soon then?"

"As soon as whenever…" said the old wizard as he disappeared in the darkness.

Blackfall raised his body up to stand tall, whipping his tail back and forth and breathing a swirl of fire into the air as he roared. He looked at the three friends of Bolstone as they still looked quite terrified, a red glint in his eye shimmered as he backed his way into the cave and into the mountain. Some of the stray Dragons who'd lingered around, flew back onto the ledge and carried on their business as if Rose, Fiddy and Furdon were part of the group. From below, a young Dragon flew onto the ledge and looked at them with amber eyes. It strode up to them and with its tail nudged them to move.

"I know you!" said Fiddy "Haven't we met before?" The Dragon puffed a cloud of smoke from its nostrils "In

Grimdell Forest, you're Hildfall aren't you?" Rose and Furdon could now see a strong resemblance to the lizard which had pulled them out of the tangled forest.

The Dragon hissed as if smiling at being recognised. He was indeed Hildfall and good friend of Troostan. Hildfall escorted them around the side if the mountain which was rocky and snow covered, making it difficult for Rose to negotiate. Fiddy and Furdon could walk and balance quite well, after all that's what their soft paws were designed for back in Cragfeld. Hildfall was getting frustrated with the slow speed they were doing, he was used to jumping around these mountains at high speed. He looked back, whipped his tail up and grabbed Rose placing her on the bumpy ridge of his back. Rose was not comfortable but they were certainly going faster. Fiddy and Furdon jumped along and only just managed to keep up with Hildfall. The Dragon's scaly skin was tough and strong and did not feel any sharpness from the rocks underfoot. He bounded round the mountain to where the late afternoon sun was casting a soft tangerine glow onto the snowy peaks above them. Hildfall came to a stop and helped Rose down off from his back. She composed herself after the bumpy ride and made sure that Fiddy and Furdon had kept up with the Dragon's strides.

"Thank you Hildfall," she said "I do hope we meet again, one day when we're in less hurried circumstances maybe?" The Dragon jolted his neck as if trying to nod. "Please let Troostan know we're are Ok won't you?" Again the Dragon jolted his neck as if nodding. His amber eyes gazed over the three friends as he flicked his tail in the air. Hildfall turned his slender body around and his scales flashed blues and greens as the sun caught them. Hildfall opened his strong jaws and instead of fire, blew a purple mist over the three friends. He then quickly bounded up the mountain in a few easy jumps, looking back at Rose before he disappeared out of sight around the mountain side. They coughed and spluttered for a few seconds until the mist had disappeared, not knowing what that was all about and decided it must be how Dragons say farewell.

"Oooo, 'tell Troostan we're Ok won't you'," mocked Fiddy. Furdon shot him a look and jabbed him in the ribs with his elbow.

"Oh shush, it's not like that," said Rose.

"Then why are you blushing?" he teased.

"I'm not blushing," she said, trying not to blush.

"Okay, but your flushed cheeks are telling me otherwise," he giggled.

"Okay Fiddy, there's no need to embarrass Miss Rose," said Furdon "Whether she likes him or not." His green eyes looked big and innocent as he subtly teased her too.

"Enough you two," she said trying to regain focus "We have a mountain to climb down and I'd like to do it before it gets dark."

"Oh look over there!" said Furdon pointing into the distance "Can you see that? Something gold is twinkling, on the horizon just as Bolstone said... It must be Ordram!"

Fiddy and Rose followed to where Furdon was pointing and there was indeed a sparkle of gold in the far distance. She felt glad to see it. At least she felt they were making some progress at last.

"Miss Rose," said Furdon in an admiring tone "Look at you, your cloak... you, you look wonderful." Rose looked down and saw her shabby grey cloak had been replaced with a rich blue hooded dress which reached to the floor and felt as soft as velvet. Her tatty old boots had been replaced with soft blue pumps which wrapped around her feet like a second skin. She smiled at her beautiful new attire, running her hands over it in surprise and admiration.

"But you too, you both look very smart," she smiled as Fiddy and Furdon looked at each other. Their black jackets, which were also worse for wear had been replaced by soft purple jackets with golden buttons. The Grocklings looked at themselves, standing as tall as they could and feeling extremely pleased with themselves.

"It must have been Hildfall," said Rose "Just then when his misty breath covered us in cloud for a few seconds… He must have magic inside him too. If it was Bolstone we would all have been clad in orange!"

"I think it's wonderful," said Fiddy as he twirled around trying to see himself from every angle.

"We were looking rather drab, a welcome improvement," said Furdon.

Rose put her hand on the locket which was safely tucked under her dress that was tied with golden ribbon at the collar.

The Ice Queen could not take her eyes off her new creations, hundreds of silver eggs were slowly showing signs of life. Some were already starting to twitch as whatever lay inside was growing and developing. The Ice Queen seemed to have become obsessed in watching them, waiting for them to break free and show their deadly qualities. Every day the Ice Queen would stand guarding her brood.

"My Queen," croaked Orme "I have brought you something." The Ice Queen looked over to the old witch who had a woman from the village by her side. The young woman walked as if she had been poisoned, with drooped head and slouching shoulders. The old witch had trapped her in a toxic gas as she wandered the streets.

"And what would I want with that?" she boomed.

"My Queen, you've become too distracted by the growth of your army. You must rest."

"How am I expected to do that, I have to look after my creatures… as they will look after me some day."

"Yes but this is why I have dragged this young lady from the village. She seemed to be wandering around with nothing to do, so I thought she could babysit?"

"Babysit? Babysit! This young woman is nothing to these creatures. They need to know I'm caring for them… from creation, to war!"

"Connect the two together Mordisan, save your strength for the day you will need it."

The Ice Queen glared at the old witch, knowing she was right. She did not like giving up control over any of her schemes. She strode over, her crystal dress swaying behind her as she moved and it glimmered in the moonlight. Taking the woman by the arm, she grabbed tight onto her and dragged her across the room. Her grip was so tight that her long sharp red nails punctured the woman's skin, causing her to bleed. The woman though delirious was aware of where she was and the pain in her arm.

"The army must feed to grow," hissed the old witch as she watched on.

"And for them to feed, they need this to bleed!" snarled the Ice Queen at the woman.

"Yes my Queen but she needs to feed from them too… She will watch over them, you must feed her one blood soaked crystal which didn't develop into an egg."

"I know Orme! I know what I must do. Don't you dare interfere with this, I will chant the magic."

Mordisan bent down to pick up a crystal which had soaked up some of the blood from the dozen men but not enough for it to start growing into anything. She took hold of the woman's face and forced her jaw open and placed the crystal on her tongue. It immediately started to bubble as it dissolved in her mouth. The young woman felt as if her tongue was freezing and the sensation moved all through her body. She was not freezing but as the Ice Queen muttered a spell, blood began to trickle from her finger nails and drip onto the floor below.

"You must bleed for my army as they will bleed for me!" barked the Ice Queen.

The Ice Queen used her magic and power to lift the woman off the ground in a shell of ice. She moved her through the air so the was hovering above the nest of silver eggs and then encased her in a clear glass like shell. Blood continued to drip from her fingernails fairly quickly and began to gather in a pool in the bottom of the crystal shell. Mordisan ensured everything was in place and then muttered the last part of the spell, a tiny hole formed in the bottom of the crystal shell and the woman's blood slowly oozed onto the eggs below. The Ice Queen set the woman's shell like cage in a very slow circling motion above the eggs, so each would benefit from the blood which dripped and eventually covered them. The creatures would get to feed whilst the woman was cursed to watch over them, slowly losing blood.

"Thank you Orme," she barked "I suppose I can focus my attention to better use."

"Indeed, the army will grow strong, that is certain."

The chandelier of crystal encased captives rattled slightly. The men trapped inside could see everything the Ice Queen was doing but could do nothing to stop her. This was her punishment for them, a cruel torment. Mordisan turned and dismissed Orme back to her chambers.

"I think I must tell my sister of this," she muttered to herself. "She would hate to hear what I'm doing, the anguish to her good heart would be too divine for me to miss." The Ice Queen laughed under her breath until it burst loudly from her lungs. Her thick blood red hair flowed behind her under the crown of ice as she hastily climbed the stairs of the tallest tower in Dark Castle.

As she reached the frozen chamber where her sister was entombed, her laughter faded as she was faced again with the feelings of hatred for Rika. She melted a doorway and stepped through into the room and just stared at her sister. She felt her frozen blood tearing through her veins as the hatred surfaced, she could barely look at her sometimes.

Rika's frozen body was neither living or dead but captive forever and at her sisters control. Rika saw and felt nothing but cold in her eternal slumber.

"Two visits in such a short space of time," Mordisan snarled "You mustn't get used to it though, I certainly won't. There's nothing I hate more than seeing you... your face. But you're my souvenir, my permanent reminder of my own power, over my throne, over my Kingdom. You were never proud of me were you? You were so concerned with yourself that you forgot about me. Maybe you'll be proud of me now... hmmm? You want to hear what I've been up to... You'll love it I'm sure! Well, your dear sister has been making herself an army, yes... an army. One so strong and powerful that man will forever regret attacking me and never be so stupid again. Of course I needed blood, so have been borrowing here and there from some wonderful volunteers from Cragfeld. But wait... this is the best bit – are you paying attention?" A hard laugh echoed from her mouth and filled the room. "My army will have pure venom coursing through their veins. No man will be able to kill my creatures. They'll defend me to the death but will never die." She looked into her sister's eyes, "What, you don't approve? No change there then, you never approved of anything I did. But just you watch, you will watch me as I fight, watch as I defend, watch as my powers overcome my enemy! Just you watch."

Mordisan mocked her sister's frozen body knowing full well she was blind and deaf to her. Yet Mordisan found something beneficial about talking to Rika this way, she could talk down to her in a way she never could when she was alive and free. Before leaving the chamber and freezing it shut, she glared at Rika and spat at her frozen coffin, the saliva hissed and bubbled, turning to blood before it fizzled to nothing.

Dragons circled overhead as Rose, Fiddy and Furdon

climbed down the steep rocky mountain path. Rose had to hold onto the sharp rocks around her to steady herself as she followed the Grocklings who were bouncing along with ease. Fiddy had a new spring in his step and felt thrilled with his new jacket, he was even softly humming to himself with joy. Furdon rolled his eyes at Rose, as much as he loved Fiddy, he did feel like it was like having an excitable child in tow. Rose smiled but made no comment, she had grown very fond of her companions in such a short space of time. After all, they had only met a few days ago.

"Rose," chirped Fiddy "Do you think us three would've become friends if we hadn't been sent on this journey? You know, if you'd have sat on your rocky ledge in Cragfeld every night and Furdon and I came to meet you but didn't take you to meet Frithad and Eady."

"I'm sure we'd have become friends," smiled Rose "Though it would've been risky to meet often what with the Ice Queen watching the border to make sure the villagers don't venture into the mountains. But our situation is different... as much as the last few days have been a surprise with not knowing what to expect – I couldn't have asked for two better friends to do this with." Fiddy beamed and his green eyes lit up with joy. They had quickly developed a strong bond and were protective of each other.

Rose was also aware that something inside her was changing. She no longer felt sad or lonely as she did in Cragfeld. She had not smiled or laughed for a long time, nor had she enjoyed good company and varied conversation. Rose was feeling happy. Of course the journey was tiring and demanding and dangers were never far away but with Furdon and Fiddy by her side, she actually felt happy. With a fresh new zest for life surging through her body, Rose was also feeling stronger and revitalised. She found Cragfeld drained her of her energy and happiness but now it felt as if she was waking up and coming back to life. Fiddy and Furdon made Rose laugh a lot, though she laughed at them more than with them a lot of the time. Furdon was sensible but had a soft side, whereas Fiddy had a more carefree approach to things.

The late afternoon felt quiet and calm as they scrambled down the mountain. The path was now less steep and vegetation was sprouting up around them. It was good to see some greenery as the rock and snow higher up the mountain was rather monotonous and grey. There were small bushes with lilac coloured leaves and yellow flowers dotted amongst the rocks and silvery blue vines and brambles which clung to the mountains. The trees further down were a lush mixture of emerald and lime greens. Along with the change of scenery there was also more animal life, birds fluttered around the trees and insects scuttled around stones and bushes. Of course these animals and insects were all new to Rose and she had never seen so many weird and wonderful things. Butterflies the size of her hands fluttered around, showing off their dazzling turquoise wings which were all patterned differently with splashes of pinks and greens. A line of ants marched across their path, on their own mission and completely ignoring the three passersby. The ants had a bright yellow spot on their back to warn onlookers they were coming through and carrying a heavy load. A centipede as long and as thick as Rose's arm wound its way along the pathway and scuttled passed without taking any notice of them. As they reached the lower part of the mountainside, grass was pushing up out of the ground and creating a thick carpet under their feet. Flowers too decorated and accessorised the landscape.

"Shall we take a break here?" suggested Rose "While it's peaceful, maybe have something to eat?"

"That sounds a great idea," said Furdon, unloading the bag off his shoulder and dropping it by his feet. "It seems a safe enough place doesn't it and it's nice that the local wildlife doesn't seem to be bothered about us."

"It's a nice change," said Fiddy "Let's eat and enjoy the view."

They dug around in their bags and found parcels of food both from the Grocklings cavern and Troostan's kitchen. Delicious and filling breads and pastries stuffed with sweet and tasty jams, chesses and pickles. It had been a long time since they had enjoyed breakfast so they tucked in with vigour.

"It feels longer than a day since we were having breakfast with Troostan and since meeting Spinbra and Betula," said Rose.

"Oh it feels weeks ago," said Fiddy "So much has happened since then, not all good but all very exciting don't you think?"

"Wonderful," said Furdon sarcastically "Being trapped in a Spiralilus and then carted off by a Dragon is just how I thought today would unfold."

"It all ended okay though," said Fiddy.

"Yes, thanks to you it did," said Rose "Thank you for calling Bolstone when you did, otherwise we'd have been thinking differently right now."

"I didn't even realise I'd called him," said Fiddy "But whatever I did without knowing was perfect timing."

"I'd say," said Furdon "That ugly flower was about to close, just as Miss Rose was pulled up and away, dangling by a thread."

"Troostan will be pleased we've made good use of the rope," smiled Rose. "It was nice to see Hildfall too, he's helped us out quite a bit."

"Oh yes," said Furdon "For a Dragon, he seems smashing. And I must admit we do look much better than we did… we are better dressed for where we are. Everything is so colourful here, the animals and the flowers."

"Indeed," said Fiddy, twirling around again and admiring

his lovely purple jacket.

"Miss Rose looks like a Princess, very pretty if you don't mind me saying?"

"Of course not," she blushed "That's very sweet of you."

"I wonder why Bolstone was meeting with the Dragons," said Fiddy "That Blackfall didn't half scare me, I thought he was going to toast us until we were nice and crispy and then eat us."

"The thought had crossed my mind too," said Rose "I wouldn't like to get on the wrong side of him, like Bolstone said never have a Dragon as an enemy. Whatever Bolstone was here for, was obviously nothing to do with us otherwise he would have mentioned something."

"Maybe, maybe not," said Furdon "Wizards can be secretive... but they can also be very forgetful too at times."

With food in their bellies and a slurp of cool water from their flasks, they packed away the food parcels for another time.

"Right then," asserted Rose "I suppose it's that way, continue on this path and into the woodland below. From here I can see that river over there is headed in the same direction as to where Ordram is, so I say we use that as a guide path."

"Certainly Miss Rose," said Furdon "Very well thought out."

"See, I'm learning," she smiled. Indeed she was learning and looking ahead.

The gentle slope guided them into the woodland. The air was warm and had sweet floral smells wafting around them. The dappled light danced between the trees as the sun was now low in the sky. Winged insects buzzed around from flower to flower. Large bluebells, pink daisies and snow-drops layered the woodland floor with colour. Toadstools huddled together at the base of the trees which twisted up from the ground and spread their arm like branches into the air. This place felt safe and untouched, there were no fallen trees which had been pushed over by Ogres and no giant flowers that could trap them. In the air was a dainty sound of chiming bells which was actually coming from the bluebells which were carpeted around them. Amongst the branches of the trees were insects which appeared to glow and light up as the sunlight faded. It was a magical place, beautiful and peaceful.

"This is a wonderful sight to see," said Furdon "I've never seen anything like it in all my life." His eyes wide open as he gazed around.

"Me too," whispered Fiddy.

"This place feels special," agreed Rose.

They wandered at a slow place to enjoy the woodland, keeping the river close by so it could guide them through the trees. Their pace was slow but they were in awe and did not want to miss anything. Rose noticed a glittery pink and gold dust had been sprinkled on some of the flowers around them. It all added to the wonder of this enchanted land.

"I wonder if the Fairies and Pixies live here," whispered Rose. "I do hope we can meet them at some point. I know Bolstone doesn't like them but I say let's see how they are with us before we decide."

"It certainly seems like the place Fairies would live and play," said Furdon "You never know who we're going to meet here, friend or foe it's always a surprise."

As the sun set it sent soft orangey peach coloured beams of light through the trees. The glowing insects seemed to shine brighter like twinkling lights sitting in the trees.

"I think here looks a good place to rest for the night," said Rose, "It's clean and dry and we can lean against these tree stumps, or I'll lean against the tree stumps and you two will lean on me. It's warm enough for us to be comfortable." Fiddy and Furdon looked at the patch of woodland around them and agreed to settle here until sunrise.

Rose pulled the hood of her dress onto her head and sat down in front of a tree stump which was over grown with moss and toadstools and had a sprinkling of shiny dust. Furdon sat to her left and Fiddy on her right, they wrapped their tails around themselves like blankets. They were all tired after the events of the day and were glad to take the weight off their feet. Chimes and magical sounds filled the forest as the sun set. They chatted for a while but soon found themselves sitting quietly listening to the tunes of the woodland. As they became drowsy, Fiddy and Furdon nuzzled up to Rose as she pulled the soft blue hood over her face and closed her eyes.

CHAPTER EIGHT

Rose slept comfortably as Fiddy and Furdon snuggled at her side and the woodland life hopped around them during the night. Insects buzzed around and Fairies danced on their shoulders. The Fairies of course were curious of Rose and the two Grocklings, not sure what to make of them at first. The Fairies delicate wings fluttered quietly as they hovered over Rose while deciding if she was welcome or not. Shortly after the Fairies had come out to play, so did the Pixies. These were Woodland Pixies, a close relative to forest Pixies. Woodland Pixies are a lot smaller and less mischievous than their forest cousins but this was not to say they weren't naughty at all. The Fairies and Pixies on their own were generally quite light-hearted and fun to be in the company of, however, when they were together they could influence each other to get into trouble.

Fiddy was first to wake, the early morning was hazy and the sun had not risen yet. He opened his big green eyes and yawned with satisfaction and a good night's sleep. Movement in the corner of his eye drew his attention to a Fairy sitting on Rose's shoulder and a small green clothed Pixie jumping around on her arm. Fiddy was startled and jumped back which woke Furdon.

"What on earth is wrong with you?" Furdon asked, wiping his eyes.

"Look, look, look," he whispered loudly as he pointed to what was sitting on Rose. Furdon unwrapped his tail and then peered up at Rose, who indeed had company. The Grocklings had no idea what to do but stare stupidly at the Pixie and the Fairy. The Pixie ran up Rose's arm to stand with the Fairy, the two of them were not sure what to do either so stared right back at Fiddy and Furdon. Rose woke to see her friends in front of her staring.

"What are you two gawping at?" she yawned.

"Shoulder, shoulder, your right shoulder," blurted Furdon at last. Rose pulled her hood back and saw two very small characters standing on her shoulder.

"Good morning," she said to the Pixie and Fairy as if it were all completely normal. The Fairy flew up into the air and then hovered just in front of Rose's face, while the Pixie jumped onto the tree stump behind her.

From here Rose could see the Fairy very clearly, she was a slender girl who could move quite quickly if she wanted to. She was wearing a pale green dress which was tied at the waist and shoulder with a pale blue ribbon. Her tousled brown hair framed her delicate face and she had a beautifully woven headdress on her head. The Fairy had ribbon crisscrossed up her legs to her knees and wore nothing on her feet. Her wings were like lace as they flickered quickly holding her in a hover. She smiled at Rose and then whizzed through the air to sit next to her Pixie friend. Rose edged back slightly so she could see them better, while Fiddy and Furdon were still rendered speechless. The Woodland Pixie was a young man dressed in an outfit made of leaves from the trees around them. His top half was bare but the leaves were wrapped around his legs like trousers. He was also barefoot as he was standing on the tree trunk. He had scruffy brown hair crowning his face and had slightly pointed ears.

"Hello," said Rose. Furdon and Fiddy edged closer.

"Hello…" said the Fairy before she giggled into her hands.

"My name's Rose and these are my friends Furdon and Fiddy." The Grocklings found themselves bowing respectfully even though they still were not sure what to say.

"I'm Gwennol," said the Fairy "And this is my friend Hullard. Don't be thinking he's a Fairy though, he's a Woodland Pixie. He's my friend but he can't fly like I can, see?!" She lifted herself into the air.

"I might not be able to fly but I can run and jump faster than you can!" He called as he ran and jumped around them quicker than Fiddy's eyes could keep track of. Gwennol then shot in front of his face leaving a sprinkling of fairy dust on his nose.

"Why are you in our forest?" asked Gwennol curiously "You don't look like anything we've seen before."

"Though we could hear you thundering through the forest last evening," laughed Hullard.

"Well, sorry to cause any disturbance," said Rose "We're just passing through."

"Passing through to where?" asked Gwennol "Where are you going? Don't you like it here… don't you want to stay with us? We're fun and we play in the woodland all day and night if we can."

"That sounds lovely," said Furdon "But some of us have to be elsewhere."

"Elsewhere…?" frowned Hullard "What's elsewhere? Why would you want to be anywhere but here?"

"Yes it's a lovely place…" said Furdon "But we don't have time to chat and play all day." Gwennol flew over to him and landed on his nose, giving him a firm slap on his cheek and he went cross eyed.

"That means you'd rather be somewhere but here," she said "And that's quite insulting to us."

"We don't mean it as an insult, you have a lovely home," said Rose trying to calm the situation and use eye contact to shush Furdon.

"This isn't our home," laughed Gwennol "Would you like to see our home? It's not too far…" Furdon glanced at Rose to encourage her to say no and grabbed Fiddy to agree with him. They couldn't be wasting time.

"That would be lovely, thank you," said Rose. Furdon rolled his eyes at her… as did Fiddy once he'd had Furdon's elbow in his ribs. Fiddy was actually excited about meeting the Fairies and Pixies of the woodland. After what Troostan had said about them he thought they would be a lot worse than they actually appeared.

"I doubt many of us will still be awake now, most of us nap at dawn," said Gwennol "But follow us and you can meet some of our friends."

Gwennol flew up into the air and hovered patiently whilst Rose, Furdon and Fiddy picked up their bags and straightened their clothes. Their new clothes showed no creases or dirt and were just as bright and as beautiful as when they first appeared. They followed Gwennol into the forest and Hullard ran in front of them, nimbly skipping over flowers and toadstools. Furdon was aware of where they were in the forest and did not want to lose their position in relation to the river, he wanted them to be able to find their way back easily if they had to, especially after the incident with the Ogre where they got completely lost. Fiddy on the other hand did not have such worries and bounced along following the Fairy without hesitation.

"Watch where you walk," said Hullard "Your clumsy feet might trample on things you can't see. Under the flowers are whole other worlds which can easily go unnoticed." Rose delicately lifted and placed each foot making sure it was not on a plant or anything that could hide or shelter tiny creatures of the woodland.

They followed the Fairy until they came to a large tree stump. The stump had obviously once supported a wide tree with a huge circumference but had fallen many years ago and was now just a bulge under the surface of the moss. That is how it appeared to Rose but she was mistaken, for the fallen tree which was mostly unseen was home to hundreds of Fairies. Underneath the fallen tree was an intricate network of tunnels where they played, slept and socialised. The Pixies lived in the undergrowth nearby, which is how the two knew each other and got along.

"Please wait here," said Gwennol indicating for Rose to stand her distance. "I'll go and see who's awake and who wants to meet you." Hullard stood in front of the entrance to the Fairy den with his chest puffed out protectively.

A few moments later the faces of four Fairies could be seen peeping out from behind Hullard. As they gradually felt braver and stepped out onto the tree stump they flickered their wings shyly. Each was dressed beautifully and slightly different in little dresses, one with a lilac dress and purple ribbons, one with a peach dress and orange ribbons, each looked dainty and feminine. They whispered and talked amongst themselves as they peered up at this lady dressed in blue and her two fury friends in purple. After a few more minutes they took to the air, glowing as they went and leaving a trail of golden light behind them.

"Who is she...?" and "What does she want...?" and "Where's she going...?" were some of the whispers that could be heard.

"This is Rose, Furdon and Fiddy," said Gwennol as she joined her friends in flight, buzzing around the odd looking bunch. "These are my friends... Bran, Edhen, Pesh and Berrin." Rose smiled at them, not sure of what to say and feeling quite outnumbered.

"What do you think they're doing here?" asked Berrin who was dressed in lilac.

"Just passing through, so they say," said Gwennol.

"Just passing?" laughed Pesh "There's no such thing as just passing by! If you come to our woodland then it's because you want to be in our woodland, not because you were heading off somewhere else."

"Oh but we are," said Furdon boldly.

"Nonsense," said Bran "Why would you ever want to leave this place, do you not find it a beautiful place to be? Nothing cruel or nasty lives here you know."

"Yes, it's beautiful," reassured Furdon "But we are honestly just passing through."

Just then they caught a glimpse of the shimmer of gold underneath Rose's collar. Hullard dashed up a tree and hung from its branches so he could see what they were chattering about.

"What's that you're hiding?" asked Gwennol. But before Rose could draw breath to answer, the other four Fairies flew towards her throat and were yanking at the chain to lift the golden locket up and into sight. They noticed the engraving of the leaf and dropped it again straight away.

"It's engraved with Ordram's Leaf," said Pesh "What are you doing with such a locket?"

"She must've stolen it," said Bran.

"I didn't steal it... and that's not very nice of you to say!"

"Then how did you come to carry such a locket?"

"It was given to me!"

"By whom?" pestered Bran.

"None of your business," said Fiddy.

"None of our business," they muttered "None of our business! Who do you think you are, none of our business indeed!" Hullard then jumped down off the branch and onto Rose's collar where he sat and admired his reflection in the gold.

"To have a golden leaf, Ordram's leaf in your possession makes you a liar and a thief... these were only given to Queens."

"I can assure you neither I or my friends are liars or thieves," defended Rose.

"You must be," said Bran "You're not a Queen are you?!"

"Well, no…" muttered Rose.

"So you are a liar and a thief," insisted Edhen who'd been quietly observing the events.

"How dare you accuse Miss Rose of being such a thing," said Furdon.

"Then one of you two must have stolen it?" accused Bran.

"How dare you be so insulting!" glared Furdon.

"Then tell us, how do you have this in your possession?"

"You tell us why it's got anything to do with you," smirked Fiddy. The Fairies were not used to being spoken to in such a way. Hullard found it all quite amusing and entertaining.

"Will you please calm down, all of you," said Gwennol "There's no point arguing. Rose, we simply want to know why you carry the golden locket with Ordram's Leaf engraved upon it."

"And we want to know why you want to know," asserted Furdon.

Before Rose knew what was happening, the four fairies were clawing at her neck to get hold the golden locket. Gwennol was shouting at them to let go but they were deaf to her calls, they were on a mission and they wanted the locket. Rose tried to flick them off her and sent them flying into the trees a few time but it backfired and made them more determined than ever to get what they wanted. They resorted to dirty tactics and were biting and scratching at Rose's neck yanking with all their might at the chain. After a scuffle, there was a snapping noise as the chain gave way and the Fairies got what they wanted. They laughed cruelly at Rose before flying up into the trees with the locket out of reach.

"It would've been easier if you'd have just given it to them," sighed Hullard.

"But it wasn't theirs to take," said Furdon firmly.

"Are you alright Rose?" asked Fiddy concerned at the

scratches on her neck.

"Yes Fiddy, I'm fine," she said "But Bolstone was right about these things, they're irritating to be around!"

"What did you say?" said Edhen "You think we're irritating, how dare you!"

"Yes, that's right," said Rose "And how dare you steal my locket, now who's a thief!"

Gwennol did not like confrontation and went to hide under a lump of tree bark until the kerfuffle was over. She was a young Fairy who was trying to get in with the older group and wanted their approval at what she had found. It was not going as she had hoped and she wanted to hide until it had all gone away. Hullard jumped up into the tree to watch the four Fairies fight each other to hold the golden locket and keep it high out of Rose's reach.

"That's just great," said Rose to her friends "I should've paid attention to what Bolstone said and ignore these so-called Fairies, he was right about them. I just wanted to see for myself."

"We know Miss Rose," said Furdon "But we're equally to blame, we didn't stop you did we?"

"I should've known better."

"Enough of this talk," said Fiddy "What's done is done, we can't change it. We simply need to find a way to get the locket back and get out of here."

"That sounds easy but the Fairies could hold onto that all day," said Rose.

"No they won't," interrupted Hullard "They've been up in the woods all night and were tired before you arrived here. They'll soon grow sleepy."

"Why are you being so nice, aren't they your friends?" asked Rose.

"What, those four? No way, Gwennol is my friend, I don't care for these four much at all. They've always been a selfish group and bully their way to get whatever they want."

"What's that?" hissed the fairies from above.

"Look at them, like vultures to a new carcass!" continued Hullard "Nope, I find them shallow and tedious. They don't really care why the locket is around your neck, they just want it for themselves." Gwennol crept out from her hiding place and flew up to hover next to Rose's head.

"I'm so sorry," she said sweetly "I really didn't mean for any of this to happen."

"It's not your fault Gwennol," said Rose "Had I known they were attracted to shiny objects like magpies then I would've tied my collar tighter."

"Magpies," screeched Pesh "Did you just compare us to magpies?"

"Yes, yes I did," sighed Rose "The resemblance is uncanny."

"Take that back, take that back right now," demanded Edhen.

"I'll take it back when you give me my locket back," said Rose cunningly.

"Ah well done Rose," said Fiddy "I see what you're doing, it's all about who has the power."

"I'm sure she's aware of that," said Furdon.

"We will not give you the locket until you apologise."

"Well I won't apologise until you return my locket. And I'm in no rush, I can wait here all day... how long can you manage?" The Fairies flapped around in disbelief at this person's cheek.

The locket began to glow and feel warm to their touch. It gradually got hotter and hotter until it was too much for the delicate hands of the Fairies to take. They squeaked in shock and dropped the golden locket, watching it fall to the floor causing the chain to jangle as it landed. The fairies looked at each other and then flew down to the locket which was now glowing with heat.

"Now look at what you've done to it, have you broken it?"

mocked Hullard.

"We've done no such thing," said Bran "Come feel how hot it is yourself if you don't believe us." Hullard jumped down and stood near the locket before leaning forward to tentatively tap it.

"It's cold," laughed Hullard "You four are losing the plot." Bran flew down and touched the locket again.

"Are you insane Hullard, it's scorching hot and could burn us."

"Not to me," scoffed Hullard "Feels cold for me to touch. Gwennol be a dear and see who's right."

"I don't really want to get involved," she muttered. She didn't want to upset her friend but equally she didn't want to ruin her chances of getting to hang around with the other four fairies.

"Oh come on Gwennol," he said "You get to say who's right." She reluctantly agreed and hovered down slowly, edging her hand closer to the locket not wanting to burn herself if it was hot. It felt cool to her touch.

"It's… cold."

"Ha ha ha, see! Oh I love being right, which is – oh yes, most of the time."

The four Fairies scowled at Hullard and then flew over to Rose to glare at her before swooping back down into the tree trunk. They were angry and upset that things didn't go their way.

"Thank goodness that's over," said Fiddy "I'll not be so enthusiastic to meet a Fairy in the future."

"We're not all bad," said Gwennol.

"Yes, erm present company excluded," said Fiddy, picking the locket up off the floor and handing it back to Rose. "Something inside the locket must've realised it was in the wrong hands and wasn't on your neck… where it belongs," he smiled.

"They've broken the chain," sighed Rose with disappointment and holding up the broken links.

"Don't worry," said Gwennol flying to stand on Rose's wrist. "With your permission of course, please allow me to fix it? Hullard if you'd be so kind to hold the two broken ends together for me and I'll see what I can do."

"Of course, you'll work your magical wonder no doubt," said Hullard, stepping forward feeling proud to be of assistance. As the friends looked on, Gwennol spun in the air until a cloud of golden dust was spinning around her. She then reached forward and with both arms pointed at the broken chain, the gold dust followed her direction and sped its way around the chain. Whoosh, whoosh, whoosh. The friends stared into Rose's hand. Once the dust had settled they could see clearly that the chain was fixed and as good as new.

"Oh Gwennol thank you," said Rose "Thank you so much."

"It's the least I could do after getting you into so much bother," said Gwennol "May I ask… Is that where you're going? Are you going through our woodlands to see Ordram and give him the golden locket back?"

"We are going to Ordram," said Furdon "…Because of the locket, not necessarily to give it back."

"Can we come with you?" asked Hullard "Neither of us have ever seen Ordram though have heard so much about the beauty of the place. We can see from our tree tops the glitter and sparkle on the horizon and often think it must be a wonderful life there."

"As far as we know," said Furdon "Ordram is only expecting the three of us… we wouldn't want to agree to let you come with us and then you not actually be invited."

"That's true…" agreed Hullard "In that case would you allow us to escort you through the forest. We would like to take you through the marshes and down to the port but it's too risky for us. The men and women of your kind might see us, we don't want that to happen."

"Why not?" asked Fiddy.

"They keep away from our woodland and we keep away from their land. We've spent so many years getting them to believe the woodland is cursed and we don't exist. They'd drain the Fairies of their magical dust and we don't want to risk it getting into the wrong hands."

"What makes them think the woodland is cursed?" said Furdon.

"Each time we see those people getting too close to us, we play tricks on them… quickly and quietly and make them think the woodland has evil spirits and is haunted."

"And they believe your tricks and games?" asked Rose.

"Yes, they have no reason to believe anything different. Since then, we've lived peacefully away from their clumsy hands. They are to us what an Ogre would be to you."

"Yes, I can completely understand," smiled Rose "An Ogre got hold of me a few days ago."

"Really?" said Gwennol "How interesting and how magnificent you got away!"

"I was very fortunate, it wasn't a pleasant experience."

"So may we escort you to the edge of the woodland?"

"Yes, why not!" smiled Rose.

"It's about a day and a half walk," said Hullard "Remember to watch where you put your feet. We might bump into a few other Fairies and Pixies along the way, those who haven't gone to bed yet… the closer we are to the far side of the woodland, the more tricky they can be. When they see you three stumbling through then they might have a bit of fun with you."

"Can't you stop them?" asked Furdon.

"To be honest we'd be expected to join in…" said Hullard.

"But we'll try our best, won't we Hullard?" said Gwennol "Don't be scaring these lovely travellers." Hullard smiled mischievously and then blushed.

They began to walk through the woodland and follow

Gwennol and Hullard. The Fairy flew around the trees and played in the branches while Rose took her time so as not to tread on or crush anything. Furdon and Fiddy were very light-footed and could scamper about quite well. Hullard ran along jumping from tree trunk to tree trunk, leaping elegantly over flowers and shrubs. The morning air felt cool and fresh and was filled with sweet floral smells which emanated from the woodland around them. Dawn had broken and the early morning sun threw soft yellow beams of light through the trees. Besides themselves, the woodland was peaceful and only stirred by the occasional bird call and buzzing insect.

"Where are you from?" asked Gwennol, hovering next to Rose as she walked.

"Cragfeld, do you know it?"

"Never heard of it. Is it as pretty as here?"

"No…" she smiled "It's very dull and grey compared to here."

"Dull and grey? I can't imagine such a place."

"Oh it's real," said Furdon "Ruled by an Ice Queen with a frozen heart."

"What!" said Gwennol with surprise "Is she not a good Queen?"

"No, she serves only herself and drains her people of life."

"Oh how awful, no wonder you have come here instead. You're going to go back to Cragfeld?"

"I'm afraid we have to," said Rose.

"Why? Why not just stay here?"

"Because we made a promise to try and help free Cragfeld from her cold grip," said Rose.

"But an Ice Queen is dangerous and can't be killed?" said Gwennol.

"That's how I understand it," said Hullard.

"Is that why you're going to Ordram, for help?"

"I think so," said Rose.

"Are you sure we can't come with you?" pleaded Hullard.

"Yes, we're sure," said Furdon, smiling to himself at Hullard's determination to join them.

The walk was a relaxing stroll and Rose was enjoying having a less stressful time of things, no Ogres, no Spiraliluses and no Dragons. Of course she knew things could change at any time in this unpredictable land which made her appreciate it while it was calm. She had not liked her experience with the Fairies and really, really did not want to meet any more if they were all like those four. Her neck was red from where they had scratched her trying to get hold of the locket, which she made sure was now completely hidden under the collar of her dress. Since arriving in Ordraskop she had noticed subtle daily changes to the engraving on the locket. What was once an engraving on the flat surface now appeared to be growing and slowly peeling and lifting itself off the surface. The engraved golden leaf was a like a growing bud slowly opening as if in the right conditions to come to life. This made hiding it under her dress more and more difficult.

They sat by the river for something to eat. Gwennol was not impressed when she saw what they were eating so she sprinkled some magic and turned dry bread into luxurious sandwiches filled with succulent slices of turkey, fresh salad and a mouth-watering dressing. She also turned crumbled pastries into ice cream sundaes with chocolate sauce and Fairy dust sprinkles. Rose had never tasted anything even close to what she was experiencing now. Hullard did not hesitate to dive in and help himself to the feast. He only had a small stomach and it only took a few mouthfuls for him to feel full. Even the frogs at the side of the river seemed interested in trying some of the treats laid out in front of their eyes. The frogs hopped up the riverbank and stared at the morsels of delight as crumbs dropped here and there and were available to whoever wanted them. It was quite a gathering that had been attracted to this sunny little spot by the river. The sound of the river running over the rocks was tranquil, splishing and sploshing as it made its way down from the mountain.

"It's lovely here," said Fiddy who was quite content with a full belly and the sun beating down warming his body from top to toe.

"It is indeed," agreed Rose, leaning back on her arms.

"It sounds like you want to stay here?" teased Gwennol.

"Maybe we will call and see you again on our way back to Cragfeld."

"Maybe," said Gwennol "If you come back the same way."

"There's another way?" asked Furdon.

"There's always another way," smiled Gwennol.

Once they had finished eating and were almost too full to move, Furdon hurried them along as he knew it was adding time to their journey. They said 'cheerio' to the frogs and then continued walking in the dappled shade of the woodland following the course of the river.

As the group meandered along, they could hear the bluebells jingling in the soft breeze. There was a slight glow around the forest as its plants and animals, all unusual and strange looking to Rose, went about their business. Most of the Pixies and Fairies hid away from the midday sun as it was too tiring for them. Gwennol and Hullard were doing well to stay awake and guide Rose and the Grocklings through the woods. The other Fairies and Pixies would be waking in the late afternoon to play in the forest and probably cause mischief.

After a few hours the trees seemed to be growing thicker and more dense the closer they got to the other side of the woodland. Less light could penetrate through the leaves and the undergrowth was dry and rusty brown. There was less of a magical and enchanted feeling about this end of the woods and they all agreed it did not feel welcoming. The air felt heavy somehow compared to when they had first met Gwennol and Hullard earlier on.

"This is why those humans from down in the port don't come here," said Hullard "They believe bad spirits hide amongst the trees."

"It certainly feels like something strange is here," said Rose.

"Not strange," smiled Gwennol "Only a magic which keeps us safe and away from them. Don't worry if you feel quite fuzzy headed, it's all part of the illusion. We will get you through it."

"Only bad news is," said Hullard "Is that we're going to have to set up a place to sleep in this part of the forest. If humans inhale too much of this air then they'll hallucinate."

"What?!" said Rose "I don't want to hallucinate."

"And what about us?" asked Fiddy "Does it have the same effect on Grocklings?"

"No, no," smiled Gwennol "You may have slight human attributes but you certainly are not human so will be okay in here. Look after Rose though, she may have a tough time depending how stressed and worried she is, hallucinations magnify any anxiety."

"Oh great!" sighed Rose sarcastically "They sound awful. We've had a few stresses over the last few days and I'm anxious of what the next few days will bring... so I'm going to be seeing all kinds of nasty things aren't I?"

"I'm afraid so, it sounds like it anyway," said Gwennol.

"Isn't there a tonic that you could give her, one she could take to ease things slightly?" asked Furdon.

"No, only the fresh air away from the woodland will dilute things for her," said Hullard.

"What about you Gwennol, is there nothing you can do to help?"

"My magic is not strong enough to compete with the strength of the thousands of Fairies and Pixies who have cast their spells here. I will see what I can do though, I promise." With that in mind, Rose was not looking forward to spending the night here.

Hullard and Gwennol found a place which they thought was suitable for the evening and night, a soft mossy patch of grass under the large trunk of a tree. Gwennol threw sparkles of magic around the area to scare away any nasty looking brambles and creeping vines. They had a small comfortable area to sit.

"How are you feeling Rose?" asked Fiddy "You look as if you need to sit down."

"I feel as if I need to sit down," said Rose. Her head was beginning to feel fuzzy.

"It's going to be difficult for us all to watch you have to go through this," said Gwennol "But we will look after you as well as we can and try to keep you as grounded as possible."

It was not long after Rose had sat down and inhaled more of the toxic woodland air that she began seeing things, images started flashing in front of her eyes. It looked as if shadows were moving around the woodland and hiding behind trees to watch her. She could hear rustling in the branches overhead and began seeing shadows of creeping animals edging their way closer to her. Rose tried to ignore them and not let her mind fall victim to the contaminated air. The harder she fought, the worse the hallucinations became. Her eyes felt heavy and she was suddenly presented with an image of the Ice Queen reaching towards Rose to grab her throat. Rose could feel her cold fingers on her throat and her sharp nails digging into her skin. She tried to pull free from the Ice Queen's grasp but it was as if she had been paralysed and could not move. The Ice Queen held Furdon and Fiddy by their tails in her other hand, dangling them over a bottomless canyon. Rose could feel her emotions rushing from angry, to upset, to terrified all powering through her she was held in the tight grip, scared for her friends and loyal companions. That image quickly faded and was replaced with Dragons swooping down on her and breathing fire at her. She tried to shelter Furdon and Fiddy to protect them all, cowering against the side of the mountain. A golden leaf then dropped to the floor, in Rose's mind this was real. The golden leaf was delicate as she picked it up. Through this leaf she could see humans and animals all together fighting with fire and ice. She was fighting too but she did not feel scared, she felt empowered, brave and a fire burning through her blood. She was fighting and had her friends by her side, the two Grocklings never letting her down. As the first wave of hallucinations subsided she was left with a very clear image of the Ice Queen staring at her, she was not touching her or inflicting any pain, just simply staring at her with anger in her eyes.

"Rose, Rose, Oh please Miss Rose, wake up," said Furdon trying to shake her out of the terrible visions.

"Please help her," pleaded Fiddy to Gwennol "Do what you can. She's going to be exhausted if it carries on like this all night. She needed to rest as best as she can, not have this draining her."

"Okay, okay Fiddy," said Gwennol quietly "Like I said, my powers are nothing compared to the ones in this woodland that Rose has inhaled. With a lot of effort Gwennol tried to help Rose. The little Fairy flew at full speed through the canopy, up, up, up to where the air was clear, high up above the woodland. She then splashed her magic Fairy dust into the clean air and small clumps began to form. Half a dozen apple sized bubbles of gold hung in the air. On Gwennol's command she raced with them as fast as she could back to where Rose was laid. Rose looked pale and clammy as her hallucinations were stirring inside her. She cracked open one of the golden bubbles over Rose's face and a blue haze leaked out and clung around her face.

"It's a fog of fresh air," said Gwennol "I hope it will relieve her, if only temporarily."

"What wonderful thinking," said Hullard feeling proud of his friend.

Rose slowly came round and woke from the vivid dreams. Gwennol then made her eat one of the bubbles to try and help purify her system.

"Good grief, you had us worried," said Furdon "You were walking around here as if wide awake."

"I saw, I saw fighting," stuttered Rose "And the Ice Queen staring at me, just staring at me, right into my soul."

"It wasn't real Rose," reassured Fiddy "It was your deep anxieties showing themselves… and to be honest if I were human, the Ice Queen would probably pop up in mine too." He smiled trying to lighten the mood.

"Here Rose," said Gwennol "Take these bubbles of fresh air, they will only last maybe twenty or thirty minutes each but it's long enough to keep the hallucinations at bay."

"Maybe we shouldn't rest," said Furdon "Maybe we should keep moving while Miss Rose feels okay. Then we will be out of this place before she has to go through all of that again."

Hullard and Gwennol were tired and struggling to keep moving. Instead, they sat on Rose's shoulder and guided her without having to fly or run ahead. This was working and they slowly trudged their way through the darkness. Hullard was so tired that he fell asleep and rolled off Rose's shoulder landing safely in her hood which hugged him like a hammock. Gwennol rolled her eyes at him as he fell, she was exhausted but had to stay awake as long as she could, at least until the oppressive air eased and the woodland thinned out somewhat. Every time Rose started to feel woozy she would eat a bubble of air, they truly helped her to feel as normal as she could in this place.

Eventually dawn broke and sunlight began to weave its way through the trees. They could see the light ahead was quite bright as if they had finally reached the other side of the woodland. Rose did not have any golden bubbles of fresh air left and did not want to ask Gwennol for more, she could see she was worn out and did not have energy to lift her head, let alone summon magic. Fiddy, Furdon and Rose trudged out of the woodland and collapsed onto a grassy knoll. They had struggled on through the night and were exhausted. They watched the sun rise through their bleary eyes. Rose put her arms around each of them, having the hallucinations fresh in her mind, she knew how much Furdon and Fiddy meant to her. She made a promise to herself there and then that no harm would ever come to them.

CHAPTER NINE

Orme was sitting in her rocking chair in a thoughtful mood. She was thinking about the Ice Queen and the army she was creating. Orme would have never been able to have an opportunity like this if she was working under the rule of the previous King who never liked or enjoyed her magic and only ever used it for good. Now she was in the position of power and influence and being able to bring more evil into existence than she ever thought possible. The Ice Queen was her perfect collaborator as they were both as selfish and as greedy as each other. Orme did of course sometime resent the Ice Queen and how she used her magic, the old witch saw no point in torture or murder for the sake of it, whereas the Ice Queen thrived off it. Each act or pain on a human caused a wave of satisfaction to course through the Ice Queen's cold veins, she felt nothing for these people. She used them to help her and once they were no longer useful then she would shrink them and encase them in a crystal of ice, some times she would add them to more chandeliers around the Dark Castle, others she would turn into jewellery… earrings, pendants and such. It was as if the Ice Queen was proud of her collection of victims and captives who were trapped by her powers forever. It was like she needed a souvenir to remind her of what was hers and how powerful she was.

The old witch was hundreds of years older than Mordisan and had been practicing magic in various ways since her school days. When Mordisan became the Ice Queen she made the old witch cast a spell on her so she would never grow old and would never die. The old witch went along with this but only after she had explained immortality would be very lonely, to which Mordisan explained she had been lonely all of her human life and it would be no different as a Queen.

Orme then found her mind wandering to when she was perfecting her magic when she was a young girl, almost a thousand years ago. There were few witches and wizards around so anyone who showed signs of having the gift was quickly snapped up and sent to the magic academy. There were only four others in Orme's class, one of whom was Bolstone the wizard. She began to remember of how they used to practice and learn how to use their magic for good, to make things better. Bolstone was always top of the class, this annoyed Orme and made her lose interest in learning. She always wanted to be the best but was never given the chance to prove what she could be. It was during this time she found an old tattered musty book on the top shelf in the library, sitting as if untouched and forgotten about for hundreds of years. She brought it down and flicked through the fragile pages only to see a kind of magic which they had not been taught or even told about, bad magic. There were spells for revenge, power, torture and other more blood curdling things. Orme's face lit up and she tucked the book under her cloak to sneak it to her room. She found she was a natural to these spells and quickly picked it up. She and Bolstone had drifted to opposite ends of the scale, Bolstone was the best at being good, whereas Orme was the best at being bad. In the time since leaving the academy they had both chosen to stay away from each other, as apart from the natural gift, they had nothing in common. On the odd occasion they had the misfortune of bumping into each other, they would completely ignore each other. The old witch smiled as she thought back over the years. She looked around knowing she was in a great position next to the Ice Queen, Bolstone certainly would not be able to say the same thing.

Orme creaked herself out of the rocking chair and hobbled through the frozen corridors to the cold chamber where the silver eggs were developing. There were hundreds of them laid out before her, covering the entire surface of the floor. Hovering above them in the shell of ice was their guardian, the woman taken from the village to watch over the eggs and provide blood for them to absorb. The woman was pale and sitting with her knees pulled to her chest, her head buried in her skirt, and blood continuing to trickle from her nails. Orme knew her blood would be no good if the woman was not properly fed and nourished, with a flick of her old wrist and a mutter of words under her breath, a basket of food appeared in the ice shell for her. The woman looked over her knees and into the basket but had no interest in what she saw, she just wanted to be set free and go home. She looked at Orme with pleading eyes, the old witch could not help her anymore than to feed her. To set her free would not please the Ice Queen at all. Orme looked back at the woman and tried to encourage her to eat. Eventually she did take a piece of bread from the basket and began to eat, trying not to notice her bloody hands. The bread looked and tasted like bread but Orme had actually given the woman a pain killer which would also make her sleepy, to try and numb the torturous thing she was experiencing. The bread also contained a drop of magic which would also nourish her properly, to ultimately ensure the eggs had a healthy supply of blood. The Ice Queen would never have done this, instead she would have ordered a replacement for when the woman was of no use anymore.

Apart from Mordisan and Orme there was very little life in the Dark Castle. One or two servants who were under a spell would potter back and forth with meals for the Ice Queen. The captives in the chandeliers were the only other sign of life in the grim cold place. The old witch thought it was quite nice having all of these eggs, growing creatures within them, for when they were ready to break free, the Dark Castle would be full of life and vile energy – just as she had always hoped for. The eggs were developing fast and some were starting to twitch and move as the life within them grew.

Orme shuffled backwards and hobbled through the corridors to the main hall where she saw the Ice Queen standing on the balcony. It was dark outside, not that it was night, it was mid afternoon but dark clouds circled the island of Cragfeld. The clouds were so thick and dark that no light could find its way through. The old witch thought nothing of it as when the Ice Queen was in a bad mood she would often blacken the clouds and create a storm. On the mountain peaks the winged wardens could be seen taking to flight to scan the mountains for trespassers. The torches burning at each station would never go out, no matter what mood the Ice Queen was in and how much rain she threw over them, they were her creation.

"Is something wrong?" asked the old witch from the middle of the main hall. The Ice Queen slowly turned her head to look at Orme, her eyes flashed with silver. Her red hair flickered like fire in the breeze.

"Are you doing this?" asked the Ice Queen suspiciously.

"Doing what my Queen?"

"This," she pointed into the sky "Cragfeld is mine, the people are mine. I control everything, even the clouds and rain… so if you are doing this, you must stop."

"I would never dare," said Orme "You know that I respect you and would never cross such a boundary." The Ice Queen looked right at her as if reading deep inside her.

"That's true," she glared "Besides, if it were you I'd be able to tell! So please tell me, if it is neither of us stirring such a black sky, then who is?" The old witch hobbled over to stand on the balcony next to the Ice Queen and stared up into the sky. Clouds were circling the island slowly and methodically and swirls of yellow and orange flashed from time to time.

"Other forces are at work my Queen. Whatever it is it must be connected to what we're forbidden from seeing. It will pass, it will pass."

"I don't want it to pass," barked the Ice Queen "I want it to be gone, I want you to clear it."

"Yes, of course," smiled Orme, knowing even though the Ice Queen had power and magic to sort this out herself, she would always want the old witch by her side. Orme took a deep breath and looked up at the clouds and waved her hands above her head in the opposite direction as the clouds were moving. She took one of the ice crystal from Mordisan's white gown and held it in her hand before throwing it up into the air. The ice crystal glowed red and shot up into the clouds. Everything went deathly silent for a few moments before the crystal burst and lit the sky. The clouds absorbed the redness and began to circle the other way and a hole appeared in the middle of them, the clouds were drawn into this hole. The sky began to clear from the outside as the circling clouds were being sucked into the middle. As the last few disappeared there was a flash of red across the sky and the ice crystal fell back down to the Dark Castle where Orme held out her hand for it to land.

"I shall destroy this," she growled as she watched the crystal go black in her old hand.

"Good," smiled the Ice Queen "See what you can get from it first, there may be a clue as to what created it."

"Yes, certainly." She made her way back through the main hall and down to her den in the deepest part of the Dark Castle.

The Ice Queen summoned the powers within her and blew her icy breath up into the sky, filling it from peak to peak with her own grey and red clouds, sending a message to the winged wardens to be extra diligent as something was brewing that was out of her sights.

Orme held the crystal tight in her hand as she stepped into her den and down the cold slimy steps. She shuffled over to her cauldron where she dropped the crystal in to see if the source magic would be revealed. The black crystal hissed as it hit the water of her cauldron and bubbled wildly as it began to dissolve. She pulled one of her dry wiry grey hairs from her scalp and dropped it into the cauldron too as she closed her eyes.

"With my own hair, Let me see, What powers beyond, Threaten me…"

She opened her eyes and saw red bubbles appearing on the surface of the water. Orme knew she had to wait a while as whatever was hiding would want to remain hidden as her powers dragged it to the surface. The old witch's eyes lit up when she saw changes stirring as the waters hissed and gurgled. When everything went quiet and the cauldron was calm, Orme peered over the rim to see what she could see. There, floating on the surface of the water was an orange sphere which burst as soon as she saw it. The old witch had seen all she needed to see and smiled.

"Ah," she cackled "My old friend, you must be getting stupid in your old age. You think after all these years that I wouldn't recognise you. I knew we'd meet again, Bolstone you old fool."

Orme now knew who she was up against and would relish the moment when she could knock him down. She would show Bolstone she was stronger and more powerful than he could ever be. She knew he would put up a good fight and would try to challenge her. Orme would enjoy the moment when he would be forced to admit that he was not as strong as she was.

The mid morning sun was warm as Rose and her friends were sleeping. After the ordeal in the woodland, they all felt as if they could sleep for days. Hullard was still tucked up in the hood of Rose's gown, whilst Gwennol was resting up a sleeve. Loud male voices could be heard echoing up from the port which was only a few miles away. Furdon was woken by some of these voices, thinking they were closer than they actually were. He stood up and stretched his arms into the air and stretched all of his muscles from his finger-tips to his tail. His green eyes cleared and he scanned his surroundings, everything was peaceful apart from Fiddy's snoring. Furdon looked down to the port and could see the boats were busy with one thing or another, he was not sure what with exactly because he had never seen the ocean before. Far out on the horizon he could see their destination, Ordram shone brightly like a beacon of hope. Furdon did not know or have any idea of who Ordram really was or how he looked but from the descriptions he had been given, he was going to be quite powerful. Frithad and Eady had described him as a magical tree but Furdon thought there would be more than just a tree when they got there. They could not have gone through all of this just to get a leaf from a tree, surely not.

Fiddy yawned with a squeak as his eyes opened and he looked around him to see who else was awake. He was pleased to see Furdon was up and about because had he been first up he would have quickly got bored and 'accidently on purpose' had to wake the others up just for someone to talk to. Rose was sound asleep so Fiddy stretched out his small frame and went to stand with Furdon who was gazing out to the horizon.

"It looks so far away doesn't it?" said Fiddy "I hope it doesn't take us too much longer." Furdon continued to stare, only nodding his head to show Fiddy he was listening.

"We've come all this way," he eventually said "Surely there is less to do than we've already done? It is good to see Ordram there on the horizon, a target to aim for."

"We've been able to see Ordram since we were at the top of the mountain with Hildfall," joked Fiddy.

"I know… but you know what I mean."

"Are you alright Furdon, you don't seem to be your usual self."

"What? Oh… erm, yes I'm fine. It's been a long few days, I wasn't expecting it to be such a tricky journey if I'm honest."

"Me too. When we volunteered to come with Rose, I had no idea of what we'd experience. But you have to admit it's been fun hasn't it? It certainly beats trudging around Cragfeld and doing the same things with the same Grocklings. I think we're doing a good job too, even if we've had a bit of help along the way."

"Yes, I think so too," said Furdon proudly "I think we're better companions than the Fighters could've been, all brawn and no brains that lot." They smiled at each other. They'd known one another for many years but these last few days had certainly tightened their friendship.

"So what do you think Ordram is going to be like? It sounds like a wonderful place to visit doesn't it?"

"It certainly does Fiddy. I don't know what to expect but he's got to be something amazing… for a tree."

"Don't say it like that," Fiddy frowned "He's a magical and powerful tree and he is the only one who can help us." Furdon looked at Fiddy and saw the excitement in his eyes.

"Yes, you are right Fiddy. I think I just need a good sleep where I can relax without anything happening to us."

"As lovely as that sounds, I think you'll have to wait a bit longer for that."

Rose stirred from her sleep, lifting her arm to her face to

block out the sun, Gwennol dropped from her sleeve and flopped to the floor with a bump which woke her up. The Fairy flickered her wings and brushed the creases off her little dress.

"How long were we sleeping?" asked Rose.

"Not as long as you think or as long as you need," smiled Furdon, turning to her.

"How are you feeling Rose?" asked Fiddy springing over to her.

"You're rather lively," she smiled "I'm okay, but can still see those hallucinations when I close my eyes."

"Really?" said Gwennol "That's odd, they shouldn't be affecting you anymore."

"I think it's just flashbacks from what I saw to be honest, it was horrible."

"Yes, I'm sure they were Rose... but they weren't real, just a creation from your own imagination about your worries."

"In that case why can't I worry about flowers, candy floss and cup cakes," she smiled.

"Where's Hullard?" asked Gwennol.

"He slipped into my hood when he fell asleep, as far as I know he's still there."

"Yes, I'm here," came his muffled voice "But you've twisted the bottom of your hood and I can't get out." This made the others laugh.

"Why didn't you say anything?" asked Furdon.

"I was so comfortable and didn't actually want to come out... but thought I'd better not be antisocial." Rose got to her feet and gently aired her hood and it twisted back around and Hullard jumped out.

"I suppose now we're all awake we should head off shouldn't we?" said Rose.

"Does that mean we can come too?" asked Hullard.

"No, it's still a no, Hullard... sorry," she smiled as he looked thoroughly disappointed. "I think we can make it down to the port okay from here."

"Be careful of the boggy marshes," said Gwennol "Stay on the stepping stones and you'll be fine."

Rose turned to look back on the woodland before leaving. She saw something move behind a tree but couldn't see clearly what it was so she rubbed her eyes and stepped a few paces closer.

"What is it Miss Rose?" said Furdon defensively "Do you see something?"

"I don't know… I could've sworn I saw something or someone hiding behind that tree."

"Let us go and see, come on Fiddy."

They walked a few metres into the woodland and checked behind all of the trees which Rose pointed to, but there was nobody there. As they were walking back towards Rose, movement caught her eye and she saw it again.

"There! there! I saw it again, there's definitely someone there."

"But we just checked all the trees Miss Rose, there's nobody there."

"Can you please look again?"

"I will look," said Hullard "I am so small that whoever it is won't see me creeping up." And so Hullard jumped from tree to tree but saw nobody.

"Maybe you're just tired and your eyes are playing tricks on you?" said Gwennol.

"No, I promise, I saw someone."

"Well whoever it is has gone now," said Furdon "Come on, we'd better get on our way. We can't be playing with shadows all day."

Hullard and Gwennol said goodbye to Rose, Furdon and Fiddy and then flew and jumped back into the trees. What Rose did not know was as soon as her back was turned they crept back and slipped into the hood of her gown. They wanted to see Ordram and were determined not to let this opportunity go. Rose could not feel them as they got comfortable, they were after all very small and did not weigh much at all.

Fiddy and Furdon lifted their bags onto their backs and began walking down the overgrown path. Rose swung her bag onto her shoulder and the flash of movement in the trees caught her eye again. This time she didn't say anything to the others but instead, stood tall to see who was playing tricks on her. Out from behind a tree stepped a girl dressed in a blue robe with a grey hood lifted up over her head, she pulled the hood back and her brown hair bounced free. She didn't step any closer to Rose but stood and looked right back at her. The girl looked exactly like Rose but had a glow in her cheeks and looked happy. She smiled at Rose and then waved before turning back into the woods and vanished out of sight. This was the second time Rose had seen herself and both times her friends were unable to see her. Rose was shocked and confused, why was this girl who looked like her following them but not making herself known. Rose looked into the trees again but saw nothing. She turned and caught up with Fiddy and Furdon who hadn't noticed she was lagging behind or that anything had caught her attention.

Hullard and Gwennol bobbed up and down in the hood of Rose's hood as she walked. After a while they were relaxed and confident that Rose did not know they were there, so they climbed up the hood and stuck their heads out to see where they were going. They could smell the stink of the marshes getting stronger as they approached, just hoping they remembered to stick to the path and not step off the stones.

The boggy marshes were full of liars and thieves, all hiding and waiting for someone to rob. These weren't human, these were creatures that had been too vile to live anywhere else but thrived in this place. Giant slugs or slippery eels were some of the better characters living here, it was the Trolls which could cause a lot of bother. They would slosh around in the smelly water, either sitting fighting amongst themselves or stomping around sending huge waves across the water. The boggy marshes was an expanse of shallow water which lead down to the port where the humans lived. They stretched for a couple of miles along the coast line but were separated from the sea by a man made wall which stood five metres tall. Humans knew the Trolls weren't going to go away but had come to an agreement that the Trolls could live in the boggy marshes as long as they caused no threat to the people. As much as the humans would have liked to catch a few Fairies from the woodlands, it really was not worth risking the pathway through the boggy marshes to get to them. Rose, Furdon and Fiddy approached the boggy marshes and felt the ground soften under their feet, it felt soggy.

"Urgh, that smells horrendous," said Rose covering her nose with her sleeve.

"I've never smelled anything as repulsive in all my days," said Furdon.

"I can feel it squelching round my feet," said Fiddy running back to a drier spot further up the bank.

"That's why there are stepping stones Fiddy," said Rose "See...? They stretch all the way to the port. Do as Gwennol said and stay on them though."

"Don't need to worry about that Rose," said Fiddy "I don't want any of that stinky water getting on my new purple jacket and especially not on my fur. I'd be able to smell it forever." Rose laughed at how vain Fiddy could be.

Furdon took the lead as usual so as to test out the stability of each stepping stone before he would let Rose move forward. The stepping stones were domed shaped rocks peeking through the surface of the brown sludge, they were sometimes slippery and had a slimy surface. The Grocklings hated every step as they could feel the gloop oozing through their toes on the smaller stones which were closer to the surface of the boggy marsh. The larger stones were cleaner and dryer but quite difficult to step on to as it seemed to take a bigger leap to get onto them. Around them there was always some kind of movement in the muddy waters as creatures skulked about and watched them. Rose had seen eels, toads, crabs and slugs which were all covered in mud, slime and stench.

The crossing of the boggy marshes was a couple of miles at least. It was a slow pace as they each stepped one at a time while the others made sure they didn't slip on landing and attract unwanted attention. Not all of the stepping stones were stable and would wobble underfoot and bubble and gurgle as they were squelched into the mud around them. Grime covered air bubbles in the marshes would slowly appear on the surface and then burst, releasing a pungent smelling green gas.

"I don't think my nostrils can take much more of this," said Fiddy from the rear "This place will have burnt away our sense of smell by the time we get to the other side."

"We know!" said Rose and Furdon at the same time. It did stink but there was nothing they could do about it so simply had to focus on the task in hand and get through it.

Rose was taking her time with each step, having to balance and judge to distance before leaping onto the next one. Leaping off was generally okay but it was the landing which was proving tricky as some stones were more wobbly or slippery than others. All of them were pleased when a large stone was next and it was dry and had a more solid position. Fiddy and Furdon benefited from their feline traits and could leap confidently from stone to stone, the only thing they did not like was being barefoot. Rose would have preferred her boots but Hildfall apparently decided dainty blue pumps were a more suitable option. To be fair on

Hildfall, the pumps were light and gripped well to the stones, even the slippery ones.

"Are we nearly there yet?" whined Fiddy "How much further is it?"

"The more you moan, the longer it will seem!" said Furdon impatiently.

"Don't worry Fiddy, just remember every step is one step closer than you were on the last one."

"Thanks but I don't find that comforting," he said "And is it me or is the water looking more unsettled?" The water gurgled as it lapped each stepping stone.

"I hadn't noticed it," said Rose "But now you mention it, it does seem quite lively." The mud gurgled and bubbled as a small wave of water moved by, it wasn't a big wave but more like a swelling as the water moved along.

"Oh, erm…" said Furdon "That muddy water has just washed over a few of the next few stepping stones and I can't see where they are."

"Urgh really? It will pass I'm sure," said Rose.

"What do you mean exactly," said Fiddy "Are we going to be stuck here while we wait for the water level to subside?"

"I don't think we have a choice," said Furdon "But you're more than welcome to take the lead and see what you think? And those stones just behind have also vanished so we can't turn back."

"No, no, it's okay," said Fiddy sensing Furdon was becoming cross at his whinging.

"Well let's just wait here," said Rose "If you two jump onto this stepping stone with me, it's bigger and then we can all wait together until we can see the path again." Her friends did not hesitate to leap onto the same rock as Rose, it was drier and cleaner than the ones they were on.

A few moments later another swell of water passed around them, then shortly after that there was another one. It did not take them long to realise that something was causing this ripple effect. They held onto each other and looked in the direction from where the ripples were coming from, they did not dare move as they waited to see what would appear through the murk. In the near distance they could hear something sloshing around in the mud, whatever it was sounded pretty big as every now and then it would grunt heavily. It was a deep loud grunt as if coming from a big pair of lungs. Out of the murk Fiddy and Furdon's sharp eyes could see a shadow moving around.

"I don't like the look of that!" said Furdon.

"No, me neither," said Fiddy holding tighter onto Rose.

"What is it, what do you she?" she asked.

"I'm not sure to be honest, it's still in the shadows," said Furdon.

"It's not an Ogre is it?" she moaned.

"It's a similar size and shape but I don't think it's an Ogre."

"Oh, it's getting closer," squeaked Fiddy "I can hear it breathing."

"Oh, oh, I can see something," said Rose "But it's only a blurry shadow to me, can you see it more clearly yet?"

"Slightly better Miss Rose," said Furdon "I think, from stories I've read, it could very well be a Swamp Troll."

"A Swamp Troll?" echoed Fiddy "What do you mean a Swamp Troll and how do you know about them?"

"A Swamp Troll… A troll of the swamps," he sarcastically said to Fiddy "I remember Frithad telling me he'd once had a run in with one."

"That's reassuring," said Fiddy "Because Frithad lived to tell the tale."

"Indeed he did, but between the Swamp Trolls and the other thieves in the area, he was robbed of anything he carried that was valuable. Miss Rose, you must hide the golden locket – if they see it, they'll take it and never give it back."

"Where am I supposed to hide it? I have no pockets and

they'll probably go through our bags."

"Here, wrap this old scarf around your neck," said Furdon as he retrieved his thin dull scarf from his bag.

"Surely this makes it obvious I'm trying to hide something?"

"Maybe but I can't think of anything else."

"Why don't you hide the locket in your shoe?" said Fiddy "It'll be out of sight and you can grip onto it with your toes."

"That's a good idea Fiddy," said Rose as she slipped the golden locket from around her neck and into her shoe. She tapped her foot to guide the locket down to her toes where she could keep hold of it.

"Did Frithad tell you the best ways to avoid these Swamp Trolls or how to get away from them?" asked Fiddy.

"Erm, let me think… I remember him saying they were easily distracted by bright lights. I suppose that's the reason for the tall wall at the other side, so they can't see the lights from the port."

"That's great, I don't suppose any of us brought a lantern did we?" said Fiddy "Shush, shush, listen… it's stopped splashing around over there – and, oh no, it's looking at us."

The Swamp Troll had indeed stopped making so much noise but it wasn't looking at them, it hadn't even seen them. It was actually just listening to the ripples in the water and gloopiness of the mud, to air bubbles popping as they heaved their way to the surface to let out even more stench. Swamp Trolls are perfectly suited to living in boggy marshes and wet lands but to them it was a case of the smellier the better. They grew to three metres tall but when they were laid down you wouldn't be able to see them because they had dark grey scaly skin which was also plated in a layer of shell. Water weeds and reeds would get caught on the shell as the trolls splashed around. Along with the weeds attaching themselves to the shell, molluscs would also find it a nice safe place to make home. Swamp Trolls were very well camouflaged when they were not stood up and they would use this to surprise a lot of the victims they chose to rob. The only reason they liked to steal things was through greed, they did not want anyone else to have anything valuable so would take it off them. This particular Swamp Troll was not as greedy as the others, he would much rather play in the mud and cover his body with smelly sludge. So when all the ripples had quietened down he carried on making new ones.

"What's it doing?" asked Rose "Do you think he's seen us?"

"I can't tell, I could've sworn he was just looking in our direction but he seems not to have noticed us," said Furdon.

"He's making more ripples though, we can't move until those ripples have settled down," said Rose "I don't suppose there's any real rush is there, a few more minutes won't make much difference."

"As long as this stone doesn't get a wave over it, we'll be fine."

"I know it smells really bad here but speaking for myself I've got used to it now and it doesn't seem as bad."

"Lucky you, it's as bad as when we first got here to me," smiled Furdon.

The Swamp Troll stumbled around the boggy marshlands and was blundering around as if quite happy with life. They could now see he had webbed fingers, large pointy ears and what looked like stumpy little horns on his bald scaly head. He was playing with a tree trunk which had fallen into the water, kicking it and throwing it about. As the tree skimmed across the water it sent waves over the stepping stones.

"I wish he'd stop doing that," said Fiddy "When we do eventually get to cross this path, those stones are going to be wet and slippery and covered in sticking swamp mud."

"I just wish he'd hurry up and move along," said Rose.

The Swamp Troll lifted the tree above his head and was about to launch it over in their direction, when he saw the blue and purple of their jackets as they were sitting on a boulder. He dropped the tree and stomped over to them to see what they were. He was standing above them and could not work out what they were, so bent down for a closer look. The three of them did not dare move as the Swamp Troll lowered his great head down to peer at them through his crocodile-like eyes.

"Have you come to play with me?" he said after a few minutes. Rose looked at her friends and then up at the Swamp Troll. She got to her feet and stood as tall as she could.

"What game are you playing?" she asked.

"What are you doing?" whispered Furdon.

"I don't know… seeing if something will work!" she replied.

"Erm, I don't know really," said the Swamp Troll "I don't usually have anyone to play with."

"That's sad?"

"No, I like it. The others won't play with me. Think it's stupid and would rather sit under the bridge at the port and rob anyone who passes. But I get this whole swamp to myself so it's okay."

"That's good then… Does this path of stepping stones lead to the bridge where the others hide?"

"Erm, I think so, it passes alongside so they can rob both."

"Oh, right."

"Have you got something they'd like to take?"

"No, not at all… but we'd like to get to the port without any trouble."

"Hmmm Urm," grunted the Swamp Troll.

"My name is Rose, nice to meet you," she said, which made the Troll smile.

"My name is Fudgel… what are they?" he asked pointing at the Grocklings.

"They are Fiddy and Furdon, my friends."

"Are you all here to play with me?"

"If we play with you, would you please help us get to the port?"

"Erm…" he thought for a few seconds "Yes, Fudgel will help you."

"Thank you," she smiled "Now what game can we play with you?" Fiddy and Furdon looked at each other astonished at what was unexpectedly happening, they appreciated help in getting to the port but were not relishing having to play games first.

"You small! Can you throw tree?"

"No, sorry they're too big and heavy."

"Can you throw boulder?"

"No… they are too heavy for us to throw."

"Can you throw anything?"

"Something small and light, yes."

Fudgel dug around in the mud and found an empty shell from a water snail which had abandoned its home or died. He swished it in some water to clean out some of the mud which had settled inside and held it up to Rose to see if she could throw the empty shell, she nodded. Fudgel smiled with excitement.

"Wait," said Furdon to Rose "How long do we have to play for before we can get help to the port?"

"As long as it takes," she said.

"You throw this for me to find," said Fudgel with anticipation. Rose smiled at his simple request which seemed to make him happy.

Fudgel handed the large empty shell to her, it seemed small in his hand but when he passed it to her it took her both hands to hold it. A hole was in the shell which made it easier for her to hold like it was a handle. Rose spun on the spot and then let go of the shell and watched it disappear into the murk and land with a splash in the water. Fudgel's face appeared to light up as his entire body was filled with energy at playing a game. He bounded off to go and find the shell where he thought it had landed.

"What are you doing?" said Fiddy.

"Oh relax the pair of you, he's harmless. Let's give him what he wants, so in turn he'll give us what we want. We might as well have a bit of fun while we're stuck here."

"I suppose so," said Furdon "But it just seems a bit silly."

"We have no way forward or back, what do you expect me to do... sit and sulk?"

"No but..."

"Shush now, Fudgel is coming back."

Fudgel had found the shell and fished it out of the boggy marshes. He splashed his way back over to where Rose was standing. Rose carried on throwing the empty shell different directions to keep it exciting for the troll and was hoping to tire him out. Rose kept going for over an hour until her arm began to ache, though Fudgel's energy level did not drop at all.

"What's wrong, why you stopping?"

"It's making my arm hurt, I'm a lot smaller than you!"

"Do you want to play another game?"

"I thought you were going to help us across this swamp to the port?"

"Yes, I will," said Fudgel "Do you want to play another game?" Rose could see she was going to have to make a game of getting to the port.

"How about you fetch over the tree you were playing with and see how far you can pull us?"

"Too easy," he frowned.

"How do you know unless you try?"

"Erm... okay," he reluctantly agreed "But I'm big, you're little... easy game!" Unenthusiastically he went to pick up the tree trunk which he had earlier been throwing around, he dragged it through the muddy waters and put it in front of the stepping stone where they were perched.

"Thank you," she smiled "This game is not only to see how strong you are but also see how close to the port you can get us without the other Swamp Trolls seeing us…"

"Oooh," he grunted "I like this game, I win, I win, easy I win."

"If the other Swamp Trolls see us or know that you have us with you then you'll not win."

"Okay, okay, I get it."

Rose jumped onto the tree trunk and balanced herself in the middle. Furdon and Fiddy hopped on so they were both sitting in front of Rose. Hullard and Gwennol were still hiding in Rose's hood and keeping as quiet as possible while wondering what was happening. Fudgel swished his hands in the waters and came up with a few reeds which he tied to a stump on the trunk so he could drag them along without tipping them off. He knew the first part of the game would be easy, getting them across the boggy marshes. Effortlessly he pulled them along and they were going much faster than they could have gone on foot. Fiddy was enjoying the ride and not having to get his hands or paws dirty with swamp mud. After a couple of miles Fudgel stopped.

"Nearly there," he said "You can see the bridge where they all hide?"

"Yes, we can see it," said Rose "The next part of the game is to get us safely on dry land without them seeing us. If you can avoid getting near them then you win a special prize." Fudgel was keen to see what the special prize was so thought carefully about where he was going to tread."

"What prize?" whispered Furdon.

"I don't know yet, help me think of something?"

Fudgel had the bridge to the far left of him and could see the other Swamp Trolls moving around. He did not like to interact with them and much preferred to be on his own and do his own thing. To the right was steep bank where Rose and her friends would be able to scramble up to the top and into the town which led to the port. He chose to drag them to the steep bank, it would be easier for them to climb up the bank than have to deal with the other Swamp Trolls. And so he turned and dragged the tree stump over the boggy marshes to a safer place for them to disembark. The other Swamp Trolls could see Fudgel dragging the tree stump around but did not take much notice of him, they were used to seeing him on his own playing with whatever he could find from the water. They were however wondering what he was doing so close to the town and the port, he never ever ventured so close normally. A few of them watched but more out of curiosity than suspicion.

"See, I win," said Fudgel as he dragged them to the edge of the steep muddy bank.

"Well done Fudgel, you did it so easily."

"Told you I would."

Rose looked up the steep muddy bank which looked quite slippery for them to climb. At the top of the climb of a few metres was a stone wall of the same height. She was relieved they were safely across the boggy marshes but felt concerned how they would climb up to the top. Fudgel used his large hands to scrape a ledge into the bank so they could climb off the tree trunk.

"Thank you," said Rose as she, Furdon and Fiddle awkwardly stepped off the tree and onto the space which Fudgel had cleared.

"My prize, my prize, you said I'd get a prize."

"I did indeed and you are a deserved winner," she rummaged through her bag to see what she could feel what might be suitable.

Fiddy and Furdon subtly did the same thing, they did not want it to seem obvious that they had not actually got anything planned. It was Furdon who found an old silver brooch in the bottom of his bag. He was not sure where it had come from but he lifted it up to Rose who offered it to Fudgel. It looked tiny in his hand but he seemed to like it. Fiddy felt around in his bag and found something cold and slimy, he pulled it out and it was a wet dead fish. He had no idea how that got in there but gave it Rose who held it up to Fudgel who was delighted with his prize. A fish was a treat for troll to eat and there weren't many in these waters, he took it from Rose and swallowed it in one gulp. Fudgel was happy with his prize. Rose dug deep into her bag and found what felt like a wooden dice, she brought it out from her bag and it immediately grew to a size similar to the shell they'd been playing with earlier. Fudgel liked this the most because it was something he could play with. It wasn't heavy and would fly through the air and float on the surface of the water, giving him hours of fun.

"Thank you," he smiled "I like my prizes."

"I'm glad, thank you for helping us."

Fudgel then threw the huge wooden dice into the air and across the boggy marsh, he chased after it with such satisfaction. They paused for a while, listening to Fudgel bound around in the water and having fun.

"I don't know where those prizes came from," said Fiddy "There wasn't a dead fish in there when I last checked this morning."

"Nor a silver brooch in mine…" said Furdon "Where did that growing wooden dice come from Miss Rose."

"I've no idea… but thank goodness they were there, we could not very well offer him nothing when we said there would be a prize. And look, here we are at the town, not far from the port on the other side. Just one question, any suggestions how we can climb up there?"

"I'm sure I still have some of Spinbra's rope," said Fiddy.

"Ah yes, perfect," said Rose.

Rose took the rope from Fiddy and aimed it up to the stone wall where it stuck like glue. The Grocklings went first and Rose followed at the back. It wasn't comfortable having her locket in her shoe but she managed to get herself up the muddy bank to the base of the wall where her friends were waiting.

"Can you hear that Rose... I think the other Swamp Trolls have caught our scent," said Furdon.

"Then let's get a move on..."

Rose flung the end of the rope over the top of the wall and used the gaps in the stone as a ladder as she pulled herself up. Fiddy and Furdon had already made it to the top and could see the Swamp Trolls sniffing the air and edging closer. Rose made it to the top, as she did so she looked down on where they'd climbed and saw a Swamp Troll looking up at them. It jumped up to try and grab her but she leapt back out of its reach. The Swamp Trolls were not allowed beyond this wall from prior agreement with the town folk.

"Blimey, that was cutting it fine," she gasped as she dropped to the other side of the wall and crouched down next to her friends.

Hullard and Gwennol pulled themselves up out of Rose's hood to have a look at where they'd arrived.

"That was a nice bit of magic you used," whispered Hullard.

"Thanks, they seemed like they needed it," smiled Gwennol.

"How did you know what prizes a Swamp Troll would like...?"

"They're simple creatures who like simple pleasures... and this one liked to play."

As Rose got to her feet, the Fairy and Pixie slipped back into her hood. Fiddy and Furdon had never seen a place like this before. Rose had never seen people like this before, the people she grew up around on Cragfeld had dull misty eyes and no zest for life... here, she could already see they had light and life in their eyes.

CHAPTER TEN

Bolstone had been busy during and after his visit to Blackfall on Drakenstop. He had spent a couple of days in Ordraskop before journeying back to his cave behind the waterfall. Alfred was spread out on the warm rug when Bolstone returned but having felt abandoned he did not get up joyfully to greet the old wizard.

"Morning Alfred... don't I even get a hello? I was only gone for a couple of days and you had plenty here to keep yourself busy. Besides I couldn't leave my home unguarded could I?"

Alfred stretched out and looked at Bolstone, he was happy to see him but did not want him to know it so rolled onto his back to layer on a bit more guilt. Bolstone knew his cat too well and was not going to fall for his little game, so he scooped him up and gave him a big cuddle. Alfred loved this but did not appreciate getting his fur messed up and eventually wriggled himself free.

"I've had a busy trip while you've been sprawled out lazing around this place. It was good to see Blackfall, yes, yes, indeed it was good to see him. I'm sure he's grown since I last saw him, maybe I shouldn't leave it so long next time. It's those pesky Fairies that I dread crossing paths with, so small yet so irritating. I know I could put them in their place but I really don't want to waste my time and energy on them… What's that Alfred, did I meet any Fairies and Pixies this trip? No actually, no, no, not at all actually, most fortunate. I'm sure Rose, Furdon and Fiddy have met a few by now in the woodlands at the bottom of the mountains. They've been in a few sticky situations you know… yes, yes, they have. Seem to be getting there though."

Bolstone conjured up a few delicious snacks for both himself and Alfred while he got his things and thoughts organised. He seemed to have gone from a quiet life shuffling through his cave, to one far too busy than he would have liked. He had got lazy in his old age without much to do, yet having to help Rose had given him a good purpose again and had awoken his spirit and love of magic.

The old wizard knew the Ice Queen and Orme would be frustrated as they could not see what was happening. He knew exactly what they could and could not see because he was helping to block the images. He knew they would be suspicious and be up to something dangerous to defend themselves but he also knew he could have a little fun with them too.

He was a very old and clever wizard and he was incredibly powerful when he summoned the magic inside himself. His appearance of being a weak old man was very deceptive and it was a clever disguise. Bolstone knew Orme and how she used her magic but he also knew her limits better than she did. She would never admit to having limits as her greed blinded her to reality sometimes.

The old wizard changed back into his shabby orange cloak and searched along the shelves in his cave until he found a little brown jar which did not look especially important. A smile crept onto his face as he thought about what he was about to do. He was just putting on a show for Orme, to spook her more than anything. He wandered out of his cosy cave and down to the waterfall where tons of water was thundering into the pool where Rose, Furdon and Fiddy had jumped. This was not any pool at the bottom of any water-fall, this was where Bolstone would practice his magic and use the water to reflect what was happening in the world around him. He could summon pictures from the past, present or future depending on what he wished to see. He had been keeping an eye on Rose as she travelled through Ordraskop but now he wanted to see what was happening in Cragfeld.

Bolstone climbed up on top of a large rock and looked into the surging waters below. With his hands he steadied the waters and made them circle like a whirlpool. He reached into his pocket and pulled out the brown jar, he poured a few drops of the thick black mixture into the pool. The waters turned dark grey and churned around and around. In the swirling waters, an image started to appear, it was a birds-eye view of Cragfeld. Bolstone could see the winged wardens in the watch towers, constantly guarding the island. He could see the people wandering without a clue about the spells they were under. His attention then fell on the Dark Castle and he could see the Ice Queen standing on the main balcony glaring into the sky at the dark clouds circling above her island. It was Orme who Bolstone was waiting to see because he knew her main concern would be to see who was doing this. She would not think about how she found out, as long as she found out. Only a few moments later the old wizard saw Orme's small hunched figure standing next to the Ice Queen. Now all Bolstone had to do was wait for her to give him exactly what he wanted. With one ice crystal from Mordisan's gown he would be able to see what they were planning. Only a minute went by before the old wizard got what he wanted. Orme had sent an ice crystal into the sky to see who was causing the trouble, it came flying through the swirling pool under the waterfall and into Bolstone's hand. The old wizard was delighted at how easy this was. He rubbed the ice crystal between his palms until it split into two and he placed one of the two pieces into his pocket. With the other, he squeezed it between his fingers with a lot of pressure until it flashed orange before turning black. He threw this back into the middle of the whirlpool, knowing he had sent a little message to Orme. As soon as she dissolved the crystal in her cauldron she would see Bolstone's signature orange sphere for a split second. This would be enough to tease her and let her think she was in control.

As soon as Bolstone had what he wanted he returned the pool to normal and went back to his cave. Alfred had finished his treats and was washing his paws and completely ignored the old wizard. Bolstone took the other half of the crystal and held it up to a lantern before putting it in a large bowl of water that he had scooped out of the sink at the back of the cave.

"Right Orme, let's see what you've been up to…" he muttered.

The waters showed several images from inside the Dark Castle from the past few days. The pictures were crisp and clear. The old wizard could see Orme and Mordisan showing concerns over the stillness of the night when Rose first met Furdon and Fiddy… yet they could not see what was causing the calm quiet night. They saw a figure in a grey cloak and were angry when they could not see more. This made Bolstone smile as he had made it so they could not see who it was. The old wizard knew years in advance this time would come, and Rose would be the one to do this journey. Bolstone then saw the Ice Queen creating her army, hundreds of eggs spread over a room in the Dark Castle. This was Bolstone's main concern as he knew what was likely to be growing inside the eggs and it wouldn't be anything pleasant. But he now knew what the Ice Queen was doing, she was preparing for a battle which may or may not happen, she would defend her crown and her Castle no matter what.

Bolstone had the power of foresight and now knew how to prepare if Rose needed an army for herself.

Rose, Furdon and Fiddy were all standing near the wall from which they had just jumped down. The cobbled streets were busy with people going this way and that, all talking or calling to one another. There was a buzz of energy flowing through the town. The three of them stood out from the crowd as everyone else was wearing more neutral colours.

"My oh my, have you ever...?" said Fiddy.

"...No, never..." said Furdon with his jaw open.

"Me neither..." said Rose.

"Let's try to blend in," suggested Furdon.

"Might be easier said than done," laughed Rose "We couldn't look more like out-of-towners if we tried."

"Okay, then let's not draw unnecessary attention to ourselves and get to the port as quickly and as quietly as we can."

"Yes, we can try," said Rose "But first I need to get the locket out of my shoe, I can't walk with that wedged between my toes without looking as if I've got a bad limp." She knelt down and caught the chain of the locket around her finger and pulled it out of her shoe. The leaf seemed to be getting bigger the closer it got to Ordram, which was fine as long as it was around her neck and not in her shoe. The clasp clicked together around her neck and they were ready.

It was late afternoon and the clouds were washed with tinges of pinks and peaches as the sun was lower in the sky. They walked in the general direction of the port and tried to stay out of everybody's way. A warm breeze wafted off the sea and through the streets. The cobbles underfoot were large and smooth, well worn from all of the people who lived here.

"Can you hear music?" asked Fiddy "I can hear music, I'm sure of it." It was a long time since Rose had heard any kind of tune as the Ice Queen had destroyed all the instruments in the villages of Cragfeld as she hated the sound of people having fun.

"It's coming from over there," said Furdon "Come on, let's get closer and have a look. We're here now so might as well enjoy ourselves."

There was a lively pub on the corner at the end of the road. As they approached the pub and went around the corner, they saw that it was actually at the edge of the town square. Dozens of people were milling around and calling for a few drinks at the pub on their way back from a day at sea. People were laughing and smiling, which Rose found contagious and was smiling back at these complete strangers. They had warm glow in their faces as they chatted to their friends, drank hearty ales and were dancing to the tunes being played. The music was joyful as fiddles, guitars, drums and flutes were all played by merry-looking folk inside the pub.

"Can we go in?" asked Fiddy eagerly, widening his soft green eyes as he pleaded.

"I can't see why not," smiled Furdon who was keen to sample the local ales and have a rest. Rose was also ready for a rest and could not resist having a closer look.

The pub door was open and people were walking and dancing in and out of the place. Young women, a similar age to Rose, were sitting in groups or dancing with the men. This is how Rose would have liked her life to have been when she was growing up, rather than being isolated and alone with people who did not do this kind of thing anyway. Fiddy found a table in the corner where they could sit and enjoy the evening in safety. As soon as they were settled, a large rosy cheeked bar lady strode over to their table.

"Right then, what can I get you?"

"Three of your finest ales please," said Furdon, looking forward to getting his hands on a glass.

"It's all fine," she laughed "Tell you what, I'll bring you

the most popular one... a thick hearty taste with a nice creamy head which will stick to your lips."

"Sounds wonderful!" He grinned with excitement as the lady went to get their drinks.

"I don't suppose they see many Grocklings in here?" said Fiddy looking around, noticing they were the only two.

"I'm sure they've seen a lot stranger-looking things passing through this town," said Furdon "As long as we're friendly then they'll be fine."

The friendly bar lady returned to their table carrying a tray of drinks for them and Furdon handed her some coins. As Furdon loved this type of drink, he was first to try the ale; it was the smoothest, creamiest ale he had ever tasted. Fiddy and Rose did not hesitate to try it and see what was making their friend melt into his chair. It warmed them from top to toe, inside and out, just what they needed after a rough night and a day playing with a troll.

It did not take long at all for them to feel relaxed and enjoy the music. Fiddy was standing on his chair so he could get a better view of the people and watch them dancing, they were linking arms and spinning around the dance floor, looking to be having a great time. The ladies were wearing long dresses which hung down to their ankles, there were very few brightly coloured dresses, none of which stood out as brightly as Rose's blue gown. The gentlemen had brown jackets or white shirts, which equally meant Fiddy and Furdon dressed in purple could not blend in. They were quite happy sitting out of the way in their corner and enjoying their surroundings.

"Maybe we should see if they have a free room for tonight?" suggested Rose. "I'd love to sleep in a comfort-able bed and start the journey fresh tomorrow."

"Oh that would be delightful wouldn't it?!" agreed Fiddy "I doubt there'll be any boats going out to sea now anyway, it's getting later and darker." The bar lady came over with three more drinks for them as she had seen they had enjoyed the first ones.

"Thought you'd like a refill," she smiled.

"Thank you," said Rose "It's wonderful. Would you happen to have a room available for us tonight?"

"Absolutely," said the lady "You look like you've had a long day. Just come and see me when you're ready and I'll get you the key to the room at the top of the stairs to the right. It's only a small room but it's comfortable."

"That's wonderful, thank you," smiled Rose, as the bar lady walked back over to the bar.

"Oh, how superb," smiled Fiddy "A comfortable soft bed, we'll sleep so well on that!"

The second drink seemed to be slightly stronger than the first but it was equally as delicious. They were having a fabulous evening and were forgetting the stress of their journey for a few hours. Hullard and Gwennol had climbed out of Rose's hood and were sitting amongst the flowers on the windowsill where they could not be seen. They were watching on and enjoying the fun and laughter in the pub. Hullard sneakily took a few mouthfuls of Fiddy's drink when he was not looking.

A tall lean gentleman wearing dark brown trousers and a white shirt which was open at the collar came over to their table. His dark hair had been tied back, and his rich chocolate brown eyes were warm and friendly. A short goaty beard framed his mouth which was smiling at them.

"Would you like to dance?" he asked Rose, who wasn't expecting an invitation off anyone to dance.

"Erm," she mumbled, looking at Fiddy and Furdon for help but saw that they were encouraging her to go. "Okay, thank you," she said at last. The gentleman took her hand and guided her through the crowd and onto the dance floor while her friends looked on.

"It's good to see her enjoying herself," said Furdon "Been

quite a stressful few days so it'll do her good to let her hair down a bit."

"Oh yes, she's looking quite happy here," said Fiddy "I don't think she's ever done this kind of thing before, dancing and laughing."

"Just keep an eye on her, we don't want to lose her now."

"Will you relax, we've got her this far, we won't lose her now. Besides, she's a quick learner and knows to stay close to us." They watched as Rose tried to remember how to dance and was stumbling about quite clumsily. The gentleman with her took the lead and told her to relax.

"Don't look at your feet," he said "Look up, into my face and feel the movement." He was right, as soon as Rose stopped thinking about where she was putting her feet they seemed to find their own way. "You see, what did I say? You've got it now."

"It's a long time since I've danced," she blushed.

"Not meaning to be disrespectful but I can tell," he smiled "I'm Ve... Victor."

"Ve – Victor, that's an unusual name," she teased.

"It's just Victor, you make me nervous," he spun her round and grabbed her waist.

"I'm Rose," she said when she had the chance.

"That's a lovely name. What brings you to this town, I've not seen you in here before."

"No, we're just passing through, we'll be leaving in the morning."

"May I ask where you are from...?"

"Cragfeld."

"Really...? It's a long time since I was there."

"You've been? That must've been a lifetime ago."

"Yes, it was," he sighed as he thought back "It was long before Mordisan took the throne. I had family there once but I'm not sure what happened to them. We couldn't get back to Cragfeld to find them so have gone separate ways. I was twenty two when I left."

"That's sad," said Rose "And you've not been able to find each other in one hundred and fifty years?"

"Our paths might cross again someday," he smiled "You never know."

They danced for a few songs until Rose was breathless and ready to join her friends again. Victor escorted her to her table and ordered another round of drinks for them. Rose introduced Furdon and Fiddy to Victor and they chatted for a while about what it was like living in this town next to the sea.

"What is it you do here?" asked Furdon.

"Me, oh… I have my own boat, just do a little bit of fishing. I don't go too far out to sea mind you, there are some odd things lurking in those waters."

"I can imagine."

"Victor used to live on Cragfeld," said Rose "Before the Ice Queen took over."

"Did you really," said Furdon "I have to admit I thought you looked familiar, maybe we used to chat when our kind were allowed to mingle with humans."

"Yes, maybe so," said Victor "If you don't mind, I'd rather not talk about that place, brings back too many memories."

"Of course, terribly sorry." Furdon knew he had seen Victor's face before and would not be able to settle until he placed him.

"It's a shame you're leaving tomorrow, I could've shown you round the town. Maybe you'd might like to live here one day? Full of fine, hard-working people… but they're not as easy on the eye as you."

"I'm sure they are," smiled Rose "But we must leave tomorrow, as soon as we're fully rested."

"Which road did you come in on?"

"We didn't," said Fiddy "We came across the boggy marshes."

"That's a brave route, you do know there are thieving Swamp Trolls out there don't you?"

"Yes, we had the pleasure of meeting one."

"And you lived to tell the tale, you must be stronger than you look."

"He wasn't one from under the bridge, he was a nice one."

"A nice Swamp Troll? You must've had a knock to your head, I don't think there is such a thing."

"Well there is... and he helped us over the boggy marshes."

"Yes, I believe you – it's just I've never heard such a thing."

Rose was beginning to feel tired so went to get the key for their room from the bar lady, while Furdon and Fiddy chatted away to their new friend.

"I won't be able to sleep until I know where I know you from," he said.

"I must have one of those faces," said Victor. Rose returned with the key which she waved at her friends to indicate it was bedtime and time to say goodnight.

"It was lovely to meet you Victor," said Rose "But as you know, we have an early start tomorrow."

"Yes indeed," he said as he stood up "Likewise, it was lovely to meet you, an unexpected evening. Allow me to escort you wherever you need to go tomorrow, at least let me see you off."

"That'd be nice, thank you," said Rose, smiling as she shook his hand.

"It'd be my pleasure," he said, pulling her closer and kissing her cheek. Rose had a strong feeling of déjà vu as they said goodnight.

Furdon took the bags to which Gwennol and Hullard had sneaked into and carried them up to their room. Rose was last to follow, turning one more time to look at Victor. He smiled and disappeared into the crowd as she made her way up the creaky wooden stairs. Rose was not used to interacting with people but she had a funny feeling about Victor which she had not felt before. When she was dancing with him and the way they moved had felt completely natural once she had got the hang of it.

"What a fantastic evening that was," said Fiddy "Dancing, singing and merriment."

"Were you having a little sing-along?" teased Rose.

"Yes, I was humming and dancing… it felt good."

It was a small bed but it was big enough for the three of them to curl up and have room to spare. Furdon dropped the bags in a heap on the floor, not knowing Gwennol and Hullard were hiding in there and were sent tumbling. Furdon jumped onto the bed and collapsed on his back, tired but happy. Hullard quietly lifted the flap on the bag so Gwennol could get out without trapping her wings. She flickered them and aired them while Hullard found a comfortable place for them both to sleep. Rose lay on the bed with Furdon and Fiddy on either side of her, the ales had relaxed them and they would sleep well.

"Why is it bothering me so much about Victor, where do I know him from?" said Furdon.

"Oh let it go," sighed Fiddy "It'll come to you when you're thinking about something else."

"It was good to dance," said Rose "I can't remember the last time I danced."

"It suited you Miss Rose, once you'd found your feet anyway."

"I know, I must have looked like a clown."

"No, you looked lovely."

As soon as they had fallen to sleep, Hullard and Gwennol found a small piece of blanket to sleep under, where they would go unnoticed for the night.

The following morning, after a solid nine hours sleep Fiddy

was first to wake. He hated being the first to wake up because he was always itching to wake the others so he had got someone to talk to. Furdon and Rose were slowly waking up but were not ready for him to go at them in full Fiddy mode yet. He did however notice a tiny little foot sticking out from under the blanket at the top of the bed. His cat like back legs were able to tiptoe up the bed without disturbing anyone. Slowly he leaned forward and picked up the corner of the blanket to see what was under there. He was thoroughly speechless when he saw Gwennol and Hullard looking back at him, both holding their fingers to their mouths, indicating for him to keep quiet. Asking Fiddy to keep quiet was near impossible. He was too pleased to see them to keep quiet and jumped over Rose and off the bed.

"Fiddy, calm down will you?" said Rose in a sleepy voice "It's not time to go yet."

"But, but Rose…"

"Like she said Fiddy, just wait ten minutes," said Furdon.

"But Rose, Furdon… We've got stowaways!"

"What are you going on about?" asked Rose as she sat up and looked at her overly excited friend.

"Look, look at the corner of the bed."

Rose did not believe him but played along in the hope he would settle down a bit. She saw the little lump under the blanket but thought Fiddy had played with the bedding. She lifted it up expecting to see nothing but was amazed when she saw her two little friends curled up there.

"What are you two doing?!" she said in shock "We told you it was too dangerous for you to come with us."

"We're sorry but we couldn't help it…" said Gwennol.

"How did you get here?" asked Rose, having been shocked from sleepy to wide awake, and Furdon the same.

"We crept into the hood of your coat and then into your bag…"

"Oh it's too dangerous," said Rose feeling confused about

the situation. "We can't send you back, if these people find you, then we'll never see you again... and it's a dangerous journey to Ordram... what are we to do?"

"Oh let them come with us Miss Rose," said Furdon "They've made it this far unnoticed. They're tough enough."

"Thanks Furdon," said Hullard "We appreciate your support."

"I never said it was a good idea but it seems we've no choice but to take you. We're certainly not taking you back, not after that unpleasant journey across the boggy marshes."

"You're welcome by the way," said Gwennol.

"What for...?" asked Furdon.

"It was me who put those things in your bags, when you were looking for prizes for Fudgel."

"See, we can help you..." said Hullard.

"Alright, alright," Rose sighed "You can come. Thank you for helping with Fudgel but I don't appreciate you sneaking along like this."

"The more the merrier," said Fiddy jumping back onto the bed.

"Yes but they must remain hidden until we are away from this town."

"That's not a problem," said Hullard "We've managed it so far." Rose didn't appreciate his cheek. There was a gentle knock on the door which sent all five of them into a panic as Gwennol and Hullard hid under the blanket again.

"Come in," said Rose, quite flustered. The door opened and it was the bar lady from the night before.

"Good morning, trusting you all slept well? Just to let you know, the friend who you were dancing with last night is waiting for you downstairs."

"Oh, right, yes... thank you," spurted Rose "We'll be down in ten minutes."

"I shall pass on the message," she smiled and closed the door behind her. They waited until they had heard her footsteps go down the stairs before they dared speak again.

"Ok, come on, let's sort ourselves out and get going," said Rose, flapping around the room.

"Deep breaths Miss Rose, he's only escorting us through town," said Furdon.

"Yes, I know that Furdon… but what happens when we have gone through town and we reach the port and have to explain why we need a boat?"

"We'll deal with that when we have to, let's just calm down and get on with it."

"You're right, you're always right… sorry, right I'm ready." She ran her fingers through her hair to try and neaten it and loosen the ringlets that had got tangled during the night. "Hullard? Gwennol? Where are you? Where would you prefer to hide?"

"In your hood, if we may?" said Gwennol flying out of the bedding "It's a lot more comfortable than bouncing around in your bags."

"That's fine, just remember to stay in there until I tell you it's safe to come out."

"Yes Rose."

"I mean it, no peeking or sticking your heads out to look at anything… stay still." Hullard and Gwennol did not want to upset her so jumped right into the bottom of her hood and would stay quiet until told otherwise.

They grabbed their bags and walked down the creaky stairs into the bar area. There were some people still in the pub who had fallen asleep at their tables or on the floor. Victor was sitting at the bar waiting for them and smiled as soon as they appeared through the doorway. Furdon went to settle the bill with the bar lady while Rose and Fiddy went over to Victor who stood up as she walked over.

"Good morning, Rose," he said, bowing to take her hand and kiss the back of it. She was not used to such behaviour and blushed.

"Good morning," she smiled with flushed cheeks.

"I hope you slept well and are ready for the day?"

"Yes, thank you."

Furdon rejoined his friends and greeted Victor.

"Where would you like to go?" he asked.

"To the port," said Furdon before Rose could answer.

"Very well, to the port it is."

Victor opened the door of the pub and the early morning sun beamed in. He guided them through the town and pointed out anything that might interest them, where he lives and such. The old cobbled streets were quiet compared to the night before and very few people were out and about. Small cottages lined the streets as they got further out of town. They walked down a hill and could see through the gaps in the cottages they were getting closer to the port.

"Do you know where we could get a boat?" asked Rose.

"A boat?" said Victor "Are you fancying a little trip around the coast? I have a boat, I can take you."

"We're actually wanting to go further out to sea…"

"Why?! I told you last night there's some strange things in those waters."

"Yes I know but that doesn't change the fact we still need a boat to go out there."

"Ok, let me get this right… You want a boat to go out to sea – but can any of you sail?"

"Well er…" said Rose looking at her friends as they shook their heads "Not exactly…"

"Not exactly? Oh dear… even the best sailors struggle in those seas but you're telling me it doesn't bother you?"

"Of course it bothers us but it's not as if we have a choice."

"What do you mean? You have the choice not to go and that's the choice I'd recommend."

Rose looked at Furdon for a bit of support.

"Yes well Victor," said Furdon "We don't have that choice… going out to sea is the only way to get where we are going to."

"And where are you going?" said Victor "Hold on, hold on… the only reason people like your good selves would risk their lives on those waters would be to get to… Ordram! Is that where you're going?"

"Keep your voice down," said Rose "We want to pass through the town discreetly and not broadcast our journey to everyone."

"Ok, yes, sorry… but is that where you're going?"

"Yes."

"Oh wow!" said Victor. He had a broad smile and a glint in his eye.

"Why are you looking at me like that?" asked Rose.

"Like what?" he laughed.

"Like you think we're crazy."

"I'd never think that about you. Can I tell you a secret… I've been to Ordram before, only once and it was a long time ago. But I know the way, I can sail a boat and I know these waters better than you do – let me take you."

"Why would you risk your boat and yourself for us, you only met us last night."

"I think I can trust you," he smiled.

Rose stopped in her tracks to kneel down and talk in whispers with Fiddy and Furdon about the offer Victor had made. Furdon was slightly more cautious but Fiddy simplified the situation and told them they were being offered what they needed. After a few minutes Rose got to her feet.

"Okay," she said "If you can take us to Ordram in safety then you have a deal."

"I said I'd take you in my boat…" he smiled "I can't guarantee the safety but I'll try my best." Rose offered her hand so he could shake it but instead, he took it and kissed the back of it.

The port was busy with lots of boats coming and going.

Most of the boats were small and used for catching fish. The larger passenger boats only went up and down to the coast to ferry people to and from another town. The shallow waters were still filled with odd looking creatures but they were not as dangerous as the ones out at sea. Victor led the way down a wooden jetty and around to where several boats were tied up. They stopped at a fairly small fishing boat which did not seem the sturdiest of contraptions.

"This is my boat," said Victor proudly.

"It's… it's err, lovely," said Rose finally.

"It's not very big," blurted Fiddy, who was shortly jabbed in the ribs by Furdon. They looked at the boat and then back at each other, neither looking as if they had confidence in the ramshackle fishing boat. Maybe it was alright for small trips but not for out at sea.

"You don't like my boat?" said Victor, noticing the uncertainty in their eyes "Let me reassure you this is a very fine boat, we've been through some rough waters together and she's never let me down. She's strong and reliable, don't let her appearance put you off. Here, let me help you on board."

He offered his arm to Rose and helped her to climb onto the wooden deck. There were patches of paint peeling off and fishing nets were piled at the back. It was not the flashiest or biggest boat but it was what they had asked for and even better that they had someone who knew how to sail it. Furdon and Fiddy leapt aboard and had a wander round above and below deck.

"Seems quite comfortable," said Furdon when he returned "There is a nice little seating area down below where we can get settled."

"Thank you Furdon," smiled Rose "But while the weather's fine I think I'll stay up here with Victor and maybe learn how to drive this thing."

"I've never had a co-captain before," laughed Victor as he

untied the ropes and they slowly began to drift.

"I don't think I like this," said Fiddy "I've never been on a boat before, it's wobbly and I don't think I'm going to enjoy this."

"Don't worry Fiddy," said Furdon "I've never been on one either, let's keep ourselves busy and try to forget where we are. Let's try to imagine we're in the mountain with our friends playing hide and seek or something."

"Thank you Furdon but I think it'll take more than that to distract me."

Victor fired up the small engine and steered the boat away from the jetty and into the harbour. There were lots of people coming and going and off, loading baskets of fish when they landed. While Furdon and Fiddy were holding hands to try and support each other through their anxiety, Rose stood at the back of the boat and looked back on the path they had travelled. She could see the top of Drakenstop covered in snow and she thought about Blackfall and Hildfall strutting around up there. She could just make out the woodland where she had met Gwennol and Hullard... and their nasty little friends Bran, Edhen and Berry and Pesh. Rose could not see the boggy marshes because of the tall stone wall which separated it from the town but she smiled when she thought about Fudgel playing with the prizes he had won. She could not believe how far they had come. Casting her eyes over the town and then down to the harbour she then saw a familiar figure standing on the jetty where only a few minutes ago they had been standing. There she was again, the girl who looked just like Rose, wearing a blue robe with the grey hood pulled back. She was standing with her arms by her sides and with her hands joined in front of her. She had a gentle smile on her face as she watched the boat carrying Rose and her friends out of the port. Rose did not take her eyes off this girl and just before the boat turned out of sight the girl waved.

CHAPTER ELEVEN

The silver eggs in the Dark Castle were starting to tremble and shake as the creatures inside them were ready to hatch into the world. Orme and the Ice Queen checked them every day to see if anything had emerged. The crystals of the chandeliers which hung over them would often tremble as the captives trapped inside watched in horror at what was happening below them. They had watched the Ice Queen create these eggs and were dreading the day when whatever was inside would burst free. If it had wings or horns, there was an obvious risk it could knock the chandelier on first flight, causing it to fall and smash into a million pieces, killing all the captives in one blow. They could see that the woman in the crystal shell was pale and thin as the eggs grew and took all of her blood and energy. The woman was cold and numb and could not feel anything anymore, she was trapped and there was nothing she could do to get away. As soon as the Ice Queen had no more use for her, she would be cast aside like the rest of them, lifeless and empty.

The old witch was the first to notice the eggs were ready to hatch and called the Ice Queen to witness the event. These creatures already knew who created them and would obey their every command. Orme had prepared the empty ballroom for their arrival so they had space to run, fly and grow bigger and stronger.

"At last the time has come," relished the Ice Queen rubbing her hands together "My babies will mature into deadly monsters and destroy anything and anyone who crosses me. No man will dare take or threaten my throne." The Ice Queen and the old witch shared an evil smile as they knew they were unbeatable.

The room began to fill with the sounds of shells cracking open, one, then another, and another. All at once the creatures broke free from their silver casing. In front of the Ice Queen was a sea of blackness rippling and bubbling to life. Out of each shell appeared black creatures covered in oil and blood. On one side of the room a Winged Goblin stretched out its wings and hissed as its strong body took to the air and flew around the room. Out of another shell came a creature with sharp horns and spikes all over its body, this would be able to crush and stab the enemy. Snakes slithered around the Ice Queens feet, dozens of snakes which would grow to monstrous sizes and strike with deadly venom. The room was soon filled with evil. The Ice Queen admired her work, what were hatchlings now would soon grow into a force like no other. Even the old witch looked excited as the Dark Castle was filled with more cruel life.

The captives in the chandelier were knocked several times by flying Goblins as they tested their wings. So far they had not been knocked over but when they saw what was appearing below them, they dreaded the day these creatures would be called upon. Even now as new hatchlings they were deadly, never mind in a few days time when they would be a lot bigger.

"What fine creatures," said the Ice Queen, bending down to pick up a snake. It slithered and curled around her arm like a jet black bracelet. It twisted up her arm and under her thick red hair which was draped over her shoulders and then settled around her neck. "See Orme, they know who their mother is."

"Yes, they do," said Orme "They'll grow bigger and stronger by the hour so we must get them to the ballroom where they have more space to become what they are meant to be."

"Feed them well Orme, they will be hungry."

"Yes, certainly my Queen."

"Oh and that woman who watched them for me is no use to me now, she might as well be their first meal. Then you can find any people in the villages who serve no purpose other than fodder for my army."

"Yes, certainly my Queen," said Orme. She didn't actually agree with the Ice Queen and would find or create an alternative source of food for the hungry creatures. There was no point killing people who might one day be called to fight for their Queen, even the useless ones would be able to hold a sword. She would conjure something for them to eat, but would still need a drop of human blood to satisfy their hunger.

As the Ice Queen and Orme walked through to the ballroom, all of the creatures had hatched and followed them like a death filled shadow. This room was long and wide and stretched high to the ceiling. The Winged Goblins and other creatures flew up to the rafters and settled amongst the beams. The snakes slid over the smooth ice floor and hid under frozen cabinets and chairs. Everything else spread over the floor and the black army soon filled the room.

"Do you have any other business Orme?" barked the Ice Queen.

"Oh yes, indeed I do," said Orme keenly "I've identified who brewed up that storm, it was Bolstone the old wizard. We've nothing to worry about, he's old and weak and has never been as powerful as me."

"Bolstone? I didn't think he'd still be alive."

"He won't be for much longer," laughed the old witch. "I

look forward to the day when he admits he'll never be as strong as me with magic… the day I finally crush him."

"Could you see anything else, what is he planning?"

"I could only see it was him my Queen. He only ever used his magic for good… and that will be no good to defeat us if that's what he's thinking."

"Good…" smiled the Ice Queen "These creatures will scare him or anyone else who thinks they can fight me. When you next see the old wizard, kill him, then we don't have to think about him bothering us again." Mordisan swung her dress round and left the ballroom where her army would thrive. She left Orme in charge of feeding them up ready to fight on command.

Orme went back to the room where all of the eggs had hatched. Crushed shells littered the room and fragments of silver were dripping in blood and ooze. The old witch clicked her old fingers and muttered some magical words under her breath and watched as the mess dissolved, turning into a gas which quickly vanished into the cold air. The room looked as it did before the eggs were created, the walls and floors were returned to their icy state and there was no sign of any shell anywhere. Orme then cast her eyes over the sorry looking state of a woman, curled up in the crystal shell, drained and no longer of any use to the Ice Queen. Orme went up to her and commanded the ice casing to lower to the floor and melt, leaving the woman in a heap on the floor. She was pale and did not have the strength to stand. Orme cast some more gentle magic over her which lifted her to her feet and carried her down to the old witch's den. Here Orme would restore her back to health and the only thing she wanted in return was one drop of blood, no more than one drop. With the drop of blood she could create food for the army of monstrous creatures.

The Ice Queen slithered along the corridors of the Dark Castle. She was pleased with how her day was going, her army had hatched and Orme had identified the trouble maker. Mordisan had met Bolstone when she was a young girl and remembered how her father talked of his magic. Since taking the throne, Mordisan had developed a hatred for the old wizard, as on the day she seized power he had tried to stop her. By this time the old witch and Mordisan had joined forces and had a formidable power that the old wizard was not prepared for and was defeated. This is not what angered her, what angered her the most what that he tried to save her sister Rika. Bolstone had interrupted her as she was capturing her sister and encasing her in ice and had tried to reverse the spell. Mordisan was fuelled by anger and threw a ball of razor sharp ice at the wizard which bowled him out of the room. Everybody had loved Rika which made Mordisan's hatred towards her even greater. People were willing to help Rika but had ignored Mordisan for too long. She would make them pay and suffer by holding onto the one thing they cared for. She would show them all never to ignore her again.

With anger running through her veins she stormed through the Dark Castle and up the tallest tower to vent the rage out of her system. She stormed through the wall of ice into the frozen chamber and stared at her sister's icy tomb. The Ice Queen raised her hands and summoned an immense strength from deep inside her before aiming her hands at her sister and throwing a thick sheet of angry ice over her again. There was no real reason for her to do this other than release the resentment she had towards Rika. The Ice Queen's frozen heart felt nothing. She screamed so loudly at her lifeless sister, the shrill noise echoed through the Dark Castle. Mordisan knew if she had not become the Ice Queen that she'd never have been given respect or even attention, let alone the throne.

"Sister, sister, sister," she hissed "How I hate you, I hate you more than you'll ever know. When you were alive you ignored me… how things could've been so different if only you'd spent time with me. But no, you were so wrapped up in being the perfect little Princess weren't you? You forgot all about me and pushed me to one side. I will never forget you, Rika… if it wasn't for you then I would've never become me. And look at me… look at me! It didn't have to be like this you know, you actually did this to yourself. All you had to do was stop taking things from me. You took all of our father's attention, he doted on you didn't he… do you remember that time he bought me a pony? I loved that pony, I called him Sugar… he was whiter than fresh snow and I used to braid his mane. But then you came along and wanted him for yourself, you didn't want a different pony, you wanted mine… and father just handed him to you. You broke my heart that day, you took Sugar and never gave me a second thought. I'll never forgive you for that! I'll never forgive you for anything. But if you could see me now Rika, you wouldn't dare ignore me now. Even Bolstone couldn't save you, could he… stupid old buffoon. I'm prepared to see Bolstone again, if and whenever he shows up then I'll have my army waiting. As much as killing him myself would be truly satisfying, I know Orme has a longer-standing fight with him so I'll let her have the pleasure of bringing him to his knees. I shall never be defeated!"

She stared through the thick layer of ice at Rika, whose face, hands and body never moved. Her skin seemed whiter and her eyes seemed bluer than usual but maybe this was because of added ice that had been layered over her. Mordisan's spell upon her sister would never be undone, Rika would remain frozen for all time. Only the Ice Queen could undo the spell and it was obvious that was never going to happen – she has too much anger and hatred towards her.

Fiddy was not enjoying his first time on a boat and was gripping tightly to Furdon's hand. Furdon did not reckon much to it either but was managing to put on a brave face as they bounced along. Rose had never seen the sea before, this vast expanse of water spreading out as far as she could see. Victor was the only one on the boat who did not look out of place as he confidently guided the boat over the waves. While they were still near the coast, Rose took the opportunity to look over the edge of the boat into the clear waters below. She could see fish of all shapes and sizes swimming along, sometimes one would pop up to the surface and show off its bright colours before plopping back into the water.

"These fish near the coast are quite safe Rose," called Victor who was watching as she admired them. "When the waters darken, it's best if you come away from the edge of the boat and stand with me. You too, Furdon and Fiddy."

"I think we're going to sit downstairs if you don't mind," said Furdon. They both wobbled across the deck to the stairwell and hopped down onto a bed where they lay flat, waiting for it all to be over.

"They've never been on a boat before," said Rose "They don't mean to be rude, it's not in their nature."

"I'm not offended, don't worry about that," smiled Victor "Either you've got sea legs or you haven't, it's not a fun journey if you haven't."

"How rough is the water likely to get?"

"It all depends on the day, some days are worse than others. If it's a bad day then I'd usually turn back... but I've made a promise to you and I'll keep it."

"Why are you doing this for us? You've only known us a few hours but here you are risking yourself and your boat for us... and I've been trying to work out why."

"Do I have to have a reason to help someone who needs it? Maybe I didn't have any other plans, maybe I had nothing better to do... maybe I was in the mood for something exciting..." he teased.

"I'm being serious," said Rose "I doubt anyone else would've been so generous once they found out where we were going. Unless, unless of course you had to see Ordram for something?"

"Why would I have to see him? Listen, I know how to get there… it's as simple as that. I've no hidden agenda."

"Okay," said Rose, she was still slightly suspicious of his kind behaviour. She went below deck to see if her friends were okay. She found them sprawled out and looking extremely sorry for themselves. Fiddy was fanning himself and humming nervously, while Furdon was trying his best not to move.

"You two have definitely looked better," she teased them.

"Oh Miss Rose, please don't joke…" moaned Furdon. "Now I know why Grocklings live in mountains, this whole water thing is very unnecessary and we are stuck on this boat with no escape until we get to where we're going, Oh Miss Rose…!"

"That thought has made me feel even worse," hummed Fiddy as he fanned himself even faster.

"Will you both try and calm down," said Rose "We've escaped Ogres, we've ridden on a giant spider, we've climbed out of a Spiralilus and been carried by Dragons… I think you're both brave enough to cope with a boat trip."

"When you put it like that, I suppose," groaned Furdon "But this feels worse than all of that put together."

"I don't like to see you both like this, I wish I could help you feel better. Gwennol is there anything you can do to help them?" The little fairy flew out of Rose's hood and landed next to Furdon. Hullard climbed up onto Rose's shoulder.

"Oh dear," laughed Hullard "What a pair… beaten by a bit of water and a boat."

"Alright Hullard, no need to make a joke of it. Imagine if it were you, would you want to feel this way for days?"

"Days?!" squealed Fiddy "I can't manage this for days, I thought we were going to be about an hour?"

"I'm sorry Fiddy… but it'll be a couple of days, maybe longer if the seas are rough."

"Oh kill me now," said Furdon "Kill me now and put me out of my misery."

"I most certainly will not," scolded Rose "Now, Gwennol… is there any way you can make them feel better while we're on this boat?"

"Yes, there are a couple of things I could do. The first is to get you to eat something which will make you feel well enough to walk around as if on dry land, or the second is send you to sleep until we get there?"

"Kill me, kill me now," repeated Furdon.

"Furdon, buck up, you're my bodyguard and I need you to be strong and fully functional. And you Fiddy, you help me see the good out of the bad. I need you both to feel okay otherwise I'll fall apart myself."

"Maybe send them to sleep," said Hullard "Then they won't remember any of this and will wake up when we reach land."

"What do you think Gwennol?"

"Going from what I overheard your friend Victor say, we could meet a few sea creatures as well as choppy waters. I think sleeping through all that would be the kindest option."

"Okay," said Rose "I'll decide for them, make it as easy as we can for them… send them to sleep." Gwennol sprinkled fairy dust over Furdon and Fiddy. Within a few minutes Furdon was yawning and Fiddy was curling up unto a ball, they both went quiet and fell fast asleep.

"I think you made the right decision Rose," said Gwennol.

"Me too," Hullard chimed in "I don't think I could've listened to their belly aching for three days."

"I know," smiled Rose "But look at them now so quiet and still, I've never seen them like this before."

"Trust me, they're fine," said Gwennol "They'll fall into a deep sleep and have no memory of being on a boat."

"Besides, they're safer below deck," said Hullard "The creatures lurking below are bound to get curious about us, these two are better not knowing anything about it."

"That's true," she said. She kissed them both on the forehead and stood up to go back up on deck. "Come on then you two, back in the hood you go… unless you can find a safe hiding place down here."

"No, we'll stay with you if you don't mind." They jumped back into Rose's hood and got comfortable again.

The sky was clear and the sea was quite calm. Rose went to sit on a wooden bench next to where Victor was standing, steering further and further away from shore. The port seemed far away now and the sea below them was growing darker and darker.

"How are your friends, feeling better I hope?" asked Victor.

"Oh, yes, thank you. I got them to go to sleep."

"How did you manage that? They seemed quite upset by the whole experience."

"I don't know really," she had to think of an answer, he couldn't know a Fairy was on board. "I just sang to them and the rocking of the boat must've helped them drift off."

"That's good, better for them. Would you like to have a go at being captain?"

"Oh no, thanks. I think I'd be rubbish…"

"That's what we thought about you dancing but you proved us both wrong about that didn't you?"

"True… okay, help me though won't you?"

"Of course, have I let you down yet?"

"No," she smiled as she got to the wheel. Victor stood beside her and taught her the basics until she was confident enough to have a go on her own.

"See, what did I tell you," he smiled "You can do anything

if you try."

Rose was feeling quite confident as she guided the boat towards the bright light on the horizon which was Ordram. After a few minutes it felt as if the boat was dragging on the seabed but this could not be so, they were far out at sea now. Victor got up and took the controls from Rose as he tried to feel if there was something wrong with the boat. Rose sat back down while he concentrated on the problem.

"Ok, I know what it is," he said at last "There's nothing wrong with the boat, it's the things beneath the boat which are rubbing against it to try and feel what we are and if we're dangerous."

"Things? What things?"

"The strange sea creatures I was telling you about, we've attracted the attention of a few."

"Do you know what they are?"

"Not yet!"

There was a great shudder as something hit the boat from below and knocked Rose off her seat. She fumbled around and stood next to Victor, they were both holding on tight to the railing near the captain's seat. Rose looked out and searched the waters for any sign of movement which broke the surface. She could see something lurking in the sea quite a distance from them, as if whatever it was, was watching them. Closer to the boat there was something moving alongside them which occasionally knocked the boat to remind them it was still there.

"It feels like we're being watched," said Rose.

"That's because we are, they're watching us and testing us… trying to scare us into going back to land."

"Why don't they want us out here, we're not bothering them?"

"It's their sea. If one of them came to land we'd be curious wouldn't we – whether they were bothering us or not."

"What are we supposed to do then?"

"Keep going, try and ignore them."

"What? How's that possible?"

"They'll get bored sooner or later, there's bound to be something more interesting than us to grab their attention?"

"And if there's not?"

"Then it looks like we'll have company for a few days."

Victor did not have a clue what he was talking about, he had never been this far out to sea and had no idea what was swimming around them. He thought Rose might feel better if it sounded as if he knew what he was doing and spoke with confidence. Victor put the boat at full speed as he also did not want to be on this journey longer than he had to be.

Out of the water right in front of them they saw the shimmering back of something huge heave out of the sea. Whatever it was, it was bending and curling in the water and all they could see was a wide grey back, its scales shimmering as it effortlessly moved through the water. Its width was wider than the boat and neither Rose or Victor wanted to guess its length. A tail flipped out of the sea and crashed down in front of them, beating the water hard as it went.

"It looks like they want to play," he said nervously.

"Play?"

"With us or the boat… See how it's swimming as close at it can without riding into us."

"That's a stupid game, if it misjudges then it'll get mad and blame us for hitting it."

"Let's hope it doesn't happen then."

This seemed to go on for most of the day, the sea creatures below did not attack them but appeared to be amusing themselves with the boat. Rose and Victor gradually relaxed as they got used to whatever it was swimming along with them. Rose had counted there were at least three of them but as she could not tell how long they actually were, there could have been more. Every once in a while she would nip down to see if Furdon and Fiddy were still sleeping, they were out for the count and looked peaceful.

The sun set and the sky grew darker, and this was when Rose began to feel nervous about what might be watching them from beneath the water. Seeing them in daylight was bad enough but not being able to see them at all was probably worse. Ordram was glowing on the horizon so the one thing in their favour was they knew which direction to go.

"Are you hungry?" asked Victor "Let's have something to eat before it gets too dark and then we'll feel good for whatever the night throws our way."

Rose rummaged through her bag but could only find a few bits of old stale cake. Victor smiled as he opened a large box which was built into the boat. He brought out some bread which had been baked earlier that morning. He had also brought along butter, jams, cakes, biscuits and fruit. It was a treat for Rose to see as she was famished. They enjoyed the food which was like a feast to them after not eating much all day. She managed to discreetly drop a few crumbs into the hood of her gown for Hullard and Gwennol when Victor was not looking.

The sun set and the sky grew darker. Victor was as nervous as Rose as to what the night could bring, but he put on a brave face to hide his concerns. They sat back, set the boat on course and felt as if they were waiting for something to happen. Apart from the sound of their boat moving through the water, things seemed too quiet. Rose could still feel they were being watched and she did not like it. She hutched up closer to Victor, he put his arm around her shoulder as if to say "everything's going to be fine".

A few hours into the night, Rose was resting her head on Victor's shoulder but was woken by a strange and creepy noise. She lifted her head. Victor had also heard it.

"What was that?" she whispered.

"It sounded like laughing…"

"It wasn't nice laughing though, there was nothing nice about that noise… like we are being laughed at."

"Yes, it feels like we are being taunted."

"Aren't you going to have a look and see if there's anything out there?"

"The waters are as black as the night Rose, and I'm not going to light a lantern, it'll attract unwanted attention… stay quiet, stay still."

The laughing continued and it was surrounding the boat, whatever was out there – there were a lot of them. It seemed to get closer and closer to their rickety vessel and then suddenly stopped and went quiet. There was a splash in the water just in front of them and then there was a thud against the side of the boat. Rose and Victor peered into the darkness. A hand appeared on the side of the boat, as whatever it was had climbed up to look onto the deck. Another hand appeared and the laughing began again. The two silvery scaly hands paused on the side of the boat, glistening in the moonlight. Rose and Victor could only watch and wait to see what it was. Slowly it gripped onto the side of the boat and pulled itself up so its head was peering over the top. With silver eyes staring at them it hissed and laughed again before diving back into the.

"I was really hoping they would leave us alone."

"What are they?"

"Mermaids, nasty horrible mermaids."

"That wasn't a mermaid," said Rosc "Mermaids are beautiful with long hair and gentle faces."

"Since when? I don't know what fairytales you've been reading but here in reality they're mean. They're very strong so don't get anywhere near them, they'll grab onto you and drag you under the water. They make you believe they're kind but they're not, don't trust them."

Rose failed to believe that what she just saw was a

mermaid, it had an upper half like a woman but was covered in a silver grey skin and scaly arms. The mermaid didn't have long flowing hair, she had no hair at all, just grey skin and scales. If it was indeed a mermaid then she only gave a glimpse her tail as she flipped back into the water.

"Why are they laughing at us?" asked Rose as the taunts continued around the boat.

"It's what they do, they work together to get the attention of sailors on passing ships. When the sailors are tired and have been away from land for many months, their eyes play tricks on them and they see what they want to. When they hear women laughing they go to look overboard to see what's out there. They are drawn in by the mermaids, thinking they are beautiful women and are lured closer and closer to the edge of the vessel. These mermaids can look beautiful when they want to attract their prey. The mermaids then grab the sailors and drag them overboard and down to the bottom of the sea, never to be seen again."

"Oh, my!"

"Which is why neither of us are going to get up or stand near the edge of the boat!"

The laughing around the boat continued well into the night as the mermaids tried their best to lure Victor or Rose to their calls. They could be heard swimming and splashing from all sides of the little boat, so Rose did not know which way to look. Each mermaid in turn scrambled up the side of the boat, sometimes one at the front, sometimes one at the back, and sometimes right in the middle. Each time was the same, they would leap from the water and grab the side of the boat and then pull themselves up enough just to look over. They were not so much bothered in Rose, it was Victor who they were after. They began to smile at him and tried to appear friendly to get his attention. They certainly had his attention but he was not falling for their tricks. The mermaids did not like the look of Rose and were quite jealous of her beauty, which meant they had to try even harder to entice him over and away from her. Victor focused his attention on the horizon, almost willing it to get closer quicker. Rose could feel he was tired of the mermaids but they just would not go away, she took his hand and squeezed it – just to let him know the night would pass, day light would come and the mermaids would go. For now though the mermaids were quite persistent and were laughing louder and faster, circling the boat more quickly. Then with a scream, one mermaid leapt up out of the sea and grabbed the side of the boat and pulled herself right up and leaned forward so her top half was balanced of the side of the boat, while her tail rested on the outside of the boat. Her skin looked smooth as the water dripped down her and onto the deck. Rose could now see why bleary eyed sailors could be drawn closer to them, when they were quiet and calm they had a magnetic aura. Victor did not give her the pleasure of eye contact and focused his attention on Ordram's light. The other mermaids began to hum a gentle tune as they circled the boat as they were trying to send Victor into a trance.

"Keep talking to me Rose, they're trying to hypnotise me… keep talking to me and I can try to tune them out."

"Why do they just want you? Won't they trap me too?"

"No, they're women… they'll be jealous of you. They'll be jealous that they can't get me away from you… and of your beauty of course."

"How can we get rid of them?"

"There's nothing that will make them go away until they've got what they came for. Only at dawn they'll go back to whatever dark wet rock they came out of."

So Rose talked to Victor all night, telling him about Cragfeld which now seemed so far away. She talked to him about the adventure she had had since getting to Ordraskop and how she could not have done it without Furdon and Fiddy. From Zwodder the Ogre to Fudgel the Swamp Troll,

Rose kept Victor's attention and he listened to every word. He loved the way she spoke and the sound of her voice as she told her tales. He had actually forgotten the mermaids were there while Rose was holding his hand and talking to him. Even Rose had got so engrossed in her stories, she had managed to block the mermaids out of her mind. The mermaids were displeased by this, they never went home empty-handed. They jumped back into water but stayed with the boat, still laughing at them, still humming a soft hypnotic tune. One at a time they would leap up and stare at Victor, watching and waiting for him to give in to their charms. He was not going to give them the satisfaction of even looking at them.

At last the darkest of the night subsided and the sky began to look lighter. Victor and Rose were exhausted, they had been awake all night. Neither of them dared go to sleep, especially Rose as she had to make sure Victor did not get distracted. The mermaids taunting laughter slowly turned to hisses of anger; all night they had tried to get their prize but all night it had been resisted. In one last attempt, a mermaid flung herself onto the boat. They never usually did this as there was a danger they would get trapped or captured but she was desperate. Her tail flapped against the wood as she composed herself, never having been out of the water before. Her tail was almost black but flashed with silvers and reds in the fading moonlight. The scales from her tail blended into those on her body. She moved forward on her arms, dragging her tail along leaving a pool of water behind her. She crawled over, closer to Victor who was still avoiding eye contact and looking out to Ordram glittering on the horizon. The mermaid edged closer to Victor and was planning on grabbing him and dragging him with her as she leapt back into the cold sea. She raised her arm up and was going to get hold of Victor's leg. Rose however became so angry at this, how dare this mermaid climb onto the boat, how dare she keep them awake all night. Rose knew they were not interested in her and their sights were set on Victor. The mermaid's arm crept closer to Victor but Rose was fuelled by anger and exhaustion, she got to her feet and with all the energy she could muster slapped the mermaid's arm away as hard as she could. The mermaid let out a shrill scream and glared at Rose who glared right back at her, she was not going to back down. The mermaid was about to launch herself at Rose when she was distracted by a pain in her tail. Hullard and Gwennol had crept out of Rose's hood; while Hullard jumped up and down on her tail, Gwennol was flicking Fairy dust which acted like tiny sparks of fire onto her tail. The mermaid hissed and spun around, flicking Hullard off and sending him flying into a corner. Gwennol stayed just out of reach as the mermaid tried to grab her, the little Fairy looked so small but she knew what she was doing. She hovered just out of reach at the edge of the boat, the mermaid leaped forward to grab her but Gwennol shot up into the air and watched the mermaid tumble over the side of the boat and back into the sea. Hisses all around the boat were heard. Dawn was breaking and the mermaids had lost, they had to admit their efforts had been wasted. Rose walked to the front of the boat but stayed away from the edge, she watched as the mermaids hissed, splashed and swam away. For the first time since nightfall things were quiet and Rose could relax.

"Oh Gwennol, Hullard… thank you for that. I don't know what would've happened if she'd grabbed either of us two."

"It's a pleasure," smiled Gwennol.

"See, bet you're glad you brought us with you now!"

"Yes, you could say so." Rose walked back to see how Victor was, he looked tired. "Are you okay? Maybe you should get some rest?"

"No, no, I'm fine now the mermaids have gone. Their singing was weaving its way through my mind and it was so difficult to ignore them. Thank you for talking to me all night, I feel as if we know all about each other," he smiled. "So, tell me... you've told me every little detail of your journey through Ordraskop, when were you planning on telling me about your little friends?"

"Oh, right," sighed Rose, suddenly realising their secret was out.

"Don't worry," said Victor to Gwennol and Hullard "I've no interest in trapping you and hiding you away to sell to Fairy collectors. Besides, you saved my life." Gwennol and Hullard shyly approached Victor and introduced themselves.

"We met in the woodland at the bottom of Drakenstop mountains, I didn't know they had hidden inside my hood until after the night at the pub." Hullard and Gwennol sat on Rose's knee and made friends with Victor.

After hiding in Rose's hood for the best part of day they had been listening into conversations and felt as if they knew him quite well. Victor did not seem at all fazed by the Fairy and the Pixie, talking to them as if he had known hundreds of them. While they were chatting, Rose went to check on Furdon and Fiddy. She went down the stairs and found them snuggled up next to each other, fast asleep and without a clue about what the others had been dealing with all night. It was also good for Rose that Hullard and Gwennol could come out of hiding and be part of the journey.

It was a relief when the sun finally rose and cast its light over them. The dark of night had been awful and it felt like it would never end. Victor grabbed his box of food and they all had some breakfast, well the Pixie and Fairy didn't need much to feel full. Rose stared out at Ordram, she could see him on the horizon, calling to them like a beacon. After sailing a day and a night, Ordram somehow did not look any closer. Rose turned back and could see the Drakenstop mountains in the far distance, they were a long, long way from the port. It was a matter of slow progress is better than no progress, as Bolstone would say. They kept moving forward and hoped they would get there soon. Rose really did not want another night with the mermaids.

Victor seemed cheerful even though he must have been exhausted after the sleepless night, he simply kept the boat on course and kept lookout for any sea creatures who were lurking around. By mid-morning the waters were calm and they were making good progress, cutting through the waters with ease. Hullard liked to sit on Rose's shoulder and look out to see as much as he could. In the near distance they saw huge sea creatures swimming alongside them, to you and me they were similar to Whales but a lot, lot bigger. They would arch their great bodies through the water and slap their tails down playfully, there were five of them swimming along gracefully.

Rose was sitting on deck with her knees pulled up to her chest and her arms wrapped around them. She rested her head on her knees and found the rocking motion of the boat made her drowsy. She nodded off for a short time, listening to her friends talking was relaxing. A few minutes later, a jolt of the boat woke Rose from her sleepy state.

"What's happening, is everyone alright?"

"Yes, we're fine Rose," said Victor, Hullard and Gwennol on his shoulder.

"Did we hit something?"

"No, something hit us, look."

Rose got to her feet and looked out in front. Right next to the boat was a school of silver flying fish which were bigger than the boat. They would leap out of the water, spread their wings and see how far they could glide before diving back into the water to do it all again. They were impressive looking, their huge silvery green bodies soared through the air, and flashes of yellow and blue could be seen under their wings. They posed no threat to the boat but were just flying past on their way to another part of the ocean. Rose looked up at them and smiled, they were magnificent. They caused a few waves which rocked the boat but it was nothing they could not cope with. Dozens of these flying fish flew and swam past them and they had quickly vanished into the distance. She wondered where they were going in such a hurry.

The heat of the sun blazed down on them all afternoon, it was nice at first but when trapped on a boat it felt relentless. Rose and Victor took it in turns to have a rest while the other kept the boat on course. Hullard seemed quite energetic so stayed with whoever was at the wheel. Gwennol would float between the two as the sun was sometimes too hot for her. Fiddy and Furdon were still sleeping through the voyage, though every time Rose went to check on them, they were always cuddling which she thought was quite sweet. She would remind them of this when they woke up, she knew Furdon would try to deny having a soft side and would never cuddle Fiddy.

In all honesty Rose was tired of being on the boat and just wanted to get there. She had no idea where they were, how far they had come, or how much longer they still had to go. Whenever she looked towards Ordram, he did not seem any closer. If it looked as if they were making progress then she might have felt slightly more enthusiastic. She knew she was being silly because the boat had never stopped moving forward since they set off. After seeing what lived in this deep ocean she felt very small and fragile. They were in a small boat which was defenceless to whatever came up next to it. One thrash of a tail and they could be smashed to pieces. Rose knew she should not think like that and had to remain positive, anything could happen out here. She could not control what might happen but she could try and remain optimistic, they would get through whatever they came up against. She knew she was tired, with a bit of rest she would feel better and recharged for hopefully their last night at sea.

CHAPTER TWELVE

In the last few days Bolstone had been busy with two things. First of all his main concern was with Rose, he kept an eye on her and tracked her progress regularly through the pictures in his waterfall. The little orange marble in her bag that she was supposed to give to Orme also acted like an eye, so Bolstone could see where they were. He had seen the sea monsters following them and the mermaids pestering them but these were not a real threat. Bolstone would never have left Rose in real danger but could see Victor was able to handle things. He could also see Furdon and Fiddy sleeping below deck and could not help shake his head and say 'tut tut tut', they were supposed to be keeping an eye on her. Yet they seemed to be making progress and on their final stretch of the journey before they would meet Ordram. It would be a relief when they got there because the old wizard had other things to do with his day, other than track Rose.

When he'd lured Orme into his little trap, he had kept one half of the crystal and sent the other half back to them. In the second half, not only had he hinted to Orme who was back in the area to cause them bother but he also wanted to see what was happening in the Dark Castle. Orme had left this crystal on the hearth in her den and thought no more about it. But Bolstone had been very clever and could use the crystal to listen in to any conversations that were spoken around it. Now, Bolstone had known Orme for many years and he knew that she tended to talk and mutter to herself. This was where Bolstone would pick up a lot of information. After the silver eggs had hatched, Orme had taken the woman from the village with her to her den. The woman was weak and could not talk but this didn't stop Orme talking to her. Bolstone was listening to every word she said.

"Come now dear, come in, come in," muttered the old witch. "Get by the fire and you'll soon warm up. Here, drink this, it will make you feel better, I promise. I know you've had a few days of torment but it's over now. It's not as if the Ice Queen doesn't appreciate you watching over her brood, she takes what she needs when she needs it, so don't take it personally. Oh dear look at you, so pale. I think you're too far gone to be let back out into Cragfeld, I think it better for you to stay here in the Castle with me, I'll look after you. If we let you out, anything could happen to you. There, there, feeling better? Good, good. You've seen for yourself how well you've done, you helped feed and nurture those eggs until they were ready to hatch. Didn't they look magnificent? Hundreds of creatures who'll grow into a strong and unyielding army. They'll protect us you know, they'll protect the Dark Castle, which is why I think you're better off staying here, with me. Don't you agree? Yes, yes, I thought as much. See, the colour is coming back to your cheeks already. You just sit back, relax, you'll feel no more pain. Now, while you rest... I must get on with things. If that blundering old wizard thinks he can get one up on me, I'll show him. We will all show him he can't win a challenge with us. Stupid man, stupid, stupid, stupid man. If he wants trouble then he's going to get trouble. Right, where's my book... no, not that one... ah there it is. I think he's forgotten that I have the darkest, blackest and most deadly magic… ha, he'll soon remember. Are you alright there dear? Wonderful. I'll be with you in a moment dear, just one more spell to find here… Ah there it is. Yes, yes, oh this will be a fun little game, for me anyway. If he shows up, I'll be ready – whenever that day comes. Oh look at you dear, looking brighter already. I told you I'd look after you didn't I? I told you I'd make you feel better. Now, all I ask in return of helping you – saving you, some might say… all I ask from you is for one drop of blood, one drop, that's all. Is that okay? Otherwise the Ice Queen would have me feed you to her army, we don't want that do we? No, good girl. Here, let me use this little needle, you'll not feel a thing I promise. There we go, good, good, that's all I wanted. See, I keep my word. Finish your drink now and have a rest, a sleep will do you good… I'll be here when you wake."

Bolstone was sitting at the back of his cosy cave in his old armchair next to a warm fire, listening to every word the old witch was saying. He knew what was happening in the Dark Castle, that they had created a vicious and vile army. He knew they were preparing for a battle which may or may not come. It would come, Bolstone knew it would come. He had been preparing for the day Cragfeld would be freed from the icy grip of Mordisan and Orme for a long time. He had been waiting for Rose for a long time and as soon as she appeared in front of him, all he had to do was set everything else in motion. The people and creatures of Ordraskop all knew about the history of Cragfeld, how the Ice Queen had heartlessly taken the throne and threatened anyone who tried to take it with the death of Rika. They all knew a warrior would come one day and fight the Ice Queen, free the island, the people, and Rika. None of them knew it would be Rose and her two little companions, Furdon and Fiddy.

Not only had Bolstone travelled through Ordraskop but he had also been to a far off land to visit a King who had tried to forget about the Ice Queen. Bolstone always told them the day would come and the Ice Queen would be avenged. This King was Rika and Mordisan's father. He always wanted to have his daughters back but knew what Mordisan had turned into. None of his men dared return to Cragfeld for fear of what she could do to them. When Bolstone had paid them a visit and told them the warrior had come forward, it was as if they had found something to believe in again. It had been told that an unexpected warrior would one day bring forward a power which would be stronger than the Ice Queen and Orme combined. The King was old now, aged more by the loss of his daughters but he could not let go of this life until he had chance to say goodbye to them. He was in his forties when he last saw them in Cragfeld, a century and a half ago. Although he was old, he had a good army who were strong and now had a cause to believe in. Many stories had been told about Mordisan and Rika, they wanted to believe they could save Cragfeld and Rika. As far as they knew, Rika might not be alive, they just had to believe the Ice Queen had not killed her. They too began to make preparations and set sail to Cragfeld, a journey of ten days.

In the Dark Castle itself Orme was completely unaware Bolstone was listening in. With the one drop of human blood she had made a powerful potion which she would use to grow their army strong and deadly. The hundreds of creatures would need a lot of food. She took this tiny jar of potion through the tunnels of the Dark Castle. She could hear cries, screeches, and animals roaring as she approached the ballroom. As she went through the door, only hours after the animals had hatched they had more than doubled in size and they were hungry. They all turned to look at her as she entered the room. Orme was not scared of these creatures, both she and Mordisan had conjured them to life so they would protect her as much as they'd protect the Ice Queen. She walked down the side of the frozen ballroom and every few steps she let one drop of the potion fall to the floor and she did the same on her way back to the door. Orme then completed the spell by snapping an icicle off the door and smashing it over the floor. From the white snow-like dust grew heaps and heaps of food for the army. Every mouthful was tainted with human blood for which they had developed a taste. She smiled as they ate, she was pleased to see their appetites were good.

The Ice Queen was happy knowing she had an army which would defend her and the Dark Castle. She was wandering around the main hall, pacing up and down as she thought about what could possibly dare try and attack her. She wanted to see if she could see anything. At the stone plinth she clicked her fingers and an ice bowl appeared and slowly from the bottom began to fill with a white liquid. She stirred it around with her finger and waited for something, if anything to appear. Only moments later an image appeared on the surface of the liquid. It was her father. She stepped back in shock as she hardly recognised him having not seen him since she threw him out of her Kingdom. This was a man whom she had tried to please all her life but had always gone unnoticed. As much as she wanted his love and respect, he never showed her any and she had always hated him for that. "Why are you appearing to me now father," she thought to herself, "after all these years, what do you want? If you think you can save Rika, then don't be a fool. If you think you can take my crown, you have lost your mind. If you think your army can defeat mine then be prepared to watch your men die." She stirred the waters again. This time the liquid changed to a soft orange colour which she knew represented Bolstone, this did not bother her as she knew he was a weak old man and could be crushed like a bug. Out of the liquid appeared another man, a younger man with dark hair but she could not see his face. "Hmm, who are you?" she wondered. No level of importance was given to this figure and she could not see if he was a King, a soldier or a warrior. She could see he was with a woman, again she couldn't see her face. What she could see around her neck was a golden locket. "Oh, I see you... it's you again isn't it? Your cloak may hide your face but I know to look out for you. I will know you as soon as I see you. Why don't you dare show yourselves to me, you can't hide forever? But be warned, when you do show yourself to me, I'll be waiting."

The Ice Queen was furious at being shown an image of her father. In one hundred and fifty years she had tried to delete his face from her memory. He looked old and weak now. When she last saw him he was strong and had the respect of his people, all apart from her. When Mordisan had developed her powers and became the Ice Queen, she chased her father and his army away. She told them she would not hesitate in killing Rika if they tried to step foot on the island again. She wanted to know why after all this time, this man whom she loathed was appearing to her. She pushed the bowl of liquid onto the frozen floor and watched it crash and shatter into a million pieces. The liquid turned to ice and the bowl dissolved into the floor.

It was early evening as Rose woke from a nap, the sun was just setting as she stepped up on the deck. Victor smiled at her as she approached, Gwennol and Hullard had been keeping him company.

"Did you get any rest?" asked Gwennol.

"A little... I had quite strange dreams."

"That's because you're in a strange place," laughed Hullard.

"Can I show you something Rose?" asked Victor, he pointed out in front of them. "Look, we don't have far to go now."

Rose turned to see what Victor was pointing at. Not far in front of her she could see Ordram looking closer, at last. There, hanging in the air about half a mile into the sky was a floating island, a very small rocky island on which Ordram stood, Rose could see the gold haze caused by the leaves. On the small island in the sky there was also a building which looked like a Fort. It was still too far for her see anything in detail but she could not wait to get there and have a closer look.

"Oh, Wow!" she was amazed. "It's beautiful."

"And still half a day away," said Victor "We'll get there in the middle of the night which isn't the easiest time to land."

"Oh but that doesn't really matter, we're nearly there!"

Rose was full of excitement as the journey was coming to an end but more immediately, the boat journey was coming to an end. She jumped for joy and hugged Victor, she was so happy. Victor wasn't expecting her to do that and was quite taken aback. "Can't we go any faster?"

"No, the sea is choppier than last night and now it's getting dark we'll have to take it a bit steadier," said Victor. Rose was too excited to really care, they were so close now.

It was a beautiful sunset that evening, splashes of reds, orange, gold and yellow mingled amongst each other, becoming darker and more intense as the sun went down. The light sparkled on the sea and the evening seemed quite tranquil. Furdon and Fiddy would have loved to have seen a sunset like this, but it was a lot easier for them to sleep through the sea crossing. Meanwhile up on deck, the four friends enjoyed the calm evening, watching the sun go down and be replaced with a bright white moon high in the sky. The sea was somewhat rougher than the night before and the rickety old boat creaked as it ploughed through the waves which rolled around them. Rose could not take her eyes off the island in the sky, the golden haze of Ordram lit the sky around it. As Victor said, they would only get there in the middle of the night and as much as she was sick of being on the boat, she knew that every minute they were getting that bit closer.

The night grew darker and the sea began to look like thick waves of treacle, which Rose felt it could be – the waves were holding them back and slowing them down. Then came the awful familiar sound which Rose knew she would hear again, no matter how much she tried to will it away. The laughter and hissing of mermaids was back, even louder and more intimidating than before. There seemed to be more of them, as if the group last night had called for reinforcements to get their man. Gwennol was standing on Victor's shoulder flicking her wings with anticipation of what they were about to face. She composed and prepared herself ready to use her magic Fairy dust to the best of her young ability. Hullard had a hatred for these fancy fish, he was a Pixie and could see them for exactly what they were – no matter how much they sang or tried to hypnotise Victor, all Hullard could see was a freaky looking fish with a human top half. Hullard sprang over to the front of the boat to peek into the dark sea below. Last night there were only a handful of mermaids that caused quite a lot of bother, not tonight. Pixies had fantastic vision both by day and by night, Hullard could see dozens and dozens of mermaids swimming beneath their fragile wooden fishing boat. Not only were they beneath the boat but they were also swimming alongside it, where they could be heard laughing at them. Hullard went back to Rose with a rather pale expression of what he'd seen. Victor and Rose could felt their mood grow heavy at the news.

"Victor, I think you should go below deck out of their sight," suggested Rose.

"It's okay, you need me up here…"

"No, we don't," said Rose "I can take the wheel, I can see where we're headed."

"But they'll do their best to tip the boat."

"Which is why you should go below deck. Up here you're too vulnerable, I don't want to risk you falling overboard and straight into their hands."

Reluctantly Victor agreed. He did not want to leave Rose to deal with this by herself as he had promised himself he would look after her as well as he could for as long as she wanted him to. Tonight she did not want him to… so he went below deck to sit besides Furdon and Fiddy who were oblivious to the entire situation. He could hear the mermaids banging on the side of the boat with their fists and tails, it was unnerving to know only a thin shell of wood was protecting him. He could hear them screaming under the water, a shrill daunting chorus.

Up on deck, Rose was at the helm, determined not to let these mermaids get what they were after. She was extremely outnumbered but was not prepared to even entertain this thought. Over the last few days, since coming to Ordraskop Rose could feel herself becoming stronger, both in body and mind. She was more determined and would not let anything stand in her way. No matter what it was, there was always a way through or around the problem. She remembered back to what Frithad had said 'Rose, we each have a warrior inside of us, it is only when we need to be really brave do they show themselves'. Rose could hear this loud and clear, she had found her inner warrior who would fight with her through whatever danger may come their way. Rose had never needed to find her inner warrior while on Cragfeld but now, through hard situations she had found hers. Rose was stronger and braver than she had ever been in her life and she was not going to let a bunch of mermaids stop her now. She looked around deck to see what she could use to defend herself and her friends against these persistent creatures. There were a few planks of wood, fishing nets with heavy metal hooks attached, metal chains and a heavy metal pole as long as her arm which she didn't have a clue about what it could be. All she needed to know was that it was heavy and could do some damage. Hullard and Gwennol looked on as their friend searched around for a weapon she could use. Rose felt calm, but she was also feeling anger towards these creatures which were getting between her and Ordram and threatening her friends. She grabbed the metal pole in one hand and a metal chain in the other, she was ready.

She could hear the singing, the humming and the hissing getting louder before suddenly stopping just as it did the night before. Rose stood on deck waiting for the mermaids to climb up and stare at her, they were after Victor but would not let Rose stand in their way. Moments later there was a lot of splashing at the side of the boat as half a dozen mermaids leaped up and grabbed the side of the boat causing it to tilt slightly. They saw Rose, a lone figure in the middle of the deck and they laughed at her. Rose could feel a rage firing up in her belly. She raised her hands in the air and let out a scream of threatening anger at the creatures who dared approach her. The mermaids screamed back at her and hissed, laughing at her pathetic attempt to scare them. That was it, Rose had had enough. With the pole in one hand and the metal chain in the other she launched herself at the row of mermaids, thrashing her arms down on the mermaids who were gripping the side of the boat. The metal chain and pole crashed down on their hands and arms causing them to let go as an intense pain shot up their arms. They had never been attacked like this before and dived back into the sea screaming in agony. Rose knew it was not over, there were more to come and she was prepared to strike them all. More mermaids leaped up to see what this young woman was doing to cause such injury to their friends. As soon as Rose saw their hands land on the boat, she struck again, breaking fingers and wrists of these wretched creatures and sent them screaming back into the sea. Over and over she did this, blow after blow Rose knocked the mermaids down. After a while the mermaids went quiet and no longer jumped up to the boat. Hullard cheered in victory. Rose however knew it wasn't over, she knew they would not give up as quickly or as easily as this.

Victor was below deck listening to what was happening. He was trying to imagine what was Rose was doing, what was causing the mermaids to scream in pain. He had no idea what Rose was doing but whatever was fuelling the power inside her was managing to push the mermaids away. The banging on the side of the boat subsided. Victor slowly moved up the first two steps and peered up onto the deck. He saw Rose like he had never seen her before, she was glowing with bravery and had a light in her eyes. He saw she had a weapon in both her hands but these faded into the background, he could not believe this was the same girl. Gwennol spotted Victor and flew over to him and slapped him on the face, telling him to get below deck and stay out of danger. Victor did not argue, the little Fairy could be quite scary when she wanted to be. He could see Rose was okay but he still wanted to help her.

The hissing laughter of the mermaids faded and the sea around the boat had settled down. Hullard rushed over to Rose to see if she was okay and commended her efforts, he too could not quite believe this was the same girl who only a few days earlier had been bullied by a few Fairies! Rose got her breath back and reassured Hullard she was fine. But then it came, the second wave of the attack she was waiting for. She could hear the hissing and singing starting all over again but this time there was something different. The hissing was the same but the singing was in a lower pitch. The mermaids had retreated but sent the mermen to lure Rose. The singing was getting into her head but she reminded herself to tune it out and stay focused, just as Victor had done the night before. Hullard knew it was mermen, they had come to get Rose out of the way and then the mermaids would come back for Victor. The splashing was getting closer to the side of the boat as the mermen readied themselves to grab this young woman. Mermaids could be heard humming in the distance while they waited until they could strike again. One merman leaped up out of the sea, grabbed the side of the boat with one hand and lifted himself up with the other. His arms and torso rested on the side of the boat while his tail balanced him there. He seemed to have a gentle face and was humming softly at Rose. To Hullard however it was like a big fish screeching at her. The merman was singing to Rose, calling her to him. Rose paused and looked at the merman and stepped a little closer, to see his kind eyes calling to her, pulling her in. Hullard watched in horror as she edged closer, shouting as loud as he could to her to wake up, step back and not to listen to the singing. Victor could hear Hullard shouting at Rose, so he crept up onto the deck and quietly picked up a large metal hammer from under the fishing nets. He turned around to see Rose and the merman staring at each other, if the merman really wanted to reach for her then she would just be out of his reach, he had to lure her forward just a bit more. Just then three more mermen jumped onto the side, singing to Rose as she was staring at the first one. The mermen were singing to her to let go of her weapons and go to them. She smiled at them, having let them think she was falling for their charms – she lifted her arms and continued where she had left off with the mermaids. She unleashed her anger towards them and thrashed the metal chain against them, then the metal pole. Their flesh was torn and bruised and bones in their hands were crushed. Victor was in shock at was he was seeing but soon came to his senses and jumped forward to help her. The mermen fell back into the sea. Victor and Rose were standing on deck both armed and waiting for the next lot who dare threaten them. As soon as Rose heard the splash as one leapt out of the sea, she swung the chain and thrashed the hands as soon as they grabbed the side of the boat. The mermen did not give up as easily as the mermaids but now Victor was helping Rose, she found it easier. There was a massive swell of water under boat. The mermen and mermaids jumped back into the sea and were gone. Hullard and Gwennol came out cheering for their heroes. Rose and Victor looked at each other, both out of breath but relieved they had won. Not a single merman or mermaid could be seen or heard, everything was quiet. They then felt another surge beneath them again, as if a huge amount of water was being displaced and causing a wave below them.

"What now?" sighed Victor.

"Your guess is as good as mine…" said Rose.

"I suggest you hold on tight, whatever it is, it is big and scared the merpeople away" said Victor. Rose clung onto the railing again and the Fairy and Pixie clung to her collar, waiting.

"Do you think whatever it is has seen us, or are we irrelevant to it?"

"It'll know we're here," said Victor. "All those damn mermaids and mermen will have caught its attention."

The sea beneath them surged again as if it were being lifted. Out of the water in front of the boat appeared the head and neck of a huge black sea snake, which towered above the boat and looked down on them. A second later another head appeared next to the first.

"A two-headed sea snake," said Gwennol "I didn't think they lived in these waters."

"Apparently they do," said Hullard "Why is it looking at us?"

"I don't know," she snapped "Why don't you ask it?"

"Fine, I will…"

"Hullard, don't," said Rose making sure he didn't go any-where or say anything.

"Why?"

"We'll find out soon enough what it wants, if it didn't want anything then it would've left us alone."

Both heads of the sea snake looked down on the little boat and hissed at it. Its two tongues were flicking in and out of its mouths as it tried to work out whether this floating contraption was a threat or not. Its black wet skin looked like oil as it stared at them with shiny eyes that flickered green. One head opened its mouth wide to show off two sharp white fangs and then lunged at the boat snapping at them but pulling back before it could touch them. The other head then did the same thing.

"It's putting on a display," said Gwennol "it's showing you who's boss, it wants to scare us back to land."

"We can't go back," said Rose "We're so close now… and we have to get to Ordram."

"Only if the sea snake lets you… and the chances of that are slim, look at it!"

"I know but what can we do against this thing, I can't exactly snap my teeth at it can I?" This made Victor laugh as he imagined her doing this. "It's not funny Victor! Do you have any bright ideas?"

"Er, me? Um no."

"Then think harder, we need to get past this thing." The two heads snapped again at the boat. "Gwennol?"

"Don't look at me," she said "I wouldn't know where to begin."

"How many times is it going to snap at us?" asked Hullard "Both of its breaths stinks." Both snake-heads came down level with the boat and flicked their tongues before hissing at them again.

"We need to think of something quickly…" hurried Rose.

"Maybe we could show it we're not a threat… like this…" said Hullard who jumped down onto the deck and did a little dance. The snake watched him for a few seconds and looked confused, wondering what this little Pixie was doing.

It hissed again.

"Yeah, that's not going to work," laughed Victor.

"I'm glad you're finding this amusing," said Rose.

"What do you expect me to do? We can't exactly cry and run away can we? We might as well laugh while we still can!"

"Very cheerful," said Rose. She was beginning to feel nervous as the snake-heads were becoming impatient and kept snapping towards them.

The snake playfully twisted its necks around each other while it waited to see what the strange things on the boat would come up with to scare it away. So far it had confidence they would turn back to Ordraskop. It didn't like anything being on these waters which did not belong here. It was the guardian of the sea and nothing got passed without proving it had rite of passage. Unfortunately none of the friends knew this. One of the heads struck again and hit the corner of the boat, making it rock horrendously. Rose and Victor were knocked off their feet and were rolling around the deck of the boat like rag dolls. Gwennol grabbed Hullard and they found a safe corner where they could hide. Rose found herself wishing Bolstone would show up but she had already used her marble to call him. Furdon had one left but that was his to use at a time when he thought appropriate. She was frustrated at being so close to Ordram but all these things kept getting in her way. She stumbled to her feet, the hood of her gown had pulled to one side slightly and her golden locket was now resting on the outside of her collar. The snake wasn't interested in gold or trinkets, all it wanted was control of the sea. The two heads snapped again at the boat, insisting they turned around and go back to where they came from and they had no right to be here. Rose wobbled around as the boat was being rocked heavily from side to side. Every movement the two headed snake made caused a rush of water and waves. The snake was standing between themselves and Ordram, Rose was not about to quit when she was so close. Behind the snakes heads she could see Ordram glowing.

Victor got to his feet and held onto the side of the boat to steady himself, he looked up at the snake and then back to Rose. He could see the locket around her neck shining brightly as if it were being lit up from within. It was lighting the dark night with a golden shimmering glow. Hullard and Gwennol also saw the light and came out from their hiding place to see what it was. Rose became aware of it when she wondered what all of her friends were staring at and found herself dropping the metal chain and pole from her hands. The snake lowered it heads down to either side of the boat to look closely at what was causing the brightness in the dark. The golden leaf on the locket which had been slowly peeling and unravelling from its case, opened up and sent a beam of bright white light glistening with gold all the way to Ordram. It was as if the leaf could feel it was almost home and calling out to say 'Here I am'. Ordram in return felt the call and glimmered twice as bright in the night sky and sent a beam of golden light straight back to the leaf. Rose was standing as still as she could, she had not got a clue of what was happening. The two headed snake had clearly seen that these were not intruders and had a right to be there. Ordram had shown the snake to back down. It hissed again at them before slowly slinking and submerging under the sea again. Hardly any movement was felt as it curled its body around and slithered away into the dark, dark sea.

The old rickety boat began to creak under their feet but was no longer rocking wildly and they could stand quite easily. The bright beam of light connecting Ordram and the leaf was dazzling.

"Can anyone tell me what's going on?" said Victor "What's that thing around Rose's neck?"

"It's Ordram's Leaf," said Gwennol. "After hundreds of years, it's finally made its way back to where it was grown."

Rose could feel there was a magnetic- type pull coming through the beam of light. The little fishing boat seemed to pick up speed, a speed not even Victor knew it was capable of. Over the sea it almost flew as it cut through the waves like a hot knife through butter. Sea creatures large and small came up from the depths and swam alongside the boat, as if escorting them in. They all looked around at the amazing sight, the seas had been lit up and Rose and her friends could see everything swimming alongside them. The huge monstrous yet harmless creatures which they had met on the first day led the way, followed by a school of flying fish. The two-headed sea snake could be seen in the distance, both necks raised tall and proud as if watching the occasion unfold. The mermen and mermaids however could not be seen and were probably too ashamed to show themselves as the golden leaf almost did not make it home because of them. Victor's worry had soon melted away and was enjoying the spectacle he was witnessing, he had never seen anything like this before and would probably never see anything like it again. The old wooden fishing boat was straining at such speed, it had not been built to cope with the amount of pressure it was suddenly under. A great crack could be heard as a split appeared at the front of the boat.

"My boat," cried Victor "It'll never survive the pace we're travelling, that split will soon tear the boat apart."

"Gwennol," called Rose "Go and wake Furdon and Fiddy, we must all stay as close together as we can, if it is as Victor says, then the Grocklings can't swim."

Gwennol flew from Victor's shoulder to the stairwell to go below deck. She could see Furdon and Fiddy had fallen into a corner having been swayed this way and that for two days and nearly two nights. She hovered down and sprinkled some Fairy dust over them to undo the spell.

Furdon was first to come round, bleary-eyed and wondering where he was. Fiddy woke quickly and jumped up.

"Where's Rose? Where's Rose?" cried Fiddy.

"It's okay, she's fine," reassured Gwennol. "She's up on deck. We're almost there but the boat isn't coping with the speed we're going, so she's told me to wake you before it disintegrates beneath us."

"Why don't we slow down then?" suggested Furdon.

"The power is no longer in our hands, come and see."

The Grocklings were not impressed that they were still on the boat and were hoping to have woken up on the safety of dry land. Yet they couldn't feel the boat rocking as it had done when they first got on board and they pulled themselves together. Gwennol flew up ahead of them and back onto Victor's shoulder, she held on tight because her little fairy wings would have struggled to keep up with the pace they were going. There was another cracking sound down the side of the boat as a panel of wood was torn off by the pressure of the water. As soon as Furdon and Fiddy heard this, they looked at each other and soon dashed up onto the deck. They saw Victor holding onto the side of the boat with Gwennol and Hullard hanging onto his shoulders. They wondered what they had missed in the last two days because the last they remembered was that the Fairy and Pixie had to stay hidden. As they edged closer they saw Rose standing in the middle of the deck with her arms relaxed by her sides. Her blue gown was wafting in the breeze and her hair blowing freely behind her. They saw the bright light coming from around her neck and beaming up towards the strange little island in the sky. Furdon and Fiddy looked at each other feeling very confused as to what was happening. They went to stand next to Victor and now they were closer could see the locket had opened like a bud to reveal a golden leaf. They were amazed at what they had woken up to but knew they would have to get all of the details later.

They were getting closer to Ordram, faster and faster they seemed to go. The small island floating in the sky was glowing with gold and silver. They were almost there, about another mile or two until they would be below the island hovering in the sky. Another cracking sound shuddered the entire boat as the crack in the front split down the surface of the deck, Rose was on one side, her friends were on the other.

"Rose, you need to step to this side of that crack in the deck," called Victor "If it gets deeper we'll be separated."

"I can't hear you…" shouted Rose, she could see him calling to her but it was if she had gone deaf, she could not hear a thing. She could not hear the wind rushing passed her face, nor the sea splashing under the boat and she did not hear the boat cracking and creaking as it was starting to fall to pieces around her. She could see them all pointing to the floor but with the bright light from the golden leaf shining below her face, she could not see anything below her chin without being dazzled.

They were now travelling incredibly fast and Victor knew it was only a matter of minutes before the boat would break apart. The split down the middle was widening. Fiddy was holding onto one of Victor's legs, Furdon was holding onto the other, with Gwennol and Hullard on either shoulder. Victor could see they were almost there, the underside of the island appearing to them as they got closer, yet it still seemed too far for his poor little boat to carry them. The five friends clung onto each other and could only look on as Rose was powerless to the situation. The sea creatures were still swimming alongside them but slightly lagging behind as even they couldn't keep up with the boat. The bright beam of light was pulling them stronger and stronger.

With an almighty bang the boat had been pushed beyond its limits and split right down the middle. Victor grabbed onto the other four who were holding onto him equally as tight as they were flung off the side of the boat and thrown into the water. It was cold and dark and Victor could not see anything in the water beneath him as they all plunged in together. He gasped for air as he came to the surface, desperately looking for his friends and Rose. He fished around in front of him and felt a chunk of wood from the boat floating nearby, he held onto it with one hand while he searched the waters with the others in the hope of feeling something that could be Furdon or Fiddy. Gwennol appeared next to him, at the last minute she had taken to the air and grabbed Hullard as she did. She dropped down onto the wood Victor had found and placed Hullard down.

"Where are they? Can you see them? I can't see them," cried Victor with panic in his voice.

The Fairy hovered above the water but could not see the Grocklings. They knew neither of them could swim and as more time passed, the chances of finding them were decreasing. Victor had a heavy heart. He knew how much Furdon and Fiddy meant to Rose, even he himself had grown very fond of them in such a small amount of time. He frantically searched through the waters but found nothing. Victor returned to the lump of wood where Hullard was waiting with Gwennol, feeling sadness run through his body. Victor could see in the distance the bright beam of light was still shining down to Rose, she was somehow, miraculously still at other end of it.

Out of the waters around him came the all too familiar hissing and humming sound. Mermaids! There was nothing he could do, he had no boat to hide on. His body was in the water, his arms and shoulders resting on the wood next to Hullard. The mermaids would just be able to snatch him without a fight. After two unsuccessful attempts and a lot of battle scars thanks to Rose, they would at last have their prize. Their hissing got closer and the waters were still as they were not having to splash for attention. Victor felt the piece of wood on which he was resting his head rock, there on the other side were two mermaids watching him. He knew there would be more of them surrounding him and swimming beneath him. Victor put his head back down, he had no fight left in him and his heart was full of sadness. The piece of wood rocked again, Victor knew it was more mermaids gathering around. What he was not expecting was the sound of coughing and spluttering. Victor looked up again and watched in disbelief as mermaids lifted Furdon and Fiddy onto the same piece of wood on which he was resting. He could not believe it, the Grocklings were okay! And the mermaids had saved them? Furdon and Fiddy were rather soggy but they were alive. The mermaids looked at Victor and then two of them started to drag the piece of wood he was holding onto towards the beam of light from the sky. The five of them could not believe what was happening. The Grocklings had never seen the mermaids before so as far as they were concerned they were wonderful creatures who'd saved their lives. As for Victor, Gwennol and Hullard, none of them could understand or believe why the mermaids were helping. However, the mermaids were dragging them all back over to the beam of light so they were not going to start questioning things. The mermaids pulled them along at a swift pace and stopped within a few metres of the light. They turned to look at Victor and smiled before diving back into the sea, swimming away back into the darkness. Three of the friends looked at each other in utter bewilderment, whilst the other two were praising the helpful fish people.

Their attention was drawn to Rose who was standing on what was left of the deck of the boat with the golden leaf fully spread over her chest. Rose was unaware of what had happened to her friends, she could not hear them call or scream as the boat fell to pieces and could not see anything other than the brightness in front of her. Through all of this she never felt scared. She felt safe from the second the leaf had connected with Ordram.

Looking up into the light they could see what looked like a bird flying down from the floating island. As it got closer the bird grew bigger but they were all dazzled by the light and could not see exactly what it was. It hovered over Rose for a few seconds and then gently took hold of her in one of its claws. It then flapped its great wings and hovered over to where Victor was floating in the water. The bird gently put its claw around him and lifted him out of the water and waited for the Grocklings to scramble on, holding onto its leg. Hullard and Gwennol leapt on and grabbed onto Victor's trousers as they were lifted from the sea. A cool air blew around them as they were lifted higher and higher. Victor and Rose looked at each other, both relieved the other was alright. The bird took them up to the island in the sky and placed them gently on the ground in front of Ordram.

CHAPTER THIRTEEN

As soon as Rose was sitting on the floor in front of Ordram the bright light around them faded and Rose was able to see and hear normally again. When she saw Furdon and Fiddy she leapt over and grabbed them in a large embrace, she was so pleased to see them. As they were her, they were baffled about what had just happened and where they were. It had been a traumatic few days for all of them and they were all thrilled to see each other safely reunited. Victor could not believe these two little Grocklings had been thrown into the deep dangerous waters, only to be saved by mermaids. He was happy and relieved they were okay and as soon as Rose let them go, he hugged them just as hard. Gwennol tried to dry her wings and squeeze the sea water from her little dress while the others were happy to drip dry. Somehow Rose did not have a single drop of water on her and her dress was bone dry.

They eventually calmed down and it gradually began to sink in that they had made it. Here they were standing in front of Ordram. After days and days of walking, dealing with Ogres, Dragons, Spiraliluses and Swamp Trolls to name but a few, here they were. The golden locket had safely come home to Ordram. However, it was no longer a simple locket and the entire top half had peeled open to reveal a beautiful golden leaf. It shimmered in the light and sat comfortably on Rose's neckline. The six friends got to their feet and slowly looked around them to see where they were. It was the middle of the night and they appeared to be standing on a beautiful cobbled courtyard which glimmered gold and yellows as bright as if it were mid morning. Behind them was a small fort type building made of stone which also shimmered with golden colours, each window was beautifully dressed with flowers. To their right was the bird which had rescued them from the sea, it stood tall and proud on a marble perch cleaning its elegant wings and preening itself. Now they could see it properly, rather than just its feet, they could see it was an impressive looking bird of prey but one none of them had ever seen before. It had the familiar strong beak with a hooked tip, powerful legs, sharp talons and yellow amber eyes... but it's wing span stretched almost as wide as the island they were on. Each and every feather looked as if it was delicately made out of silver or gold filigree. It was a beautiful bird. However, it did not seem at all bothered about them and simply carried on preening itself and enjoyed listening to them saying how handsome he was.

They then turned around to see the reason they were here, Ordram. An ancient-looking magical tree stood on front of them with its golden leaves rustling in the night's breeze. Ordram's trunk was as wide as it was tall and would've easily taken ten men stretched from hand to hand to make a circle around him. The bark on his truck was old and knotted as it had twisted and grown through the years. In the moonlight the trunk appeared bronze but by day a bright golden light would glow from his core. The branches grew tall and strong and were laden with stunning golden leaves, none of which looked like the leaf around Rose's neck. The leaves on Ordram's branches were two or three time the size of Rose's and seemed somewhat sturdier as they wafted around. The one that had grown from the locket was a lot lighter and more delicate to look at.

As the six friends were standing in front of Ordram, he shivered his branches as if he was stretching. Then the most incredible thing happened. There was a deep groaning noise coming from far inside Ordram as he slowly began to untwist his knotted trunk. Fiddy grabbed hold of Rose's dress as he did not like this at all. Gwennol was flying cautiously next to Rose's shoulder. The other boys were trying to act cool as if this was perfectly normal, Hullard on Victor's shoulder and Furdon by his side. Ordram's trunk creaked slightly with age as he stretched himself up taller. The giant bird of prey again paid no attention to this and stood on his perch watching on with his beady eyes. As Ordram's trunk untwisted, there before them they could see a small doorway appearing into the magical tree. Fiddy's jaw dropped to the floor, as did everyone else's. They were all speechless at what they were seeing before them. The creaking noise ceased and the untwisting motion stopped as the little doorway glimmered at them invitingly.

"What now...?" whispered Victor "Are we all supposed to fit through that gap."

"I don't know," said Rose "I suppose so, I can't see where else we'd go."

"What about the fort behind us, shouldn't we see if there's someone home?"

"Whoever's in there knows we're here, otherwise this glorious bird wouldn't have collected us. I say Ordram is inviting us in and it's rude to keep him waiting."

Rose led the way and walked up to the magnificent tree that was Ordram. Fiddy was right behind her with Furdon on his tail. Gwennol flew above the Grocklings and then Victor and Hullard followed at the back. The doorway in the trunk only came up to Rose's chest but it was wide enough for her to squeeze through. She poked her head through first to have a look inside and then popped back.

"What can you see?" asked Furdon.

"A spiral wooden staircase slowly going around and down but I wouldn't be able to say how far."

"Oh I'm getting that feeling again," said Fiddy "I don't think I like this."

"Fiddy you come from the mountains, you'll be fine," Rose smiled.

She ducked down and squeezed herself through the gap until she was standing tall inside Ordram's golden trunk at the top of the wooden staircase. She took a couple of steps down and waited for the rest of her friends to join her. Fiddy and Furdon had no problems with the size of the doorway but Victor found it quite difficult as he was the tallest and widest of all of them. Once he had eventually found a way to bend and edge his way though, Ordram twisted back the other way and closed the doorway behind them.

"Down we go then," smiled Rose.

"Like we have any other option," huffed Fiddy.

The spiral staircase was quite wide with shallow steps. The inside of the trunk had a natural golden glow in the grain of the wood which naturally lit their path. The golden leaf around Rose's neck had started to shine again, though this time a lot more gently than before. The steps were evenly cut and the sides of the stairway were smooth to touch as if carpenters had done their finest work. They spiralled down a few times and when they got to the bottom there was a heavy wooden door on gold hinges. Rose knocked on the door and they waited. They couldn't hear anything on the other side, no shuffling of feet or murmuring voices. After a few seconds the door slowly and quietly swung open.

They stepped down into a small circular, well-lit wooden room. There was nothing inside the wooden cavity beneath the ancient enchanted tree, apart from the six friends of course. The door closed behind them. Above their heads was a tangled mass of roots, all twisted and looped around each other. The room in which they had found themselves was not at all dull or wet, it actually felt warm and comfortable. The golden locket was shining beautifully around Rose's neck as they waited for something to happen or someone to show themselves.

After several minutes they could hear a movement coming from the other side of the wall, rather inside the wall. There was a creaking of wood all around them and they did not know which way to look. Out of the smooth curved wall on the opposite side of the room, they could see something pushing through the wood. It was not actually pushing through the wood, it was all part of the wooden wall. A large wooden chair appeared before them, it was a large throne which looked as if it had been carved perfectly into the wall. A few seconds later a tall figure could be seen standing next to the throne but was also part of the wall. The figure moved through the wood and took a seat on the throne. It was as if it were a perfectly sculpted man had been carved to sit on the mighty chair. The figure was that of an old wise-looking man, his wooden beard hung long down his chest and his eyebrows twitched as he looked at them. Around his head sat a thin band of what appeared to be a crown. He looked almost human but he was clearly part of the great tree of Ordram in which they stood. He creaked in his chair as he got comfortable and cleared his throat to talk to them.

"Welcome," he boomed in a deep yet gentle voice "I've been waiting for you for a long time. I trust you're all safe and uninjured after your journey?" They all nodded.

"I'm Rose and these are my friends."

"Yes, I know… I know you all. I knew three of you would be here but the other three are a surprise… and you two little Grocklings only just made it didn't you? Rescued by mermaids, they'll never live that down!" Rose looked concerned at her friends, she did not know about them being thrown into the sea

"What happened?" she whispered to them, they just smiled

as it was not the best time to be exchanging stories.

"Rose, don't worry about your friends," said the old man "You all arrived safe and well, that's the main thing. Here you are standing within the tree of Ordram, I am Ordram." All the friends muttered to each other in excitement at meeting this wondrous being. "I do believe you've brought me something?"

"Oh, er yes," said Rose as she unclasped the chain which had held the golden leaf around her neck. She stepped forward slightly and offered it to him in the palm of her hand. Like one of his own arms, a large root broke free from the ceiling and dangled down in front of Rose, scooped the locket into its grasp and held it in front of Ordram's eyes. The old man stared closely at the leaf locket as if it brought back many memories.

"I never thought I'd see this again," his voice was gruff but he smiled at the leaf and his guests. "Forgive me, you must be weary, here take a seat and I'll get you something to eat and drink while we talk."

Some chairs appeared up through the wooden floor for Rose and her friends to sit on. The roots above then twisted around for a while before handing them some bowls of stew and bread rolls and hot refreshing beverages. They were very hungry and started to tuck into the food with thanks and appreciation. While they were eating, Ordram admired the golden leaf while he waited for them to satisfy their hunger. The friends chatted quietly amongst themselves, Rose wanted to know what had happened to Furdon and Fiddy. They in turn wanted to know what happened on the boat while they slept through everything. Once they had finished eating, the roots dropped down and removed their plates, whisking them up and out of site through the ceiling.

"Do you know why you're here Rose?" asked Ordram.

"I only know it's something to do with that locket," she said pointing to the leaf.

"Indeed it is my dear girl," he smiled "I made this leaf a very, very long time ago for a dear friend of mine. He was the King of Cragfeld and he wanted something special for his daughters…"

"I didn't steal it, I promise."

"Why would I think you'd stolen it?" he laughed.

"The Fairies in the woods seemed to think I did, they said only a Queen or Royalty would have an Ordram's leaf."

"Yes, that's true," he said "I only ever made two and gave these to the King, for his daughters Rika and Mordisan."

"Mordisan? The Ice Queen?" asked Rose.

"Yes, the very same. As soon as I saw what Mordisan had turned into I had to try and get them back because they're full of my magic. The old witch, Orme took Mordisan's golden locket and forced it open so she could use it in her curses and magic, she crushed it, flattened it and burned it so she could try to tap into my powers and to be able to see into the future. Fortunately her magic was never able to do this but I knew when she was trying to use it and would show her what she wanted to see."

"And what happened to Rika's locket?" asked Victor.

"I have it here in front of me now," said Ordram.

"But the Ice Queen froze Rika in a tomb of ice, how did it leave her and finds its way to Rose?" asked Victor.

"Haven't you worked it out?" said Ordram "You've been given a lot of clues since you started your journey. With this leaf here I've been able to listen to every word you've heard or spoken since you entered Ordraskop." They all looked at each other with confusion. "The reason Mordisan and Orme couldn't see you in their foresight was partly because of this magical golden locket and also, you don't have simple human blood running through your veins. They can only see human blood clearly, it can't be disguised at all. Because of this… you climbed the mountain to the Grocklings cavern without being detected, even the Silvertips could smell that you don't have simple human blood."

"What do you mean I've not got human blood running through my veins, of course I have."

"Rose, you've never felt as if you fitted in on Cragfeld have you? The Ice Queen's spells never seemed to work on you did they?"

"No, but…"

"But what Rose?" he leaned forward. "You grew up in the same house as your friend Amber, whose parents kindly took you in? Is that right? Well I'm afraid this isn't the full story."

"What? I think I know my own childhood…"

"Or so we let you believe."

Rose and her friends were perplexed and trying to make sense of what Ordram was saying. Rose was Rose and she grew up on Cragfeld, how could it be any different.

"What do you mean…?" Rose felt nervous. She did not know what Ordram was talking about but did not dare doubt him because he was the great Ordram.

"You, my dear Rose… are Rika!"

Silence fell on the room.

"I beg your pardon," muttered Rose "I'm Rose… Rika is Mordisan's sister, frozen in a tomb in the Dark Castle. She was a young lady when her sister did that to her. I have memories of my childhood, growing up in the villages of Cragfeld. You are mistaken."

"Are you sure about that?" said Ordram, he had a stern look in his gentle face. "You are Rika, there's no doubt about it."

"Okay, hold on" said Victor, "How can Rose be Rika, please explain because I'm not following."

"Ah yes Victor," said Ordram "You ran away from Cragfeld didn't you? You have had sorrow and the loss of your loved ones, for one hundred and fifty years haven't you?" Victor nodded. "If you don't mind, I'll come to you in a moment. First I must help Rose to understand, she needs to hear the truth. Rose, I'm afraid you've been under a spell for the last one hundred and fifty years. You've been under one of Bolstone's spells, not one of Mordisan's. She had such rage and jealousy of her own sister that she turned her to ice, this we all know it true." They all nodded. "Bolstone interrupted this spell and extracted most of Rika's life-source from her body before Mordisan could complete the curse. Bolstone brought me Rika's life-source and we created you, a place where Rika would be safe until the day we could unite you with the rest of your body and soul again. You don't have simple human blood, you have Royal blood."

Rose's eyes glazed over, all she had ever known had been a false truth. Her childhood and been a memory created by Ordram who had blocked out her real history. A small portion of Rika's life had remained in her body. Rose thought back to her hallucinations in the woodlands when she had had vivid images of the Ice Queen scowling at her, this was what her other self was seeing and Rose could see this when they were reconnecting with each other.

"So… I'm not me, I'm not Rose? I have no idea who I am then."

"I know this is a shock and a lot to take in," said Ordram kindly "But what you are today, standing there in front of me is who you are… You are strong and determined and won't let anything stand in your way, you've proved that over the last few days. You have wonderful friends by your side. As soon as you're reunited with your other self, everything will feel clear again."

Victor was in shock himself and could see confusion running through Rose, he put his arms around her to comfort her. Furdon and Fiddy did not know what to say. They had been in the company of a Princess for over a week. Gwennol flew over to Rose, she knew something about her was different when she had first met her in the woodland.

"So, my whole life has been a lie…?" she said.

"No, no, not at all. When you're reunited with your other self then you'll still be you, the strong determined person I see before me. But you'll feel complete again, as if you know yourself better than you've ever known yourself. All of your questions will suddenly be answered and everything will have meaning and make sense. I'm sure over the last few days you've been aware of your other self?"

Rose thought back and realised what Ordram was talking about. She had first seen herself as another person though the gap in the wall they had walked next to after Troostan had dropped them at the edge of Grimdell Forest. She saw her again at the edge of the woodland after her hallucinations, and again standing on the port as they sailed away from the town. This was the other part of her, whose body was frozen but whose consciousness was alive and aware of Rose. Ordram then explain that Rika, frozen in the Dark Castle will have been dreaming about what life Rose had been living. When the two were connected again then they would feel like one complete soul, not like two separate people. Over the next few minutes Rose thought back over all of the life she had been aware of. What Ordram was saying was gradually sinking in but she was in total shock.

"Ordram, why did you wait until now for all of this?" she asked "Why not call me and your leaf to you sooner?"

"I couldn't bring my leaf home alone," smiled Ordram "Only you could do that. Only when you were ready and the stars were properly aligned would you feel it was time. Only you can destroy Mordisan. Up until now you haven't been ready."

"But I thought you were the most powerful and magic being? Couldn't you have destroyed her long ago?"

"I could have done many things to her," said Ordram. "I could have done the same to her as what she did to you, I could have imprisoned her, even tortured her but she would constantly be fighting back. Only with your blood and my powers can her powers be destroyed."

The small group of friends huddled around Rose as this shocking truth was revealed. None of them could really believe it but they knew it had to be true. Ordram was a powerful being and he would not lie to them.

"If what you're saying is true, then why didn't Mordisan recognise me as her sister in all these years?"

"She wasn't looking for you was she? As far as she was concerned she had you frozen and held in the tallest tower of the Dark Castle. We did change your appearance to her, but to the rest of the world you still look like you. In turn you wouldn't have given her any reason to question who you were." Ordram's eyes moved from Rose to Victor, "However I thought you might recognise her?"

"Me?" said Victor "Why would I recognise her?"

"You knew something was unusual about this girl when you met her, something drew you to her didn't it?" Victor blushed. "There's no need to be shy young man. You two actually know each other very well, you have danced with each other many times."

"But if you excuse me," said Victor "I only met Rose three nights ago."

"This isn't Rose, remember?" said Ordram.

"What am I supposed to remember?"

"Oh dear," said Ordram in a deep gruffly voice "It seems you've tried to block out your memories of Cragfeld, which is a shame because you were happy there for a time. Only when Mordisan became the Ice Queen did your life seem to shatter and fall to pieces. Come here young man, let me help you see."

Ordram held out his hand to Victor who cautiously and nervously walked over to him. Ordram used one of the roots on the ceiling to push up through the tree and bring back a large golden leaf to give to Victor. Ordram told him to take a bite of the leaf, just one corner and then look into the reflection on the leaf. Victor looked back at Rose who was still befuddled but encouraged him to do as Ordram said. He took a bite of the golden leaf and was surprised when it tasted sweet. He then looked into the leaf and could slowly see a picture forming. There were people dancing in the great ballroom of the Dark Castle, laughter and joy filled the room. His eyes were then drawn to a young couple dancing in the centre of the picture, this was Rika and her Prince. They swayed and moved and looked happy together. Then as if a heavy fog had been lifted, Victor's memory came flooding back and he turned to look at Rose.

"Rika? This is us…" he said becoming emotional. "This is you and me dancing in the ballroom. I knew there was something familiar about you when we met the other night."

"Rose, come here," said Ordram "Will you please do the same? Take a bite of the leaf and then tell us what you see?"

Rose got to her feet and moved over to stand next to Victor. She tore a piece of the golden leaf and ate it, she thought it tasted like honey. When she looked into the reflection of Ordram's leaf she could see herself as Rika on the balcony of the Dark Castle with a young man who looked just like Victor. They looked very much in love and seemed very happy. However, in the background she could see the dark shadow that was her sister. Mordisan was waiting in the shadows for the perfect time to strike her sister down. Just as this was about to happen Ordram blocked the picture and said it wasn't necessary to see everything as it would be too upsetting for everyone. Rose turned to look at Victor.

"Vecter?" she whispered.

"Rika!" he smiled.

It was as if they'd been transported back all those years to the time when they were standing on the balcony, holding each other and feeling utterly happy. Only now, at this point did they recognise each other. Ordram brought them back to the present.

"Now, do you see?" he said. "Victor, you are in fact Prince Vecter! Mordisan hated how happy you two were so she cast a spell on you to forget Rika so that you'd never even contemplate going back to Cragfeld to save her."

Furdon and Fiddy, Gwennol and Hullard were all mesmerised as the story unfolded piece by piece. They couldn't believe what they were hearing but could also see it was all true. They could see Rose and Victor change in appearance for just a few seconds into Rika and Vecter as they realised who they were.

Rose felt her heart start beating, as if she had been half dead all her life up until this point. She felt heat running through her veins as she looked at Vecter, into the eyes of the man she had once found and lost. Victor too suddenly felt alive as he looked at Rika, he had lost her for many years because of the Ice Queen, he was not prepared to do that again. It was as if time had stood still for them and would only start ticking again when they found each other.

"Do you see?" said Ordram "Now can you see who you both really are?" They both smiled as the realisation was no longer a shock but actually felt as if it were supposed to happen.

Fiddy jumped off his chair with joy and ran over to Rose and Victor, bouncing up to them and hugging them both. Furdon was also feeling a rush of excitement but disguised it well with a cooler exterior.

"I felt that I knew you from somewhere!" said Furdon "I think you and I've shared many a conversation in the past." Victor bent down to the Grockling.

"Yes, you know what Furdon, I believe we were good friends long ago." They smiled and hugged each other as if long-lost friends had been reunited.

Ordram looked on and smiled at the scene in front of him. He knew it would be a lot of news for them to process and had to show them the truth in the easiest way possible for them to understand. Only when Rose had come to Ordram with the golden locket would they have the right ingredients to attack the Ice Queen and the old witch. Rose had to do this journey to Ordram to realise how strong she actually was and that she could take on things that she had never even dreamed of. Ordram now only needed a strand of hair from Rose to be able to create something that would stand up to the Ice Queen's powers. Rose had found the fight deep inside her over the last week or so, she had found her inner warrior. Looking back, she would not have recognised herself as the lonely girl sitting on the ledge at the bottom of the mountains of Cragfeld. She now had friends and a zest for life. After finding out who she was and what her sister had done to her, she felt an anger within her heart towards Mordisan. Rose would do whatever it took to get her revenge on her sister who had cost her one hundred and fifty years of life and happiness.

"You must get some rest," said Ordram as he got up from his wooden throne and walked around the edge of the room, still blending into the wall. "Not only have you had a long journey but also a lot of information to take in. Please don't think about your revenge on Mordisan, it's too negative a thought to let into your mind. Rather think of freeing Cragfeld from her grasp. We have a long and busy day tomorrow my friends. Get some rest." And with that, Ordram vanished into the wall and it was as if he was never there.

The door from which they had entered opened but instead of the spiral staircase which they had come down on, there was a corridor with some steps at the other end. The six friends walked along this corridor, Fiddy was nudging Furdon as he noticed Rose and Victor holding hands. Gwennol flew ahead whilst Hullard bounded after them, lagging behind at the back. When they reached the bottom of the stairs they noticed them flashing all different colours, soft pinks to bright blues, pastel purples to vibrant yellows. Gwennol flew up the flight of stairs which seemed to go on and on and on. When she came back down she told them there was another large wooden doorway at the top. As they walked up the stairs each step played a beautiful little tune as they trod on them. Fiddy was running up and down them like a child, trying to make them play faster. Hullard was frustrated because he was too light in weight to get much of a tune out of the steps so he whistled at them instead and they echoed back his tune. Rose and Victor smiled at their friends, it was good to see them relaxing after a strenuous journey.

At the top of the staircase the large wooden door slowly opened itself. On the other side of the door was a room with stone walls, a large wooden table and six beds. Two large beds were for Rose and Victor, two small beds were for Furdon and Fiddy, and the two tiny beds were for Hullard and Gwennol. The room was well lit and had lanterns hanging from the walls. On one side of the room, wide open windows looked out over the sea and let a cool night breeze waft around the room. A fireplace in a huge stone hearth came to life as soon as they entered, a sweet scent of honeysuckle was coming from outside.

"We must be in the fort that we saw when we got here," said Victor.

"Yes, must be," agreed Rose, taking a seat in a big armchair that squished around her.

Fiddy and Furdon ran over to the windows and looked out at the magnificent views.

"Oh look Miss Rose," said Furdon "the ocean looks so calm and I think I can just see Drakenstop far, far over there."

"I can see things swimming down there," said Fiddy "Huge beasts breaking the ocean surface as they go."

The two Grocklings had never seen anything as beautiful and enjoyed the sweet scent of the flowers swaying by the windows. They enjoyed the view for quite a while before turning back into the room to settle down by the fire with their friends. The table in the middle of the room began to shake on the spot, very gently until it was laden with a feast. There was a roast turkey taking centre stage of the display and a wide selection of perfectly cut and cooked vegetables. Salads with fresh ripe tomatoes were like jewels around the other bowls of goodies. Ice cream sundaes covered in chocolate, vanilla and strawberry sat at the edge of the table. No matter how long the feast sat there, the hot food stayed hot, the cold food stayed cold and the ice creams did not even melt a drop. Fiddy was always hungry and did not hesitate about diving into it, fitting as much as he could fit into his mouth. Hullard was not far behind him. They ate and ate until they could not find space in their bellies for anymore. In fact they rather over-did things and had to go and lie down for a while to let it all settle. Furdon rolled his eyes in disgust at his friend, there was no need to be so greedy. He jumped onto Rose's lap and got comfortable next to her. Victor went over to the table and picked up three glasses of ale which had a beautiful creamy head inviting them to taste. Victor handed one to Rose and Furdon before taking a seat in the armchair opposite Rose. They sipped their ale and stared into the fire, thinking about everything Ordram had just told them.

"Here's to new friends being old friends," said Furdon as he raised his glass.

"Yes, strangely a perfect toast," said Victor clinking their glasses.

"Who would've thought?!" said Rose "I still can't get my head around it all, it's unbelievable. How can I be Rika? I don't feel any different."

"What were you expecting?" smiled Victor "To suddenly

feel like a Princess?"

"Maybe? I don't know," she smiled back and looked into his eyes.

"I can't believe after all these years…" said Victor, he leaned forward and took her hand, holding it tightly within his.

"I can't believe you didn't recognise each other," laughed Furdon. "But I knew I recognised Victor's face, I knew it, I knew it, I knew it!"

"Indeed my old friend," smiled Victor "I also had a feeling that we'd met before, but knew it couldn't have been possible."

"Seems anything is possible," said Rose, sipping on her drink.

"But now we know why we came here," said Furdon "Now we know what it was all for. You are going to help try and free Cragfeld, isn't that an incredible thought. After all these years the sun might shine on it again, melt the ice in the Dark Castle and have the sound of laughter dancing through the streets."

"It would be a wonderful thing to see," said Rose. "I wonder what Ordram is planning, surely we can't just waltz in there and take back what she took."

"No, it would never be that simple," said Victor. "Ordram and Bolstone will have known this time would come eventually and I suppose be getting everything ready into place."

"What 'everything'?"

"I don't know, magic, armies, who really knows…? We'll know sooner or later."

Gwennol flew over to the window sill and sat quietly watching the sea sparkling in the moonlight far below. She was an exhausted little Fairy. She couldn't believe how she and Hullard had hidden away in Rose's cloak, how things would have been different for them both had they stayed in the woodland like they were supposed to. Now rather than having petty squabbles with the other Fairies, she was friends with a Princess and would do all she could to keep her safe. Whatever Ordram had planned would not be an easy task for Rose and she needed all of her friends to support and encourage her through the days ahead. She flew over to the table and grabbed a couple of pink grapes before curling up on her bed for a rest.

Furdon finished his ale, it had warmed him through and completely relaxed him. The three new old friends chatted for a while. Rose and Victor told Furdon about all of the sea creatures they had come across while he and Fiddy were sound asleep. He realised the mermaids had not been very nice to his friends but would always be grateful to them for saving him and Fiddy from the deep dark waters. Victor said how he thought the mermaids had taken his friends and had come back for him… but actually they came to help. It must have been Ordram's leaf keeping them all from harm as he was calling it home.

Rose looked down and saw Furdon had dozed off. She smiled at him as he slept and gently scooped him into her arms, carrying him carefully over to his bed. He sank into the sheets and she covered him with a blanket. She looked at all of her friends as they were snuggled up in bed, sound asleep. She smiled at them and gave each of them a kiss on the forehead. Rose was grateful to have such good friends, the journey would not have been the same adventure without them. She turned around and saw Victor had moved over to the window and was leaning on his arms as he looked out. Rose softly walked over to him, it was as if she knew him really well but not at all. Like they knew who and what they were to each other but as if they were learning it all over again. She reached out and took his hand. Victor took her hand and put his other arm around her shoulders. It was as if they had done this everyday for the last one hundred and fifty years but also strange that they had not done this at all. Rose and Victor felt a sensation of calm as they stood together and looked out of the window at the view. She was his Princess, he was her Prince… they knew this. Rose and Victor were very slowly getting used to reconnecting with Rika and Vecter.

CHAPTER FOURTEEN

The Ice Queen's army of creatures was growing bigger and nastier by the day. Orme was in charge of feeding them and seeing to it that they had a taste for mankind. The Ice Queen would look in on her creations several times a day, hour by hour they grew bigger and stronger. Black snakes slithered around the room, Winged Goblins sprang along the rafters and snarling hounds the size of elephants would get into fights numerous times a day. They would be encouraged to fight, it would make them stronger and not be able to feel pain. Wounds were never bad, they could not kill each other even if they tried because they were all made with the same poison and blood. Cuts and bites would heal up in a matter of minutes. These creatures were made for fighting and nothing would be able to get in their way.

Orme still had the young woman hidden in her little den at the bottom of the Dark Castle. The old witch had kept her word and brought her back to health, in exchange for a few drops of blood a day so she could create a food potion for the army. This had been kept a secret from the Ice Queen, she did not have a heart and saw no reason in saving someone who she had used and was now redundant. In fact the Ice Queen would often disguise herself as a villager and mingle with the crowds, carefully selecting the weak and useless who would be no good to her but they would make food for her army. She would lure them closer, looking like a beautiful woman who had been hurt. As soon as the man or woman was close enough and offering help, she would stab them with her dagger of ice and whisk them back to the Dark Castle for her creatures to play with. Orme hated seeing this but knew it best not to argue with the Ice Queen. The old witch would not be able to save them but as soon as she saw that another person had been brought in, she whispered a spell which would ease their pain and suffering. Of course the Ice Queen knew what Orme was doing but didn't argue with her, in a way they were both getting what they wanted. The ultimate goal was to grow a strong army and everything they were doing was working to plan.

Howls, hisses and screeches echoed from the frozen ballroom all around the Dark Castle. They were blood-curdling sounds. It was like the calls of death were booming through the corridors. The Ice Queen loved to hear these sounds, it reminded her of her actual strength. She was feeling more powerful every day, every minute. Any army who would try to take what was hers would be in for a painful reality as they stepped onto Cragfeld. Her dark army would strike down any threat and would not fall at any mans sword. The Ice Queen was feeling pleased with herself.

The Ice Queen had summoned her winged wardens who guarded the mountains to tell them what to look out for. They all flew down from their posts like bats of the night, hissing and snarling as they gathered. Their bodies were covered in a thick matted black fur and they had large horns protruding from their scalps. They were ugly-looking things but were very protective and had been loyal to the Ice Queen. She had seen a picture of her father, the only significant thing this could mean is that he was bringing an army to claim what was his. Even though she was his daughter, she did not know what he would do. After what she'd done to Cragfeld, her sister and the family – he might feel nothing for her and try with all his might to kill her. The winged wardens were told to watch the seas and look out for any ships that may bring an army to fight them. She reassured them that their army was the deadliest force and would defend the Ice Queen and the Dark Castle against whatever fool tried to attack them. The winged wardens sneered and laughed before bowing to their Queen and taking flight back up to the mountain tops.

The Ice Queen was feeling indestructible and full of power and rage. How anyone would ever dare threaten her was a ridiculous thought, especially her own father who was old and weak. She thought it was pathetic. She strode down the corridors of the Dark Castle, icicles formed on the ceilings wherever she walked and snowflakes drifted behind her. Her white gown seemed to be brighter and more encrusted with ice crystals than ever before and it trailed behind her longer than before. Her thick long red hair draped around her shoulders like a scarf of blood beneath her crown of ice. She walked powerfully down to the ballroom to take another look at her army. The howls and screeches could be heard for miles around but to her it was like sweet music to her ears.

When she opened the door the army gathered around her. Snakes effortlessly moved across the room and out of corners to wrap themselves around her ankles. The flying goblins would jump and scream uncontrollably in the beams above her head. The bulls and the hounds all came up to her for attention. As they growled, drool would gather in their mouths and drip onto the floor like a toxic poison, it would freeze immediately on touching the frozen floor. As vile as these creatures were, they knew what they were to do and who they were to protect. Their eyes were full of eagerness to fight and they were chomping at the bit for the time they could run out into Cragfeld and destroy the enemy. The Ice Queen was very pleased, very pleased indeed at what she saw before her.

Orme scuttled around the Dark Castle as she was busy with potions and planning. She was ready for whatever they would face. Orme was not actually interested in any army who would attack them, they were just a glitch to her as she knew she would be able to crush them with or without the help from the Ice Queen or her army. It was Bolstone who she was interested in and she had made it her task to get rid of the blundering fool once and for all. She was tired of him thinking he was better than she was. She had been in her den stirring, creating and practicing her magic ready for facing the old wizard. As always she muttered away to herself as she went about her business and was actually liking having a bit of company in her den. The young woman was terrified of being in the Dark Castle but the old witch seemed to make it sound better than being freed back into the villages. A lot of people who went into the Dark Castle were rarely seen again and completely forgotten about. She realised as long as she was with the old witch then the Ice Queen could no longer hurt her or drain her blood. Orme muttered to herself more than her companion so she had learned to stay still and quiet and hopefully everyone would forget she was there. Neither of them even noticed the little black crystal on the hearth, it actually looked like a speck of soot and was easily looked over. The old witch was muttering her plans and thinking out loud, without a shred of idea that Bolstone was listening in.

Hullard was the first to wake from a very deep sleep, he felt refreshed and full of life and energy. He sat up and stretched out his arms while he yawned, having not slept so well for a long time. As he looked around he saw all of his friends still sleeping even though the sun was blazing through the windows. The table on which the previous night's feast was laid was now covered in a vast variety of breakfast goodies, bacon, sausages, eggs, tomatoes, fried mushrooms, breads, jams and pastries. The delicious smell had woken him up and he soon bounced off the bed and jumped onto Fiddy, his eating companion. Fiddy took a while to wake up and tried to shove Hullard off the bed as if he was being bothered by a fly. Hullard persisted and began whispering into his ear what tasty food they could be scoffing for breakfast. Fiddy's ears pricked up and then his nose began to twitch as he too could smell the bacon and sausages. Fiddy sat straight up and jumped to his feet, knocking Hullard out of his way as he went to see what was smelling so good. The rattle of plates and bowls soon woke the others who looked over to see Fiddy spoilt for choice and not knowing where to start. His eyes were fixed on the table in front of him and his mouth was watering with eagerness of tasting this breakfast. The others were sitting up in their beds and watching Fiddy's dilemma as he couldn't fit everything onto his plate. Rose had also slept incredibly well despite the evening of surprising revelations, she felt safe now they had made it to Ordram. They eventually joined Fiddy at the breakfast table, before he tried to eat everything in front on him.

"I don't think I've ever slept that well," said Rose.

"Me too," they all agreed in unison.

"There's something about this place…" she continued.

"It's magical isn't it?" said Furdon "Just how Frithad and Eady had described."

"Yes, it's certainly magical," smiled Rose.

Victor poured out some glasses of fruit juice for each of them and took a seat next to Rose.

"I wonder what today has in store?" he said.

"I hope nothing as out of the blue as last night," said Rose "I don't think I could take anymore news like that. Furdon, you're not secretly a King are you? Fiddy, you're not secretly a Prince?"

"Prince Greedyguts," laughed Furdon at Fiddy.

"Huh? me?" said Fiddy with a mouth full of sausages as he

paid no attention to the rest of them.

Gwennol daintily sat on a strawberry cupcake and dipped her finger into the pink icing. She had never tasted anything so sweet and creamy before as the blast of strawberry flavours tickled her tongue. Her wings fluttered with enjoyment and sprinkles of fairy dust fell from her dress as she was in taste heaven.

Once they had all had breakfast, the table wobbled again on the spot and all of the breakfast foods disappeared. Fiddy made one last grab for a jam-filled pastry but was too late as he disappointedly grabbed hold of thin air. The friends then moved away from the table as it folded itself flat and moved out of the way to the edge of the room. The rug on which the table had been placed began to twitch at the corners. Victor looked around at his friends and then took hold of the rug by the corner and flipped it out of the way. There underneath the rug was a round wooden door, like a trapdoor and presumably covered a round hole. The wooden doorway lifted up on its gold hinges by itself and opened outwards until they could see what it was covering. There appeared to be a golden wooden helter-skelter slide which spiralled back down into the centre of Ordram.

"You can go first," said Fiddy to Rose "We'll be right behind you."

"Oh Fiddy come on," said Furdon "We're all in this together aren't we? Miss Rose, if you step down the hole and sit down, allow me to join you?"

"Of course Furdon," said Rose as she stepped through the trapdoor and took a seat at the top of the slide. Furdon then jumped onto her lap. Rose shuffled forwards and then whoosh, they slid down the slide and out of sight.

Victor was next. He stepped down to the slide and waited while Fiddy jumped onto his lap and then Hullard and Gwennol right next to Fiddy. Victor shuffled forward and then slid down this golden tunnel behind Rose and Furdon.

They all landed in a pile at the bottom.

"Very graceful," laughed Rose as she straightened her dress.

They were now somewhere similar to where they had been before in the heart of Ordram. This empty wooden room was larger than where they had been previously but still had Ordram's roots tangled around each other on the ceiling. There was the familiar rumbling noise coming from within the walls as Ordram made his way to them. However, before Ordram appeared to them in the walls, they heard a voice above them at the top of the slide which they had all just slid down. "Woohoo," said this voice from the top of the slide. Only moments later an orange lump landed in a pile at the bottom of the slide where they were standing. There was muttering coming from within the ball of orange material and Victor went to help whatever was tangled up in itself. There was Bolstone looking rather flustered as he rearranged his orange cloak so it hung more comfortably from his shoulders.

"Bolstone," they cheered, pleased to see him.

"Yes, yes, it's me," he grumbled, still displeased at his rather inelegant entrance.

"Don't worry," smiled Victor pointing up the slide, "It did the same thing to me!"

"Yes, yes, well I don't remember it being quite that steep before," he said.

"It's good to see you Bolstone," said Rose. "These are our friends Victor, Hullard and Gwennol."

"Right, nice to meet you all," said Bolstone. "See Rose, I told you how well you were doing didn't I when I last saw you. Now look at you, here in Ordram."

"Bolstone, why didn't you tell me?"

"Tell you what?" he said innocently.

"Why didn't you tell me who I was or what you'd done?"

"Would you have believed me?" he smiled "When I saw

you, you didn't need to know, it would've distracted you from getting here wouldn't it. So I thought it best to pretend that I'd never seen you before and let Ordram break the news."

"But you saved me," smiled Rose "Thank you."

"Oh any old wizard would've done the same," he said modestly.

There was a rumble in the walls as Ordram appeared in front of them. He was standing in the wall like a beautifully carved statue, looking out at his guests and at Bolstone.

"Glad you could make it," said Ordram to Bolstone "I would ask what kept you but think I know the answer to that already."

"Yes, yes, that's right Ordram, busy, busy, busy."

"What with?" whispered Victor

"Never you mind," frowned Bolstone.

"Here we are at last," said Ordram "What was created has come forward and what created them has come forward. Tell me Bolstone, what news do you have from the Dark Castle?"

"Ordram, I have good news and I have bad news. On the plus side, I've been listening in to what the Ice Queen and old witch have been planning. On the down side they've been making a deadly army of vile animals."

"Do you know how many?" asked Ordram.

"From what I can make out there must be two or three hundred creatures. She's feeding them human blood and they have a taste for it, so they can't be killed by mankind."

"Typical…" huffed Ordram.

"I've also been to see the King and he's preparing his troops to join us."

"Ah that's good."

"The King?" interrupted Rose "What King?"

Ordram and Bolstone exchanged glances and weren't really sure how to respond.

"The King of Cragfeld of course," said Ordram finally.

"What King of Cragfeld? Is he something to do with the Ice Queen?"

"Yes my dear, he's her father."

"Her father? My father?"

"Yes Rose, Rika."

"But, you mean... he's alive?"

"He's alive," smiled Ordram "But very old and weak."

Victor put his arm around Rose. She'd always thought she was an orphan so to find out she had a father was quite overwhelming and emotional for her.

"Does he know about me?" she asked.

"No, not yet," said Bolstone "But you will see him again when you are at full strength."

"You mean when I'm reunited with what's left of me in the Dark Castle?"

"Yes, yes, exactly," Bolstone smiled at her comfortingly.

"When will that be?" asked Victor.

"Sooner than you think," said Ordram "As soon as we are ready, we have no time to waste."

"Can we help?" asked Fiddy keenly.

"Of course you can," said Ordram "We're going to need as much help as we can get."

Fiddy was giddy at the thought of being part of such an important gathering.

"What can we do? what can we do?"

"Keep calm and quiet for now," said Ordram "It's Rose who we need first, the rest of you will have to be by her side as we face Cragfeld together." Ordram walked around the wall and came to Rose, holding the golden locket which she had carried. "Thank you for returning the locket my dear, it was in perfect condition. I just need one thing from you to turn this into something incredible, all I ask is for one hair from your head."

"Is that all?" she sounded surprised as she plucked a hair

from her scalp. "You said yesterday that only with my blood and your powers could we face the Ice Queen?"

"I didn't mean it literally," laughed Ordram. "Your hair has the same basic formula as your blood which has the same formula as Mordisan's blood… this will be her antidote." He curled the hair around his fingers into a neat little ball and placed it in the back of the locket. Rose had never been able to open the locket, only Ordram could do that.

The locket glimmered with reds and greens as soon as the hair had been sealed inside it. Ordram then held out his hand and the leafed locket floated into the middle of the room in front on them and began to spin around and around, faster and faster. It was like a golden globe spinning for a few minutes until it stopped as quickly as it started and fell into Rose's open palm. She looked down and saw that the open leaf had been folded back into the locket. It didn't look the same as it used to, rather than a simple oval shape with engraved shell, it was now round with a spiky gold case. It was a stunning thing to behold. Bolstone took it from her hand and fastened it around her neck.

"What do I do with this?" she asked.

"Keep it safe until you need it," said Ordram. He placed his hand on her shoulder and smiled at her, he knew she was tougher than she thought and would know exactly what to do with the locket when the time came.

"Sorry to be a party pooper," said Furdon "But how do you expect us to re-enter Cragfeld without the Ice Queen, her witch, the winged wardens or any of her other spies seeing us or sniffing us out?"

"A fair question," said Bolstone "It won't be easy but they won't be looking everywhere all of the time. They won't even notice you and Fiddy, you're mountain dwellers so can slip under the radar with the rest of your colony."

"The rest of the colony?"

"Yes, I've been to see Frithad and Eady to tell them of the situation," said Bolstone. "They'll do all they can to help us." The two Grocklings looked pleased with themselves and knew their friends would back them up.

"What about us three?" asked Hullard. "The Ice Queen will know as soon as a Fairy, a Pixie and a man have stepped foot in her Kingdom."

"Which is why you won't be setting a foot in her Kingdom," smiled Bolstone.

"But we want to help Rose," he said.

"And you will… but you'll be flying in on Dragons. Rose, that's why you saw me at Drakenstop with Blackfall when you did."

"Ahhh, right," she said "Blackfall terrified us three!"

"I hope he and his troop have the same effect on Cragfeld," said Bolstone.

"And what about my father and his army, she'll be able to smell then coming for miles won't she? And this army she's created are thirsty for human blood but cannot be killed by any man… it sounds like they are all walking straight to their deaths without a fighting chance?"

"It does seem that way," said Ordram "But things never go as you'd expect them to. There is more good teaming together than Mordisan would ever expect. Her dark army may be strong but we are stronger." None of the six friends were convinced.

"So…" said Victor "What do we do now?"

"We plan," said Ordram "We plan how we're going to get to Cragfeld, plan how we approach and plan how we fight the army to get to her. The goal is to get the frozen Rika from her tomb and safely away from the Dark Castle. The Ice Queen mustn't know you're doing this, you need to keep her distracted… and Orme too, she will no doubt be on the look-out for you."

"Aren't you coming with us?" asked Victor.

"No, no young man I'm not, I can't leave this place… but I'll be there in spirit. Bolstone will be there with you."

"And don't worry about the old witch," said Bolstone "She and I have an old score to settle so I'll keep her distracted while you climb the tall tower for Rika's tomb… I suggest Victor does this while Rose keeps the Ice Queen busy and can get close enough to… to do what she needs to do."

"Agreed," said Ordram in a bold voice.

"Well… er, are we all supposed to just go along with this?" said Fiddy.

"Do you have any better ideas?" said Furdon.

"Not right this minute, no…"

"Then keep quiet. Ordram's leaf got us here safely didn't it?"

"Umm Yes…"

"Then Ordram's leaf will keep us safe, won't it?"

"I suppose so…" huffed Fiddy.

Ordram smiled at Furdon's encouragement and could see he would be the one for keeping their spirits high when their moods were low.

"When will all this be happening?" asked Rose in a quiet voice.

"As soon as we're ready," said Ordram "Maybe today if Bolstone can confirm Blackfall and the King's army are ready." Ordram could see Rose and her friends were nervous and apprehensive. "I understand a lot is being asked of you, you're being asked to do things you've never done before, things you never thought you'd do. But believe me, we are all fighting for the freedom of Cragfeld and for the Ice Queen to lose her crown and her throne. Keep reminding yourself of the ultimate goal and nothing will stand in your way."

The six friends looked at one another, they knew what they were being told and knew what they had to do but it was still a daunting mission. Nobody ever wanted to see the Ice

Queen let alone make a mission to go straight to her.

Ordram and Bolstone were both incredibly powerful and as they were joining forces... this meant a formidable strength between them. They knew the young group of friends had no knowledge or experience of war but ultimately believed they would have to overpower the Ice Queen and her army. The time had come, the stars were lining up and their Rose had come forward. The newly made locket from Ordram's leaf now held incredible magic as it contained Rose's DNA and Ordram's power, if it fell into the wrong hands it could cause destruction on a massive scale. Bolstone and Ordram had to put all their trust in Rose.

"Excuse me," said Gwennol "Please don't think I'm being disrespectful but it seems you're sending us all in unarmed, how are we supposed to look after ourselves, defend ourselves from the Ice Queen and the old witch?"

"That's a good point..." said Hullard and Fiddy nodding together.

"Ordram won't see you struggle," said Bolstone "But here are my gifts to you. Now let me see, I'm sure they were in this pocket... or maybe this pocket, ah here we are." He pulled out five orange marbles. "Do these look familiar? Yes, yes of course they do, don't they. Well here you are, one each, apart from Furdon – you still have the one I gave you when I first met you don't you?" Furdon nodded proudly at not using his yet. "Good, good, that's marvellous. And Rose, you still have the one for Orme don't you? Whether you see me with her or not, use that marble won't you? Yes, yes, jolly good. You of course get a new one for yourself. Right then, these new marbles aren't quite the same as the last ones, you won't be able to call for me to help you because I'll already be there fighting with you. Each of these marbles will turn into the weapon of your choice as and when you need it. Be careful though as you can only use them once, you can't go changing your mind once you've made your decision of what you want. Yes, yes, there you go. Lovely." They each took their marble held them tightly in their hands. The ones for Hullard and Gwennol immediately shrunk in size to fit in their tiny palms, otherwise they would not have been able to carry them.

"Well presented," said Ordram, looking at each of them from under his bushy eyebrows and stroking his beard. "Rose, you must be careful with the locket as it is now a precious and powerful device, keep it hidden until it is time to use it. Bolstone has kindly given you each a weapon of your choice, I however will provide you each with one of my golden leaves." With his roots he brought down a small golden leaf for each of them from his branches. "With these you can make one wish to help you with the tasks ahead... You could wish for invisibility, to be able to jump high as if flying, to be able to disguise yourself, or to be able to throw your voices to make it sound as if you're in a different room. Again like Bolstone's marbles, you'll only be able to use them once and make one wish. So choose wisely... when you've made your wish, eat the leaf and see your wish come true. I can help you this way." The roots handed each of them a golden leaf.

"Thank you," said Victor as he folded the leaf and put it in his pocket. They were all grateful for as much help as they could get.

Rose was putting on a brave face but was actually feeling terrified. She had found a good group of friends and had been happier in the last few days than she could ever remember. She would have been quite happy staying with Ordram forever, it was calm, peaceful and safe. Why would she want to go to war, it was not in her nature to fight. It was however in her nature to stand up for what was right, she knew it was the right thing to help Cragfeld and its people, whatever that entailed.

The Grocklings had never been to war or fought in any

battle but the fact that they were about to go to one didn't seem to faze them. Of course they would rather be relaxing with their friends with good food and drink but they were also stubbornly loyal and would stand by their friends through the good times and the bad. Furdon and Fiddy had never liked the Ice Queen for what she had done and were actually looking forward to giving her a taste of her own medicine. They had grown used to Cragfeld being a miserable place and would much rather have it be restored to how it used to be. Grocklings and humans get on incredibly well and it was very sad when the Ice Queen forbade them from interacting.

Gwennol was a young Fairy and her magic and dust was not as strong as it could have been compared to her friends. This wouldn't stop her though, she would do what she could. She and Hullard were very small and could probably move around the Dark Castle unnoticed.

Victor, like Rose was terrified. He had never wanted to go back to Cragfeld once he'd left. He'd come to terms with the fact he had never go back and never see Rika again. However, since seeing what he saw in Ordram's leaf the night before, he knew anything was possible. Here he was standing with Rika who he thought he had lost forever, now with determination in his veins he would help Rose with her task. He would do whatever it took and if that meant facing old demons, then so be it.

"I've still much to do Bolstone," said Ordram walking back around the wall. "Please, take our friends here up onto the patio. The fresh air will do them good and help clear their minds. If you will all excuse me…" And with that he turned around and disappeared into the wall of gold tinged wood.

"Yes, yes, I agree," said Bolstone. "Come now, Ordram has a lot to do and so do we. It'd be rude to keep him from his business. And it's such a beautiful day, wonderful sunshine, clear blue skies… it's a shame to miss it. Yes, yes, come, come. Right then, each take each other's hand so we're all connected, that's right, lovely. Okay then, after I count to three just hold on tight... ready, one... two... three..." They each felt a pull on their arms as Bolstone whooshed them back up the helter-skelter all the way to the top. They found themselves all heaped back into the room where they had slept and still holding hands.

"Forgive me," said Bolstone "But that was a lot easier than getting back up here via the stairs. I'm an old man you know, it's rude to ask an old man to climb so many stairs. Anyway yes, here we are. If we go through that door there it will take us right outside." They looked over in the direction he was pointing and saw a small round door with a large gold handle and flowers growing around it. The door looked tiny, far too small to fit through.

Victor led the way to the door so he could open it for the rest of the group who followed politely in single file through the door. Apart from Gwennol and Hullard, the others seemed to shrink in size to fit through the little doorway, once on the other side they returned to their normal size. This doorway opened up onto the courtyard where they had first landed having been rescued from the sea. The enormous bird was sitting on his perch and shrieked at them when he saw them approaching. He flapped his wings in a fluster at the disturbance.

"Alright Bargos, settle down," said Bolstone firmly to the bird.

"You know him?" asked Furdon.

"Oh yes, I know most animals, birds and creatures in Ordraskop, though I'm rather selective on the creature with whom I make an acquaintance. Bargos has lived here for as long as I can remember, he's Ordram's most favourite companion and they spend many a day together."

"He saved us from the sea," said Fiddy with excitement "Do you think he'd let us get any closer to him?"

"I'm sure he'd be grateful for your thanks but be careful Fiddy, he can be quite snappy."

Fiddy cautiously approached Bargos and held out his hand to reach up to the bird, he could only reach his talons. Bargos lowered his head and stared at Fiddy with his beady eye and squawked at him, making him jump back a little. After a while and persistence from Fiddy, Bargos allowed him to stroke his neck. Fiddy smiled with joy at having such a privilege.

Ordram would often untwist the trunk of the ancient tree and sit in the doorway talking to Bargos. They were old friends and had been together for many hundreds of years. They had seen Ordraskop have good times and terrible times but whatever happened they would see it through together. Ordraskop had been peaceful for many years and things had settled into a calm natural rhythm. There was no King, Queen or throne to fight over but everybody seemed to see Ordram as the one they would turn to if they needed leadership or guidance. Although Ordraskop was calm, Ordram still felt as if he should look after Cragfeld. The Ice Queen and old witch had never shown him any respect and in turn he had also tried to forget about the depressing place. However, Ordram had been good friends with the old King and had respect for his daughter Rika, so felt an obligation to help them and the people left on Cragfeld.

The seven friends were sitting on a very small and neatly manicured lawn next to Bargos, all enjoying the warmth of the sun on their skin. Bargos got used to them and as usual went back to preening himself and completely ignoring the guests. They were all fairly quiet, each thinking to themselves about where they had come from and where they were going to next. None of them had ever thought or planned anything like this venture but somehow, no matter how scary it was they were all ready for it. Rose in particular was thinking about how she used to think she was nothing,

nothing special anyway. She used to live alone and spend time away from the rest of the villagers because she never fitted in. But now, her entire life had changed. She had friends, she had seen creatures and worlds she could have only dreamt about and she was the daughter of a King.

"So my friends," said Bolstone as he lay back on the grass "Do you feel ready for what lies ahead?"

"No…" said Fiddy.

"I don't think we'll ever feel ready," said Furdon. "But we have to do what we have to do. It's our duty as friends of Rose to do this."

"Good, good," said Bolstone.

"What happens now?" said Victor. "Are we just to wait here until we are told otherwise?"

"Yes, yes, what else would you rather do. I say enjoy the peace and calm while you can. You'll not be able to sit in such calm for a long while. You must prepare mentally for what you'll face." The old man sat up "There are things, creatures which will be hunting you and trying to kill you. You must avoid or attack these whilst never forgetting your mission. Rose, to take on the Ice Queen. Victor to track down Rika's tomb in the tallest tower of the Dark Castle. While you're doing that… I'll pay my old friend Orme a visit and give her a piece of my mind, the ridiculous old woman!"

"And what about us?" asked Hullard.

"Don't you worry Hullard," said Bolstone. "There'll be plenty of ways you can help. You'll find where you need to be when we get there. You and Gwennol have the advantage of being tiny and can make your way through the Dark Castle with less risk of being spotted. And the Grocklings, I don't want you two to leave Rose's side, do you hear me?"

"Yes, we understand," said Furdon "Don't we Fiddy?"

"Oh, of course. We've never left her side yet since we met her."

"That's good," said Bolstone "Keep up the good work."

As they were sitting on the grass discussing what lay ahead, they could hear deep rumblings beneath them as Ordram was working and planning for the days ahead. There was nothing they could do now apart from wait. Fiddy and Hullard were childishly playing and chasing each other around the sunlit courtyard, they jumped along the walls and onto rooftops trying to catch each other. Gwennol stayed with Rose and lay down on the grass next to her.

It was tranquil and relaxing as they listened to the breeze rustle the leaves on Ordram's branches. The air smelled of sweet honeysuckle and Rose could feel herself drifting off to sleep. She had slept incredibly well the night before and was hoping to rest her mind for a while before leaving the safety of Ordram. However her thoughts were troubled and her dreams were disturbed, she was picturing everything that Ordram and Bolstone had described to her. All sorts of flashing images popped into her mind, she had happy ones where she and Vecter were dancing through the Castle and walking through the gardens, then there were those where she and Mordisan met again for the first time in one hundred and fifty years, she could almost feel the venom from her sister.

While Rose looked peaceful the others let her rest as much as possible. Bolstone, Victor and Furdon watched on as Fiddy and Hullard dashed around and kept themselves entertained.

"How do you think we'll do…?" said Victor "When we get to Cragfeld, how do you think we'll do against the mighty force of the Ice Queen?"

"I wish I could tell you Victor," said the old wizard. "Both Ordram and myself have the power of foresight where we can see into the future… but neither of us can see beyond this battle for Cragfeld."

"What does that mean?" asked Furdon "Does that mean

there isn't a future for Cragfeld?"

"Let's not think like that my little friend," said Bolstone "Ordram and I can only see a black veil, nothing more. No matter how far we try and see into the future, all we can see is the black veil."

"But we do have a chance, don't we?" said Furdon, his big green eyes searching for hope from Bolstone.

"We will always have a chance," sighed Bolstone "While ever we have a chance we have hope to succeed. The Ice Queen and Orme will throw all they've got at us, in turn we'll throw all we have back at them. They may think they've an army but when I look around me right here… I can see we have warriors." He winked at Furdon.

Furdon and Victor could see the old man wasn't holding anything back just to make them feel better and maybe more positive. There was no point in holding back anything, they might as well know what they are in for so they can prepare themselves accordingly. They each had one of Bolstone's marbles and one of Ordram's leaves, which they would keep safe until they were needed.

CHAPTER FIFTEEN

While the six friends slept, Bolstone and Ordram had been working through the night with plans of ways in which they could approach Cragfeld. They knew they would be seen by the Ice Queen's spies but wanted to leave it as late as possible for her to get notice of their presence.

After another night in their comfortable beds, they were woken by Bolstone creaking the door open and calling them all outside. Dawn was only just breaking and the morning air felt cool in their lungs, it was refreshing. Fiddy and Hullard were last to rise and trailed behind the others into the court-yard. Bolstone steered them to sit on the grass next to Ordram's great tree of magical leaves. Bargos could tell something was stirring and couldn't get comfortable on his perch.

"Haven't you slept Bolstone?" asked Rose as she rubbed her eyes.

"No, no. No time for sleep my dear. Besides you need it more than me. An old man can't sleep as well as he used to."

"What have you and Ordram been doing?"

"Planning, planning, planning," he smiled.

At that moment Ordram rumbled underneath them and un-twisted his gnarly old trunk and stretched the tree up and up until the little doorway appeared. It had only been a couple of days since they had ventured through that doorway, yet somehow it felt longer. Rose found she could quite easily stay with Ordram forever and easily forget about Cragfeld. They could see the wood and bark of the trunk shifting as Ordram appeared and took a seat in the doorway of the tree trunk.

"Good morning my friends," he said in a deep warm voice "I hope you're all well-rested?" They all smiled and nodded, none of them had ever slept as well as they did here. "Good, that's good. Because my friends, the time has come. The King's ships are only a day away from Cragfeld where Bolstone and Victor will meet them. Rose, you are to go with Furdon and Fiddy and stay with the Grocklings out of sight as long as you can. Hullard, Gwennol... you two must stay with Victor."

"This is all very sudden," said Victor.

"No, I'm afraid it's on schedule," said Bolstone "Everything and everyone is ready, you must be too."

"Well, yes, we're ready," said Rose "I suppose we were just getting comfortable here."

"Understandable," smiled Ordram "But now you must go, go back to Cragfeld and fight for the people." He twitched his eyebrows and stroked his beard while he looked over at the small group he was putting all his trust in.

"I'm sorry to state the obvious," said Victor "But how are we supposed to get back to the mainland? My boat was destroyed getting here, we have no way back."

"You don't always have to go back the same way you came," said Ordram "No, it would take too long by boat, we need to get you back there in less than one day, if you go by boat it will take at least two, maybe even three days. You need to go by air. Bargos will take you, won't you Bargos?" The huge bird shifted uncomfortably at the idea but agreed to take them. "Good, I knew I could rely on you my old friend."

"Why can't I stay with Victor and Bolstone and meet my

father?" asked Rose "Doesn't he want to see me?"

"I'm sure he can't wait to see you Rose," said Ordram "But not yet, not yet. You must stay out of sight for as long as possible. You'll see him soon enough, soon enough my dear, when you're back to your full self." He tried to reassure her but she felt frustrated. As Rose, she had never known what it was like to have a father. Maybe when she was reunited with her other self she would understand.

"We've no time to waste," said Bolstone as he got to his feet and walked over to Bargos. "Come on now, don't dilly dally." They were all quite surprised at how quickly this was happening but realised it would be dangerous if the Ice Queen heard whispers of their plans.

"Will we see you again Ordram?" said Rose, walking up to him as he stood in the doorway in the tree trunk.

"I'm sure you will," his beard hid a smile and his eyes glinted. "Now you look after that locket won't you? Good luck Rika." He winked at her.

Bargos stretched out his wings and flapped them ready to take flight. Rose, Furdon and Fiddy climbed up and sat on his back between his wings, whereas Victor found himself in the talons of one foot and Bolstone was in the talons of the other foot. Hullard and Gwennol were safely tucked into Victor's pocket and were hanging on for dear life.

"It's very rude to make an old man travel this way," moaned Bolstone.

"Oh shush," said Ordram "You enjoy it really."

"I'd rather be up there where Rose is…"

"I'm sure you would. But even though you're an old man, you're still a gentleman and wouldn't switch places with a lady would you?"

Bolstone frowned but agreed. He thought it a very uncomfortable way of getting around. It may have been uncomfortable but they were all very safe, Bargos would not let go of them until they reached Cragfeld.

Bargos stretched out his wings and with an almighty thrust, lifted into the air. Rose was quite comfortable and held on to a couple of golden feathers, more for her own balance than for safety. Victor and Bolstone were safely wrapped up in Bargos' strong feet as they were lifted higher away from Ordram. Rose looked down and could see Ordram looking up at them as they took to the sky. They could barely see each other but they exchanged smiles, a thank you for each doing their part to save Cragfeld. Bargos lifted higher and higher and then turned to face the mainland, he then flew with grace and elegance through the clean air. He was flying towards Ordraskop with ease. Rose looked down and could see the sea sparkling far, far below them.

"Do we have to be this high?" asked Fiddy as he covered his eyes.

"I suppose so," said Rose "If we didn't have to be, then I doubt we would be."

"I say up there," called Bolstone. "Don't worry, yes we are supposed to be this high. Don't you remember how you got to Ordraskop from my waterfall under the mountain?"

"Yes, the bubbling whirlpool," confirmed Furdon, he had not enjoyed that one bit.

"Well Bargos here has to do a similar thing to get back to Cragfeld... He has to drop through a whirlwind which is out at sea and he needs to be this high to get it right. It's not going to be pleasant but he's done this a few times, haven't you old chap?" Bargos screeched in agreement, he was not looking forward to the whirlwind as it would be quite a blustery experience. He would have to dive through the centre of it like a bullet so as not to get his wings caught up in it. It was the safest way of getting all of the companions back to Cragfeld from Ordraskop.

In the distance Rose could see a long spiralling tower of wind which seemed to link the sky and the sea. As they got closer she could see that it was in fact the spinning wind tunnel that Bolstone had told them about. Bargos flew towards it, screeching as he went, dreading having to fly down it. Coming back into Ordraskop from Cragfeld was always a lot easier as the winds were less aggressive. Bargos soared above the whirlwind until he was in the perfect place, ready to dive through the centre. Rose looked down briefly but it soon made her dizzy, the greyish purple tube twisting around and around really quickly. Fiddy and Furdon wanted to have a look but Rose told them not to bother as it would make them shaky. She knew she would have to lean forward and stay as still and as flat as possible in order to make it as easy as possible for Bargos. Furdon and Fiddy tucked themselves underneath Rose ready for the dangerous part of the flight. Bargos stretched his legs back until he was like a streamlined arrow. Bolstone and Victor looked at each other and then down into the spiralling tunnel below, they each thought it best to close their eyes for the next bit. Gwennol and Hullard pulled themselves deeper into Victor's pocket and held on tight, ready for the bumpy ride. Bargos screeched out a couple of times as if readying himself and his passengers. He pulled back his wings and plunged straight down in a vertical line, right down the centre of the tunnel. Winds were gushing at incredible speeds around them and they could hear it whistling passed their ears as they clung onto Bargos. They were travelling at such a speed that they had to tuck their heads down so they could breath. Bargos confidently powered through the whirlwind like a beautiful golden arrow. The noise all around them was getting louder and louder as the winds were spinning faster and faster, then all of a sudden there was a great Boom Bang noise as they broke through the sound barrier into Cragfeld. The spinning grew calmer and the winds were less angry as Bargos continued to fly perfectly straight. Rose did not know whether to look up or down because when she last looked they were diving downwards from Ordraskop, now they were flying upwards through the tunnel into the seas surrounding Cragfeld. It was a double ended whirlwind, no wonder they all felt dizzy. Bargos called out as he reached the top, letting them all know it was over. He flew high over the whirlwind to make sure they weren't going to get sucked back in.

As they looked down and around them they could see Cragfeld in the far distance, looking like a little spec in the ocean. Rose never thought she would get to see Cragfeld from the outside but she always knew there was more life and excitement over the mountains that she could never see beyond. Down below she could see small clusters of islands which until now she never knew existed. She wondered who (if anyone) lived there and if they had ever sailed to Cragfeld.

Victor and Bolstone had now dared to open their eyes as the winds gushing by had stopped once they got to the other side. They were soaring above the ocean, not too high to make them dizzy but high enough for them to enjoy the views and have a comfortable ride.

"Look!" shouted Victor. He could see ships in the distance ahead of them, sailing towards Cragfeld.

"Ah wonderful," said Bolstone "It appears we are all going to be on schedule."

Rose peered into the distance and could just make out the shapes on the ocean. She had a strange feeling in her stomach as she knew her father was down there amongst them. She had the same feelings as she had with Victor. To Rose they were strangers but to Rika they were family and best friends. When Victor looked at Rose he could see both Rose and Rika and feel what he felt for Rika. Rose felt strange when he wanted to hold her hand because it was as if she hardly knew him. She knew she could trust him but it would take time for her to see him in the same way he saw her. As soon as she was reunited with the frozen Rika then everything might just click into place for her.

Bargos was flying at a gentle speed and had seen the ships in the distance a long time before Victor had pointed them out. The huge bird had incredible eyesight and could see the detailing on the ships which looked like blurry blobs to Victor. Furdon and Fiddy were actually enjoying the flight, they could not wait to get back to Frithad and Eady to tell them all about their adventures. Their Grockling friends would be hanging onto their every word, knowing they themselves would never have got to experience such an amazing journey.

With grace they cut through the air and were soon approaching the King's fleet. Bargos kept his distance but flew close enough so the King would know it was them with Bolstone on board. The King could just see Bolstone's orange cloak flapping in the wind as the huge beautiful bird soared by. Rose tried to looked down on the ships to see if she could see the King but Bargos' wings blocked her view. It was probably a good things as Ordram said, she just had to be patient.

Cragfeld was not far away now and they could see the mountains encircling the island standing tall like soldiers on guard. On the top of each mountain they could see the seven fires of the watch towers burning, where the winged wardens would be scanning the sea for any threats. They had to try and stay out of sight as long as possible. The winged wardens were looking for ships, so Bargos would be able to go unseen as he flew close to the sea. The glimmers of his feathers would blend into the glimmers on the sea and the winged wardens would not be able to see him. Bargos flew close to the surface of the water, almost skimming the surface with his feet and drenching Bolstone and Victor who had to remind the great bird they were there. He lifted slightly but was still a bit too close for their liking.

As they approached the island, Rose could see the

mountains had sheer vertical cliffs. Bargos flew as close to these as he could to stay out of sight from the watchful eyes above them until he found a safe place to land. He gently placed Bolstone and Victor on a rocky outcrop where a thin rarely used path led from the sea to the island.

"Yes, well, erm thank you Bargos," said Bolstone "Thank you for getting us here safely even though a tad wet, I know it's not your most favourite journey. Now, Rose my dear you stay up there with Furdon and Fiddy – Bargos will take you up to the secret entrance to the Grocklings cavern, alright?"

"Ok," said Rose "I suppose it's goodbye for now then?"

"Yes, yes, indeed. Not for long though. We'll see you on the other side of these mountains when we face that dreadful woman!"

"See you soon Rose," said Victor. He smiled at her to cover his sadness, he did not want to say goodbye to her again but knew it was a short sacrifice for a long term gain.

"Yes, see you soon Victor," she said.

Furdon and Fiddy waved goodbye to their friends as Bargos took to the air again. Gwennol and Hullard could be seen standing on Victor's shoulders as they said their goodbyes. It was quite a sad moment because this was the first time the group of six friends had been apart, they had grown quite close over the last few days.

Furdon, Fiddy and Rose were still together though and were being taken to the hidden doorway to the Grocklings cavern. They flew out of sight of their friends and around the edge of the mountains. Bargos knew exactly where he was going and silently took them to a cave half way up the mountain. They each carefully climbed off their new friend and thanked him for getting them there safely. He proudly bowed his head to them and swooped off the mountain and flew at great speed away from Cragfeld back to Ordraskop.

They looked around at the cave where they had been dropped off. There was a vertical drop into the sea and no pathway around the outside of the mountain. Rose remembered the first cave she had found herself with Furdon and Fiddy, where the doorway was hidden under a boulder. However, this cave was empty and did not have any boulders to hide any doorways.

"Well I never," said Fiddy "I never knew about this entrance, did you?"

"I'd heard about it," said Furdon "But never actually been to it."

"How do you suppose we get in?" asked Rose.

"That's a good question," said Furdon as he began feeling the walls for a potential handle or lever which would reveal to doorway. He and Fiddy were both doing this but could not find anything and were looking very puzzled.

They were all fumbling around the cave for a few minutes before Rose tripped on an unexpected tree root. It was un-expected because they were in a cave, in a mountain with no trees. By chance Rose tripped on it and tugged it with her foot which then set of a few rumbling sounds. Above them in the roof of the cave appeared a round hole. Rose lifted Furdon and Fiddy up through the hole and onto a ledge but couldn't quite reach the hole to grab it and pull herself up. Fiddy reached into his little bag and dug out his trusty web rope of Spinbra, he tied it around a rock next to him and lowered the rest down to Rose. Between them they lifted her up and she climbed up far enough to get her tummy onto the ledge and pulled herself round. They were in an old unused tunnel which appeared to be quite dark and dull. The Grocklings could see better than Rose so took the lead down the tunnel. There was dust, dirt and cobwebs in this tunnel which made it quite apparent that it had not been used for a long, long time. Grocklings were usually quite proud of their home and kept it clean. It was a long tunnel which curved slightly to the right but didn't rise up or down. After a while Rose's eyes became accustomed to the dark and she could see where she was going without tripping on uneven bumps in the floor. Towards the edge of the tunnel Rose could see a soft yellow light as if they were getting closer to the Grockling's cavern. As they approached the end of the tunnel, they found themselves standing in a very small hole above the room where they had started their journey, the misted well was below them casually circling around and around. Furdon and Fiddy jumped down first into the empty room, things felt very quiet. Rose had to sit down and then squeeze herself through the small hole before dropping to the floor with a thump.

"Why does it feel so quiet?" asked Rose.

"I'm not sure," said Furdon "I've never known it this quiet, you can usually hear the rest of the colony talking to each other and the voices echo around."

They climbed the steps out of the room where their journey had begun and up into the main cavern. It was early evening so there should have been a lot of hustle and bustle as the other Grocklings went out for their night walks on the mountain. Furdon called out but there was no answer. It was very strange because their home had never been this quiet. He called again but they were greeted with silence. Furdon then ran round to where Frithad and Eady slept but their beds were empty.

"This is very peculiar," said Fiddy "Where is everyone?"

"I don't know, but I don't like this at all. There's usually someone around."

Just then they could hear movement in a tunnel at the top of the stairs and peered up into the doorway, not knowing what to expect. The silence was deafening and the wait seemed endless, who was up there?! A small shuffle of feet could be heard getting closer and the wait was unbearable. Slowly a Grockling peeked its head around the corner, it was Eady. When she saw who it was who had been calling from the cavern she jumped down the stairs to greet her friends.

"Oh, welcome back," she smiled, hugging them all "Welcome, welcome back. It is good to see you. Are you all alright, none of you are injured at all?"

"No, we're fine," said Furdon "Where is everyone?"

"Oh so much has happened in the time you've been gone. Rose, the lovely Rose… You now know the truth now don't you, that's good."

"Eady, where is everyone and what's happened," repeated Furdon.

"We're all fine," said Eady looking quite flustered. "We're all sitting out on the mountain, we daren't go into the mountains or stray further than our own doorway."

"Why?" asked Rose.

"Here, come with me," said Eady, directing them to follow her. "The Ice Queen, since you've been gone, has been up to something in the Dark Castle and well, we don't want to think what she's been concocting. But come, come with me and see for yourselves."

They followed Eady through some corridors and up a few stairs that came out into the cave where Rose first entered their cavern. In the cave and closely surrounding it on the cliff side were hundreds of Grocklings from inside the mountain. They were all cuddled close together and sitting quietly as the moon rose higher into the sky and night fell on Cragfeld. Eady took them over to the edge of the cave where Frithad was sitting. He greeted them with a huge welcoming smile but there was something worrying him.

"Why are all the Grocklings here and not out on patrol?" asked Rose, taking a seat on the rocks.

"Wait, just wait," said Frithad, staring towards the Dark Castle, "You'll soon understand."

They all settled down with the other Grocklings and waited for whatever it is that was scaring them. They did not have to wait long. As they night grew darker the air was filled with the most haunting and chilling sounds possible.

The Ice Queens army were restless at night, screaming and howling as they grew bigger. The creatures were bursting to be let out of the Dark Castle to chase and kill whatever was a threat to the Ice Queen. The Grocklings could hear these creatures and could tell they could break free at any time.

"What's that?" whispered Furdon to Frithad.

"It's her army, she created a deadly army."

"Bolstone came to tell us what she was up to," said Eady "But we could never have imagined it would be like this. We don't know what they will be chasing but as we aren't friends of the Ice Queen, we presume to be on the menu." Fiddy's green eyes were filled with terror as the cries boomed out of the Dark Castle and echoed around the mountain. With every blood curdling howl and scream, the Grocklings huddled closer together.

"How long has this been going on?" asked Rose.

"For the last few nights," said Frithad. "I've advised we all stay closer together. If we stay put then we're closer to home and can escape underground at a moment's notice. We've been underground all day, we need to get some night air."

"We don't know what she's been creating with her frozen heart," said Eady "But whatever's in the Dark Castle has been created to protect the Ice Queen and the old witch."

The Grocklings sat in the mouth of the cave with Rose and balanced on narrow ledges on the mountainside. They listened for hours to the chilling sounds coming from the Dark Castle. It was only a matter of time before whatever was in there would be unleashed.

Bolstone and Victor were waiting at the coast for the King's ships to edge closer. The ships set anchor and one by one released rowing boats onto the sea, carrying the King and his men. Bolstone and Victor watched as their allies approached, slowly and steadily on the quite choppy seas.

When the boats reached the shore, the King and his soldiers disembarked, leaving one man in each boat to row back to the ships.

"Greetings Bolstone," said the old King, bowing to the old wizard.

"Good evening," said Bolstone "And welcome to all your soldiers. We must keep very quiet, I'm sure your arrival hasn't gone unnoticed but let's try to be as quiet as we can, just in case…"

"Hello," said Victor, bowing to the King "I'm V…"

"I know who you are young man," smiled the King "It's been a long time, hasn't it Vecter, far, far too long."

"It has, yes Sir," said Victor.

"Tell me Vecter, have you seen her? Have you seen Rika?"

"Yes Sir."

"And… is she well?"

"She is well. She's looking forward to seeing you again."

"Ah, as am I. As am I."

"Yes, yes, yes," interrupted Bolstone. "We are all fine and it's good to see us all, yes, yes, yes! But we don't have time for pleasantries, no, not at all. We've come together to face an enemy. The Ice Queen."

"Mordisan…" sighed the King.

"She was Mordisan," said Bolstone "But I fear what you remember as your daughter is long gone as her powers made her into what she is today."

The old King looked at Bolstone and understood what he was saying. He would love to see his daughters again even if they were not how he remembered them. He was old and frail and certainly would not be the man they remembered to be their father.

Bolstone led the King and his soldiers down the narrow path to the rocky cliffs of Cragfeld. The sea had eroded the base of the cliffs which had made a safe and sheltered pathway for them to walk in single file. The old King and Victor exchanged polite conversation but did feel quite awkward after not seeing each other for one hundred and fifty years. The last time the King saw Vecter he was asking for his permission to marry Rika. How things had changed, lifetimes had been lost and nothing was how it used to be.

There were easily four hundred soldiers who stood by the King to come with him on this quest. They knew it was dangerous and none of them ever would have volunteered to return to Cragfeld, but they knew it was to save the King's daughter. They also knew Ordram was behind it all and they would never question him. The soldiers knew what the Ice Queen was capable of but they had to try and put that out of their minds and focus on the task in hand. Bolstone was explaining that the soldiers would have to fight the Ice Queen's army and distract them from Victor who would have to find a way into the Castle and up to the tallest tower. As they marched along the craggy coast of Cragfeld, they became aware that they were not alone. The night sky was dark and they only had moonlight to see where they were treading. They could hear something out at sea but it was too dark to see what it was. Their first thoughts were that it was the winged wardens, having seen them they would strike from the air, grabbing each soldier and tearing him apart. However, in the moonlight they could see dark shadows in the night sky as if they were circling the island. Bolstone did not seem at all bothered by the noise because he knew it was his old friend Blackfall. Blackfall and several other Dragons had come in to see what was happening and wait out of sight until Bolstone called for them. These Dragons were as black as the night itself and were almost impossible to see. The soldiers were muttering amongst themselves as to what it could be, but none of them could guess as they had never seen Dragons before. The old King told them to keep their voices down, they did not want any of the Ice Queen's spies to hear them.

Both Gwennol and Hullard were sitting back in Victor's shirt pocket. Pixies and Fairies did not like King's or men because they had always had a rough history. Mankind failed to believe there were such things in their worlds, turning them into stories as if they never existed. If a Pixie and a Fairy were to suddenly appear in front of their eyes, not only would they all frighten each other but they would make enough noise for the winged wardens to hear. It was a lot safer for them to keep still and stay quiet. They bounced along in Victor's pocket and listened to what he had to say to the King. They whispered to each other so nobody would hear them, commenting about what Victor was talking about. When conversation turned to the old days when the King ruled Cragfeld, both Hullard and Gwennol got a bit bored. They began thinking about Rose and were wondering how she was going on with the Grocklings. They did not like having to be split up from their friends. Either way, even though they had been split up, both paths would meet again on the other side of the mountain.

Bolstone walked into a clearing, like a beach at the base of the mountains with a vertical cliff above them. The King hobbled along with the help of Victor and one of his soldiers. They gathered in the clearing in the dark of the night and waited for Bolstone to say something. Before Bolstone could open his mouth the echo of howls and screams from the Dark Castle made its way to their ears. This was an unsettling sound and scared the soldiers to their core. They didn't know what was making those sounds but they were not the sounds of anything friendly. Bolstone and Victor looked at each other, knowing that Rose could probably hear these noises too.

"My friends," began the old wizard "The Ice Queen has been busy making an army to fight us. Granted it will not be the kind of army you'll be expecting. She's made creatures who will fight you until the bitter end." The men shuffled uncomfortably. "She's given them a thirst for human blood and they cannot be killed by your swords."

"You've brought us to our deaths!" said one soldier, with the agreement of dozens of others.

"You may think that," said Bolstone "But you're not alone in this fight. Ordram, the Dragons and myself will do everything in our powers to keep you safe and help you to fight these monsters."

"Why should we fight if they can kill us but we can't kill them?"

"Yes, yes, a fair question," muttered Bolstone "But please, trust me. Yes it will be difficult. Yes it will be exhausting. But remember why you're doing this, for the King and for Cragfeld. Trust me, trust Ordram. The Dragons are here to help, they can fight these ghastly creatures without such an unfair disadvantage as yours. Dragons aren't human… so they can kill them. Are you all with me, with us?" They all nodded.

The sounds of the creatures in the Dark Castle were calling out into the night, it as if they could tell something was about to happen. The Dragons waited in the darkness for Bolstone's signal.

The Ice Queen could tell something was wrong. She was used to hearing the deadly creatures of her army screeching and calling into the night but they seemed more agitated this evening.

"Orme, Orme!" She yelled at the top her voice from her throne. She was getting impatient and yelled again as the old witch scuttled into the great frozen hall.

"Yes, my Queen," she hissed under her breath.

"What's wrong with the animals, why are they making such a noise? You have fed them haven't you?!"

"Yes, they're well-fed," said the old witch. "They have good appetites but are always hungry for more."

"Then maybe you should give them more if it will help quieten them down!"

"They have plenty of food, an endless supply. They're not hungry, they're bored."

"Bored, what do you mean bored? How can they be bored?"

"The air carries a scent tonight, that scent is calling to them."

"Scent... stop talking in riddles and tell me what you mean."

Just as the old witch was about to explain herself, three large winged wardens swooped in through the balcony and landed hissing into the room in front of the Ice Queen.

"Your Majesty," said the largest winged warden, bowing to her.

"Yes, what is it?" she snapped.

"You told us to look out for ships and those ships have come. A dozen tall ships are anchored off the coast and four hundred men have come to shore."

"This is what the army can smell," said Orme. "They can smell fresh food that hasn't been tainted with our magic. The villager's blood tastes quite stale compared to that of an incomer."

"Is that so...?" said the Ice Queen getting up out of her throne. "Tell me, who are these men, who do they serve?"

"We believe there's an old man leading them, my Queen," hissed another winged warden.

"An old man? Would this old man look like he used to be a King?" she grinned.

"Yes, yes my Queen."

"Good! It seems my father has gone mad in his old age. Thinking he can come to see me, to come unannounced and try to take my throne. Stupid, stupid old fool." She strode over to the balcony and looked out into the night. "Thank you my dears, you may go back to your posts now – and watch the show begin." She smiled and dismissed the winged wardens who hissed as they flew around the room and then out into the night, back to the mountain tops.

"What will you have me do my Queen?" said Orme.

"Prepare my army, if they're hungry... then they shall feast. There is fresh food walking right up to us. Orme, are they coming over or under the mountain?"

The old witch reached into the pocket of her cloak for her ice crystal ball. She stared into it for a while until she could see the shadowy figures of the soldiers lining the coast of the island. She waved her hand across the ball again until she could see which path they were taking.

"My Queen, they will split their force, half over the mountain and half underneath."

"Which path is the old King going to take?"

"He'll be going underneath the mountain," she croaked.

"Good. Make sure no harm comes to the old man, I'll deal with him myself!"

"Yes, certainly."

"Let's prepare Orme. I thought this day would never come. I didn't think anyone, especially my own father would bring four hundred men straight to their deaths."

The chandeliers around the room began to quiver as the captives inside each crystal began to applaud. They knew someone would come one day, someone would come to free them as well as the rest of the island. The Ice Queen glared at them as she walked under them, telling them not to get their hopes up for they would be trapped in their crystal shells for all eternity. Nothing could help them. These captives had been trapped as souvenirs of Mordisan's triumphs and she would never let them go.

The old witch hobbled behind the Ice Queen as she glided elegantly down the frozen corridors to the ballroom. She opened the door and saw the snakes writhing and hissing impatiently, the fierce hounds thrashing their horns at the walls trying to get out, and the flying goblins tearing through the rafters. For anyone other than the Ice Queen they would have been faced with a terrifying sight. The Ice Queen smiled, she knew her army was ready and hungry for the attack. She knew her father was out there and just seeing these creatures might kill him but she did not want her army to touch him, they were to find him and escort him back to her.

Mordisan was feeling quietly confident. She knew how strong she was, she knew how strong Orme was – between them they couldn't be overpowered. She sped through the corridors of the Dark Castle, laughing to herself at what was about to happen. She felt like a child, one who had been given the best toy to play with. Her father and his army were her toys and she was going to play with them until she got bored with them. She even thought about how she would re-unite her father with Rika, she might do the same thing to her father as she had to her sister. Then they could be together forever like a perfectly happy family, just like she always wanted. The difference this time would be that she'd be in charge and they would not be able to do anything but watch on with their pathetic sad eyes. The anger she felt for her father and Rika fuelled her strength, the more rage that was building up inside her would make her stronger than ever. Nobody in fact knew how strong and powerful she was, nobody had been back to Cragfeld to challenge her since she took the throne and the crown. She walked powerfully through the Dark Castle and stood on the balcony of the main hall, looking out into the thick black night. He eyes were focussed in the direction of where Bolstone was standing with the King and his army.

The terrifying calls coming from the Dark Castle were getting more angry and fired up as the night drew on. Victor could remember there were two ways through to the other side from where they were.

"Which way are we going then?" he asked Bolstone.

"Yes, yes, I think the King would be safer to stay out of sight as long as possible and go through the underground tunnel to the other side. Half of his men will go with him and the other half shall climb up the mountainside, if I remember correctly there's a set of steps up there somewhere."

"Yes, I remember them too," said Victor. "They are too steep for an older man to climb."

"What are you trying to say," smiled Bolstone. "You know it's rude to tell an old man that he's old!"

"Erm, I wasn't saying that exactly," said Victor trying to back-pedal out of the insult.

"Don't worry Victor, I'm fitter than I look. Besides, I'll not be climbing those steps, no, no, no. Like you, I'll be travelling by Dragon. We need to get over to the Dark Castle as quickly and as safely as possible. Going up or under the mountain would be slower and a lot more dangerous. Yes, yes, Blackfall and his friends will help us and then go back to fight alongside all these men here, yes, yes. That's right, yes."

"When do you propose we attack?" asked the King in a slow deep voice. He was sad to return to Cragfeld in such a negative way.

"Well, yes, yes, you and half your men make your way through that tunnel over there, the other half up the mountain. As soon as you get through the tunnel, call my name."

"Then what?"

"Then I will show the sign and we will charge at full force towards the Dark Castle and face whatever the Ice Queen throws at us."

"Forgive me but I'm an old man and can't be charging anywhere."

"Yes, yes, I know, I know," said Bolstone "And you won't be. The old witch needs to see your presence in her crystal bowl or ball or whatever she uses these days… oh yes, which will tell them how to prepare for battle of their side. You will be pulled to safety by one of the Dragons before anything can happen to you, yes, yes." The old King did not look so sure but went along with the old wizard's plan.

The King set off with half of his soldiers into the dark tunnel under the mountain, They did not want to be seen from the Dark Castle so only lit one torch to help them find their way. The other half of the men were directed up the mountain path, it was a slow steep climb. Bolstone and Victor waited on the beach and watched the brave soldiers trudging to the positions ready for battle.

Blackfall loomed out of the dark sky, they could hear his wings above them as he hovered and lowered himself to the floor. He was very difficult to see but his glistening eyes and sharp white teeth could be seen in the moonlight. Bolstone walked up to him and greeted him like the old friends they were. The wizard magically changed his cloak from orange to black and Victor could hardly see him. The old wizard climbed up Blackfall's strong scaly legs to his back, sitting at the base of the Dragon's neck, between his shoulder blades. A second Dragon came to land next to Blackfall, this was Blackfall's brother Trennfall. Trennfall was equal in size and shape to his brother, in fact the only difference Victor could see was that Trennfall had a red tinge to his otherwise black eyes.

"Are you ready?" said Bolstone.

"As ready as I'll ever be," smiled Victor.

The Dragons raised their wings and wafted them in the air a few times before lifting themselves slowly off the ground. As soon as they were airborne they twisted and turned in the skies, Victor was surprised how agile they were for such huge Dragons. Gwennol and Hullard peered out of Victor's pocket to try and see what was happening and where they were. Victor told them to hold on and stay still while they were on the Dragon's back. He reassured them they would be fine, they just needed to get over these mountains and to the Dark Castle as quickly as possible. Blackfall and Trennfall circled the skies, waiting for their call, their sign to attack.

CHAPTER SIXTEEN

Rose was sitting at the edge of the cave with hundreds of Grocklings around her, perched on any bit of ledge they could find on the cliff face. Furdon was sitting on one side of her and Fiddy was on the other, with Frithad and Eady just in front of them staring into the darkness. The chilling calls from within the Dark Castle were getting louder as the creatures were becoming agitated and ready for battle. The Grocklings had incredible night vision and could see movements and shadows over Cragfeld.

"I can't see anything," said Rose "What's happening out there?"

"There's something out there causing the Ice Queen's army to get riled up," said Frithad.

"It must be the King and his army," said Rose. "We flew over them out at sea, they must've reached the shore. Maybe the Ice Queen's dreadful army can smell them?"

"It is quite possible," said Frithad.

"What are we all sitting here waiting for?" she said, frustrated "Those men need help, they can't fight and kill whatever is about to be unleashed from the Dark Castle."

"All in good time Rose," said Eady "Bolstone will know what he's doing. Besides, we need to get you ready?"

"What do you mean? I am ready!"

"No, no you're not," smiled Eady "You can't go down

there, dressed like that. Come with me all three of you –
Furdon, Fiddy come on." They followed Eady into the
cavern and left the other Grocklings watching and waiting
for battle to commence. Waiting for Bolstone to declare war
with the Ice Queen.

Rose, Furdon and Fiddy followed Eady into a room where
only the fighter Grocklings had been to before. This is where
they would go to be fitted for uniforms and armour once they
had finished their training, they had to earn their burgundy
cloaks. The well-trained fighters were out there on the
mountainside with Frithad, keen and ready to put their
training and skills to good use... as long as they did not have
to leave Cragfeld of course otherwise they would have been
more willing to help Rose in the first place.

"Here we are," said Eady "If you're going to face battle
then you must be dressed accordingly, that blue dress is
lovely but it just won't do."

"But Hildfall gave this to me, as with Furdon and Fiddy –
their purple jackets."

"Yes, I know," she smiled "You can keep those here for
now but you should be dressed more appropriately. Furdon,
Fiddy here are two burgundy jackets for you..."

"Burgundy jackets..." said Fiddy "But only the fighter
Grocklings get to wear these."

"And what do you think you are, you've proved yourselves
and have earned these jackets." Furdon and Fiddy bounced
with joy and surprise at being given such an honour. "Rose,
this is for you, I made it while you were gone." She handed
a long burgundy dress to Rose and then a long black cloak
with a beautiful deep hood and a gold clip at the front. Rose
took the dress and loved it, she thought even this was too
beautiful to go to battle in.

"Oh, thank you," said Rose "It's gorgeous."

"It is my dear," said Eady "But it's also our troops' colours,
wear it with pride. You'll all be well camouflaged down

there in these. Now get changed and I'll meet you back up on the surface." They did as they were told.

The dress fitted Rose perfectly and it moved easily with her. She tucked her spiky locket of Ordram's leaf out of sight. Furdon and Fiddy emerged from their changing holes and looked very smart. They all admired each other in their new outfits. Rose knelt down on the floor to talk to her friends.

"You both look wonderful," she smiled, feeling quite emotional. "We've been through so much together already and I know that our friendship is for life. I wouldn't have been able to get this far without either of you… and I just want to say thank you."

"Oh Miss Rose," said Furdon "We feel the same. If we'd never have met you or spoken with you then we never would've got to see what we saw and do what we did…"

"Absolutely!" agreed Fiddy, giving Rose a hug.

"I'm terrified," said Rose "But as long as we stick together and look out for each other then I know we can do this. There are so many people out there depending on us… Your troop, the King's army, the people of Cragfeld… and of course Bolstone and Ordram."

"Don't worry Miss Rose, we won't leave your side," said Furdon.

They climbed back out of the cavern and onto the ledge. The Fighter Grocklings saw Furdon and Fiddy wearing burgundy jackets and scowled with jealousy. Frithad and Eady smiled proudly at their three warriors who would enter the Dark Castle while the rest of them were fighting with the King's army against the Ice Queen.

"It's almost time," said Frithad "We can see a very soft glow in the tunnel under the mountain, it must mean the King and his men are almost through to this side. And on the top of that mountain there, we can see more of the King's men getting into position."

313

"And what about Bolstone and Victor?" asked Furdon.

"Blackfall and Trennfall are circling overhead," said Frithad "From what we can see, Bolstone and Victor are up there with them. As soon as the King's men are in position then Bolstone will call out for us to charge the Dark Castle and fight whatever comes out of it. It's not long now, I can feel it. Remember Rose, find your inner warrior and nothing can stand in your way!" Rose smiled nervously at Frithad and Eady.

All of a sudden out of the dark skies above them Blackfall roared and sent a flash of fire from his great lungs into the sky. Bolstone had given the sign and now the battle for Cragfeld was declared

The Ice Queen and Orme were standing on the large balcony of the main hall waiting for the King to call out to his men to fight. When they saw Blackfall in the sky above them throw flames into the night sky, they knew it was time.

"Let's unleash my army," demanded the Ice Queen "And bring the King to me… alive!"

"Yes my Queen," said Orme.

They stood hand-in-hand and between them lifted their arms into the air and sent a shockwave through the Dark Castle. This shockwave blasted open every door and shattered every frozen window in the Dark Castle. The deathly screeches filled the hallways and the vibrations of thundering footsteps shuddered through the Castle. Giant snakes slithered and hissed out of the Dark Castle, hundreds of them oozing out of every window and doorway. Flying Goblins screamed with excitement as they were freed into Cragfeld to attack the King's army and kill to their hearts content. The stampede of bulls and beasts poured out of the Dark Castle and they could be seen in the moonlight like a black veil moving out over the land. The King's army could be heard chanting and building themselves up for the fight even though they did not know what to expect.

The Ice Queen was smiling to herself as she saw her evil creatures spreading over Cragfeld. She had no doubt in their abilities and knew they were a terrible force that would stop at nothing until the job was done. They would keep going, keep fighting until the Ice Queen told them to stop. And she would not do that. She would make sure the King's army were so terrified of her that they would not contemplate coming back for more. The ships waiting out at sea for their soldiers would be sent home, their tails between their legs in dismay and defeat.

As her army quickly spread over Cragfeld the chanting of the army soon turned to yelling and fearful cries. The two armies had clashed, it wasn't a fair fight as the men only had shields, swords and arrows; the Ice Queens army slithered, flew and barged at them from every angle. The men could fight, stab and attack but their weapons were useless on these creatures. Wounds would heal within seconds and the beasts would never tire.

A Winged Goblin could be seen diving at the King's army from above and screaming with pleasure as it grabbed the old King by the scruff of his neck, lifted him up off the ground and carried him back to the Dark Castle. The Ice Queen could see clearly that the King had been captured and she was looking forward to showing him why he should have left her alone.

"Ah, do you see that Orme," she hissed "Did you see how effortlessly the King was taken?"

"Yes, I did my Queen," smiled Orme from under her hood "Maybe this fight won't be as much fun as you'd hoped, it will be far too easy?"

"To see my father's army suffer… that will always be fun!" The flying Goblin swooped towards the balcony and dropped the old King onto the freezing hard floor. The Ice Queen praised the goblin as it drooled black blood from the corner of its mouth. She sent it back to fight.

"Would you like me to stay here with you?" asked Orme.

"Why, where would you rather be? What could you possibly find to do that was more exciting than this?"

"No, nothing my Queen," she stuttered "But I can see what's happening better from my cauldron, I want to see where Bolstone is so I can get to him before he can get to me."

"Ah, yes, I understand," she had a cruel twinkle in her eye. "You go and do what you must to rid that buffoon for good. I can handle things here. Besides, I think I should have a bit of quality time with my father, don't you?"

"Certainly, it's long overdue…" she chuckled and hobbled away through the freezing castle.

"Ah, hello father," said Mordisan, she bent down and looked at the sad old heap of a man on the floor. "How the mighty have fallen, you're nothing like how I remember." The old King was bruised having been dropped from quite a height by the goblin – he did not hurry to get up. "Don't you have any respect for me father? Don't you know you should bow in front of a Queen?!" She used her magical powers to lift the old King up off the floor and made him bow in front of her. She had control over him like a puppet as he was lifted off the ground in a crystal sphere of ice.

"Mordisan… please…" he managed to mumble at last.

"Mordisan? Mordisan! She was lost a long time ago father. Can't you see with your pale old eyes, I am a Queen now! And you're trespassing on my Kingdom. Why come here after all these years, didn't you learn to leave us alone."

"This isn't a Kingdom," said the King "This is a sorrowful place where you're cruel to the people. If they weren't all under your dreaded curse then they would've retaliated years ago."

"How dare you speak to me like that! My people are happy, Cragfeld is happy."

"And are you happy?"

"Don't be so ridiculous. I am a Queen, I have power and rule over my people and I have their respect. I've got what I always dreamed of."

"Oh but do you…? Your people serve you no purpose to you, you chew them up and spit them out."

"And how would you know, you haven't been here for years. How would you know what happens here you old fool."

"There are ways of seeing my dear…"

"Don't you dare call me 'my dear', I am a Queen."

"You're still my daughter…"

"Really…? You never made me feel like I was your daughter when you had the chance. You never looked at me in the same way you did Rika, you always loved her more than you did me. You gave her everything… so I took it all away!"

"How can you say that? You were always loved and treated the same."

"You have no idea how you made me feel do you? You ignored me for years. You wanted to spend time with your precious Rika and throw all of your affection on her, especially once you knew the darling Prince Vecter had asked for your permission to marry her."

"That's not true."

"Don't you dare tell me I'm wrong. I was there, I grew up in the shadows. Which is where Rika is now, in the shadows, never seeing the light of the warm sun again."

"Where is she…?"

"Where is she? That's all you have to say? Not even an apology! You're more concerned about your precious Rika!"

"She's your sister, your very own blood. You used to love each other as children and play until long after sunset." He was in pain from his fall but the Ice Queen kept hold of him with her icy grip.

"She's not been my sister for a long time, in fact – I don't have a sister."

"Yes you do Mordisan, you have a sister called Rika, and I'm your father… I'm sorry I wasn't the father you wanted or deserved."

"An apology? Now we're getting somewhere. Would you like to see her, your precious Rika?" The old King nodded, he would have loved to see both daughters as he remembered them but knew Mordisan had been lost for a long, long time. The Ice Queen was actually preparing to send her father to the same place as Rika, cast in a tomb of ice.

The Ice Queen pushed the floating ice sphere in which her father was trapped along the floor of the main hall of the Dark Castle. Screams and cries could be heard in the distance by both man and beast as the fight went on. She smiled to herself, she knew she was powerful but until she had to use her powers in a battle, only now she knew what she was capable of. She was controlling an army which could not be killed and now she had her old father in her grasp. Thoughts went through her mind that she could seize him and take control of his kingdom too.

Blackfall lit the sky with a blast of fire as he circled above Cragfeld with Bolstone holding onto his back. Trennfall swooped after them while Victor tried his hardest just to stay on, it was a long way down. Below them they could see the small light of the King's army at the base of the mountains, coming through the old unused tunnel. As Bolstone saw everyone was in place he took a deep breath and readied himself for what lay ahead. He knew it was going to be a hard fight between the armies but they had to do whatever necessary for Rose to get to the Dark Castle as quickly and as easily as possible. The Ice Queen would be distracted by the King's army and Rose could slip into the Dark Castle to face her. Bolstone's main concern was Orme, he had to find her as soon as he could before she saw him. Their ongoing rivalry would come to a head tonight, Bolstone was not going to back down and knew it would take all of his strength to knock her down.

With an almighty roar, Blackfall twisted and turned in the night's sky and flew towards the Dark Castle, with Trennfall right behind him. Below them they could see the Ice Queen unleash her army as the Dark Castle shook below them. A sea of blackness could be seen passing over Cragfeld like a wave as the dark army approached the King's men. Bolstone knew the men were weak in comparison but just had to believe in themselves to fight long enough to distract the Ice Queen from seeing Rose approach from the other side. As they looked down they could see the old King who had never seen anything like this before shrink in terror as a Winged Goblin headed straight towards him and grabbed him. Bolstone's heart sank, this is the last thing he wanted to happen. He had made a promise to the King and his army that Blackfall and Trennfall would go back for the King as soon as they had been dropped at the Dark Castle. It was too late now and the old King was being carried over the fighting straight to the Ice Queen. Bolstone dreaded to think what she would do to him, she had a bitterness inside her that would only deepen with anger and resentment when she saw her father. The old wizard could not do anything to help the King right now, he had to get to Orme first and just hope the Ice Queen did not do anything too harsh in the mean-time. The two huge black Dragons landed quietly on the back courtyard of the Dark Castle. Bolstone and Victor climbed down and ran over to a corner under some steps where they would go unnoticed while they decided the best way to go. Blackfall and Trennfall jumped up into the air without a sound and flew over the Dark Castle, circling a few times before flying back to help the army. The Ice Queen's army could not be killed by man but there was nothing stopping the Dragons from attacking and killing a few. The Dragons would be able to hold back some of the evil beasts with burning fire.

Bolstone and Victor waited for a few seconds until they knew they had not been seen by anyone or anything in the Dark Castle. The light from the moon was bright and cast a pale blue glow over the courtyard. The Dark Castle sounded deathly quiet, all they could hear was the distant cries of battle in the Lowlands.

"It's a long time since I've been here," said Bolstone.

"Yes, me too," smiled Victor "Can you remember your way around?"

"I think so, an old man doesn't forget these things easily you know. How about you, can you remember your way to the tallest tower?"

"I'm sure it'll come back to me once we're inside. Which way are you going?"

"I need to find that wretched old witch. I doubt she'll be watching the show like Mordisan, she'll be in a hole somewhere keeping her head down. I'll find her, yes, yes, I will certainly find her." With that they wished each other luck and crept off in opposite directions.

As Victor climbed some steps, he began to remember his way around as if he had only been away for a few days. The Dark Castle was covered in a thick layer of solid ice which made it difficult for him to tread carefully and quietly without slipping and falling. Gwennol climbed out of his pocket and flew close to him but cast enough light from her little body so Victor could see the way. Hullard jumped down onto the floor but as soon as he realised it was ice cold, he jumped back up into the warmth of Victor's pocket. The Dark Castle was quiet but they knew they were not alone. Some of the creatures of the Ice Queens vile army had not gone out to fight, some had stayed back to guard the Dark Castle and their Queen. The halls and corridors echoed with hisses and growls but Victor could not see what was making these noises. Even the sharp eyes of the Pixie failed to see in the darkness, they could not even see their own hands in front of their eyes. It was a concern that even though Gwennol was trying to help light their way, she was actually leading whatever was wandering the Dark Castle straight to them. Victor told Gwennol to get back in his pocket and he would try and negotiate the corridors from memory. All of a sudden they felt something swoop by, causing a cold waft of air on their faces.

"Okay, what was that?" said Hullard "Did anyone else feel that?"

"Oh yes," said Victor "We aren't on our own in this place, we're being watched... maybe even hunted."

"Well that's a nice cheery thought Victor," said Hullard.

"Why don't we use Bolstone's marble or Ordram's leaf to help us see what we're up against?" suggested Gwennol.

"I was hoping not to use them until absolutely necessary," whispered Victor.

"It's either use them now or not at all... because whatever is watching us will have killed us by then," said Hullard.

"Alright, alright," snapped Victor "Which one shall we use... the weapon or the wish?"

"The wish, definitely the wish," said Gwennol.

They each reached into their pockets and pulled out each of their leaves from Ordram. As they pushed the leaves into their mouths they each made a wish. Victor and Gwennol wished for invisibility while Hullard wished to be able to throw his voice, so whatever creatures were watching them would think they were elsewhere. Hullard was only invisible by default to Victor's wish (if he stayed deep in the pocket), if he peeped out even a little bit then his head could be seen as if it were floating along. Of course with it being pitch black, they could not actually tell if the wish had worked, but from going off the noises around them, they were getting less attention. Out of the darkness came the sound of something large and heavy running down the corridor towards them. Victor pushed himself as close to the wall as possible as the huge beast cantered by. It was a bull of monstrous size with horns curled around on its head so it could crush anything in its way. It left a stench of death in the air wherever it went, as did all the evil creatures in the Ice Queen's army.

"I really, really don't like this," said Hullard.

"Trust me, you're not the only one," said Victor.

"Come on," said Gwennol "Let's try and get out of this corridor. I know we're being followed, I can feel it."

The floor was slippery and Victor was struggling to get any kind of grip underfoot. It was slow going and incredibly frustrating. Victor could hear footsteps, like hooves following them step by step. When they stopped the hooves stopped, when they walked the hooves walked. It was an un-settling feeling. Whatever it was that was behind them might not have been able to see them but it could certainly smell and hear them.

They eventually made it through the long dark corridor and into the main entrance of the Dark Castle. The ballroom was to their right and the main hall was to their left. Spiralling up and around them was a beautiful ornate stair-way which had been frozen in ice and time, ice crystals and icicles were delicately hanging off the banister. Moonlight shone through the open doorway and windows so the three friends could at least see where they were. They could see the small doorway at the back of the room which led to the staircase which wound its way up to the top of the tallest tower. They could hear the Ice Queen's voice echoing around the main hall but they could not see her or who she was talking to. Her voice echoed around, sounding cruel and heartless with every icy breath. They crouched down at the bottom of the stairs and listened for a while. They could hear the screams and fighting in the distance, they could almost feel the pain that the men must have been feeling. Every now and then there was a reassuring roar as the Dragons threw fire over the Ice Queen's army. The Ice Queen's voice drifted through the Dark Castle and they could hear her saying the word 'father' a few times. It quickly became clear that the flying Goblin had taken the old King straight to their Queen. Gwennol flew over to the main hall and hovered in the door-way, she was invisible and made no sound as she watched the Ice Queen tormenting her father. She could see the old King being held in a ball of ice while the Ice Queen talked at him with venom. Gwennol turned to fly back to Victor and Hullard but as she did so she saw a black shadow out of the corner of her eye. Two goblins had followed them along the corridor and into the grand entrance. However, now Victor and Hullard were sitting still, the goblins couldn't hear them, so they were trying to sniff them out. Gwennol flew over them and straight to Victor's pocket where she whispered to Hullard to throw his voice as there were two ugly goblins trying to pick up their scent. Victor could hear the footsteps of the goblins, tiptoeing and edging closer, he could smell the stench that they carried with them into the room. Victor did not want to waste Bolstone's marble because whatever weapon he chose he could not kill these things. Gwennol could see the two goblins getting closer and closer to her friends. Hullard was too scared to make a sound in case he couldn't throw his voice at all and it brought them straight to them instead. Gwennol flew up and then swooped down and hit a goblin on the back of its head, which made it spin round thinking it was his friend who did it. She then did the same thing to the other one. Hullard suddenly found his voice and threw it into the ballroom. The two goblins weren't really listening now because they were fighting with each other, thinking they had each started the fight. While they were bickering Victor inched away from them and stood next to the doorway to the main hall. The Ice Queen then came storming through from the main hall with King trapped in a swirling ball of ice. The two goblins saw her and scarpered, if she knew they were squabbling instead of guarding the Dark Castle then they would be in trouble. Victor looked on as the Ice Queen disappeared through the doorway with the old King, up to the tallest tower. Victor had hoped not to meet Mordisan, he wanted to slip in, get Rika and then get out as quickly as possible. It wasn't going to be that easy.

As soon as Bolstone and Blackfall had announced battle to commence, all the Grocklings who had be sitting patiently waiting suddenly jumped into action. Hundreds of them leaped out of the cave and off the side of the mountain to run down to Cragfeld and fight the Ice Queen's army. These were just the regular little Grocklings without any fighting skills. They did not think themselves small, even though they were tiny in comparison to what had been unleashed from the Dark Castle. They might be small but their courage was big and they would help out as best they could. Like the Dragons, the Grocklings could help the King's army because they did not have human blood running through their veins. The Ice Queen and the old witch must have thought the King's army would not have any support or help from any other being, be it foreign Dragons or domestic Grocklings. The throng of Grocklings sped down the mountain, each carrying a sharp little dagger, their only weapon against the vile creatures. These little daggers would actually do more harm to the Ice Queen's army because they were not held by human hands so the wounds wouldn't heal.

Frithad and Eady were the only two Grocklings left in the cave with Rose, Furdon and Fiddy. As the heads of the family they were not allowed to fight but wished Rose and their two friends luck. Frithad reminded Rose to concentrate on getting to the Dark Castle as quickly and as quietly as possible and avoid the Ice Queen until the very last minute. Frithad could see Rose wanted to do this but was also scared, he reminded her not to forget her inner warrior who would push Rose to keep going even when she thought it was a hopeless task. They said their goodbyes and began their descent down the mountain. Furdon and Fiddy went first, scrambling effortlessly down the sharp craggy mountain side. Rose found she was a lot more confident in doing this now than she was the first time.

As the side of the mountain rumbled far beneath them, shifting in the night as it always had done, the path became easier and less steep. The howls of the Silvertips could be heard all over the mountain, they also knew something was happening and were gathering together in packs around the mountains. Rose and the Grocklings stumbled upon five Silvertips, all snarling and growling with anger. They had seen Blackfall in the skies and could smell the reek pouring out of the Dark Castle. One of the Silvertips saw Rose and ran up to her, still drooling and snarling. Furdon and Fiddy were not fond of Silvertips so hung back and hid behind Rose's legs. Rose put her arm up towards the Silvertip and it immediately calmed down and almost purred at her. She did not know if it understood her but she spoke to it anyway and told it what was happening, with the King's men and the Ice Queen's army, and that they were trying to end her cruel reign. The Silvertip raised itself up on its back legs and yelped and howled into the air, its calls were returned from the other sides of the mountains. The five Silvertips dashed down the mountain to join the Grocklings in their fight against the Ice Queen. Furdon and Fiddy were quite surprised by this, they had seen a different side to the Silvertips when Rose was around.

The moon was bright in the night sky and they could see silhouettes moving down on Cragfeld. They could seen the army pouring out of the Dark Castle and over the villages to the Lowlands of the mountains where the King and his army were waiting. Rose could not see clearly what was happening but knew the Grocklings and Silvertips would join together and help the King's men. In the sky, they could see Blackfall and Trennfall circling and then disappearing behind the Dark Castle. Only a few moments later they were back in the air and throwing flames down on the battle site, attacking the creatures who were thirsty for human blood. They knew once they saw the Dragons back in the air that Bolstone and Victor had been dropped off behind the Dark Castle.

As the three of them approached the villages of Cragfeld, which they had to walk through to get to the Dark Castle they could see the people walking around as if nothing was happening. There were men and women carrying on with their lives completely oblivious to the fighting in the Lowlands. The people of Cragfeld did not even seem to see Rose and the Grocklings as they moved through the streets. Rose had now got used to meeting people with life in their eyes, Troostan, Victor, Bolstone… but now she was back here, she was quickly reminded how these people had lifeless eyes, misted over by the Ice Queen's magic. It actually felt as if they were walking through a ghost town, a place which was once full of life was now full of the lifeless. People were sitting in pubs or in their homes utterly unaware and unresponsive to anything apart from each other around them. Furdon and Fiddy did not like it, the last time they had been down in the villages of Cragfeld it felt like a different place – they hardy recognised it now. They strolled through the streets unnoticed by anyone.

In front of them stood the Dark Castle, it's tall silhouette soared above them. The steps leading up to the main entrance were covered in a thick layer of ice and they each struggled to climb them. Fiddy pulled Spinbra's rope out of his bag and threw one end as far as he could up the steps to see if it would grab onto anything, with a tug he felt it was latched onto something so they could now try and pull themselves up the slippery steps. One step at a time they shuffled their way to the top. They could hear the fighting in the distance and it sent a chill to their core. They knew their friends were out there fighting for them, which meant they had to succeed in getting Rika out of the Dark Castle and face the Ice Queen and her wrath.

When they approached the top of the steps they could now see that Spinbra's rope had looped itself around the leg of the biggest bull they had ever seen. It had not seen them but was standing guarding the doorway of the Dark Castle, it was looking out towards the Lowlands where the battle was in full force. This bull had long black fur which dangled low from its body and hung around its eyes and ears. Six mangled horns grew from its head, four were for pounding and crushing, two were for stabbing and prodding. Its large hooves stood firmly on the ice which creaked under the weight of the beast. Rose did not want to get its attention so they left the rope where it was and tried to sneak around the back of it. Just then they heard a hissing sound as a big black snake slithered in front of the bull and down the steps which they had just climbed up. The bull did not like the snake as it make him jump and he stepped back out of its way, almost trampling on Rose, Furdon and Fiddy. The snake flicked its black tongue into the night air, it had picked up their scent. It turned back on itself and slowly slithered back up the steps. The three friends now found themselves standing between the two back feet of this monstrous bull and being sniffed out by an evil black snake. The bull had not caught their scent so was wondering what the snake was doing, whatever it was doing the bull did not like it dancing around near its feet. As the bull pranced on the ice to avoid the snake, Rose could see the situation could get a lot worse.

"We're either going to get trampled to death or bitten by that snake if we don't think of something," said Furdon.

"Let's share one of Ordram's leaves," said Rose "That way we still have more if we need them once we're inside…"

"Ok, let's share this one," said Fiddy pulling a golden leaf from his pocket. "Now we all have to make the same wish at the same time as we eat this…"

"I suggest we wish to be able to get out of here as fast as we can," said Rose "Let's wish for the ability to be able to jump as if we can fly?"

"Yes, perfect," said Furdon.

They ate the sweet tasting leaf and edged further back behind the bull. Furdon spotted a low rooftop which they could aim for. The snake was getting closer and closer and the bull was getting more agitated so Rose and the Grocklings did not have time to waste. They looked at the rooftop and leaped with all their might and flew effortlessly through the air, landing safely out of the way. It was just in time too because the snake had now truly spooked the bull which slipped on the ice as he bolted out of snakes way. The snake pounced but hissed with disappointement when nothing was there. It flicked its tongue trying to pick up their scent again. Before it had the chance to do so, Rose, Furdon and Fiddy had jumped up and further around the sides of the Dark Castle out of the black snake's reach.

"That was a bit too close for comfort," said Fiddy.

"Let's try to be a bit more careful," said Rose "Let's avoid the main ways in and try and get in through an unguarded window."

They scrambled around the sides of the walls of the Dark Castle and quickly felt the effect of Ordram's leaf wearing off. They were supposed to have one leaf each, so the effect of having one between them had split its strength in three. This was not a major disaster as they had got out of danger and were managing to climb down to an open window. Like the floors of the Dark Castle, the walls both inside and out had a thick layer of ice, making it quite difficult to grab onto anything. They ended up sliding down a shallow rooftop and in through a window with a bump.

"Not the easiest way… but we're in," said Furdon in a low voice "Do you know where you are Miss Rose?"

"Er, no I don't know where we are," she whispered "I've not been here for a long time and Ordram helped me forget a lot of this place. Maybe it will come back to me as we walk around." As soon as she stood up she fell down again, the ice inside the Dark Castle was just as solid as outside.

"Maybe we should stay low and crawl Miss Rose," suggested Furdon "It might be easier for us to move along these dark corridors."

"Ok, good idea."

"Which way do you think we should go?" asked Fiddy "Down to the left into darkness, or down to the right into darkness!"

"Let's go this way," said Rose "If we go down to the right it will hopefully bring us back to the main entrance and things might start looking familiar again."

As they crawled along the frozen corridors they could only just see where they were going from the moonlight shining in through the occasional open window. Through these open windows they could hear the fighting echoing down from the Lowlands, it was not a pleasant sound. Howls, screams, cries and roars sent an awful tingle down Rose's back.

Eventually the corridor began to feel as if it was opening up as they approached the top of the main entrance. They found themselves next to an ornate banister which went along a landing and down a beautiful curved staircase to the main entrance of the Dark Castle. There were many large open windows letting moonlight in so they could see down to the ground floor. They could hear the Ice Queen's voice coming from the main hall and terrible screeches coming from the ballroom. They sat quietly watching and waiting to see if they would be able to get down the stairs without the Ice Queen walking out and seeing them. As they peeked through the frozen banister rails they could see two dark figures skulking along the hallway below. These two dark figures appeared to be looking for something.

"Goblins," whispered Furdon "Trust the Ice Queen to have goblins wandering the corridors, tear you to bits before you have chance to look at them. Horrible things!"

"They look as if they're looking for something, do you think they've already caught out scent?"

"I doubt it," said Furdon "They haven't got the best sense of smell, they track their prey by sound."

"Best we keep quiet then," interrupted Fiddy.

Just then the Ice Queen burst out of the main hall with an old man in a frozen ball of ice, he was in her control and there was nothing he could do about it. Rose looked down at the old man but could not see through the blurred spinning of the ice ball as to who it was. The two goblins ran back down the corridor out of sight. The Ice Queen strode across the main entrance of the Dark Castle with hatred in her face and anger raging through her veins. Her white gown of ice and crystal glittered in the soft light and her red hair looked like fire blazing around her.

"Sorry you had to see him like that Miss Rose," said Furdon.

"Sorry to see who like that?"

"That was the old King, your father. Looks like the Ice Queen picked him up before Blackfall could."

"Oh no, what? Where do you think she's taking him?"

"I wouldn't know."

"Should we follow them to find out, we have to help him."

"No Miss Rose, we don't. We have to help Rika remember, we can deal with the Ice Queen as soon as we know Victor has got Rika out."

"And where do you suppose Victor is? He could be any-where in this dreadful place. I feel as if we're being watched all the time in here, I can hear footsteps all around us but when I turn around there's nothing there. Now we're here in the main entrance it feels worse than ever, those noises coming from inside the ballroom sound horrendous."

"I know Rose, it's creeping us out too," said Fiddy as he comfortingly stroked her arm.

"Look, what's that down there now... another goblin?" said Rose. They saw a lone figure at the bottom of the stair-case near the door of the main hall slowly walk across the floor below them. It moved towards the doorway which the Ice Queen had gone through.

"Maybe it's one of her servants," said Furdon "It doesn't have the same posture or smell as a goblin."

Just then out of the blue, Gwennol appeared in front of them and made them all jump. Gwennol had forgotten she had been invisible as she flew up the staircase. She had heard the voices of her friends and made a bee-line for them. As she got to the top of the stairs the magic of Ordram's leaf wore off and she suddenly became visible again and a flash of the Fairy dust appeared in front of them.

"Gwennol! Thank goodness it's you," sighed Rose in relief "I'm hearing noises all around us and feeling we're being watched, thank goodness it's you my little friend."

"I've only just heard you... so came straight up. There are other things around us though, Victor was followed all through the Dark Castle, that's why we had to wish for invisibility."

"Wait, was that Victor down there? Walking from the bottom of the staircase to that little doorway over there?"

"Yes, the magic from the golden leaf seems to have worn of now, so we'll have to be careful because we haven't got any left."

"We didn't use all of ours," said Fiddy "And we still have

all of Bolstone's marbles."

"As do we," said Gwennol "Good to see you got here okay though. I must go and tell Victor you're here, he'll be glad to know you're safe."

"Where's he going?" asked Rose.

"He's going up into the tallest tower to get Rika."

"So why is he following the Ice Queen?"

"Because that's where she's going too."

"And she's taking the King up there?"

"Yes, so it seems."

"I was hoping we could distract the Ice Queen from that tower so Victor could get Rika," said Rose "This is going to be a lot more complicated if we all end up there together. Have you seen Bolstone?" The little Fairy shook her head.

Gwennol told her friends to follow them through the doorway, they had no option but to go up into the tallest tower. The little Fairy darted over the bannister and flew after Victor to tell him that Rose, Furdon and Fiddy were in the Dark Castle and would be following them.

Rose was beginning to remember where she was. The last time she walked down these stairs was as Rika, when Vecter met her at the bottom and linked arms with her before walking over to the balcony and asking for her hand in marriage. That was a very long time ago though. She now stood at the top of the staircase and looked down into the cold dark gloom, it did not feel like the same place that she grew up in. As they walked down the stairs they could hear Blackfall and Trennfall blasting fire in the distance. She had to remember what Frithad had told her, when she was feeling weak she had to summon her inner strength to fight the hardest fight.

CHAPTER SEVENTEEN

Bolstone made quick progress through the Dark Castle. He used his magic so that he could float through the frozen corridors, he was silent and did not make a sound. Bolstone knew Orme would be hiding away down in the belly of the Dark Castle. Fortunately Bolstone knew his way around very well and had a vague idea of where he would find her. As he moved through the lower corridors he could hear the tormenting calls from the Ice Queen and her army as they stormed around above him. In his black cloak he was well-hidden amongst the darkness of this cold place.

As Bolstone approached Orme's den he could hear her hissing and muttering to herself. He was going to try and coax her out into the open so they could sort out their squabble once and for all. Now he knew where she was, he knew exactly what to do. He dropped a small orange marble onto the floor and let it roll with his guidance through the door of her den and bounce to the floor… tap, tap, tap it bounced. Orme heard and saw this straight away and screamed at it, she knew what it was and who it was from. She knew Bolstone was here. The old witch hobbled up the steps in search of the old wizard but she could not see him. Bolstone dropped another marble, then another and another until she was following the trail he had left. Orme was hissing and puffing along the corridors, she would soon have hold of Bolstone and he would regret being so bold as to coax her out into the open. Orme followed the marbles through the Dark Castle until they came to the main hall. Here in the main hall they had space to air their magic and have a final show down.

"I'm glad you could join me," said Bolstone, standing tall at the end of the room.

"I wouldn't miss it for the world," she snarled.

"You think all of your dreams have come true don't you, being partner to the Ice Queen?"

"It's a lot more successful that what you have, you old goat – let me guess, you're still living under the mountains with your silly white cat?"

"Alfred's not silly."

"So you are still living your sad little life."

"I wouldn't say that. I think this is more depressing than anything I've ever seen – craving power and control over a Kingdom and settling for a Queen who sucks all the life from her people... No, no, no, your story is a lot more depressing."

"You're wrong," she growled. She stood tall and swung her cloak around her and turned into a young woman. She looked like the young woman she was when she and Bolstone were at school together. "I'm still me but with magic which is darker than you could ever imagine."

"Is that so?" said Bolstone, spinning around and turning himself into the young man he used to be. "I think it's time we end this argument as to who's best, don't you?"

"Indeed it is... I hope you're ready for failure."

"I don't know what you mean, I'm looking at it right now!"

Bolstone, now looking like he was in his thirties with thick brown hair and a long orange beard had the strength returning to his limbs. The old witch was now a beautiful young woman with golden hair swishing over her shoulders and down her slender frame. It was a long time since they had both looked liked this, pushing a thousand years or so. Orme was muttering under her breath, summoning dark magic to her hands. She looked up and saw Bolstone standing and looking at her as he played with three apple-sized orange balls in his hand.

"Now what are you messing at?" she glared at him.

"Oh nothing, just waiting for you to get yourself and your magic together. When your magic is as strong a mine, it's automatically in one's hand."

"We'll see!" she hissed.

Orme summoned a magic from deep within her, a dark power she had been building stronger throughout her life. Between her hands she called up an electrifying thunderbolt of dark magic which would knock Bolstone off his high horse. She spun the thunderbolt playfully between her hands and arms before lifting it up and throwing it at her rival. It was supposed to knock him to the floor and pin him down so she could torment and torture him while he lay powerless and defenceless. Bolstone raised his hand and exploded the thunderbolt in front of him, he did not seem fazed. He then played with an orange ball, throwing it up in the air and catching it in his own little game. With both hands he threw the orange ball which had absorbed some of the old witch's magic right back at her, shortly followed by his own power ball, both exploded at they reached the witch. She held her arms up to protect herself but was knocked to the floor by the blast.

"Are you sure you still want to play this game?" he jested.

"I've never been more certain," she got her breath back and stood tall once more. "It will take more than that to beat me."

"Hmmm, from what I can see you're all bluff and bluster."

Orme then launched seven thunderbolts at Bolstone which he fended off well until it got to the last two which pushed him across the floor to the other end of the room. Orme laughed at him. She laughed because she had the upper hand and was going to enjoy pushing him down again and again until he admitted he was not as powerful as she was.

Bolstone go to his feet and marched back to the middle of the main hall. The chandelier above their heads rattled as the captives in each crystal cheered and supported Bolstone, this angered Orme even more.

"You only think you're powerful when you have the Ice Queen by your side don't you?" said Bolstone "You're nothing when you're on your own are you?"

"That's what you think. I seemed to have kept you at bay for all these years."

Bolstone rubbed his orange beard and saw out of the corner of his eye, a small orange marble rolling across the floor from the doorway towards Orme. He knew it was Rose, she had remembered what he had said. Bolstone was filled with relief that Rose had made it to the Dark Castle and the fight with the Ice Queen would almost be done. The feeling of knowing he was not alone filled him with a great warmth. This was a power that Orme would never know, it was a power that came from goodness and would always over-power any other sort of magic, especially dark magic. The little orange marble that Rose had carried with her had absorbed some of her kindness and it rolled slowly and quietly towards Orme, stopping by her foot. The old witch did not even notice it because she was full of so much anger. Bolstone relaxed his shoulders and took a step back as if he had all the time in the world. Orme found this incredibly frustrating, she just wanted to get this over with. Bolstone let go another orange ball from his hand and it slowly floated over to Orme until it was above her head. She turned to Bolstone and gave him a look of 'Is this all you've got?" Bolstone clicked his fingers and both the orange marble and the orange ball burst around Orme and splattered her in a bright orange gunk.

"Is this the best you can do?" she snarled "Orange slime?"

Bolstone stood back and smiled as he watched Orme begin to squirm. The orange slime as she called it began to spread all over her like paint. She watched as her skin was covered in Bolstone's signature orange which she hated because it represented the rival she detested. As the orange gloop smeared itself all over her she screamed insults at the old wizard. She summoned another powerful blast of fire within her hands and threw it at Bolstone. He was knocked off his feet and covered in a blue powder, Orme's signature blue. It enraged both of them to be covered in a colour which represented their enemy. Orme used the anger she felt to create powerful spells which would really test Bolstone. As angry as he was, he knew it wouldn't help him and he had to focus on Rose and her mission. What Orme did not realise was the marble which Rose had rolled over, (the one that had exploded) was slowly blocking the old witch's pores and seeping through her skin. Orme thought it was a cheap trick from Bolstone to cover her in orange slime, she did not realise what was happening as they fought on. Thunderbolt after thunderbolt, strike after strike and blow after blow they fought each other. This fight had been building for hundreds of years and now it was time for them to clash head on. These two old rivals were as determined as each other to win and have the upper hand. They would fight as long as they had to, until one of them won.

The main hall was filled with flashing lights as they struck each other with lightning bolts and fire balls. The Dark Castle shook around them as they went on blow after blow for hours. Flashes of oranges and blues filled the room with every attack from each side. A couple of goblins were standing in the doorway watching but could do nothing, they would be turned to dust if they got in the way.

Up in the tallest tower of the Dark Castle the Ice Queen had taken her father to see Rika. As she marched up the frozen spiral staircase she could have sworn she heard a voice behind her but realised it must have been the cries from her creatures as they guarded the Dark Castle. In front of her she pushed the ball of ice in which her father stood helpless. Up and up they went, higher and higher until they reached the frozen chamber in which his precious daughter was trapped. The Ice Queen raised one hand in front of her and melted a hole in the wall through which she would force her father to face the reality of her anger.

"You want to see your darling Rika," she growled "Then here she is... just how you remember her!"

The old King was still trapped in the ice sphere but he could see Rika perfectly clearly. It was as if what had happened to her had only been done to her the day before, she had not aged a day and looked exactly as she did on the day he lost her. Mordisan watched his face carefully as he looked at his daughter.

"Mordisan... you did this, you did this to your own sister?"

"Of course I did! Who else would want to destroy her? She caused me so much pain, now look at her... no use to anyone now is she? I would've thought you'd have wanted to fight for her though. Neither you or her dearest Vecter attempted to get her back." As she mentioned Vecter's name she saw the expression on her father's face alter slightly. "Oh no, really this is too good to be true. Vecter is here too isn't he? He's joined you on your silly little quest. Where is the oh so wonderful Prince charming?"

"He's out there... fighting whatever monsters you've created."

"Is he indeed. He won't be out there long, in fact he may even be dead by now. Such a shame, it would've been lovely to see him again, like a little family reunion." She smiled a cruel smile, full of venom and hate. Mordisan stepped over to her sister's frozen tomb and glared at her and then back to her father. "It didn't have to turn out like this you know, if only you'd have seen me and shown me some love as a child. If you think about it, all this is because of you."

"No, no it's not Mordisan, don't be thinking you can blame anyone else for this... it's all your doing."

"Hmmm, yes I suppose you're right and I did such a great job too, didn't I!"

"You call this sorcery a 'great job'? You're deluded! Take a good look at what Cragfeld has become because of you."

"Oh, please! Who cares about this little insignificant island really? It just happened to be the perfect place for me and Orme to grow strong off the weak population... they'd do anything for me."

"Only because you've cursed them all and they don't have a choice."

"Again, that's your fault, you left such a pathetic population when you deserted Cragfeld, so easy to manipulate. It was so easy in fact, it actually became boring."

"So you did all of this out of boredom?"

"Don't be stupid. I did all this because of you father, so you couldn't ignore me anymore. In the last one hundred and fifty years I doubt one day has gone by without you thinking of me, even indirectly your thoughts of Rika and Cragfeld would always lead back to me."

"What do you want from me Mordisan? You've had your apology, why don't you just let me go?"

"Let you go? Why would I let you go? You've come to see Rika and here she is. Oh no, father dearest... you're staying with me now. Surely you didn't think a little insincere apology would make everything better, make it all go away. You came here tonight for Rika didn't you? You didn't want to come back for me!"

"I hoped to have you back too... but now, even though

you're my daughter, I don't recognise you at all."

"Good! Maybe now I'll have some damn respect off you!"

"Just let me and Rika go, we'll leave you in peace and never come back to Cragfeld."

"And what would be the fun in that? No father, like I said – you're staying with me now and there's nothing you can do about it. Wouldn't it be nice to stay here with your daughters, here in the tower with Rika! Your army can't save you, they're all being slaughtered out there, listen to their cries," she pointed out towards the Lowlands. She was about to speak again but was stopped when a strange smell caught her nose "What is that stench you brought with you?"

"I don't know what you're talking about."

"I can smell… I can smell Pixies. Is it one of yours or is it a stowaway from one of your little ships."

"Mordisan… I don't know."

"Don't call me Mordisan, I am the Ice Queen! Have some respect."

At that moment Victor stepped into the doorway with Hullard on his shoulder. Gwennol was hanging back in the stairway out of the way, she hated the Ice Queen and didn't want to see her.

"Hello, Mordisan…" he said boldly, stepping into the frozen room "It's been a while."

"Vecter, well, well, well, look what the tide has washed in. It was only a matter of time I suppose before you showed yourself. Let me guess, the heroic Prince comes to save the day and rescue the King and his long-lost Rika?"

"That sounds about right, yes."

"Very bold, very bold." Her eyes flashed with silver as she looked him up and down. Her red hair almost came to life as it swished around her shoulders like a hundred poisonous snakes. "I see you've brought a little friend with you, a Pixie for luck maybe? I could smell that stinking thing a mile off. That Pixie will bring you no luck, nothing can bring either of you any luck now. You've both walked straight into my Castle as if you wanted me to have such an easy job taking you and tormenting you, torturing you."

"We've not come for you Mordisan, you can have Cragfeld, just let us take Rika. I promise we'll leave you alone."

"Ha, you are just as silly as the old King here. If either of you think I'd let Rika go then you're seriously deluded. Now I have you both here, I'm sorry to inform you that you'll both be joining Rika in a comforting tomb of ice... for eternity. It's what you really want after all, to be with your darling Rika!" Her silver eyes lit up and she snapped her fingers at Victor and encased him in a swirling ball of ice, just as the King was in.

"Mordisan stop this," said Victor "You can't do this!"

"Oh I assure you I can. You're forgetting this is my Kingdom and I can do whatever the hell I like. I'm the Ice Queen and you're trespassing." She hissed at Victor and her father as they were both trapped in balls of ice, they could still move but they certainly couldn't get out.

"Let your father go, he's an old man. He doesn't deserve this."

"He deserves everything I throw at him Vecter, he made me this way. You should be glad I have him here with me now, goodness knows what else he's capable of."

"You could let the Ice Queen go," said the old King "Be Mordisan again, be my daughter again."

"It's too late for that father," she snarled "It's too late for that happy ending you've always wished for. There's some good news for you both though, you're both going to be here with Rika for all eternity... the bad news is you'll be frozen in time and forgotten about. Oh and father, as your only surviving heir then I'll take those ships of yours and what's left of your army... and take your Kingdom too!" She watched as the old man looked pale and lost.

"Mordisan," said Victor "Don't do this, why would you do this?"

"Let me see," she growled "Maybe because I hate both of you too, almost as much as I hate my sister. And now look, you can have your happy ever after with your beloved after all, I might even perform a wedding service for you…!"

The Dark Castle shook around them, the Ice Queen thought her creatures were becoming restless but it was actually the blasts that Bolstone and Orme were firing at each other. The Ice Queen ignored the vibrations and started to cast the spell to send the King and Victor to their frozen lifeless coffins. The room went dark and both Victor and the old King looked at each other helplessly. Hullard was cursing under his breath and wishing he had stayed with Gwennol, out of sight and out of trouble. Victor had not seen things going this way, he thought Mordisan would be so busy with her father that she would not even notice him. Unfortunately the Pixie smell of Hullard gave them away before they had chance to assess the situation. They were all frustrated at themselves as well as each other, having both failed Rose and Rika. A dark purple glow filled the room as the Ice Queen began to spin the balls of ice in which Victor and her father were trapped. Her victims could not move and could not speak, all they could do was watch as the magic took its hold. They felt cold like they'd never felt before as ice began to form around them. Mordisan closed her eyes and spun the ice quicker and quicker, her eyes went black as she summoned the cruel magic. She looked up and saw it was working exactly as she wanted, she smiled to herself at finally getting what she had always wanted, the three people who had ruined her life now altogether forever. Once the spell was cast the purple glow in the room disappeared and the dim light returned. The old King and Victor (and Hullard) were now trapped, encased in solid ice. She did not want to kill them, that would be too easy, she much preferred to keep them alive and haunt their dreams. For Victor and the old King it was as if they had been put in a constant state of drowsiness, they could not wake up but they could still hear everything around them. They could hear the Ice Queen walking around the room, they could hear her voice growling at them with hatred. It had been said that the Ice Queen's heart had frozen over when she captured and trapped her sister, now she had got her father and the Prince – it was as if she had not got a heart at all.

Now the spell was over, Gwennol did not dare see what had happened to her friends. She had been listening to what the Ice Queen was saying and knew her friends could not be helped, her Fairy magic was nothing compared to that of the Ice Queen. As much as Gwennol wanted to help her friends, there was nothing she could do and would have ended up in the same state as Hullard. The little Fairy was in tears as she turned back and flew down the stairs to find Rose who was somewhere behind her. She was flying at such a speed and in such a state that she flew straight into Rose. Rose had climbed halfway up the tallest tower when Gwennol crashed into her.

"Rose, oh Rose, oh deary, deary… not good, it's not good."

"Whatever's happened Gwennol?"

"It's too late, we're too late…"

"What do you mean?" asked Rose, looking down at Furdon and Fiddy who were equally baffled.

"The Ice Queen, she's, she's got them… She's got Victor and Hullard and your father. She trapped them in ice and did the same thing to them as she did to Rika."

"Has she indeed!" said Rose "Well, she's not going to do that to us, is she?" The Grocklings shook their heads, they did not know what was going to happen but certainly did not relish the idea of being frozen, neither living or dead.

"But what can you do? She's full of so much anger and hate."

"I'm sure she is," smiled Rose "But nobody does that to my friends."

Rose continued up the hundreds of steps of the tower, she was racing up as she was fuelled by anger at what the Ice Queen had done. Furdon and Fiddy ran after her, with Gwennol finding herself going back up to where she had been hiding. As they got to the top of the stairs the corridor felt freezing cold, even colder than the rest of the Dark Castle. They could hear the Ice Queen in the frozen chamber talking to the old King, Victor and Rika. Her voice sounded cruel as she taunted her new prisoners, welcoming them to the family. As she spoke to Rika, it was as if Rose was hearing her whispering in her ear which was unsettling. Rose told her friends to wait at the top of the stairs, she did not want them getting hurt or frozen. She told them to use Ordram's leaves to help them get out of the Dark Castle, if the worst came to the worst.

"But Miss Rose, we've sworn to protect you…" insisted Furdon.

"And you have done a great job," she smiled "But I have to face her on my own, don't worry, I'll come back for you as soon as I can." Fiddy and Furdon smiled at her courage but were scared for her.

Rose crept over to the door of the frozen chamber and peered in. She saw the Ice Queen standing tall in her gown of crystals and staring at her frozen family. As Rose stepped through the door, Furdon and Fiddy crept over to the doorway and crouched as low as they could to stay out of sight while they watched Rose and Mordisan face each other. Rose could feel her heart racing as she got closer to the chamber, stepping through its thick walls of ice and seeing the Ice Queen for the first time. At first glance Mordisan looked how Rose remembered with thick red hair pouring over her shoulders and down her back. When she looked closer she could see her eyes were silver and her skin was whiter than snow as no warm blood ran through this woman's veins. Her skin had not aged a day and to all who did not know her she would look quite beautiful with her plump red lips and slender figure draped in ice crystals. Rose quietly stepped into the room. Mordisan sensed there was someone there but did not turn around to see who it was, she had nothing to fear.

After a few seconds, which felt like hours to Rose, the Ice Queen turned around to see who was bothering her now. To Furdon, Fiddy and all her friends she looked like Rose but to the Ice Queen she looked like Rika. As Rose stood still and quiet, the Ice Queen stared at her in disbelief, how could her sister be standing in front of her when she was a frozen captive.

"Hello sister," said Rose. Now she looked at her sister she felt strange, it was as if Rose was reconnecting with Rika and her memory of Mordisan was coming back.

"Rika?" she hissed "That's not really you is it?"

"Yes. Have you missed me?" Rose was beginning to feel her nerves fade and be replaced with confidence. All the time she reminded herself of her inner warrior, she could do this. She looked over at the three frozen bodies of Victor, the old King and her former self and felt sad to see them in that way. She looked back at Mordisan and saw her steely silver eyes staring back at her.

"No, I haven't missed you! What, how are you standing over there… when I have you frozen here?"

"Ah, the wonder of magic," said Rose "You didn't manage to capture all of me, Bolstone stopped you remember… and saved most of my life-source. Only a bit stayed here with you."

"That's a lie. Bolstone is up to his old tricks again…"

"No, I assure you he's not been up to anything. I am your sister and I've come to claim the remaining part of me… and my friends."

"Your friends? You mean this silly old man who used to be our father and this stupid little boy who was your handsome Prince. Well, you can't have them, they're mine now. As for you, then I think we need to unite you with your true self and get you inside this tomb with what's left of you."

The Ice Queen scowled at Rose and her eyes flashed with hatred as she summoned two huge spinning balls of ice in her hands to throw over Rose. She released them with a powerful heave, to trap Rose in ice as she had done with Victor and the King. However, the balls of ice burst like water balloons before they could hit Rose and it was like she had an invisible protective shield around her. The Ice Queen scowled and did the same thing again, only for them to burst and cause no harm to Rose. This infuriated Mordisan, she hated her sister and the last thing she wanted to see was two of her. She screamed in frustration, why wasn't her magic working, was she so unsettled that it had affected her powers?

"What's wrong Mordisan? You don't seem quite as strong as you were…"

"Urgh, I despise you Rika. Why can't you just leave me alone, I wish I'd killed you when I had the chance. I hated you all those years ago and that hasn't changed, only that I hate you more. Where have you been hiding all these years, tiptoeing around me like a coward I suppose?"

"I've been right here on Cragfeld, right under your nose and you never saw me."

"Why haven't you stepped forward before now?"

"Because only now I've been given what I needed to destroy you."

"Ha, you can't destroy me. You are weak, you've always been weak. Your gentle heart always left you vulnerable."

"No, my gentle heart has made me stronger than you could imagine."

"I doubt that very much. You don't have the courage to go

up against me."

"Are you sure about that? Maybe you would rather release your captives and we can go home and forget today ever happened. Unless of course, you're scared of what I could do to you?"

"You can't do anything to me!"

Furdon and Fiddy were hanging on to every word being spoken and could not believe their Rose was being so courageous. She seemed fearless as she spoke with her sister.

"What makes you think I can't do anything to you?" said Rose softly.

"Because I am the Ice Queen and I am immortal, this is my Kingdom and Castle. You're just my pathetic sister who was and still is, full of daydreams."

Rose could feel the spiky locket under her collar becoming warmer. She loosened the ties on her cloak and pulled the golden locket out of hiding so Mordisan could see it. Mordisan looked at it and thought nothing of it.

"What's that, your lucky charm?" she snarled.

"Something like that, yes. I doubt you'll recognise it but you used to have a locket made from the same gold... our father had one specially made for each of us."

"I doubt that! He probably gave one, or both to you. He never gave me anything, which is why I took his every-thing..."

"You think you're so strong, don't you? If you actually took a good look at yourself, you're actually quite pathetic."

"How dare you speak to me like that," the Ice Queen stormed over to Rose and grabbed her throat with her cold hand, her red nails digging into Rose's skin. "Now can you feel how strong I am? I have more power than you could dream of." As her hands touched Rose, a strong dark haze passed through Rose. In those few seconds she could see into the sinister depths of her sister, her blood was like poison and her heart was frozen solid. Mordisan squeezed her hand tighter around Rose's throat and sent another wave of darkness over her, this time she could see all of the deathly things her sister had done since taking the throne.

"Whatever you do to me," said Rose "Will never bring you the love you so crave from our father. He came here to show you that he still saw you as his daughter... but look what you did to him. Your selfish desire for control is getting you nothing you actually want."

"Is that what you think? You think all I wanted was some affection and attention? Oh no dear sister, I wanted far more than that. I wanted respect, I wanted to be feared... can't you see I have that? And now I have you, every last drop of you – I hate you more today than ever before. Which is why I'm going to throw you back to your cold grave where you belong, out of sight and out of mind. Don't worry though, you have company this time with those pathetic figures over there. Send them my hate won't you!"

As Mordisan squeezed her cold hand around Rose's throat she sent a cold pulse through her body. Ice crystals began to form on Rose's skin and frosted their way slowly up to her face. Mordisan was taking her time with this one, she wanted her sister to feel the pain and darkness that she had felt all of her life. Rose felt the ice running through her body and she could see and feel the cruel heart of her sister overwhelming her and choking her like a black fog.

Rose could feel she was being suffocated by her sister. Rose closed her eyes and blocked out the image in front of her, she needed to focus and dig deep inside of her for the strength to fight back. Like a fire inside her heart, she felt life coursing through every cell. As she opened her eyes, Mordisan saw flames within her sister's eyes which were burning away the ice which was being pushed into her. Mordisan smiled and pushed harder and deeper, sending a stronger wave of ice into Rose. In turn Rose fought back and felt the fire like an inferno inside her, she screamed out at her sister and flames appeared around Rose like a shield. The Ice Queen could not understand how Rose was fighting her off, nobody could do this and never had done before. Mordisan took her hand away from Rose's throat stepped back in wonder at what had happened to her sister. From memory she hated Rika's kind and gentle nature, yet now standing in front of her was a young woman with fight inside of her and fire around her. Fire always melts ice but Mordisan was not going to let that be the case this time, her ice may melt but it would turn to water which would put out the fire inside her sister.

"Well, well, well," smiled Mordisan "It's about time you stood up for yourself, you were always so wishy-washy."

"Not any more sister, not anymore!" The golden locket around Rose's neck was also glowing as if there was a fire inside it. The golden locket began to slowly open, all by itself and it filled the frozen room with a bright light.

Furdon and Fiddy were dazzled as they watched what was happening, they could not believe what they were seeing. Through the brightness they could see the Ice Queen standing tall and proud, her blood red hair swirling up around her, ready to take on any fight with her sister. Rose was surrounded by a shield of fire and was lifted off the ground, only by a few inches. From the corner of the frozen chamber they saw a white figure step forward, it was a slender female figure in a blue dress and she was full of light. The Ice Queen and Rose's friends watched as this ghostly figure went to stand beside Rose and the burning shield engulfed them both. A blast of heat and flame burned around Rose. The Grocklings were scared that their friend was being burned alive. They could see Rose through the flames, standing tall and not moving, she did not appear to be in pain. Indeed she was not in pain at all. Ordram had released Rika from her frozen slumber and reunited her with

Rose. The fire burned around them as the two entities became one. When the fire died down, Rose was standing like a powerful woman in front of the Ice Queen. They were both incredible figures, on one side there was the cold white ice of Mordisan, on the other the fire of Rose. Fiddy and Furdon could not take their eyes off the sisters. Gwennol had opted to stay out of the way until it was all over, no matter how many times the Grocklings called her over, she refused to leave the stairway.

"This is going to be one hell of a fight," whispered Furdon.

"I know, I can't believe that's Rose, she looks amazing!"

"She looks like she could be a Queen."

"Shh, best keep quiet… it's not over yet."

The bright light in the frozen chamber died down, as did the burning fire around Rose. The golden locket however, still burned from within and was slowly beginning to unfold again. The spiky appearance was now looking like a rosebud.

The Ice Queen looked at the frozen tomb where Rika had been kept for all those years, it was empty. She then looked over at her sister and saw her as she had never seen her before. There was a determination in her eyes. Rose felt different, she felt a strength like she had never felt before, she had life in her veins and a purpose in her heart. She had to take on her sister for the sake of Cragfeld. As Rika, she saw her father and her Vecter imprisoned in ice and knew the only way to free them and all the other captives on the island was to defeat the Ice Queen. It was not an easy task but now she felt complete, she felt and looked fearless. She knew Ordram was with her, to help and protect her but ultimately it was her fight. The Ice Queen felt bitterness towards her sister, there was no love, only hate. She would end this once and for all and get her Kingdom back.

"I hope you're ready?!'" said the Ice Queen.

"I've been ready for one hundred and fifty years, do your worst!"

"Oh I will, and then some!"

The Ice Queen launched herself at her sister and grabbed her by the throat and pushed her back through the doorway. Rose took hold of her sisters hair and hung on tight, pulling it as they both rolled out of the frozen chamber to where Furdon and Fiddy were watching on, open-mouthed. The Ice Queen and Rose did not see them as they were too enthralled in fighting each other. Mordisan was wrapped in snow and ice which spun around her like a white haze. Rose was fighting back with fire, it looked like she was wrapped in flames. They spun across the corridor screaming at each other.

Gwennol who had been hiding out of the way now saw the Ice Queen and Rose at loggerheads. The sisters were holding onto each other, fighting with ice and fire against each other. As they burst out of the frozen chamber they skidded to the top of the stairs and were balancing on the top step. The Ice Queen raised one hand and slapped Rose around the face and they both went tumbling down the staircase. Furdon and Fiddy ran to the top of the steps to join Gwennol, watching as the ball of fire and ice fell down the frozen steps into darkness. The three friends looked at each other in disbelief as to what they were witnessing and then all stared down the stairs.

"What's going on?" said Gwennol, in surprise and wonder.

"I'm flabbergasted!" said Fiddy.

"It looks like Ordram has released Rika from being frozen…"

"Oh she was a ghost, a white ghost walking over to Rose," interrupted Fiddy.

"And then in a blast of fire they were somehow put together as one person and now Rose looks like a… a…. I don't know!"

"She's found something inside her that is prepared to fight the Ice Queen," said Gwennol.

"She's magnificent!" said Furdon.

"Come on," said Fiddy "Let's follow them, we can't miss this."

Just before they flew down the stairs after Rose, they caught a glimpse out of the open window of fire blasting from Blackfall over the Lowlands. They were reminded that this was not just a fight between Rika and Mordisan, the whole island was fighting for freedom.

At the bottom of the stairs in the main entrance to the Dark Castle, Rika and Mordisan were now standing at opposite sides of the room and facing each other with equal determination. Mordisan summoned a huge spinning globe of ice with deadly frozen shards which looked like deathly daggers, she fired it at Rika who moved out of its way. It went crashing through the wall into the main hall where Bolstone and Orme were still in battle.

Bolstone and Orme were distracted for a second as to what could have been causing such a commotion. Orme could not believe it was Rika she was seeing taking on the powerful Mordisan. Bolstone was thrilled to bits to see Rose and Rika fighting as one, it filled him with a new found energy. Whilst Orme was distracted, Bolstone dug into his pocket and pulled out a large orange globe which looked like glass as he smashed it over his rival. Orme seemed in shock as the glass cut her skin. With these cuts, the orange serum penetrated through her skin and into her bloodstream very quickly. Her arms and legs became stiff and she couldn't move. With creaking and crunching sounds, Bolstone watched on as Orme changed back from her beautiful young self to the old witch she really was.

"What have you done Bolstone? You'll regret this!"

"No, no, no I find that highly unlikely. You my old friend, have lost."

"Lost? I've not lost!"

"Then how will you get out of this little pickle. If you're

stronger than me, as you've claimed for so many years…
then getting out of this will be a doddle."

The old witch squirmed around but could not move. With
every struggle she started to shrink in size until Bolstone
could pick her up by the scruff of her neck between his
fingers. He could not help but laugh at seeing the old witch
looking so useless. She may have lost the ability to move
but she certainly had not lost the ability to talk, she was
cursing the old man. Bolstone shrank her down so she could
stand on the palm of his hand and wafted his other hand over
her until a little gold cage appeared around her. Bolstone
carried her over to the stone steps near the frozen throne. He
clicked his fingers at her and the orange paint like substance
disappeared from her skin and she could feel she was able to
move again, still shouting and cursing at him.

"Now, now, now Orme, there's no need for that. If you're
going to make such a noise then it might as well be a pretty
one." He tapped the cage with his hand and saw the
wriggling old witch turn into a bright orange canary and her
voice was replaced with it's song. Bolstone laughed from
his belly. He knew he could beat the old witch. Before he
felt too smug, a swarm of flaming daggers flew through the
room as Rika was throwing all she had at her sister.

Mordisan looked at Bolstone as he turned himself back
into the old wizard and she wondered where Orme was. Out
of the corner of her eye she saw the birdcage and realised
what Bolstone had done. This filled her with even more
anger and she threw hundreds of sharp icicles at both Rika
and Bolstone. These were met with shields of fire as each
sharp shard melted off them. Rika bent down and picked up
one of the Ice Queen's razor sharp icicles, cutting her hand
as she did so. A petal from Ordram's golden rose
blossoming around her neck fell onto the icicle she was
holding. Bolstone was looking at Rika, Mordisan was
looking at Bolstone, when Rose powerfully hurled the shard

back at her sister.

The Grocklings and Gwennol were watching from the landing at the top of the stairs. It was as if everything slowed down as they watched the frozen shard, covered in Rose's blood and a glimmer of gold fly towards Mordisan. By the time Mordisan turned to face Rika, it was too late and the icicle plunged into her chest like a blade.

Rose stood up slowly and saw what she had done, she only intended to hurt the Ice Queen, show her she could be defeated – they were sisters after all. The Ice Queen looked down at the blade in her chest and saw it was covered in her sister's blood. The golden petal began to glow as Ordram's magic came to life. The crown of ice fell from the Ice Queen's head and smashed into a million pieces on the floor. Her white skin started to look grey and her red hair grew dull. The powers of the Ice Queen were fading and they could all see Mordisan slowly collapsing to the floor.

"Only your blood and Ordram's leaf could stop you Mordisan," said Rose "We are sisters, your blood is my blood."

Mordisan looked at the Dark Castle around her and saw the walls melting and water flowing through the corridors. Crystal chandeliers fell from the ceilings and dropped into the torrent of water. Bolstone ordered all of this water out of the Castle. As they looked through the entrance to the Dark Castle they could see the stream washing over the land, picking up every single dark creature from her evil army, turning each and every one of them into water. Bolstone ordered the water to leave Cragfeld and never return, and in a swirling tower it leapt up into the sky as if it were being sucked away. The cries from the Lowlands turned to cheers as the King's army and the Grocklings realised the Ice Queen had been defeated. Rose walked over Mordisan and knelt down next to her sister, who now looked like an empty shell with no powers. By her own wish, Mordisan had insisted the old witch would make her immortal, she could not be killed.

"You knew this day would come, didn't you Mordisan?" said Rose.

"Not by your doing Rika, I thought I had you..." she wheezed as the icicle melted through her heart. "What will you do with me?"

"We're sisters Mordisan – I know that doesn't mean as much to you as it does to me, but I won't be cruel to you... even after everything you've done."

Bolstone walked over to the sisters who were crouched on the floor. Rose put her hand on her sister's shoulder and as she did so she saw ice crystals forming all over her. Mordisan felt cold. Ice slowly crusted around her body and she knew that she was facing the same fate she had sent her sister to all those years ago. She was not going to go quietly, with one last effort before she lost movement in her arm she reached out and grabbed a shard of ice from her dress and thrust it into her sister's side, twisting it and laughing as she did so. Seconds later Mordisan was frozen, her arm at her sisters side and an evil smile on her face.

CHAPTER EIGHTEEN

As dawn broke over Cragfeld it was if the island had been woken from a deep sleep. The people in the villages woke up feeling refreshed as if they had been brought out of a hazy dream. It had not been a good dream either, all they could remember was a dark fog around them. The misty greyness had been washed away from their eyes like the water from the Dark Castle. They looked at each other more clearly than they could remember. When they stepped out into the streets, the grass on the Lowlands looked greener than they had ever seen it before. The mountains seemed at ease and it was as if Cragfeld was able to breathe again.

Blackfall and Trennfall were clinging to the mountain side like two great war heroes. Their black scaly skin glistened in the morning sun, smoke dancing from their nostrils. They had been fighting all night against the evil creatures of the Ice Queen's army but knew as soon as the water washed them away, the Ice Queen was powerless. The Dragons swished their tales playfully down the cliffy ledge of the mountain and waited for Bolstone to announce their victory.

All of the Grocklings cheered when they saw the Dark Castle had lost its frozen coat and the black mist evaporated from the villages of Cragfeld. They had fought side by side with the Dragons and the Silvertips who were cleaning their paws after the battle. Some of the Grocklings were overcome with excitement and ran down the mountain, over the Lowlands and into the villages. It had been far too long since they had mingled with the human folk. As they reached the houses, people could be heard cheerfully greeting them as if time had stood still and they were welcoming old friends.

Frithad and Eady were sitting at the edge of the cave waiting for Bolstone to call them all down to celebrate. Eady was flapping about trying to make herself more presentable for such a momentous day. It had been a long time since they had seen the King and did not want to look shabby after the night's events. For the first time in one hundred and fifty years, Cragfeld looked, smelled and felt healthy. The grass was greener and the trees seemed lush. The sky overhead was clear from grey clouds for the first time since the Ice Queen took her throne, a beautiful clear sky welcomed in the dawn of a brand new day. The winged wardens were hiding out of sight until they knew what had happened.

The Dark Castle had been restored to how it used to be, strong grey stones towering up from the ground with colourful flowers hanging from each window. The tallest tower however looked as if it was still frozen and covered in a thick layer of black ice.

Not only was it the dawn of a new day but the dawn of a new era for Cragfeld and everyone who lived here. The people, the Grocklings and everything in between were all excited to see a new injection of life fill every corner of their land. The people were gathering in a crowd at the bottom of the steps up to the Castle, waiting eagerly for their King to step out onto the balcony and greet them.

Inside the frozen chamber of the tallest tower, Victor and old King felt warmth again. The coffins of ice in which they had been frozen were beginning to melt. Victor was the first to force his way through the shell of ice, he and Hullard then went to help the King get out of his. The old King was tired and looked weak and pale after the ordeal but whatever was going to happen he needed to see Rika, it was his dying wish.

"Are you alright?" asked Victor.

"Er, er, what happened? Are we alive?"

"Only just," smiled Hullard "My word that Mordisan is a cruel one isn't she, didn't hesitate in freezing us with her magic spells."

"From what I can gather, Rose has been successful," said Victor "Otherwise we wouldn't have ice melting off us."

"Who's Rose again?" asked the old King.

"Sorry my King, Rose is Rika…"

"Oh my darling Rika… take me to her," he gasped trying to catch his breath.

"Certainly, let me carry you."

Victor lifted up the old King in his strong arms and carefully walked down the dark stairway. The last time he walked on these stairs it was frozen solid and he did not want to slip, especially carrying the old King.

"It's alright Victor," said Hullard "These steps don't have any ice on them, they're bone dry."

"That's good, another encouraging sign that the Ice Queen has been beaten."

As they made their way down the stone steps they saw Bolstone standing over both Rose and Mordisan. Fiddy and Furdon flew down the staircase from where they had watched the traumatic events unfold. Rose was collapsed in a heap on the floor while Mordisan was frozen in the evil pose of stabbing her sister for the last time. Furdon and Fiddy ran over to Rose to see if she was okay but she lay lifeless before them.

Bolstone was filled with fury and with all his might he cast a deep unbinding spell on Mordisan. The frozen figure of Mordisan melted into a pool of black water, where it hung in the air for a few seconds before Bolstone sent it up the tallest tower. Mordisan would be frozen in time, just as she did to Rika for all those years. The frozen chamber was resealed. Nobody could go and see her even if they wanted to, the wall was a solid block of ice which nothing could get through. Nobody could go to taunt her like she did to Rika, she would be alone in silence for the rest of time with only her cruel thoughts and memories for company. Her wish for immortality had come back to bite her as she would now be lonelier than she had ever been before.

Back in the main entrance of the Castle, Victor carefully sat the old King down on a wooden chair near the main hall. He ran over to Rose and joined Furdon and Fiddy in their state of disbelief. After all Rose had been through and defeating her sister, Mordisan had to have the last laugh and take Rose away from them. Victor picked her up and held her closely but her body hung limp in his arms. Fiddy and Furdon had tears running down their faces. Gwennol and Hullard failed to believe what had happened, Rose was too strong to let this happen. They knew she had so much to live for now. Yet Rose grew white and her skin felt cold. Victor carried her over to the large stone table in the main hall and lay her down.

"Let me see my daughter," said the old King. Victor helped him over and sat him down next to Rika. The King saw Rika but the rest of them saw Rose.

"I'm sorry…" whispered Victor as he stood next to the table.

"Oh Rika," said the old King "If only I could've seen you one last time to say goodbye… Not like this, not like this. I had so many things to tell you. Hmmm yes, so many things. I wanted to tell you before I died, I never thought it would end like this." Fiddy was in tears and leaning on Furdon for comfort. "I wanted to tell you that I'd never left you… Whatever Mordisan told you. I thought of you every day and tried many, many times to come back for you. Yet each time your sister grew stronger and more cruel, overpowering our army every time." A tear slid down the old man's face as he looked upon his daughter who was laying before him. He reached out and took her cold hand. "How I wish we could've had more time together Rika, I'm so sorry I wasn't there for you when you needed me. Rest in peace my beautiful girl."

"I'm sorry I let you down too," said Victor, taking her other hand "I should've come back for you, I shouldn't have abandoned you for all those years. It should not have turned out this way, we had so many memories still to make and adventures of our own to go on. I'm so sorry I let you down, my love." He kissed the back of her hand and grief took hold of his heart and he had to walk over to a window to get some air. He looked out and saw all of Cragfeld had turned out and were waiting for their King or Queen to step out onto the balcony.

Bolstone could hear the crowd gathering and walked over to where Victor was looking out. There were people from the villages, the King's men and hundreds of Grocklings gathered. They could be heard muttering their curiosities, would it be the old King, or a new King, or would it be a Queen?

"I can't face them…" said the old King "I can't face them Bolstone, not after this."

"Yes, yes, I know, I'll go and tell them… something," said Bolstone, trying to keep himself together, he'd never imagined it would end this way. He slowly walked over to the balcony and was welcomed with a great cheer from the crowds below. "Welcome, welcome… People of Cragfeld, Grocklings of the mountains and all other residents of this island, thank you for your warmth. It is with great pleasure that I can tell you that the Ice Queen is no more and her dark curse has been lifted." The crowds cheered. "She has been banished to the tallest tower of the Castle where she will remain for all of time."

"Can we see our King?" shouted one voice from the crowd.

"Your King thanks you for your warm wishes, yes, yes. But he's currently very tired, he'll be with you once he's had some rest." The crowd cheered as Bolstone walked back into the main hall where his friends were gathered around Rose.

The Grocklings, Hullard and Gwennol had all climbed onto the table to say their goodbyes to their beautiful, kind-hearted friend. Bolstone walked over, feeling a loss in his heart of their brave girl. In turn, they each kissed her forehead but couldn't bear to say goodbye. Fiddy saw the blade of ice still in Rose's side which upset him even more, knowing the Ice Queen had taken the final fatal blow. Fiddy gently put his little hand on the blade and pulled it out, letting it fall to the floor and turn to dust as it landed.

Orme, in the form on the orange canary started singing with laughter at what had happened. They'd taken her Queen so it was only right for them to lose something they loved. Orme and Mordisan had worked side by side for over one hundred and fifty years. As much as she wanted more power, she would have preferred to be the Ice Queens faithful witch than the old wizard's canary. Bolstone glared at the old witch as she sang her song from her cage. From under his cloak he pulled out Alfred, his white cat and told him to go and play with the canary. Alfred was not stupid and knew what Bolstone had done, he knew it was Orme and he would enjoy hissing and clawing at her until she kept quiet. Alfred ran over to the little cage and immediately Orme stopped singing and was quiet. She was not able to speak to summon and magic and she was not able to concoct any spells… she was powerless and knew a cat could do her a lot of damage if it so chose. Without her powers or her spell book she was in Bolstone's hands, which upset her more than losing Mordisan. Bolstone threatened her, if she did not keep quiet then he would send her to join Mordisan. As much as the old witch liked Mordisan, it was the lesser of two evils to be a canary; it was better than having to put up with her friend whinging for eternity.

"What do we do now?" asked Furdon, wiping away his tears.

"I don't know..." said Fiddy "I don't want to leave Rose's side."

"Me neither."

"Nor us," said Hullard.

"Come on," said Victor "It's been a long night, let's go and get some fresh air."

"Yes, yes, good idea," said Bolstone "Let's go and sit out in the garden, it's been a very long night. Yes, yes. An old man needs his rest."

With that, they went slowly out of the main hall of the Castle. Victor helped the old King get to his feet and walk along the passageway to the enclosed garden at the back of the Castle. Bolstone picked up the little cage in which Orme sat quietly staring at him and Alfred who followed closely behind. Gwennol flew out with them and Hullard sluggishly wandered after her. They were in shock and loss. They knew they should be elated at their victory but could not have expected to lose Rose after all they had been through together. Fiddy and Furdon refused to move, they were not going to leave Rose on her own. They curled up next to her, hoping it was all a bad dream and they would wake up soon.

Out in the garden, they walked into the morning sun which was warming the stones and grass around them. They found a stone table with tall stone chairs to sit on, these had not been used in years having been frozen over with ice and snow. The old King sat forward and leant on his arms, he was tired and felt broken. Losing Rika felt as if he had been torn apart and truly could not take anymore. Bolstone was exhausted after his fight all night with Orme and he felt deflated on what should have been a glorious day. They sat at their table in silence. Victor could not settle, he was restless and upset. He could not believe he had found Rose only to lose her again. Hullard suggested they take a stroll around the garden. Gwennol and Hullard joined Victor and took in the fresh morning air. The grass was long and overgrown, covered in dew drops as they walked through it.

"I can't believe she's gone..." he said finally.

"No... we can't either," said Gwennol.

"It's hard to take in," said Hullard "I just feel... numb."

"Yes, me too," said Victor "Why did I go up into the tower after Mordisan, why couldn't I have waited for her to come back down before I went up for Rika. If I'd done that then I could've been there for Rose when she needed me."

"We can all look back and see things we could've done differently," said Gwennol "But none of us were to know what was going to happen."

"I know," he sighed "But I don't think I'll ever be able to forgive myself for this."

"It wasn't your fault," said Hullard "Mordisan is the one who killed Rose, not you. We all knew she was a cruel and evil force and Rose was brave to go up against her."

"I should've been by her side..." he said, staring up into the sky. They walked around the garden a few times, staring into space and wearing a path into the overgrown grass.

Bolstone and the old King were sitting quietly, thinking about everything that had happened the previous night. Bolstone was replaying his fight with Orme, thinking if he had sorted that out sooner, then he could have helped Rose. The old King thought about everything Mordisan had said to him, her final words to him were full of hatred. He was saddened that Mordisan thought of him without even a shred of love, she hated him as much as she hated Rika and she was not ashamed to say so. The old King only wanted to love his daughters but now he had lost them both.

There was a huge roar coming from the sky above them as Blackfall and Trennfall circled overhead, spreading their wings and enjoying the morning sunshine.

"I don't know how I'm going to break the news the them all..." said the old King.

"No, no, me neither... their faces are full of hope at this new beginning," said Bolstone.

"I have my Kingdom back Bolstone but I'm not sure I can rule it. I'm too old."

"You are their King," said Bolstone from under his bushy old eyebrows "Take your time, they will understand."

"The one thing I don't have is time, this journey has taken everything I have, and I have nothing left to give. I won't be going back... I'll end my last few days here."

Bolstone did not say anything to the old man, he could see he knew his time was coming to an end and now the deep sorrow would only shorten it. Bolstone played with three orange marbles in his hand while he watched Victor walking around the garden. Alfred was sitting at the edge of the table keeping a close eye on the orange canary, Orme was keeping quiet.

The Castle had never felt this quiet or empty, the rooms and corridors were silent as if in shock and mourning at what it had hosted. The crowds outside had settled down but there was still excitement buzzing over them. The Grocklings were mingling with the people and seeming to pick up where they left off. People were slowly getting back to their old ways and were getting to know a few new faces. The captives which the Ice Queen had trapped in her chandelier had been set free as the ice melted from the Dark Castle. They had fallen into the water and had been washed outside onto the steps of the Castle. When the sun rose and hit the chandelier crystals, the frozen glass around them cracked and they broke free and were reinstated to their former selves. They had tried and failed to attack the Ice Queen and had been held captive for many years, so they joined in with the crowds who were gathered at the centre of the island near the Castle. As they were chatting and coming to terms with the fact they were suddenly free, they noticed a small figure at the top of the steps. It was a young woman in a tatty white dress who was dazzled by the sun as she stepped into the light. A woman from the heart of the crowd stepped forward when she saw the girl and ran up the steps.

"Amber? Amber? Is that you?" she cried.

"Yes," said the girl in a soft voice.

"What happened to you? Where were you?"

"I can't remember," she looked at her bloodied fingernails.

"We woke up this morning and you weren't in the house."

"I think I've been in there a while…"

A tall gentleman came up the steps and stood next to them. He had been held captive in the chandelier and thought the woman deserved to know the truth as he had witnessed it. He told her what the Ice Queen had done to her and how she had been used to feed and watch over a growing army. The woman was saddened by this but grateful to know the truth. She had woken up in the deepest part of the Castle, not knowing where she was or why she was there. She had somehow found her way out of the Castle, fortunately for her it all felt like a strange dream and she could barely remember it.

Furdon and Fiddy had heard footsteps shuffling along the corridor and passed the main hall. They did not know who it was and thought it might be Victor or Bolstone coming back inside. Had they been to have a look, they would have seen Amber strolling dizzily towards the main doorway. Furdon and Fiddy knew there was someone there but also knew it would not be an enemy, as they had all been washed away into the night sky. The two loyal Grocklings were not going to leave Rose, anyone could wander into the Castle and see her. Fiddy had a found blue velvet shawl and pulled it up over Rose, covering her feet all the way up to her shoulders. Furdon had pulled the hood of her cloak over her head. She looked peaceful. Neither of them could sit comfortably, the events of the night were haunting their thoughts. They were listening to the people outside, the creaks around the Castle and the breeze swirling through the open windows. Furdon was staring with no direction or purpose at the gold locket from Ordram. The closed golden bud from Ordram had blossomed into a glorious golden rose that sat proudly on their friends neckline. The gold was shimmering in the light that was dancing through the Castle, as if a million specs of glitter were spinning around each petal.

"Fiddy, look…" said Furdon, pointing at the golden rose petals.

"What… What are you looking at?"

"There! Can't you see it? The locket made from Ordram's leaf has opened up into a wonderful flower."

"I saw that earlier."

"Was is glowing last time you looked?"

"No…?" Fiddy turned to look at the locket and saw that it was as Furdon said, glowing.

They watched as the golden locket lifted up and freed itself from the chain around Rose's neck. The beautiful golden flower hovered for a while and then slowly floated down and hung a few inches above Rose's fatal wound. Three petals then fell from the flower and landed on Rose and after a few moments the petals melted into liquid gold and seeped through the blue velvet shawl to Rose's stab wound.

"What's going on?" asked Furdon.

"How should I know, I've never seen anything like this

before. Gold doesn't just melt."

"Apparently it does… because unless my tired eyes are deceiving me, that gold just melted."

They peeled back the blue shawl so they could see what was happening. The liquid gold had spread itself all over the bloody wound in Rose's side and began to soak through her skin and into her body. Fiddy took hold of her left hand and Furdon took hold of her right hand.

"Can you feel that?" asked Furdon "She doesn't feel as cold."

"I think I can feel it…" said Fiddy, thinking hope was tricking him to feel what he wanted to.

After a few minutes the liquid gold had disappeared and there was no sign of it. The golden flower rested back down on Rose's chest and she lay as peacefully as before. The two Grocklings looked at each other both puzzled as to what had just happened and why. After almost an hour had dragged by, the golden rose on their friend's chest looked dull and the glittery glow faded.

Another hour ticked by and Fiddy and Furdon were sitting on the edge of the table with their little legs dangling over the side. They were talking about the adventure they had been on and all of the magical creatures they had encountered in Ordraskop. They discussed all of the things they found hard… the Ogre, the Spiralilus, and the Swamp Trolls. It was not all bad though as they had enjoyed meeting Troostan, Betula, and Bolstone. They could not quite decide how they felt about the mermaids because even though they had saved their lives, they had been rotten to Rose and Victor. A few nasty things had happened out at sea and they were actually grateful to Gwennol for sending them to sleep. Neither of them felt as if they would sleep that well, if ever again after the loss of their friend.

"You didn't mention Blackfall or Bargos in your little story," said a soft weak voice.

Furdon and Fiddy swung around and saw Rose laying there with her eyes open. She lifted her head up and looked at her little friends and smiled. Fiddy shot like lightning to her and squeezed her as hard as he could. Furdon thought he was seeing things, it had been a long night and maybe he was seeing what he wanted to see.

"Rose, Rose, oh Rose," squeaked Fiddy kissing her cheek a hundred times.

"How can this be?" said Furdon, slowly realising his wish had come true, to see Rose alive. He jumped over, hugged her and gave her a hundred kisses on her other cheek.

"Alright you two," she said softly "Would you please tell me what's happened?" She tried to sit up but felt a sharp pain in her side. She looked down and saw her clothes had been ripped and had bloodstains on them.

"Well the good news is that you did it, you killed the Ice Queen," said Furdon.

"And the bad news?" asked Rose.

"She killed you too," said Fiddy looking bemused.

"Right….? I'm going to need a little more detail."

"You threw the Ice Queen's deadly sharp icicle back to her," said Fiddy excitedly "It was covered in blood from your hand as you picked it up, and, and Ordram dropped a petal from the necklace onto it… and, and…"

"It's okay Fiddy, take your time."

"And she fell to the floor," he continued "The ice on the castle melted and her army was washed away."

"So how did she kill me…?" asked Rose.

"I can't talk about this bit, it's too upsetting – Furdon, you tell her."

"Well, let me see… You went over to Mordisan who'd been drained of her powers and you said you wouldn't be cruel to her, regardless of how she'd treated you. As you put your hand on her she slowly started to turn to ice but she grabbed an ice dagger from her dress and stabbed you before she froze completely."

"Where is she now?"

"Bolstone sent her to the tallest tower to be frozen in ice for all eternity like you were."

"And then we all realised what had happened to you," said Fiddy, "The others are outside but we couldn't bear to leave you."

"I'm glad you didn't," she pulled herself up slowly into a sitting position, the wound in her side was painful. "But we did it didn't we? The Ice Queen is gone and Cragfeld is free?"

"Yes Miss Rose, absolutely," smiled Furdon. The two little Grocklings were holding onto Rose's arms and holding her tight.

"Okay then, can you please tell me how if Mordisan stabbed me, why am I not dead?"

"Oh but you were," said Fiddy "It was awful. Bolstone and the others outside still think you're dead."

"We should go and tell them…" said Furdon.

"Wait," said Rose "Please tell me how I'm not dead."

"Right, yes, of course. From what we saw… we think Ordram healed you," said Furdon "His magic from the locket melted into you and healed you… I think."

"Oh let's go and get the others," screamed Fiddy.

"Actually, if you don't mind I'd rather go to them. They might think you've gone doolally if you tell them what you've just told me. Anyway, I think the fresh air would do me good."

The three friends walked slowly through the Castle hand-in-hand until they reached the top of the steps which looked down onto the garden. Rose could see Bolstone and her father talking at a large stone table, while Victor was wandering around with Gwennol and Hullard in the over-grown gardens. Fiddy cleared his throat to get their attention and they all turned to see the two Grocklings standing with Rose. They all looked at her in amazement, she was alive and smiling at them all. She looked at Bolstone and could tell he was smiling at her as he gave her a wink from under his bushy eyebrows. She then looked at her father who she was looking forward to spending some time with. Her eyes then moved over to Victor who could not believe his eyes, he had been given another chance to be with her.

Rose held Ordram's leaf in her hand, she and the golden locket had gone a long way together and she was not going to let it go now. Ordram had helped her through the toughest times and hardest battles. Rose was looking forward to the future with her father and friends. There was a warmth running through her veins that she had never known before and she felt more alive than she could remember. Rose had so many things to look forward to and many more adventures to go on. She knew she would go back to see Ordram soon.

THE END